TILDA IS
VISIBLE

TILDA IS
VISIBLE

A NOVEL

JANE TARA

CROWN
NEW YORK

CROWN

An imprint of the Crown Publishing Group
A division of Penguin Random House LLC
crownpublishing.com

Originally published in Australia by Affirm Press, South Melbourne, in 2024.

Library of Congress Cataloging-in-Publication Data
Names: Tara, Jane, author.
Title: Tilda is visible: a novel / Jane Tara.
Description: First edition. | New York: Crown, 2025.
Identifiers: LCCN 2024008953 | ISBN 9780593799444 (hardcover) |
  ISBN 9780593799451 (ebook)
Subjects: LCGFT: Humorous fiction. | Novels.
Classification: LCC PR9619.4.T33 T55 2025 | DDC 823/.92—dc23/eng/20240514
LC record available at https://lccn.loc.gov/2024008953

Hardcover ISBN 978-0-593-79944-4
International edition ISBN 979-8-217-08622-1
Ebook ISBN 978-0-593-79945-1

Editors: Amy Einhorn and Shannon Criss
Editorial assistant: Austin Parks
Production editor: Liana Faughnan
Text designer: Aubrey Khan
Production manager: Dustin Amick
Copy editor: Sibylle Kazeroid
Proofreaders: Chris Fortunato and Tess Rossi
Publicists: Dyana Messina and Lindsay Cook
Marketers: Chantelle Walker and Hannah Perrin

Manufactured in Canada

9 8 7 6 5 4 3 2 1

First US Edition

For my two drifters,
Indy and Raffy

Things as they are, no mortal has ever seen, though the words be familiar as household words, and perpetually on the lips of men. We cannot see things as *they* are, for we are compelled by a necessity of nature to see things as *we* are. We never can get rid of ourselves.

—Author unknown, from an article titled
"Things as They Are" in the *Atlas,* 1831

TILDA IS
VISIBLE

1

It started with her finger.

It was not quite nine a.m. when Tilda realized that the little finger on her right hand was missing.

She knew it was impossible. How could she lose a finger? But the hand that rested on her computer keyboard now had only four fingers attached.

She blinked, unable to comprehend what was so preposterous. Waiting to see that it was a trick of the light. But it wasn't. Her finger was actually gone. Without her knowing, it had . . . what? Dropped off?

Tilda searched the room for answers. Or, rather, her finger. There was no sign of an injury. No blood. No pain.

Her gaze skimmed over the piles of paperwork she'd been meaning to file, and the prints she had yet to frame, and the camera gear that lay scattered around. Her eyes rested on an empty can of kombucha she had drunk earlier.

Had someone spiked the kombucha?

She'd done acid once back in her early twenties and thought she was stuck in a bubble for six hours. It was a horrendous experience, and it not only put her off hallucinogens for life but also gave her a deep-seated fear of losing her mind. A surge of adrenaline coursed through her limbs now—pure fear. What if she had been drugged and was losing her mind?

Breathe.

She turned her attention to things that were real. Her home office with its pitch-perfect wood floors, earthy colors, and natural light from the large windows. Her gallery wall, where over a dozen of her favorite photographs hung in mismatched wood frames. There were photos of her twins, Holly and Tabitha. Her girls had shared a womb but couldn't be more different. One photograph showed Holly, in all her green-eyed, auburn-haired beauty, head thrown back laughing, and tiny blond Tab, a step back from her spotlight-stealing sister, content in the background. Not that Tabitha was unsure of herself—she had a quiet confidence and was, in fact, the more self-assured of the two.

There was the photo of them both at Angkor Wat.

Holly dressed for the lead in a school play.

Tabitha as she was awarded the citizenship medal at her high school graduation.

The two girls with their grandmother Frances at their twentieth birthday dinner, nearly a year ago now.

And then there were other images. Tilda's closest friends, Leith and Ali, dancing barefoot in her garden, wineglasses in hand. An average Friday night.

Her dog, Buddy, his large paw across Pirate, the cat, both curled up in front of a winter fire.

Pirate was watching her now from on top of the printer. He seemed normal, and she met his gaze. Pirate had only one eye, but it was steady and all-knowing. From the moment Tilda first saw Pirate four years earlier, she knew he was a cat who had seen things and survived them.

"He'll be a lifer," the woman at the animal shelter had said. "No one wants a damaged cat."

But Tilda knew how it felt to be discarded and alone, so she'd brought him home. On his papers, it said he was wary of all human interaction, but he'd jumped up onto her lap that very night and their three eyes had locked. Tilda's fears, stresses, and worries had all melted away, as if he'd drawn them out of her.

"You're special," she'd whispered, tears rolling down her cheeks.

Pirate had curled up on her lap and fallen asleep, as if relieved that finally someone had seen him.

Even now, he calmed her. She wasn't tripping—the kombucha had been fine. Everything but her hand was normal.

Then what?

She mentally ran through her day so far, trying to remember the last time she'd looked at her hand. She'd used it to hit her alarm, get dressed, and then take Buddy for a run on the beach. He'd been the one running, not her. Tilda always joked that the only time she'd ever run was if something was chasing her.

She'd used her hand to pat him, to clip and unclip his leash. It was an unusually cold day, even for late May, so she could remember rubbing her hands together for warmth while she let him bolt up and down the beach. Then she'd returned home and searched for her keys behind the potted plant and opened her front door, letting Buddy bound past her down the hall. She'd pottered around the kitchen, made a coffee, and then sat at her desk, taking a moment to savor the sun streaming through the window before turning her attention to her emails.

"All that and I'd notice a finger missing, right?" Tilda said to Pirate, an edge of hysteria in her voice.

Pirate couldn't answer that question. Or didn't want to.

Tilda held her fist up in front of her face and, one by one, unfurled her fingers. She wiggled them. Her thumb. Check. Her index finger, and then her rude finger, as Holly had called it when she was little. All good. Her ringless finger, as her mother, Frances, called it. Check. And then . . . tentatively . . . her pinkie. Check.

What?

She could still feel it. It was there. She hadn't *lost* her little finger—she just couldn't see it.

Tilda pushed back her chair and stumbled through the house to the bathroom. She clutched the basin and searched her eyes in the mirror. Wasn't it Susan Sontag who'd said, "Sanity is a cozy lie"? What if Tilda was suffering a psychotic episode or mental breakdown but didn't realize it? Was she unhinged? Surely even asking that question ruled it out. Years ago, an old friend of hers from university had been certain the CIA was following him—it was this certainty that led to his spending time in a clinic. From the little Tilda knew about the matter, people who were having a psychotic episode didn't think there was anything wrong with them. But if her mind was fine, why couldn't she see her finger? A brain tumor? She'd read that a tumor could affect your vision.

A sense of tumor, Tilda thought. *Good to see I still have my sense of tumor* . . .

Perhaps it was her vision that was playing a trick on her? Was she going blind? She looked over at the wall above the toilet, at the framed print of a meditating monkey that Leith had given her. Underneath his serene image, it said in small, ornate lettering, "Let that shit go."

The fact that she could read the poster gave Tilda some comfort. Her eyes seemed fine. She turned back to the mirror and stared into them again. No visible weird shadows or spots. And then, to her absolute horror, Tilda noticed that her right ear was missing too. She raised her hand—the one missing the finger—and drew back a lock of hair to touch the spot where her ear used to be. She could feel her ear. It was still attached to her head. But as with her finger, she just couldn't see it.

And with that, Tilda turned to the toilet and threw up.

2

Time moves slowly, but passes quickly.

—**ALICE WALKER,** *The Color Purple*

The bathroom tiles were hot, as if hell itself were under the house. Tom had been worried about the cost of underfloor heating, but Tilda had wanted the comfort. Now, as she lay on the floor for what felt like an eternity, she was glad she'd won that fight. Tom wasn't around to worry about the investment anymore, and she really needed the warmth today. It was as if she were separate from herself and observing herself lying there. Dissociation. The first time she'd ever felt anything similar was when, at thirteen, she found her father dead in the garden. Finding his lifeless body had been so inconceivable that now, when she recalled that moment, the memory came in slow motion, as if she'd been moving through mud. Or perhaps that's exactly how she had moved at the time.

Her current situation was similar: she had seen something so absurd, so unthinkable, that she felt disassociated from it. Once again, time moved slowly, waiting for her brain to catch up. It didn't. Instead, it turned to Tom.

. . .

"You're leaving?"

"Correct."

Tom had responded "Correct" when she'd asked if he was leaving her. As if she'd repeated a phone number or was asking to confirm the time of an appointment. She stared at the man she'd been married to for seventeen years. *"Correct"?*

She noticed the new clothes. He had the usual three-day growth, but it was more manicured. This was not the result of simply forgetting to shave—this was a look that was crafted. Same brown hair, but his cut seemed more styled. The mess of waves she'd always loved and thought of as "wild and sexy" when they'd met was now tamed, and combed in a way that men believe covers the thinning of their hair. How could she have been so blind?

• • •

Five years had passed since then, and despite everyone talking about how time flies, those first years after he left had been built from countless pro-tracted days. Heartbreak was heavy and slowed the march of time to a snail's pace. And yet Tilda's mind was now back on the tiles he hadn't wanted, contemplating how quickly the years had raced by. Perhaps Einstein was right and time was nothing but a stubbornly persistent illusion. She spread her arms out, embracing the warmth. Who would've thought that grey Moroccan Bazaar tiles could be so comforting?

Not Tom, that's for sure.

He also wouldn't know if she spent the day on them. No one would. But then she felt three eyes watching her. Buddy and Pirate were at the door, one with a look of worry, the other with weary disdain.

They needed her.

So Tilda pulled herself to her feet.

Again.

3

Nothing in life is to be feared,

it is only to be understood.

—MARIE CURIE

"It's good to see you, Tilda."

Tilda almost laughed out loud at Dr. Majumdar's choice of words. Turned out her meltdown on the bathroom floor had lasted twenty-seven minutes, disproving her theory about time flying, because it felt like she had been there for hours. Once she'd fed Buddy and Pirate, she'd called her doctor. There was no point getting all worked up until she knew what was happening. Tilda had a propensity for fear. Tom always called her thinking black and white, but Tilda's mind was actually a complex palette of many shades, including *deep anxiety azure*. That, combined with a *vivid imagination violet*, meant that she was constantly worrying about something—her kids, the state of the world, the possibility of a zombie apocalypse. Age had, however, given her the experience to not let fear get the better of her, and to instead search for a solution. And that's what she needed now. Elucidation. Her missing finger might be something quite minor. Only recently she'd read online about an Irishwoman who'd hit her head and started speaking Polish, despite never having studied it. The internet was filled with similar stories, so there must be a reasonable explanation for Tilda's current situation. She had walked the three blocks to her doctor to find one, eyes downcast in case she ran into someone she knew.

She and Tom had moved to Middle Bay not long after the twins were born, when it was much cheaper to buy there. Life with kids was easier in the beachside suburb, so Tilda had talked her best friend into moving to the area as well. Once Leith and her husband, Ziggy, arrived, Tilda found herself putting down roots. Leith and Tilda then met Ali, and those early days revolved around her girlfriends and their young children. Tilda was enlaced in happiness and dreams of the future. And it had been good, for a while, but all good things come to an end. Tom left first, and then the twins moved back to groovier pastures, an hour away in the city. For Tilda, however, Middle Bay was home. It was where her dearest friends lived. It was where she'd built a business. It was where she knew people at the dog park and the local café, bookshop, and hair salon. It was where she knew her doctor by her first name.

Now she watched as Gurinder Majumdar brought up Tilda's records on the computer. She hadn't seen Gurinder since her pap smear eighteen months earlier. Just one of the many things in life she found uncomfortable but knew needed to be done. There was the added awkwardness that Gurinder's daughter, Prisha, had gone to school with Tilda's twins. Over the years, the two women had been on several fundraising committees together, and it always seemed strange to Tilda that the woman she was discussing the sausage sizzle with had seen her vagina.

Not that Gurinder was anything but professional. Every examination included a friendly chat about gardening or Indian spices. Tilda had tried another clinic once, but Gurinder was the only doctor who'd been able to diagnose her eggplant allergy, which is why Tilda had stuck with her. She was an excellent physician, and Tilda resisted change unless it was absolutely necessary.

"How can I help you today, Tilda?" Gurinder's voice was low, with the melodic tones of her accent. She'd once told Tilda she was from Mumbai.

"This is going to sound crazy, but . . . I can't see my little finger." Tilda slapped her hand onto the desk.

Gurinder peered at it over the rim of her glasses. "It's missing."

Tilda breathed a sigh of relief. "Thank god you can see that."

"Or not see it."

"Quite right. I thought I'd lost my mind, but obviously if you can't see it either, that would rule out my eyes or my mental health."

"So it would seem." Gurinder had one of those piercing stares that made you feel she was watching for any inconsistencies in the information you gave her, trying to catch you out. She was always able to get the truth as the patient knew it, and then use her medical knowledge to dig deeper. Yet another quality that made her such a good doctor.

"Are you in pain?"

Tilda shook her head. She'd been holding it together up to this point. "I do feel like I could have a panic attack, though."

"Just breathe. We'll work this out."

Tilda did as she was told while Gurinder reached over and took her hand. She checked her fingers one by one, just as Tilda herself had earlier, and then when she got to the little finger, she gave it a good yank. "Still there. It's just invisible," Gurinder said. "When did you first notice this?"

"A couple of hours ago." Tilda pushed her hair back off her face. "My ear is missing too."

Gurinder looked at the side of Tilda's head, her mind clearly working overtime, just as it had when she diagnosed the eggplant allergy. She reached across and gave Tilda's ear a yank, and then made an *mm-hmm* sound. "Can't see it, but it's there."

Finally, she sat back in her chair and stared at Tilda. Really studied her.

"How old are you, Tilda?" She turned to her computer screen and began entering Tilda's answers.

"Fifty-two."

"Do you feel well?"

"I thought I did."

"How would you describe your quality of life?"

Tilda's four-fingered hand flew to her chest. "Are you suggesting euthanasia?"

Gurinder didn't even try to hide her frustration. "That's a giant leap from a simple question. I just meant are you happy?"

Tilda's brain recalibrated and then came to a standstill. This question was more confusing than the last. *Was she happy?* She'd always considered herself to be a positive person, especially when she was younger, but Tom erred on the side of intellectual and had accused her of being "irritatingly Panglossian." Of wearing rose-colored glasses. So, over the years, she'd removed them. She'd adjusted her optimism to suit him, at first purposely, but then habitually. And now . . .

"I'm not unhappy," she said.

"How are the twins?"

Tilda was a little thrown by the shift in questioning, although this was much more comfortable territory. "They're great."

"Is Tabitha still studying veterinary science?"

Tilda nodded. "And still volunteers with the rescue group. You know Tab, always involved with different animal causes, even when she was in high school."

"I think she got that from you," Gurinder said.

It was true. Tilda was a rescuer; it was something she shared with her daughter. "It will certainly lower my pet-care bills once she's a vet."

Gurinder chuckled. "I bet. Do you see her often?"

"Most weeks," Tilda said. "She comes for dinner with her partner."

"Do you like him?"

"Her. Jess. And yes, I like her very much." Tilda knew Gurinder was quite conservative and was pleased to see that she didn't bat an eye at this information.

"I watched Holly's show recently. Is she back in Sydney now?"

"Yes, they're filming here. She's got a place in the city, and she loves her job," Tilda said. "How's Prisha?"

Gurinder smiled, clearly delighted to talk about her daughter. "Final year of medicine but is going into infectious diseases and immunology."

"Smart girl. Give her my best." Tilda felt like they should be ordering a couple of flat whites to go with the chitchat. She glanced at her hand, eager to move on to a diagnosis.

Gurinder continued to drill. "Have you been in a relationship since the divorce?"

"No . . . nope."

"When was the last time you had a sexual partner?"

What did that have to do with anything? "Eighteen months ago. I dated someone briefly, but it didn't work out."

Gurinder kept typing. "Was he your last sexual partner?"

"Yes, he was," Tilda lied. There had been one other, but she did her best to forget him, so naturally, he didn't count.

"Are your periods still regular?"

"A few days out on either side."

"Any hot flashes?"

"No." Apart from now, with all these questions that had nothing to do with her finger—or ear, for that matter.

Gurinder stood. "Come, I'll examine you."

Tilda sat on the table while the doctor checked her reflexes, her heart, pulse, and blood pressure. She did a breast exam and felt her glands. And then she pulled the curtain around the bed. "Undress and I'll do a smear."

Gurinder returned to her desk while Tilda removed her clothes, folded them neatly on a chair, and slipped on one of the gowns provided. Then she lay on the table.

She hated this.

A long moment later, the doctor stepped into the cubicle, snapping rubber gloves on.

"Knees up, Tilda."

Tilda did as she was told, looking around the room as if she had a renewed interest in the same décor she'd seen countless times. Her gaze rested on a faded print of an old woman feeding a duck and Tilda gave it her full attention, as one would an original Monet. Meanwhile, Gurinder took a speculum and spatula from their wrapping and then turned her attention to . . .

"Dear god, your vagina has gone too."

Tilda bolted upright, and the doctor laughed and guided her back down.

"Only joking. It's still there, dear."

Tilda faux laughed, but she felt like punching her in the face. Today was traumatic enough, but at least she could explain a missing finger to a date. She stared at the woman and duck until Gurinder finished the inspection with "All looks good down there."

"That's a relief." It was. In Tilda's experience, men often found it difficult to find her clitoris when it *was* visible.

"Get dressed while I organize some referrals."

Tilda took her time putting her clothes back on. She listened as Gurinder made a call. "Kate, Gurinder speaking. I have a patient here who needs some tests as soon as possible . . . bloodwork and a CT . . . hmm . . . yes . . . yes . . . excellent. Name is Tilda Finch. I'll let her know."

Tilda yanked the curtains back and returned to her seat while Gurinder typed something and then printed out the paperwork.

"They'll fit you in," she said.

Tilda tried to decipher the doctor's face, but today, with her glasses and thick black hair pulled back in a tight bun, Gurinder wasn't giving anything away.

Fear came over Tilda again. Marie Curie said that nothing in life is to be feared, it is only to be understood, and Tilda tried to remember that whenever this all-too-familiar state consumed her. When fear's long, gnarled fingers clutched at her skin, she tried to find practical ways to break her fear down and address it. What was she afraid of? Would more information help? Was the fear a reasonable one? While that didn't work for huntsman spiders, it certainly helped with flying. But now panic was rising.

"Do you think I have cancer?"

"Cancer is unlikely."

"Then what?"

Gurinder's expression gave nothing away. "Let's not jump to conclusions until we rule everything out."

"But it could be serious?"

"Best we wait."

"Gurinder, please. I'd rather have some idea of what your suspicions are, otherwise I really will just jump to the worst possible conclusion."

Gurinder nodded. She understood. "I suspect it's invisibility disorder, from the Latin *invisibilis morbus*. You have all the symptoms, but I can't be sure until we run these tests."

Tilda's eyes narrowed. "I don't understand."

"Invisibility," Gurinder said. "You're becoming invisible."

Tilda stared at the doctor. "I've heard of it. I know women talk about it, but I thought it was more metaphorical. Or at the very least, incredibly rare."

Gurinder forged on. "Actually, it's not uncommon in women as they get older."

"Are you serious?"

"Unfortunately, yes. Most women who suffer from invisibility notice the symptoms in their early fifties, but I had a patient recently who was still in her thirties. That poor girl suffered a dreadful case of it. Woke up one morning and couldn't see her own head."

"I'm disappearing?"

"We don't use that term anymore. Invisibility advocates are very much against it. Women who suffer from invisibility don't literally disappear. You may be invisible, but you're certainly not disappearing. There's a difference."

"People won't be able to see me?"

"Correct."

There was that word again, although used in a more appropriate setting.

"My daughters won't be able to see me?" Tilda's voice now had a shrill edge to it.

"Impossible to predict, Tilda. It depends on how it progresses."

"How can that be?"

"We don't know. I'm reluctant to say this, but it is a disease that affects, predominantly, older women, so research is dreadfully underfunded."

"Why aren't more women talking about this?"

"It's frustrating, but there is a movement to educate ourselves. Along with perimenopause and menopause, invisibility mostly affects older women. And yet, until recently, we didn't even discuss this issue between ourselves. That's all changing now."

"Could it be something else?"

"Possibly, which is why I want to rule everything else out. Let's not jump to conclusions until we complete these tests." Gurinder handed Tilda the folded referrals. "And for goodness' sake, Tilda, do us both a favor and stay off Google."

4

Some say Google is God. Others say Google is Satan.

—SERGEY BRIN, co-founder of Google

Pinot noir or Shiraz? What was the appropriate wine of choice for someone who was disappearing? Tilda grabbed one bottle of each, and then, juggling the bottles with her laptop, she legged it up the stairs. Her bedroom was the refuge she needed now. It was her retreat from the world. After she and Tom separated, Tilda hated sleeping in the room they'd shared, so she'd done what they'd always planned to do but never got around to and converted the attic into a bedroom. While her cottage was situated two streets back from the beach, it was on a rise, which meant Tilda's bedroom now had ocean views out the large windows. The high, sloped ceilings and white beams, wood floors, and natural colors soothed her soul. She stripped her clothes off and wrapped herself in a wool robe. She was well under her quilt when she realized she'd forgotten a glass, but she figured no one was going to witness her drinking out of the bottle . . . so she did just that.

Pirate jumped onto the bed and made himself comfortable at her feet while Tilda took a swig of courage and comfort and, ignoring Gurinder's advice, began to google. The results were disturbing.

A much higher percentage of women suffer invisibility than previously thought.

Usually affects women over fifty, as the ovaries stop producing estrogen; however, no research yet indicates a correlation between invisibility and hormones.

Early symptoms include not being served in shops and bars and being overlooked at job interviews or for promotions at work.

Over eighty percent of sufferers report some form of invisibility or the experience of "not being seen."

Approximately seven percent of sufferers have body parts that disappear.

One in one hundred women diagnosed with invisibility will disappear altogether.

More studies needed.

Underfunded.

Little research.

On and on and on . . .

Tilda knew that searching for reputable information online was like asking a fish how to fly, yet she was still disheartened to see that most sites agreed there were no treatments, apart from one natural health site that said:

There is no truth to the information out there about the link between invisibility and dairy products. In all my years of being a naturopath, I have seen no evidence that it is connected to diet. On the contrary, there appear to be many physical, emo-tional, intellectual, and spiritual reasons why a woman will manifest invisibility. In treating it, first and foremost, every woman who has successfully managed this disorder has been proactive about healing. This is the key. You must be proactive right from the start. Are you?

Proactive?

Tilda's hackles rose even thinking the word. She'd come to truly dislike those nebulous terms that belonged in urban dictionaries, not Oxford ones. *Hack* was another one. Hack really got her hackles up. One of the marketing coordinators at work had recently called her packed lunch a *life hack* that saved her hundreds of dollars a year. Tilda couldn't help snapping back, "Jesus, Min, a packed lunch is not a *life hack*."

Mantra was another word she hated. #LifeMantra . . . Unless it was in Sanskrit, it wasn't a mantra.

Proactive sounded similar. Whatever proactive meant. She realized she was having a very strong reaction to something she didn't really understand, a habit of hers.

Tilda did a search.

Proactive: Initiating change rather than simply responding to events.

Antonym: Reactive.

Reactive, she understood. Most of her life seemed reactive. Lying in bed in her robe taking swigs from the Shiraz bottle seemed reactive. It also felt therapeutic. But if studies showed that being proactive helped with invisibility, then Tilda wanted to be proactive. She'd be proactive about being proactive. She just needed to work out how. Normally, any type of self-development or deep self-reflection was outside her comfort zone. Ironic, considering what she did for a living.

Drumroll, please . . .

Tilda made her living from mantras, life hacks, and inspirational memes. Her business, This Is A Sign, sold posters, T-shirts, mugs . . . anything, really, on which an inspiring quote could be plastered. Tilda and Leith were more than just best friends; they were also business partners. They'd met in the bathroom of a nightclub in the late eighties when they noticed they were both wearing the same supposedly one-off crochet hot pants and then, in the mirror, they bonded over a love for Revlon's Wine with Everything lipstick. They'd been inseparable ever since, with a series of boyfriends and then their husbands having to accept that the relationship came with a nonnegotiable third wheel. They were always discussing creative ideas together, but it took the utter mind-numbing boredom of early motherhood to really motivate them to follow through. Leith, a lover of anything metaphysical, came up with an idea for the two of them to save their sanity.

"Some days I wake up knowing it's another day of breastfeeding and the Wiggles, and I want to scream," she said. "I love Lulu, but mothering is hard work."

"Imagine having twins," Tilda slurred, exhausted. "Some days I can barely dress myself."

"You're a goddamn warrior." Leith's face lit up. "Let's create a pack of inspiration cards, for mums."

"Like tarot cards?"

"Quotation cards. You pull one card a day, to motivate and inspire you. To help you face the day. To help you get dressed."

Tilda was catching on. "Or so you don't stab people."

"Exactly. I know it's a silly idea," Leith said. "But we'll design each card with a beautiful photo. You'll have an excuse to take photos, and I love inspiring quotes. We can sell a few packs at the markets or something."

"No one will buy them." Tilda didn't need tarot cards to predict that.

"Maybe not, but it'll be fun making them."

Leith was right, and Tilda did love the idea of having a project to work on that didn't include crayons or children's songs. "I'm in!"

The "silly idea" was now a very successful business.

Over the first few months, Tilda shot seventy-eight stunning images (loving every minute of doing so), while Leith matched each one with an inspirational quote.

Leith believed in the cards one hundred percent. Caught up in her enthusiasm, Tilda started to believe in them too. Plus, she enjoyed doing something creative with her best friend, their daughters nearby. It was a very special period in her life. It was a bonus when, to her disbelief, the pack sold out at their very first market stall. So did the reprint, and soon they were printing more. Before long, their pack of cards was a hit, spawning a successful market stall selling inspirational posters, cards, diaries, and mugs. Aldi contacted them and asked for their collection in a weekly special, something they'd done annually ever since. They knew then that they were really onto something. They named their business, and Ziggy, whose passions included marketing and meditating, came on board, driving their quirky little idea forward. Success didn't come overnight, but it did steadily build. They worked hard for years, first from their kitchen tables, then in a shopfront office, and now out of a local commercial building. Covid-19 had, ironically, been excellent for business. Everyone needed inspiration.

Tilda's success felt more a fluke than fate. Her life was now built upon a paradoxical contradiction—there was a divide between what she believed personally and what she created professionally. To say she subscribed to any of the inspiration she peddled would be stretching it. Whereas Leith and Ziggy lived and breathed it. In their minds, they'd manifested the success of the company. Tilda felt she'd just kept taking great photographs and hanging out with her friend until there was a lot of money in it, which had been a pleasant surprise. For Tom, who thought they were delusional, it had come as a shock.

"Time to be proactive!" Tilda shouted at Pirate, who jumped off the bed and walked out of the room. She called after him, "When have I been proactive about anything?"

Pirate disappeared around the doorframe, so she had to search for the answer herself.

Her divorce? Tom had left but then never served her papers. He got on with his life, and she was left in limbo. So finally, eighteen months ago, she'd instigated the divorce. It was her response to the events thrust upon her years earlier. It was reactive. And heartbreaking.

Proactive. What else? She took a daily multivitamin and some collagen. Did that count?

She hadn't put a lot of thought into these things, but was that wrong? She had a nice life and wasn't unhappy. Was she?

The confusion she'd felt when Gurinder asked her if she was happy returned.

Tilda knew she *should* be happy. She went through the motions in a life she'd willingly created. She lived in a gorgeous beach suburb buzzing with fabulous people and excellent coffee. Apart from the lack of parking spaces on weekends, she really had nothing to complain about. She had the luxury to overanalyze her life and emerge dissatisfied, so normally she avoided even going there. But with a looming diagnosis, and the terror that went with it, perhaps it was time to reflect.

She knew unhappiness. She'd lived it for years when she was married: I'd be happy if . . . I'll be happy when . . . Fill in the blanks. And years flew by. It hadn't always been like that. Meeting Tom had felt destined. Those early days were heady. Electrifying.

They'd met at a writers' festival where Tom was speaking. At forty-one, he was ten years older than Tilda. He was a journalist. He'd had some success with his first novel, a political thriller that was popular with both the literati and airport readers. Tilda sat at the front during his session and watched him speak, mesmerized. He was one helluva man. Rugged, with dark hair, muscular arms, and an endless chest. And he knew how to work a crowd. He was articulate and erudite, but he also had the audience in stitches. At one point, his eyes rested on Tilda and her whole body filled with fire. Afterward, to her surprise, he came over and introduced himself.

"I find it unfair that you know my name and I don't yet know yours."

"I'm Tilda." She shook his hand, and a jolt of pure energy shot straight through her. She covered her surprise with nervous chat. "I enjoyed your talk. I absolutely agree with—"

Tom cut her off, as was to become his habit in their relationship. "Have a drink with me."

Tilda agreed without hesitation, something that became another pattern in their relationship. Right from the start he was challenging, but Tilda found it refreshing to be challenged. From that moment, he had swept her into *his* life, into *his* bed, into *his* plans. The books he'd write. The success he'd have. Tilda had slammed into a star, not noticing that there was room for only one star in his sky.

Seventeen years and one very combative marriage later, Tom moved out, and Tilda realized just how *unhappy* she'd been. Initially, she was hit by a tsunami of grief for the ending of their marriage, grief that lasted on and off for two years. But then something new emerged from the ashes: a hard-won contentment. She recognized how much she'd given to him. And she was relieved that she no longer had to give. She'd emerged feeling battered and bruised, and that was that. She didn't have time to question what she'd been through or learned. After all, she was still raising children and running a business. Like countless women before her, she just got on with it, and tried to convince herself that she was okay. Only, clearly, she wasn't.

Tilda shook off thoughts of Tom. She shook off thoughts of unhappiness. Instead, she tossed off the bedcovers and stumbled over to her phone. Seconds later, her Friday night playlist filled the room. "I'm Every Woman" was exactly what she needed right now. She began to dance . . .

"Eyeyaaaaaaam every wooooooomaaaaan . . ."

Tilda realized she was quite drunk, so she took another swig of wine—the final swig in the bottle, as it turned out. No wonder she was stumbling. She used the empty Shiraz bottle as a microphone—"I'm nevfbutptime, entowap heeee . . . Wo wo wo wo . . ."—then tossed it aside. She'd never known those lyrics.

Chaka Khan gave way to Helen Reddy singing "I Am Woman" and then, right on cue with the word *roar*, and a dramatic swing of the arms, Tilda gave an actual roar and collapsed onto the bed, where she passed out.

She woke four hours later to a dry mouth and pounding head.

"Oh my gawd." She peeled herself off the bed and headed for the bathroom, where she drank water straight from the tap. The mirror was not kind. She wore barely any makeup, yet her eyes were rimmed with it. Her hair looked like she'd spent a week in a meth lab. She grabbed an elastic and scraped it back from her face, noticing her hand as she did.

Her thumb was now missing; black despair took its place. Her thoughts turned to her daughters. Was this condition hereditary? Her own mother certainly never had a problem with being seen. Even now, in her late seventies, Frances was beautiful, the type of woman that men opened doors for, and that other women rallied around. But perhaps there had been other women in Tilda's family who'd had the disorder. There was a great-aunt on her father's side who'd supposedly been placed in a sanatorium in her fifties. No one ever saw her again. What if she'd had invisibility? What if Tilda's girls were at risk?

Tilda quickly searched online, clicking on a university medical website.

> There might be some environmental influence, but there is no known genetic cause. More research needs to be done in this area.

Tilda exhaled. No known genetic cause.

Now that she'd allayed that fear, what else did she need to know? She opened the second bottle of wine and continued her internet research. There were so many rabbit holes to go down. One suggested that Greta Garbo had suffered from the condition. Another led her to advice on addressing the condition with plastic surgery. One online user said there was a cure to be found on the dark web.

"I'd rather be bloody invisible," Tilda told her computer as she backpedaled through pages.

She quickly turned her attention to a subject that was more relatable to her own life and searched:

INVISIBLE WOMEN—WHAT TO WEAR

> Age-appropriateness is key. No short skirts, nothing that accentuates the cleavage, and always steer clear of bold patterns, which draw attention to your disappearing body parts.

"Perhaps I'll need a hazmat suit," she wailed to no one in particular. "I'll live in my robe," she threatened the wall.

Another article told her to wear low heels. Stilettos create the illusion of saggy breasts.

"It's no illusion!" Tilda shouted, slapping her sagging breasts with her disappearing hand.

One video extolled the virtues of a nice scarf to deflect attention away from a missing limb.

"How nifty. It can deflect a defect."

On and on she read. For three days, Tilda danced and cried. She responded to calls from friends with a quick text saying she had laryngitis and all was fine. But she wasn't fine. She spiraled down a well of despair. She went down the rabbit hole of invisibility and aging in a world that seemed to mostly celebrate youth. She left the house only to have the tests done, aware that the woman doing the MRI could smell wine sweating out of her pores. Tilda reminded herself that no one could make her feel inferior without her consent, a quote from This Is A Sign's Eleanor Roosevelt series of cards, and told herself it didn't matter if the technician thought she was drunk. Because she was. Afterward, she returned home to her internet rabbit hole, and by the time she arrived at Dr. Majumdar's office for her follow-up appointment, she was praying for another diagnosis and a week in rehab to be the fix.

5

We are half of the world, mothers to
all of the world, and still we are invisible.
—**LYNETTE LONG,** psychologist and author

Gurinder had that look on her face. *That* look.

"You have that look on your face." Tilda stated the obvious.

Gurinder swiveled her chair to face Tilda. "I'm afraid it is invisibility."

Of course it was.

"I'm sorry, Tilda . . . I know you were hoping for—"

"Anything else? Rectal cancer?" Tilda said.

Gurinder raised an eyebrow. "I can assure you, that's a pain in the arse."

Tilda gave a half snort, appreciating Gurinder's attempt at humor. "I bet it is. Okay, is there a cure?"

"There's no cure."

"I read somewhere on the internet that—"

"Tilda, I told you not to google this." Gurinder said "google" as if it had four o's.

"I only googled once." *For seventy-two hours straight.*

"You can find anything you're looking for on the internet," Gurinder said with a stern look.

"I've tried online dating, so I know that's not true."

It was obvious that Gurinder hated being the bearer of this news. "I'm sorry, Tilda, but the reality is that there is no cure."

"There must be something. A treatment to delay progression?"

"There's no magic pill, if that's what you're asking," Gurinder said. "Some doctors prescribe Botox, but I don't see any evidence that it helps."

"If I disappear, my wrinkles go with me," Tilda said wryly. "How can there be nothing? How can women all over the world be disappearing and no one is doing anything about it?"

"Women have always been poorly represented in medical research. There *are* some pharmaceutical trials, but nothing I'd recommend yet."

"Where does that leave me?"

The tone was final. "We'll see how it progresses."

"So that's it. I leave here and wait?"

"We'll book an appointment for next month, just to monitor things. Right now, you have stage 2 invisibility. You might stabilize there."

"How many stages are there?"

"Four. Stage 1 is incredibly common; being overlooked for a promotion at work, that kind of thing. As you're experiencing, stage 2 comes with some minor appendage visibility issues."

"And stage 4?"

Gurinder sidestepped the question. "By next month, we'll have more of an idea of how your invisibility has developed. We might find it's a mild case and, beyond your ear and finger, there will be very little change."

Tilda gave Gurinder a thumbs-up.

"And your thumb," Gurinder added. "That might be it."

"Or I might end up with stage 4 and totally disappear."

"You won't disappear, Tilda. You just won't be visible."

"It's the same bloody thing."

Gurinder remained calm. "It's important to look at the positives, dear."

"Positives?" Tilda pretended to think for a moment. "I'll be able to pull off that bank job."

Gurinder laughed. "You're very funny."

"Great, I can be the first invisible stand-up comedian in history."

"No, I saw one at the Melbourne Comedy Festival a few years ago. Well . . . I didn't see her, obviously. I heard her. Also a very funny woman."

Tilda traced her invisible pinkie with the index finger on the opposite hand. "Gurinder, I looked online for any information about this being hereditary . . ."

She didn't need to say any more. Gurinder turned to the computer and opened a web page.

"Tilda, I was concerned too, so I've already looked at the latest research. I'll email you this link. There's nothing that suggests Holly and Tabitha will end up with this. There are no definitive genetic markers. No one knows the cause. Only the symptoms."

"I bet if erectile dysfunction was a symptom, we'd all know more about the cause."

"The gender health gap is alive and well. Just last week I saw that a famous footballer negotiated a new salary that's infinitely more than this country's entire funding for research into endometriosis. I despair when I read these things." Gurinder opened her desk drawer, shuffled through it for a moment, and then drew out a flyer. "There's a local support group. The meeting details are at the bottom."

"You mean there are more of us? Locally?"

"You'd be surprised at how many. Go and meet some of these women. You're not alone."

Alone. She was used to being alone. Tilda had been alone long before Tom left her. If anything, she'd felt less alone since he'd left.

Defeat weighed heavy. "What will I do?"

Gurinder reached out and gave Tilda's shoulder a squeeze. "You'll find ways to live with it. And I'll support you in whatever way I can."

Tilda took a moment to gather herself. Her eyes drifted to her hands. Faint lines ran in rivers across her skin. They weren't old hands, but they weren't young anymore either, no matter how much vitamin E cream she slathered on them.

Gurinder took a book that was sitting on her desk and handed it to Tilda. "I don't usually give my patients . . . It's just we've known each other for so long."

They'd never spent time one-on-one, but years of school events and class parties had created a special bond and Tilda was touched.

She read the title of the book aloud. "*The Truth About Invisibility.*"

"I haven't read it, but I know the author. She's an excellent doctor whom I worked with years ago. I thought she'd retired, but apparently she just . . ."

"Disappeared."

"Became invisible," Gurinder corrected.

Tilda slipped the book into her bag. "Thank you."

Gurinder was clearly upset for Tilda. "Please don't hesitate to contact me if you're overwhelmed. It's normal to struggle with this diagnosis."

"I see."

"I think that's the key."

Tilda's brow furrowed. Had she missed something?

Gurinder smiled kindly. "When you say 'I see' . . . I've broken the same news to numerous patients. I've watched how they cope, and what I'm about to say is merely my observation over many years. The ones who do well appear to have one thing in common."

"What's that?"

Gurinder looked at her over the rim of her glasses. "They maintain a positive perspective."

Tilda nodded as if she understood. She didn't, though. She didn't understand what was happening to her or what was about to happen to her. In this moment, she just felt the weight of her life, of her past, and the dreadful expectation of what her future would be.

She had invisibility. She let that word sink in.

And as it did, she realized . . . she'd felt invisible for years.

6

STRESS RESPONSE IN WOMEN: BEHAVIORS AND HORMONE CHANGES IN TIMES OF NEED

K Whiley, C Barton, L Newton, L Hourigan, J Hinchey, M Hinchey
PMID: 00001234NM

The study on female friendship showed that in times of stress, when the body goes into fight-or-flight mode, women experience something men don't—a release of oxytocin, compelling them to gather their children and female friends together. This gathering of loved ones buffers the stress response and has a calming effect.

*   *   *

Tilda instinctively ran straight to Ali's bakery. She needed her friend.

When Ali saw her, she called for her son, Jack, to take over at the shop counter. She then grabbed Tilda's arm and led her out the back of the shop, into the kitchen.

Ali's husband, Geoff, spotted Tilda and made for the back door. "I'll just step out for a smoke." Geoff didn't smoke.

Once they were alone, Ali held Tilda while wracking sobs tore through her. "What the hell's going on, Tilly? Is it one of the girls?"

Tilda shook her head so hard her hair fell out of its elastic.

"Has someone died?"

"I've been diagnosed with invisibility. My finger, thumb, and ear have already disappeared." Tilda held her hand up in front of Ali's face.

"Oh, shit." Ali was visibly horrified, but she quickly regrouped. "I believe it's quite common. I recently saw a feature on *A Current Affair* about a preschool teacher who lost her job because her invisibility was frightening the students."

This set Tilda off even more. "I'm going to frighten children!"

Ali grabbed Tilda by the shoulders. "No, darling, you won't. And even if you do, you've always said that you hated kids."

Tilda nodded. "That's true."

"Apart from yours, mine, and Leith's," Ali reminded her.

"You're right—I don't like any kids but ours."

Ali adjusted the green cap on her head, part of the uniform that included a green shirt and a white apron with the Bread Basket logo across the front. "So who cares if you scare them? If anything, it could be fun. Especially at Halloween."

Tilda calmed down, a half-smile emerging through her tears. "Finally, a plus."

"There must be a treatment?"

"Zero funding for research or a treatment. It's right up there with the arts in this country."

Ali shook her head in sympathy with her friend. "I'm here for you, by your side, every step of the way."

"Unless you can't see me, and then you won't know if you're beside me."

"We've always said we're going to be two ole birds together. You'll be invisible and I'll be known as the crazy old lady who talks to herself, because people won't know you're there." Ali handed Tilda some tissues. "Jokes aside, we're going to sort this out."

In their group of three inseparable women, Ali was the organizer. Over the years, she'd been the one to arrange all the kids' birthday parties, and the big birthday bashes for each of her girlfriends. Besides running the family bakery, she also worked in the school cafeteria one day each week and headed up the parents' committee. Geoff was very nice but always exhausted from the early shifts at the bakery so didn't speak much (and often fell asleep at social events). Their son, twenty-one-year-old Jack, also worked at the bakery.

Tilda realized he was standing at the door, wary of the outpouring of emotion.

"I'm okay, Jack," she said.

Jack watched her for a moment, his eyes narrowed. "Remember, Tilda, tomorrow will be a better day."

"You're absolutely right."

"I'm happy to help." With that, he retreated to the shop.

"I probably scared the shit out of him."

Jack was autistic, and uncomfortable with extreme emotion, but he had several well-rehearsed responses to manage it.

"He said exactly the same to me last election," Ali said.

Tilda spotted a tray of *pains au chocolat* on the stainless-steel counter and made a beeline for them.

"Another positive," Ali said. "You can eat the whole tray, get fat, and no one will notice that you've gained weight."

Tilda shoved one in her mouth.

"I almost envy you. I'd love my fat arse to disappear."

"Don't say that about yourself."

Ali waved her hand as if brushing that conversation away. "Geoff loves my bum. He can't get enough of it."

Ali was open about her healthy sex life. Perhaps that was why Geoff was always so tired.

"You're lucky. You have a man who adores you," Tilda said through a mouthful of pastry. "You'll never be alone."

"You're not alone. You have us. We'll work this out together." Ali walked over to a fridge. A moment later, Tilda heard the clink of ice.

"You keep alcohol at work?"

"Geoff and I sometimes end the day with a tipple and a shag on that counter."

Tilda stepped away from the counter.

Ali handed her a glass. "Drink up. It'll take the edge off."

Tilda grabbed a wet wipe from a box on the counter and used it to remove the flakes of pastry from her fingers. Gone were the days when people licked their fingers. She then tossed back her drink, which was clearly a double shot. She could feel the warmth of the liquor seep into her veins.

"You're right, that helped."

Ali did the same. "Yep, that's better. I'm rattled too. Gawd, if any of us were to disappear, you'd think it would be me."

"Why would you say that?"

"Well, look at me and look at you. You're gorgeous. I don't know much about invisibility, but I've felt invisible to most people my whole life."

"You're the most highly visible woman I know, Ali."

"I force myself into everyone's line of sight. All the committees and volunteering at the school . . . people have no choice but to see me."

"Maybe I've got invisibility because I never volunteered," Tilda joked, but then said seriously, "You don't have to worry about being invisible. Every single day, you climb into bed with a man who sees you and adores you." Tilda shook her head. "Now we sound like Leith; as if there's a reason for this. There's not. Shit happens."

Ali looked at Tilda, as if she really was trying to see her. "You're strong, Tilly. You'll get through this."

"I don't have much choice, do I?"

"No, but you have support. Let's call Leith."

Tilda shook her head. "Not yet. Leith will have a shitfit that I haven't told her first."

"She'll get over it."

"I just need a few days to absorb this, before Leith sweeps in to 'heal' me."

"You get two days," Ali teased. "After that we'll come and find you."

"Not if you can't see me." Tilda gave Ali a wry smile. Just talking to her friend had given her strength. "See my ear?" Tilda pulled her hair back.

Ali's face fell. "You can just wear your hair over it." Ali picked Tilda's hair tie up off the floor and passed it to her. "Leave your hair down."

Tilda put the elastic around her wrist and patted her hair. "It's just an ear."

"I won't be getting you earrings for Christmas." Ali slapped her hand across her mouth. "I'm sorry. I shouldn't joke."

The two women looked at each other in horror, and then Tilda began to giggle. Eventually, Ali joined her. The laughter got louder until they were doubled over in the middle of the bakery's kitchen.

"Stop," Tilda hissed through her laughter. "I haven't done my Kegel exercises for a decade. I might pee my pants."

"Oh, darling, at least you have your sense of humor," Ali said, howling.

"I promise you, that'll be the last thing that disappears."

7

To be fully seen by somebody, then, and be loved anyhow—
this is a human offering that can border on miraculous.

—ELIZABETH GILBERT, journalist and author

Buoyed by vodka and hope, Tilda resolved that she would gather information, work out a plan, and, importantly, continue to live. She had her friends. Her daughters. A successful business. Money. A bag of pastries. She just needed to keep things normal. She resisted the urge to retreat to the safety of home and stopped at her local café instead. She found a vacant table at the back and ordered a flat white. Then she opened the book Gurinder had given her to the author's note.

> If you're reading this book, you've probably been diagnosed with invisibility. You're not alone; it's just that you can't see the others. Invisibility is more common than you think. Statistics show that ninety percent of women over fifty suffer from undiagnosed stage 1 invisibility without realizing it. They spend years missing out on social and career opportunities because of the impact their mild invisibility has on them.
>
> A small percentage of women experience stage 2 invisibility, where their appendages disappear. With stage 3 there is a loss of limbs, and then full invisibility is stage 4. It's difficult to know the percentage of women whose invisibility develops to

the later stages because of the tendency of those affected to withdraw from normal life.

Surprisingly, this is not a modern-day disorder. Leading invisibility academic Jill Pigeot spent her career deciphering coded mentions of the disorder in the Bible, and later wrote about it in her bestselling book *The Day My Head Disappeared*. Egyptologist and antiquities academic Farrah Ahmad maintains that the hieroglyphics on the walls of the tomb of royal priest Wahtye make mention of his mother disappearing. And yet despite the medical establishment's having known about the condition for centuries, and the many women who continue to be diagnosed each year, research into invisibility—its causes, its impacts, and any reliable treatments—remains almost nonexistent.

I was a practicing doctor for twenty years before my diagnosis, and I knew very little about invisibility. Until it happened to me.

In this book, I share what I've discovered, including which medications will help you manage any symptoms of depression and anxiety, both common with this disorder. This is a practical handbook for sufferers. But let me be clear, this is not a story of triumph; it's one of truth and a journey of immense suffering. You're not going to beat invisibility, so if that's what you're looking to do, close the book now.

Huh?

Tilda stared at the page she'd just read in disbelief. She knew things were going to get tough, and she didn't need a book about a cure, but what was wrong with hope? She'd felt so hopeful after talking to Ali. Now she regretted not asking Gurinder for a prescription for antidepressants. She slammed the book shut and pushed it across the table.

"That bad, eh?"

The man at the next table was speaking to her.

"You slammed that book shut as if it contained a new strain of Ebola. A one-star review?" he said.

Tilda politely smiled. "You can tell that just from how I closed my book?"

"I read between the lines."

Tilda looked at the stranger for a moment. He was in his forties, with tousled brown hair and a chiseled jaw lined with stubble. She couldn't quite gauge if he was hitting on her or being friendly. Usually, she could tell from someone's eyes, but his were hidden behind sunglasses. *Trying to be cool*, thought Tilda. Although he didn't look like someone who would try to be cool, or anything else. He obviously *was* cool.

"Bad editing? Unpalatable font?" he asked.

Tilda slid her hand under the table, already self-conscious about her missing fingers. "A friend just gave me this book, and I was expecting . . . something more."

"Like what?"

"Hope," she blurted.

"Hope is a beggar," he said. "Faith is key."

"This isn't one of those conversations that will end with you handing me a Bible, is it?" Tilda asked.

The man laughed. "Hardly. But I was going to say something cheesy about anything you're looking for in a book, you can also find . . ." He paused.

"On Google?" The banter felt light, and Tilda was smiling.

"One option, I guess. I was going to say the answers you're looking for . . . they're probably in you."

This threw Tilda a little. "Oh my god, Yoda, I barely recognized you."

A very sexy grin. "Next time I'll wear a robe."

"And bring a wooden cane."

He paused for a moment. It was difficult to read him. And then, "Do you come here often?"

Tilda's eyes narrowed. "This is a café, not a bar."

"Does that mean I won't get that whisky I just ordered?" he said.

Tilda laughed. "To answer your question, yes, I do come here often. You?"

"Most days."

"I've never seen you here before."

"Perhaps you weren't looking." His smile was disarming. "I usually come in earlier, after a surf, but it was a lake out there today. Not a wave in sight."

Tilda felt her guard coming down. This man was not only handsome and nice, but he was talking to her. Hell, he'd initiated their conversation. *Take that, invisibility!*

He reached his hand across the table, and without hesitation Tilda thrust hers out and took it. His fingers were long, his handshake firm.

"I'm Patrick."

"Tilda."

"What a great name."

Tilda blushed. It had been a long time since a man had paid her a compliment. She suddenly felt warmer than she had all day.

"As much as I've enjoyed chatting, Tilda, I have to get back to work."

Patrick stood. He was of medium height and lean, with shoulders you could land a plane on. Surfer's shoulders.

She tried not to stare as he gathered his bag. Then, to her mortification, he picked up a white cane.

"Nice to meet you, Tilda."

"You too, Patrick" was all she could manage to stutter out.

He made his way over to the register, where Tilda watched him chat with the waitress and pay his bill. Then, tapping the cane in front of him, he turned and left the café with more grace than she'd ever been able to muster despite having full sight.

Tilda pressed her forehead with the palm of her hand. The Yoda joke about the cane! Oh no . . . what had she said? *"And bring a wooden cane."*

Oh. My. God.

Tilda sat quietly for a moment. A painful knot had formed in her gut. She was so stupid. Not only because she'd said something so utterly awful, but also because she'd thought he'd seen her and had found her appealing enough to talk to. But no, he was no doubt the type of man who struck up conversations with strangers all the time. Didn't blind people have heightened senses? He could probably smell her desperation and was just being nice. She couldn't even run after him to apologize, seeing as one of her feet was shoved in her mouth. She'd trip!

The waitress appeared and started wiping down the table. She stopped mid-wipe. "Oh, sorry, Tilda. I thought you'd left."

It was happening faster than she'd thought it would.

"I wouldn't leave without paying."

"Patrick paid for yours."

"He did?" Nausea washed over her. Was buying her a coffee classified as charity work? Could he claim that as a tax deduction? "Does he do that a lot?"

"Nope." The waitress gave the table in front of Tilda a quick swipe and walked off.

Tilda shoved the book into her bag. Today was officially over. A big serving of invisibility with a humiliation dressing. But just as she reached the café door, she noticed a sign. One of hers. Or, rather, of her company's. A print of a woman staring out to sea, with the words *Your reality is a reflection of your thoughts* across it.

She turned to the waitress, who was now back behind the counter. "Is that new?"

The waitress gave a disinterested shake of the head. "It's been there for ages."

Tilda closed the door behind her, realizing she had no idea what This Is A Sign's bestselling poster meant.

8

It's my women friends that keep starch in my spine and
without them, I don't know where I would be.

—JANE FONDA, in *Vanity Fair*

Tilda rubbed the fog off the bathroom mirror. Her nose was blurry. It was the only way to describe it. It was still visible, but only just. Could today get any worse? It wasn't even seven o'clock—surely there was still time for a comet to hit the house, or a clown to climb through her window, or a plague of huntsman spiders to invade? She slipped into her pajamas and made her way into the living room. White-painted cathedral ceilings, wood floors covered by a large Tuareg rug. Art she'd collected over the years hung on the walls. The fireplace crackled but did nothing to remove the chill. Her home was usually a warm, wonderful, creative space, but tonight it felt empty.

Tilda liked her own company. Being alone had been difficult after Tom left. In the early days, going to bed by herself after a long marriage had been hard, hard work. Some nights she clutched a pillow and cried. Not that she wanted Tom back. She just didn't know how to be on her own. To learn that, she'd walked through flames, but the phoenix always rises, and now she enjoyed her bed, her space, and her independence. Most nights. Tonight, she'd give anything for a caring ear.

"Open up!"

The doorbell buzzed as Leith's voice rang through the house. Flooded with relief, Tilda made her way to the entrance and opened the door to find her two best and dearest friends, looking worried but each holding a bottle of wine.

"Yay, we can still see her!" Leith had clearly been filled in. "I can't believe you didn't tell me. And I can't bloody believe you're disappearing."

Tilda stepped aside so they could enter. "Apparently, it's not called disappearing . . . just invisibility."

"Exactly the same thing."

"I told you not to tell anyone yet," Tilda said to Ali's retreating back.

"I didn't tell anyone," Ali shot over her shoulder. "I told Leith."

Ali and Leith marched up the hall toward the kitchen, while Tilda locked the front door. The house instantly felt warmer again.

"I need to put a bra on," she called out.

"Don't bother." Ali gestured at her oversize cardigan. "I didn't."

Leith popped the cork. "Everything feels better braless."

"We should put that on a T-shirt."

Tilda loved her kitchen—French blue cabinetry, a limestone countertop, and traditional blue-and-white Portuguese tiles behind the stove were a nod to the ocean nearby. But the kitchen was especially wonderful when these women were in it, bringing light and raucous laughter with them.

Leith and Tilda had already been friends for years when they joined a local playgroup with their kids and met Ali. She just fit. It was the start of a wondrous journey, as the three women forged their friendship as their children grew up together. Weekly dinners. Walks. Afternoon wine, morning coffee. If their friendship was a shape, it would be a slightly wonky triangle, which also joined their houses. It took twenty-two minutes to walk in a clockwise direction. Counterclockwise was up a hill so took a little longer.

"Grab the cheese board, Leith. And open the crackers and dip." As always, Ali was in charge. Tilda could relax.

Ten minutes later, Tilda sat center stage on her green velvet couch while her friends sat on either side of her. Snacks and wine were on the coffee table and glasses were at full capacity. The fire crackled and a couple of scented candles wafted subtle musk through the room. The women toasted to friendship, clinking carefully so they didn't spill any wine, and making sure they all made eye contact as they did. They'd heard that it was seven years of bad sex if you didn't lock eyes during a toast, and no one was going to risk that. (Although Tilda did worry that she'd once forgotten to lock eyes with someone, and that's why her sex life had been so atrocious.)

Then, finally, Leith said it.

"You've got no bloody nose, Tilly."

Leith was a drop-dead gorgeous redhead, with a yoga-toned body, a whip-smart brain, and the spirit of a sixties hippie. Tonight, she was in faded blue jeans and a caramel blouse, topped with a rust-colored crochet shawl and matching beanie. Despite the boho clothes and spiritual and philosophical beliefs, she had absolutely no filter.

"I always wanted a nose job," Tilda shot back, making them both laugh. Then she gave a quick show-and-tell of her invisible fingers and ear.

Leith visibly blanched. "Bloody hell. How are you holding up?"

"Better than when I was waiting for the diagnosis," Tilda admitted. "At least I know now."

Leith turned to Ali. "Didn't Jennifer Ginsberg have it?"

"I thought she moved to Melbourne."

Leith shrugged. "Then who am I thinking of?"

"No idea." Ali pulled a paper fan out of her bag and began waving it. "Why don't we know more about invisibility?"

"Same reason you're using that fan right now," Leith pointed out. "Women's issues."

"These hot flashes will be the death of me," Ali sighed. "Is invisibility a symptom of menopause?"

"No, but it's prevalent in menopausal women," Tilda said.

"Like my thinning hair," Leith moaned. "You'll be invisible, and I'll be bald."

"Pretty sure you can get a wig and no one will know the difference," Tilda said.

"Jenny Pearsall!" Leith interjected with a clap of the hands.

Ali gave her fan a flick in acknowledgment. "That's right, she had invisibility. Whatever happened to her?"

There was an awkward silence, and then Leith turned to Tilda, almost defiant. "We're not going to let you disappear."

"I bet Jennifer Pearsall's friends said the same," Tilda mumbled.

"We need to work out what you did to bring this on."

"I knew you'd say that." Tilda glared at her. "This is somehow my fault?"

"Every disease has an emotional root cause."

"Tell that to a toddler with brain cancer," Tilda snapped.

"Point taken," Leith said. "But I'm just trying to help you."

Ali, always the mediator, jumped in. "Let's not argue. We're here to support you, Tilly."

Leith looked at Ali in disbelief. "I *am* supporting her. If she's going to beat this thing, she needs to work out what caused it. My money is on that bastard Tom and the way he treated her."

"That, I'm willing to believe," Tilda mumbled.

Ali topped up everyone's glass. "We don't know what caused this, and I think any speculation should be left to the experts in the field."

"I agree." Leith drew a business card out of her pocket and handed it to Tilda. "This is where you start."

Tilda read the card. "Selma Nester—Visibility Neurotherapy. Redefine what you see." She glanced at Leith. "A therapist?"

"Not just a therapist, but an expert in the field of female invisibility disorders," Leith said. "She's developed a treatment—"

Tilda cut her off. "Gurinder said there are no treatments."

"No mainstream treatments. Selma's approach is alternative and she is very well-known. I got you an appointment next week." Leith sipped her wine. "Details on the back of the card."

Tilda was clearly unimpressed. "I think I'm busy that day."

Leith shot daggers at her. "Then don't take it, but at least have the decency to cancel. There's a twelve-month waiting list to see her."

Tilda laughed in disbelief. "Right. How did I magically jump to the top of that queue?"

Leith rolled her eyes. "Because she's one of our biggest clients. Her conferences are huge."

That shut Tilda up. She placed the card on the coffee table.

"I'll keep it in mind," Tilda finally said.

"You need to be careful what's kept there." Leith sniffed.

"Kept where?"

"In mind." Leith pulled her shawl tight around her body, visibly annoyed.

Ali pulled out a notebook and pen and handed it to Tilda. "Let's get organized. I know how you love lists."

It was true. Tilda was the queen of lists.

"I thought it would be a good idea for the three of us to brainstorm. What are some things you need to do to manage this?"

Tilda was touched. Ali really got her. She grabbed the pen and opened the notebook—one she'd designed—to the first page. A new notebook held a world of possibilities.

"One," she started, writing as she spoke, "gather as much information as possible."

"Excellent. Good place to start," Ali said.

Tilda stalled, the pen hovering over the paper.

"Diet and exercise?" Ali suggested.

Tilda wrote both down. "Absolutely. Perhaps I should start juicing."

Ali murmured her support, while Leith let out a dramatic sigh.

Tilda's head shot up. "Do you have a problem with me juicing?"

"Nope. I'm all for it."

"Then what?"

Leith looked emotional, which stopped Tilda in her tracks. "There's nothing new there."

"What do you mean?"

"The definition of insanity is doing the same thing over and over again but expecting different results."

"You're quoting a mug to me?"

Leith waved a hand at the notebook. "You are an obsessive researcher. You always need to know the answers to everything, so I'm guessing you've already done that."

"It's important to know what I'm up against," Tilda said.

"And does your diet and exercise really need addressing? You're active, you eat well." Leith slapped at the notebook. "This is your comfort zone."

Tilda had to disagree—she was feeling incredibly uncomfortable. She and Leith often fought but always resolved things. In fact, Leith had always been the one person who could pull Tilda up or tell her she was wrong, and vice versa. They were each other's voice of reason and call to action. But tonight, Tilda wanted comfort and Leith was pushing her instead. "What are you trying to say?"

"There's no need to write those things on a list. You already do them." Leith moved across to Tilda and wrapped an arm around her. "I don't want you to think I'm not supportive. I'll do whatever you need to get you through this. I'm just concerned that . . ."

Tilda felt defensive. "That what?"

"That if nothing different goes on that list, nothing will actually change." Leith locked eyes with Tilda, as only best friends can.

After a long moment, Tilda wrote, "Do something different." And then said to her friend, "Better?"

Leith nodded. "It's a start."

9

Enjoy the little things in life, for one day you may
look back and realize they were the big things.
—ROBERT BRAULT, poet

Empty nesting had been a difficult adjustment for Tilda, particularly that first year after the twins moved out. She still missed their chaos, their laughter and light. She even missed those early years: the long nights with two small bodies sprawled across her in bed, the schlepping around from one after-school activity to the next, making endless school lunches, the incessant and often inane chatter—all of it. She simply didn't see how precious it was until the twins had carved out lives of their own, leaving her behind to reflect on just how many moments she'd missed. Oh, she was there, but she wasn't really *there*. Most of the time she'd been too busy watching all the balls she had in the air, afraid she would drop one. She never took time to understand how juggling was meant to be fun. Her days were a cortisol-fest of long work hours, the kids' busy schedules, arguments with Tom about money, and tiptoeing around his moods.

Now, years after all the drama had abated, much of Tilda's grief over her marriage was not over Tom but over the many precious moments she'd missed with her daughters along the way. Irreplaceable moments. She could never get back those lost moments, so instead she deeply valued the ones they had now. One of the posters at work said, "There are no perfect families, just perfect moments." Unlike some of their quotes, this one Tilda understood well.

Today, Tilda felt buoyed by her daughters' chatter and laughter. She used a gloved hand to adjust the mask on her face. She'd fibbed and told the twins she was worried she was coming down with a cold, which they didn't question. She'd decided that she wanted some normal time with them before they freaked out over her missing appendages. Which they would. Especially Holly, whose middle name was melodrama. Tabitha was more contained. She'd go silent. Tilda would tell the girls about her diagnosis after lunch, but it had been nearly two weeks since she'd seen them and she wanted to just bask in their company first.

She watched as they both bustled around the kitchen, along with Tabitha's girlfriend. At twenty-six, Jess was a few years older than Tabitha, but Tab had always been an old soul and was drawn to Jess's steady nature and maturity. Tilda watched Jess now: attractive with lovely brown eyes and an open, warm face, her dark hair cropped close to her head, multiple piercings in each ear, arms covered in tattoos.

"How's the studio, Jess?"

"Going gangbusters," she said as she crumbled feta over a roasted veg-etable salad.

Tabitha handed her some dressing. "Jess tattooed one of the Hems-worths the other day."

Holly's eyes lit up. "I know Liam. Was it him?"

Jess clearly wasn't impressed. "I was too busy looking at his butt to really check out his face."

"*Kelp* wants to run a piece on Jess and her work," Tabitha said proudly. "But she doesn't want to be featured."

Tilda nodded her approval even though she had no idea what *Kelp* was, if not seaweed.

"*Kelp* is a total wankfest," Jess explained, clarifying nothing for Tilda.

Holly grabbed a bottle of kombucha from the fridge and took it over to the table. "We're in our peak career years and need to leverage that."

Holly's time in Los Angeles had rubbed off on her in some of the lan-guage she used.

Jess gave Holly a flick with a tea towel. "You sound like you write for them."

Holly laughed, but then stopped and looked at her mother. "I don't care if you have a cold. Take the mask off."

Tilda finished slicing the still-hot sourdough bread and did her best to act normal, placing the loaf on a large breadboard.

"You girls don't need a sore throat."

"As long as it's not the rona, we'll be fine," Holly said.

"It's not the rona," Tilda assured her, as the dread crept back in. She'd need to remove her mask to eat. She hadn't thought that through. "But I'm also fasting, so the mask stops me from putting food in my mouth." Quick thinking.

Tilda carried the bread to the table and checked out the spread—salad; some dips and veggie slices; Gorgonzola, Edam, and Brie cheeses; some strawberries. Weekend lunches were always thrown-together fare.

Tilda sat, the cue for the others to follow. Holly poured four glasses of kombucha and passed her mother a glass, her eyes narrowing suspiciously at her mother's glove. "Does this break a fast?"

"How's work?" Tilda diverted Holly's attention away from the glove and back to her daughter's favorite subject—herself.

"Exhausting," Holly said dramatically.

Tabitha snort-laughed into her glass.

"Did I say something funny?" Holly snapped.

"You're starring in a TV series, filmed fifteen minutes from where you live. You get picked up every morning and driven home every night. And in between, you pretend you're a nuclear physicist who can fly. You're hardly on a factory floor."

The twins were close, but Tabitha still liked to take Holly down a peg or two.

"Don't argue," Tilda said. "Holly has early calls, and you know she's not a morning person. And Holly, Tabitha had a rough day yesterday with a litter of parvo puppies."

Tilda felt she'd got their attention, with the sniping coming to a stop and all three pairs of eyes now locked on her.

"That's better," she said. "Let's not ruin lunch."

Then Tilda realized it was too late; lunch was already ruined. The strap on her face mask had fallen and the mask was now dangling to one side of her face, revealing her blurry nose. Three very shocked young women stared at Tilda in disbelief. A moment passed and then Jess jumped up and ran around the table to Tilda, taking her by the arm as if she was ill.

"I think we should go into the bathroom," Jess urged.

"If that's because you want to show me that my nose is missing"—Tilda shot them a toothy smile—"I already nose." Tilda removed her glove and showed them her hand. "In fact, my finger has disappeared too. I finger it's run off with my nose." She gave them a thumbs-up with her invisible thumb.

And that's when Holly fainted.

10

It's not what happens to you,
but how you react to it that matters.

—EPICTETUS, philosopher

Holly had always been a drama queen. Right from birth, three minutes after Tabitha, she'd screamed like a banshee while her sister looked on in silence. And nothing had changed. After fainting, she'd cried for half an hour, while Tab clammed up.

"What's happening to you?" Holly bawled.

"Holly, please calm down," Tilda said.

Holly clearly wasn't going to acquiesce, so Jess, ever the peacekeeper, moved around the table to the seat next to Holly and put her arm around her. Holly turned her head and sobbed into Jess's shoulder.

Tabitha was more difficult to read. "Have you been diagnosed with invisibility?"

"You've heard of it?" This surprised Tilda.

"I've read about it, yes."

"Then you'll know it's not terminal."

"There's also no cure." Tabitha's measured tone was the opposite of Holly's hysterical one.

Now it was Tilda's mask of confidence that dropped. "No, no cure."

"When did this happen?" Tabitha asked.

"Just over a week ago. I was going to tell you today, after we'd enjoyed lunch."

"Can someone please explain what's happening?" Holly's hands were wiping the tears from her eyes, a pointless exercise as they continued to flow. The gesture just made her look overwrought.

"Parts of my body have started to disappear," Tilda said in a measured tone, now afraid Holly would have a panic attack. "It's a condition that is quite common in women my age. It's called invisibility."

Holly's eyes were wide and wild. "Will you completely disappear?"

"I don't know. I went to Dr. Majumdar . . . She says hello, by the way."

"I don't care about that!" Holly snapped.

"She'll monitor me over the next few months. But yes, it's possible I might disappear."

"Oh my god, this isn't happening." Holly started to retch, and then she vomited all over the table.

Now she was tucked up in bed, too distraught to go back to the city just yet, so Jess had suggested she get some rest and she'd drive them all back at dawn.

It had been an interesting journey parenting Holly. Ali often joked that Jack was a breeze comparatively, and she had a point. At least Jack's intensity had a name. Ali was able to explain away any behaviors with that umbrella term of autism, but Tilda didn't have just one label to use. Holly had been assessed as twice exceptional, or 2e. She was highly gifted but also had dyslexia and ADHD. So instead of having an easy ride through school and life, she faced her own set of unique challenges. Holly's sensitivities and behaviors that stemmed from her neurodiversity were either ignored or excused for another reason—her looks.

Tilda was aware that all parents thought their children were beautiful, and she certainly thought Tabitha was too, but the difference was that Holly's beauty had given her a pass to all sorts of benefits her entire life, including the well-paid success she now experienced as an actress. Tilda had watched it unfold. From her first day at preschool, when the teacher had said, "My goodness, what a beautiful child," Holly had been treated as one of the special ones. Anyone who said that what was on the inside was what counted had never borne witness to the currency of beauty in their child.

Tilda had overcompensated for this by drilling into Holly the importance of manners and kindness. And while Holly often lacked the former, she did have the latter in spades. She'd been Jack's protector all through school, and still considered him to be her best friend. Even today, she'd dropped by to see him and pick up the bread he'd baked for her. Holly and Jack were as close now as they were when they were children. It had, around puberty, concerned the two mums, who felt Jack was at risk of being hurt. But Ali had spoken to Jack about it.

"Do you love Holly?" she'd asked at the time.

"Yes." Thirteen-year-old Jack was quite up front about it.

"Love . . . like a . . . girlfriend love?"

Jack looked confused. "Holly and I were born to protect each other."

And that was that. It didn't matter if no one else understood their bond. They did. Ali believed it was because they balanced each other out; and were both misunderstood. Whatever the case, people who didn't know Holly were often surprised by the depth of her loyalty to Jack. Not Tilda. She knew her daughter's strengths. After Tom left, Tabitha had been the more considerate one, but Holly was the one who hugged her. Long, tight embraces, just at that point in Tilda's life where human touch meant everything. Holly was wild and creative and would make her laugh. For every frustrating, exhausting behavior, Holly had ten traits that brought joy into your world. She was sensational, and it often baffled Tilda how she'd managed to have any genetic input into such a creature.

Or how Tom had, as he was less than average in so many ways.

Tilda sipped her wine by the fire with Tabitha curled up on the sofa beside her. Her relationship with Tabitha brought her peace and calm. Tab had always been mature for her age, at any age, perceptive and self-aware. Growing up, she'd been the leader of all the kids: Holly, Jack, and Leith's daughter, Lulu. The four of them were still close, with Tabitha being the person they all turned to in a time of need, the one who organized their regular catch-ups and, importantly, the one who kept all their secrets.

Tab had her sister's tiny frame, but her eyes were more almond-shaped and her nose slightly longer. Her pixie cut showed off her high cheekbones and full lips. She'd grown up in Holly's shadow, constantly being compared to her twin by others, so she was unaware of just how beautiful she also was. In fact, the older she got, the more beautiful she became. Her face reflected her qualities of reliability, trustworthiness, and kindness. And love. The love that she shared with Jess showed on her now.

Tilda felt a tug of envy in her gut. Good envy. And relief. She was relieved that despite the ashes of her parents' marriage, Tab wasn't repeating those patterns in her relationship. Tabitha and Jess shared an easy love. Tilda wished she knew the secret to that. She'd never experienced easy love, but the older she got, the more she admired it. Desired it.

She could hear Jess in the kitchen, cleaning up. It gave Tilda and Tabitha the space to talk.

And they had. Tabitha's reaction had been as predictable as Holly's—silence giving way to thoughtful questions and practical suggestions, followed by a wait-and-see approach.

"We really won't know how this will present in you for some time."

Tilda felt a surge of pride. "You sound like a doctor now."

"And in my field, if things get bad, I'm allowed to euthanize you."

Tilda laughed. "Not if you can't find me."

Tab giggled, and then took her mother's hand. It was a big move for her. She'd missed out on the affection gene while Holly got two.

"You know, Mum, you don't have to be so together about this. It's okay to lose it."

"When I found out, I spent three days drunk, dancing to seventies disco hits and howling," Tilda admitted.

This surprised Tab, who grinned. "Good on you."

"It was definitely cathartic."

"I'm here if you need me."

"I know." Tilda gave Tab's hand a squeeze. "This is probably stating the obvious, but please don't tell your father about this."

The girls were close to Tom, and Tilda suspected that, like her, he had the time to enjoy their company more now that their marriage problems weren't taking up so much time and space.

"Gawd, of course not," Tabitha said. She gazed at the dying embers in the fireplace. "You know, I understand what it's like to feel invisible."

Tilda's heart hurt at the pain in her daughter's voice. "Do you mean because of Holly?"

Tabitha chuckled. "No. I'm sure some people view me as being in her shadow, but I'm happy to hide there in the shade. I'm talking about growing up queer."

Tilda searched her daughter's face. "I hope I never made you feel invisible because of that."

Tabitha didn't respond. She waved her hand in the direction of the kitchen. "Jess sees me. Maybe you just need someone who sees you."

"Maybe the point is to see ourselves."

Tabitha absorbed this for a moment. Ever thoughtful. "Want my advice?"

How quickly that moment comes when your baby becomes your adviser.

"Of course," Tilda said. "I welcome your advice."

Tabitha looked her mother square in the eye. "I can't help but think about that card you got me for graduation, with the H. Jackson Brown Jr. quote on it."

" 'Throw off the bowlines'?"

" 'Sail away from the safe harbor,' " Tabitha said. "Take a risk with this thing and try something *different*."

"Try something different . . ." Tilda gave her daughter a resigned smile, noting the coincidence. Although Leith would call it a sign. "I promise I'll do that."

11

It is not the answer that enlightens, but the question.

—EUGÈNE IONESCO, playwright

Early the following morning, Tilda gave all three girls a tight hug and watched as they bundled into the car and drove off. No one mentioned that her nose and her whole hand were now completely missing. The car rounded the corner and Tilda felt that all-too-familiar tug in her gut. Things had been so much easier when the girls were younger and she always knew exactly where they were.

She put on a mask, pulled her hoodie as far over her head as she could, slipped on a pair of gloves, and, with Buddy yanking at the leash, headed to the beach.

Her beach.

It had been this stretch of sand that had sold her on the house. When she and Tom had bought it, and for years after, the house was in disrepair. They had plans to renovate but no money to do so. But the moment she'd stepped onto the beach, she'd known that she'd found her forever home. Her place in the world.

Over the years, her footsteps had eroded the sand as she walked out her worries about building a business. She was a photographer, and while creating those early products with Leith for their market stall was fun, the more successful their little company was, the more she found herself making business decisions instead of creative ones. Decisions that over time provided for her family financially but took her further and further away from her own artistic dreams. And then there was the stress and heartbreak of her marriage. She'd pounded countless kilometers out on this beach, clearing her head after one of their arguments, trying to unravel the knots he tied in her brain. Tom was self-absorbed and difficult but also fiercely intelligent and interesting. He didn't have a romantic bone in his body, but he was passionate. He didn't tell her she was beautiful or desirable, but he showed her. From the moment he'd first kissed her, she was his. His very presence excited her. And ultimately subsumed her.

Today, her brain was working overtime again, but the space that had once been filled with marriage and work problems was now a repository for even more complex problems, including her diagnosis.

She had invisibility. And she was terrified.

How? Why? Was there a purpose to this?

Had she somehow created it? Leith believed that most illnesses had an emotional root cause.

To Tilda, that seemed like a double whammy for the sufferer. "You have this incurable disease, and not only that, but guess what? You caused it."

"Don't you get it?" Leith would say. "It doesn't make you more of a victim. It hands your power back. If you created it, you can uncreate it!"

Leith and Ziggy had eventually stopped trying to convert Tilda to their way of thinking. Now their tradition, every birthday, was to create a new "unspirational" product for Tilda. The first year, they'd printed a poster that said, "The key to happiness is to lower your expectations."

The birthday after Tilda's divorce spawned a T-shirt with "There's someone for everyone, except for you." Tilda's favorite item was the mug she used most mornings: "You're only as deep as your most recent inspirational quote." She loved the unspirational products, as did a lot of people— when, a couple of years ago, the team decided to release the whole series, everything sold out in two days. Now they always kept the unspirational line in stock and sold a ton each year.

Tilda's feet hit the sand and she unclipped Buddy's leash and let him loose to run. He was a mutt but could run like a greyhound. She shot a few images of him, tempted to push all these troublesome thoughts from her mind and escape into her camera. That was her normal modus operandi. When she was "in the zone" shooting, her mind was blissfully empty. But today, she slung her camera back over her shoulder. Both Leith and Tabitha had suggested she try something different, and asking unsettling questions was certainly different. They had started with what would happen if she disappeared. Not on a physical level, as she was already experiencing, but existentially.

If something can't be seen, does it still exist?

If she was invisible, would she still exist? Perhaps some people wouldn't think so, but she knew she would. And if that was the case, didn't that point to the existence of other things that couldn't be seen?

How can you prove something exists if it can't be seen?

Tilda had always been dismissive of this exact thing—Leith's deeply held belief in the unseen.

"Our world is full of things you can't see and never question," Leith would say. "Gravity, consciousness, dark matter, black holes, electricity . . . radio waves. Ever actually seen those crazy things that make your internet work?"

Tilda knew she'd lost the argument but gave it one more shot. "But 'spirit' is different. There's no data on that."

"Do you know what data is?" Leith challenged. "Experience. Not just one, but many. So I don't just believe in spirit, I know it to be true based on the data I've collected through multiple experiences. It's no longer my 'belief,' it's my 'experience.'"

Tilda still thought measuring gravity and measuring God (or Universal Life Force, as Leith preferred) were worlds apart.

But what if she was wrong?

She knew she wasn't breaking new ground. These questions had been asked for thousands of years, more recently on the very products her company created. Often the questions had no answers. Needed no answers. Asking the question was the point. Or, to paraphrase Socrates, perhaps accepting that you don't know anything is the only true wisdom.

Tilda didn't view herself as a religious person. She also wasn't an atheist. She saw both as flip sides of the same coin. Each side was so certain they knew the truth of God's existence. Tilda sat somewhere in the middle, on the spin of the coin as it floated in midair before being caught. When it could go either way. That was her . . . she could go either way. She believed that something, a higher consciousness, could exist, and there was a lot of beauty in the world to indicate that it did. Surely such beauty could not just be random. But then how to explain the opposite? The pain in the world.

In the past, she'd never really contemplated these things. At work, she was surrounded by people whose lives revolved around digging into those questions. She left the words and ideas to others and focused on the photos.

Today, Tilda's invisible hand clutched Buddy's lead while he ran ahead of her. An icy wind whipped along the sand. Being on *her* beach calmed her, and the panic she'd felt since being diagnosed subsided and made way for one question to rise above all the others: Why me?

The only answer she had was Why not?

Was it an odds game and her number had been called?

Was it simply random bad luck?

Or was there a reason? A purpose?

Tilda noticed two surfers leaving the water up ahead. She lifted her camera and pressed the shutter button. For a moment, her mind switched off and she existed in that space—that creative moment. The surfers continued to walk toward her. She called Buddy back and clipped his leash on. She pulled the glove off, praying her hand would be visible again, but if there was a god, they weren't taking requests. No miraculous reappearance of appendage to report.

If nothing would change until she tried something different, then what was it she needed to do? What might produce a different outcome in the progression of this disease?

Tilda knew she needed support. She had her friends, but she had no intention of burdening them constantly, especially if she really did disappear. In lieu of faith, she needed something else. A therapist? She had that appointment Leith had set up. And then she remembered the flyer for the support group that Gurinder had given her. A group of this kind was not a place she'd ever envisioned herself, which made it *different*. The idea of attending a support meeting made her uncomfortable, but one of the mugs at work said that real change happens when you're watching your comfort zone disappear in the rearview mirror. It was on a mug, so it must be true.

The surfers were now close by. They walked side by side, the wind carrying their voices along the beach. She was just about to head back up the path to her cul-de-sac when she realized the taller of the two was Patrick. His cane had been replaced by a surfboard under his arm. Wait a minute . . . had she been duped? Was he not blind?

And then she saw the other man raise his hand and guide Patrick by the elbow. He dropped it and repeated the action a short time later.

Tilda secured her mask up over where her nose should have been and decided to make a quick getaway, but before that happened, Buddy, who had no social skills whatsoever, lurched toward the two men to say hello. He pressed his head against Patrick's hand, demanding a pat.

Tilda couldn't blame him. Seeing Patrick in his wetsuit, she felt like doing the same.

Patrick laughed. "Hello there." He gave Buddy's head a rub and turned in Tilda's direction. "What's his name? Or hers?"

This was awkward. "His. Buddy."

Patrick moved his head slightly to one side. "Tilda?"

Did he see her? Or did he recognize her voice? Either way, it was nice. "Hi, Patrick, yes, Tilda here . . ."

Okay, humiliating—they weren't on a phone call.

She gestured at the dog. "And this is my very needy mutt, Buddy."

Patrick thumbed in the direction of his companion. "This is my very needy mutt, Stephen."

Stephen grinned at Tilda. "I'm also his brother."

"Fancy meeting you here." Patrick rested his board on the sand, one arm leaning on it. "You come here often, Tilda?"

"This is a beach, not a bar."

"Does that mean I won't get that whisky I just ordered?"

They both laughed. Tilda noticed Stephen watching them curiously.

"I bring Buddy here most mornings and take photos." Tilda lifted her camera to show them and then awkwardly dropped her hand again, unsure what the protocol was when showing a blind man an object you're holding.

"Are you a photographer?" Stephen asked.

"I am."

"What sort of photography?"

"I started in portrait photography but now take all sorts of photos. I have a business that creates inspirational posters and products."

"This Is A Sign?" Stephen asked.

"Guilty as charged," Tilda said, embarrassed now. When people heard about her business, they immediately assumed she was all fluff, no substance.

Instead, Stephen said, "My wife loves your stuff. It's all over our house." He turned to his brother. "Tilda made your favorite mug."

The penny dropped for Patrick. "Oh right! I love that mug."

Now it was Tilda's turn to judge. Please don't make Patrick a *Live, Love, Laugh* kinda guy! "Which one?"

"'You're only as deep as your most recent inspirational quote.' I use it every day."

Tilda stared at him.

"Stephen bought it for me," Patrick explained.

"I have that mug too," Tilda finally managed to say.

"Our mugs should meet for coffee."

It was the first day of winter, yet one look at Patrick, his damp curls and *that* smile, and Tilda suddenly needed a dip to cool off. Either that or she was suddenly menopausal.

There was an awkward pause, until Buddy (thankfully) made a snuffling sound at Patrick, who grinned and gave him a pat. Tilda watched his long fingers curl around Buddy's ear. Tilda needed to escape before she made a fool of herself.

"Anyway, nice seeing you, Patrick." Shit, do you say "nice seeing you" to a blind person? And are they called blind or sight impaired? Geez, life was difficult. Obviously more so for Patrick, who was blind . . . or sight impaired. She bumbled on. "And lovely to meet you, Stephen." *Meet* was a safe enough word, unless he was a vegetarian.

Patrick gave her a wave. "Catch you soon, Tilda. Third time's the charm."

Tilda yanked Buddy's leash and started walking up the beach, trying not to trip. At least Patrick wouldn't see it if she did.

12

If we are to love our neighbors, before doing
anything else we must see our neighbors.

—FREDERICK BUECHNER, author and theologian

On the way home, Tilda made a pit stop at the end of her street, to visit her neighbor Maeve. She clicked the rusted clip on the gate and then opened the letterbox. As always, it was filled with catalogs and flyers. Not that she was allowed to throw them out. Maeve felt that Chemist Warehouse had printed them for her and Australia Post had delivered them to her, so the very least she could do was read them. And she did. Once she'd finished, she placed them on the ever-growing pile beside her laundry door and used them for cat litter.

Maeve had lived in this home for sixty-five years. She'd raised her son here, but he now lived in Dublin. Her husband had died here, although he'd also been gone for decades. All the other homes in the street had been renovated over the years, but Maeve's weatherboard cottage stood firm in its original state. The front grass needed clipping, weeds sprouted through the path and from the steps, and her guttering was rusted.

For years, Tilda had just known Maeve to wave to as she passed by, or to have a quick chat with at the front gate. But when the pandemic hit, Tilda knocked on her door to see if she was okay and if she needed any groceries. She'd been knocking on her door a few times a week since.

Tilda had never realized how alone the elderly woman on her street had been. Perhaps because she was busy herself, raising kids, fighting to save a marriage, building a business. But in recent years, she'd had more time to notice others around her, and she'd noticed Maeve. Alone at eighty-eight, apart from eleven cats.

Which was another reason Tilda was now so involved with Maeve. During those first months of visiting, Tilda discovered that Maeve had built up a colony of underfed cats who kept breeding. She'd taken them, pair after pair, and arranged with Tabitha to have them spayed and neutered. Tilda paid, of course, but told Maeve it was a community service program. Then she nursed the cats at her place for a few days, much to Pirate's disgust, until they were ready to be released back into Maeve's clowder.

Tilda removed her mask and shoved it in her pocket, gave a sharp rap on the door, and then bent down and pulled some weeds from around the steps while she waited for Maeve to open it. Depending on what chair she was sitting in, it could take some time. Finally, Maeve appeared. As always, she was fully dressed, wearing stockings with a ladder up the leg and badly applied makeup. Tilda suspected Maeve's eyesight wasn't so great. Which was a relief today, because she didn't have to explain her own appearance—or rather, disappearance.

"Morning, Maeve." Tilda tossed the weeds she was clutching into the overgrown garden and then handed over the catalogs. "There's a Dick Smith one in there."

"Can't stand the man. Total commie. I'll enjoy watching the cats crap on that."

Spending time with Maeve was often a lesson in patience. "I just wanted to see if you need anything. I'm putting my grocery order in."

"Just the usual. Plus add a lemon cake. Come in and I'll get my purse." Maeve limped up the hall toward the kitchen. She had a bung hip, as she called it, but otherwise was in very good health. She always paid for her groceries, but Tilda told her the cat food was free from the charity. It wasn't. Tilda knew that despite living in a house that was now worth a fortune, Maeve had to pinch pennies.

She looped Buddy's leash over the fence post, just in case he decided to follow her in. Unlikely. He'd met Maeve's cats. "And you were low on tea," Tilda called, following her up the hall.

The smell of cat urine enveloped her. She always felt like she needed a wash after visiting Maeve, but she felt responsible for the old woman now. What had started as "the neighborly thing to do" had turned into a complex relationship: she not only felt obliged to help Maeve but also liked her. Not always on the same day. She'd had some great conversations with Maeve over the years. When the older woman got talking about her past, you couldn't stop her. Maeve had been raised by a single mother after her father didn't return home from the war. Then, when her own husband died at thirty-three, she'd sworn to never remarry.

"That doesn't mean I was celibate," she'd told Tilda. "He croaked just in time for the sexual revolution. And I was quite a looker. But the more men I knew intimately, the more I realized . . ."

"Realized what?" Tilda encouraged.

"You couldn't pay me to give up my freedom and marry again."

Maeve never said if the price she'd paid for that freedom had been worth it now that the only person who saw her regularly was a neighbor.

Still, Maeve often surprised Tilda with her experiences and views on life, so despite the state of the house, she did enjoy their conversations. Summers were easier, when they'd sit outside and have a whisky—Maeve's secret to good health, apparently—and Tilda didn't have to deal with the oppressive dankness inside.

Tilda sidestepped Miss Piggy, Maeve's favorite cat, who waddled up the hall. She had a mean streak that served her well in the cutthroat feline community out the back. She was always fed. "I'm going to pick up another big bag of that kibble, and some more flea treatment, so I'll come by with that too."

Maeve handed Tilda a twenty. "You're a dear."

Tilda waited, to see if Maeve noticed anything different about her. But Maeve said nothing, which confirmed Tilda's suspicions about her sight. She obviously wasn't like Patrick—she still did her weekend sudoku and could name all eleven cats at a distance—but she had been made to surrender her driver's license.

"Should we book you for your annual eye check?" Tilda asked.

"Nothing wrong with my eyes. I don't need to see far, stuck here like I am."

"I don't want you tripping over a cat," Tilda said, watching as Gandalf jumped onto the counter and licked Maeve's breakfast plate clean.

"They keep out of my way," Maeve said, ushering Tilda back down the hall and out the door.

Tilda untied Buddy, and he yanked her out the gate. "I'll be back tomorrow, Maeve."

"Don't you worry about me," Maeve called.

Maeve said that a lot, but if Tilda didn't worry about her, who would?

13

The meeting for the Invisibility Support Group was held at the local town hall on Main Street. Tilda entered the room, and a woman missing the whole bottom half of her body floated over to her.

"I often wonder if Michael Jackson suffered from it, you know." The woman gave Tilda a knowing look. "It's rare in men, but he had the signs."

Tilda had no idea what she was talking about, and it showed.

"The glove," the woman explained, looking down at Tilda's hands. "It often starts with the hand, and we all wear gloves."

"Ah, right, Michael Jackson. I guess he couldn't beat it," Tilda joked, but she quickly realized the woman across from her didn't find it funny, so admitted, "I wear the glove because I don't want to scare anyone."

"There's no getting around it. You'll eventually scare someone. Mine started in my hand as well, and now look at me."

Tilda found looking at the woman disturbing.

"If this doesn't frighten people, what will?" The woman jutted her chin out, as if challenging Tilda to answer.

She didn't. Instead, she asked a question. "Why are your trousers invisible?"

The woman nodded—approving the question. "I have late stage 3. What we know is that invisibility affects the body first. Sufferers can get away with wearing clothes that mask the issue, as you're doing today with your glove. Over time, though, it doesn't matter what a woman wears . . . nothing makes us visible."

Tilda's eyes widened in horror—would this happen to her?

"I'm Brenda. Come in and I'll introduce you to the others."

Tilda followed Brenda into the room. There were about a dozen chairs in a circle. Some were taken. Other women milled around a table with tea and cookies.

"Ladies, we have a new attendee today." Brenda turned to Tilda. "I'm sorry, I didn't catch your name."

"Tilda."

The other women nodded and murmured their greetings. Tilda scanned the room. It was a diverse group of women, with differences in race and religion, and what appeared to be socioeconomic status. There were even some differences in age, although all of them were over forty.

Brenda motioned for Tilda to join the circle. "We're about to start, if you'd like to take a seat."

Tilda made her way over to the chairs and was just about to plonk herself in one when another woman stopped her.

"Carol is sitting there."

The empty chair spoke. "Not a problem. Happens all the time."

Tilda was aghast. Poor Carol was completely invisible. Tilda moved over a seat, next to a woman who didn't have any specific limb missing but just looked hazy, in general. She introduced herself, but Tilda had to blink a lot to keep her in focus.

"I'm Belle. Just diagnosed?"

Tilda nodded. "You?"

"I've been suffering with it for fifteen years."

Tilda looked shocked. Belle was an attractive brunette, albeit with an air of weary defeat about her. "Fifteen? You don't look old enough."

"That's very kind, but I'm fifty-five."

Tilda swallowed the urge to scream, "That's not old!" Instead, she turned to the rest of the group, who were now seated.

Brenda ran the group. Tilda had the feeling that she ran a lot of things.

She looked efficient with a clipboard in hand. Everyone waited patiently while she walked over to a large monitor connected to a laptop and launched a Zoom meeting.

"Some members attend virtually," Belle explained to Tilda.

Tilda realized there were half a dozen more participants on the call, but all but one of the screens were blank.

"Afternoon, ladies," Brenda said to an underwhelming response apart from the one visible attendee who waved. She turned back to the women in the room. "Perhaps we should start with Tilda. She can share her story, and then we can open up to questions." Brenda gave Tilda the go-ahead. "Tilda, all yours."

Tilda disliked speaking in front of groups but, remembering her decision to be proactive and do things differently, forged ahead. "I'm still absorbing my diagnosis. It's been a shock."

Everyone nodded in sympathy.

"I'm trying to understand what it means for me."

Another group nod. Sympathy was dripping from the walls.

"But I intend to do everything I can to beat this."

There was a collective gasp. The other members glanced at each other and then turned to Brenda for guidance. Brenda snickered.

Tilda fought back a wave of rage. She'd had the courage to show up and introduce herself, only to be ridiculed. "Did I say something funny?"

Brenda's tone bordered on patronizing. "Not funny, just uninformed. We hear this so often, just after diagnosis. Women who think they can somehow beat this."

"You don't think I can?"

"I have suffered this dreadful disease for many years now." Brenda's forehead furrowed. "I'm pretty sure that if there was an effective treatment for it, I'd have heard about it."

Brenda had just pushed Tilda's insubordinate button. Tilda *would* beat invisibility, just so she could show this silly cow how wrong she was. "A friend told me about Selma Nester—"

This time a few of the other women tittered along with Brenda.

"That woman is a charlatan," Brenda said. "I went to her once, and she barely even discussed my disorder. Instead, we had a ridiculous conversation about neural pathways in my brain, and my personality."

Tilda bit down on her bottom lip to stop herself from smiling. She noted that she needed to add Selma Nester to her list and at least research the woman before canceling the appointment Leith had made for her.

"I wanted an antidepressant to help me cope. But she made a distasteful joke about how if she gave me what I asked for, I still wouldn't be happy. She was very rude." Brenda pursed her lips.

Tilda refrained from mentioning her own appointment with Dr. Nester and let Brenda continue.

"You're reeling from the shock of diagnosis, Tilda. You might even be a little delusional. That can happen."

Tilda raised an eyebrow. Her body might be disappearing, but her mind was fine.

Brenda had the floor and worked it. "I'll tell you the reality of invisibility. I'm in a constant state of despair about my legs. I might as well be naked from the waist down."

Tilda couldn't help herself. "Are you?"

Brenda looked horrified. "Absolutely not."

"I imagine it would be a bit nippy going half naked, but you could probably get away with fleece tights in winter and no one would know," Tilda said.

Brenda went on, seemingly ignoring Tilda. "It's important to maintain a sense of who you are and to continue wearing what you like, even if no one can see it." Brenda gave her cardigan a little tug, as if to emphasize that fact, and then waved a hand at Carol. "Carol favors expensive designer labels, but obviously we can't appreciate that now."

"I'm still in my pajamas today." Carol's voice came from nowhere. "What's the point?"

Brenda stared at the empty chair in frustration. "But I waited for you to get dressed when I came to pick you up."

"I had a brandy instead."

"Would you like to share your week with the group, Carol?"

"No, I have nothing else to say."

Brenda turned to the others. "Let Carol's deterioration be a lesson for us all."

Carol was silent, but the others couldn't wait to tell their stories.

Claire jumped to her feet. "I had a bad week. The automatic doors at the supermarket wouldn't open for me. I just stood there for ages, waiting for someone to enter or exit so I could get my groceries." She was crying inconsolably. "What will I do? I don't want to starve."

"Have them delivered," Brenda suggested.

Claire's crying let up. "Yes, of course. Why didn't I think of that?"

"Because you're under enormous stress dealing with this condition," Brenda reminded her.

"Thank you. Not sure what I'd do without this group."

Claire returned to her seat, while Waris stood. Tilda recognized her from various television commercials.

"As you know, arriving here as a refugee has meant I've often felt invisible. My modeling was my way of being seen. But now that the work has dried up, I've also realized how precarious my financial situation is."

Brenda jumped in. "Have you ever worked as a makeup artist, Waris?"

"No, but I could. I'd enjoy that."

"Come and speak to me after the meeting. There's a group I volunteer with that can help you find work."

"That would be amazing, Brenda. Thank you."

Waris returned to her seat and the one visible woman joining via Zoom spoke next.

"Brenda, I know you've explained the different stages of invisibility before, but I'm still a little confused."

"I'm happy to reiterate, Lara." Brenda walked over to the side of the room and grabbed hold of a large mobile whiteboard, pivoting it into the center of the space. Then, with a blue marker in hand, she began to write.

Stage 1: 90% of women over 50

"We all understand this stage," Brenda said. "It crept up on us, somewhere in our forties. While there are no visible affects during stage 1, we're overlooked at work for a promotion, despite being the most qualified person for it. Many of us deal with financial disadvantages. We're ignored in certain social situations. A dawning occurs at this point. Most women remain at stage 1, but for some of us, somewhere around fifty . . ." Brenda scrawled across the board.

Stage 2: Appendages disappear

She was on a roll now. "It's devastating. We cover the missing appendages with clothing and detract from the condition using bright accessories, but nothing helps because stage 3 follows quickly."

Stage 3: Loss of limbs

"During stage 2 and early stage 3, we cover up our invisible limbs as best we can, until late stage 3, when our clothes become invisible as well. From this point on, nothing we wear helps. And inevitably, stage 4 arrives."

The marker scrawled across the whiteboard.

Stage 4: Complete invisibility

Brenda paused for a moment, tapping the marker against her palm. "Any questions?"

"Yes, does anyone want to buy my collection of Camilla kaftans?" Carol called out. "Total waste of money now."

Tilda cracked up, but when she realized she was the only one laughing, she stopped. "Sorry," she mumbled.

"You've just won a free kaftan," Carol quipped.

Tilda could see that participants benefited from Brenda's advice and help, but the overall atmosphere was weighted with negativity. Apart from Carol, no one made a joke or said anything that wasn't despondent. Tilda clutched the edge of her plastic chair and fought the urge to leave. Was this her future? Surely something funny had happened to one of them. In fact, every story was so ridiculous, they should be laughing at themselves. At one another. If this was a support group, where was the laughter? Wasn't that the best medicine?

"Tilda, how did you feel when you realized your ear had disappeared?" Brenda said.

Tilda decided to try to lighten the mood. "I've got to say, it was a little ear-ie."

Ba dum tss.

Nothing.

"It's how I ended up 'ear.'"

Still nothing. Although, to be fair, Carol might've been grinning from ear to ear. There was certainly a chuckle from that direction.

Brenda nodded. "I understand. You're desperate to make light of the situation. That will change."

Tilda felt defiant. "I was horrified, Brenda. And frightened. I still am. But I also intend to maintain my sense of humor. Otherwise, what's the point?"

"That's definitely a question you'll be asking yourself before long," Brenda said.

Tilda kept her mouth shut. Who was she to judge? Perhaps years of living with invisibility had worn them down. Tilda tried to have some empathy for these women but felt suffocated by their hopelessness. Everyone howled and moaned and cried, and by the end of the meeting Tilda felt completely depressed. Yet she'd be lying if she didn't admit that she was also relieved—relieved that she wasn't the only one. Despite sensing that this was an unhealthy environment for her, she took comfort from being around people who were in the same situation.

After the meeting, Brenda approached her. "We'll see you at the next meeting." It was a statement, not a question.

Tilda would return, not because she wanted to, not because the meeting had inspired her in any way, but because she didn't want to be alone.

14

We're so focused on being beautiful,

we don't learn how to be visible.

—SELMA NESTER

Later that night, curled up in front of the fire, Tilda flipped open her laptop and searched for Selma Nester. She was surprised by what she found. There were tens of thousands of mentions of Selma. There were clips of Selma speaking on various television shows, at conferences, at the UN, and at a TED talk. She couldn't have such a high profile and be a complete charlatan, could she?

> I too was diagnosed with invisibility. I lost the whole right side of my body before I discovered the key to beating it. Since then, I have dedicated my life to helping thousands of other women return to visibility. Here's what very few doctors will tell you: invisibility is a curable condition.

A shiver of excitement ran through Tilda. Hope.

What had Patrick said? Hope is a beggar, faith is key? It reminded her of the oven mitt at work embroidered with a Napoleon Hill quote: "Nothing is impossible to the person who backs desire with enduring faith."

There seemed to be a leap between the two, and today, hope was a start. Tilda trusted Gurinder, but what if she was wrong? What if there *was* a cure?

Selma's biography added to Team Hope.

> Selma Nester studied medicine at the University of Wrocław
> before emigrating to Australia, where she completed her mas-
> ter's in medicine (psychiatry). Her work in the field of invisi-
> bility and female disappearing disorders is renowned. In 1982
> she was awarded the Australasian Prize for Women's Health.
> Nester was diagnosed with invisibility in 2002. By 2005 she
> was completely visible again. Her memoir, *Now You See Me,*
> *Now You Don't,* was on the *New York Times* bestseller list for
> seven months. In 2007 she was featured on the *Oprah Winfrey*
> *Show,* forging the way for a successful speaking career. Nester
> has clinics in the UK and Australia and holds weeklong work-
> shops around the world. She has helped cure countless women
> of invisibility.

Tilda stared at the photos of Selma. One photo had been taken in 2002
and was of a rather mousy-looking woman with one arm missing. The
second photo was from three years ago. While much older, the woman in
that photograph was clearly visible.

Tilda clicked on a YouTube link to a clip of Selma speaking at a
conference—the clip had over five million views. How had she never
come across this woman before? She reminded herself that until she'd
been diagnosed with an eggplant allergy, she'd never been to an allergist
either.

She pressed Play. Selma was a fiery redhead, with a magnetic presence.
Her speech was a call to arms that had the very large audience of women
clapping and cheering.

"For most women, invisibility starts somewhere in their forties. Forty
is not, as many will tell you, the new thirty. That completely diminishes
the powerful lessons the forties bring with them. It is a decade of great
change for women, in a society that wants women to remain the same:
youthful and submissive. This completely goes against how Nature designed females—to step into our power as we age. The systemic denial of

aging, and the rejection of the power that comes with getting older, results in most women taking an emotional and psychological beating in their forties. An enormous amount of pressure is placed on what is nothing more than a number. Aging is not the enemy. A great gift is forged in the flames of mistakes and mess-ups and the pain and tears that weave rivers of lines across our skin. Once we've grown used to the weight of loss and the impermanence of everything, something shifts. Take this journey and on the other side you will find something so important, so extraordinary, and so freeing, which is this: how the world sees us, how other people see us, is meaningless. What's important is how we see ourselves. We must be visible to ourselves."

Tilda closed her laptop and stood. She felt restless. She was fifty-two, and newly diagnosed with invisibility. But she'd felt invisible for years. Her forties *had* been tough. Every month, there'd be a few days when she'd swing between despair and rage. Tom never understood it. If anything, he amplified it. He wasn't the type of man to ever ask why she felt a certain way, or if there was anything he could do to support her. Instead, he'd make it about him—she was crazy, she was difficult. She was *wrong*, about everything. She tried continuously to resolve their problems and reignite their relationship. He retreated even further.

Tilda had started doing research online: Was she crazy? Was something wrong with her? The countless articles and online communities pointed to perimenopause. Leith suggested bioidentical hormones, so she asked Gurinder about them but was offered an antidepressant instead. Tilda turned it down. She wasn't depressed. She felt like Medusa three days a month. The rest of the time . . . well, she didn't know whom she felt like, but certainly not herself.

Selma was right. Hitting forty was pivotal. The whole decade had been like visiting a country where nobody could hear her, understand her, or see her. Tilda was an attractive woman, but somewhere in her mid-forties that currency had waned. She was often overlooked in a queue. She would enter some restaurants or bars and feel like a dinosaur. Male heads that had once snapped to attention as she walked by now failed to turn, which wasn't in itself a bad thing, but then Tom too joined that throng. He barely noticed her, never looked up when she entered the room. And then he had an affair with a much younger woman and walked out the door. Before she knew it, she blinked and fifty arrived, and she recognized just how fabulous she'd been at forty.

Tilda walked into the bathroom and stared at her reflection in the mirror.

She realized that she'd felt like she was disappearing well before her first finger did. She'd spent her forties clawing to be seen. All around her, women were erasing their age from their faces. She too had been increasingly critical of her appearance, but why? What a waste of time.

Turning fifty had been easier. She'd been alone for long enough to savor her hard-won contentment. There was an undeniable acceptance that wasn't there at forty. She didn't fight the lines or grey hairs as much, although she was still self-critical. But now, right now, looking in the mirror watching herself disappear, she desperately wanted to see herself grow old. The thought of missing out on that shook her to her core.

She reached out and touched her reflection. It was as though a great gift had just been taken away from her. And she'd do anything to have it back.

15

Whether you like it or not, there's a voice inside your head.
That's out of your control. The voice will either make you
happy or unhappy. That's what you can control.

—SELMA NESTER

There was Helen Mirren. And Jennifer Lopez. Another one with Michelle Obama standing on one side of Selma and Oprah on the other. If the framed photos on the walls were anything to go by, Selma Nester had met a lot of very visible women.

Tilda couldn't help but be a little in awe of her. Considering the research she'd done, and now taking in all the photos hanging around the room, how could she not be starstruck by Selma? Even her waiting room was impressive. The woman was clearly unafraid of color, with burnt orange and walnut furnishings and a blue rug. Stylish and bold. And the view from the twenty-first floor was sensational, stretching right across the city to the ocean in the distance.

The receptionist dressed to match her surroundings. She was an attractive woman in her seventies (as she told Tilda) wearing red and green, which on paper sounds more appropriate for an elf from Santa's workshop, but on Pam, with her long silver hair and slash of red lipstick, the result was sensational.

"I was a patient once," Pam said. "Now look at me."

Indeed. She was fabulous, and very visible.

"Dr. Nester won't be long," Pam said.

It had been an hour. Tilda checked her messages.

Ali: Let us know how it goes with Selma.

Tilda: I'm here now . . . waiting ages.
Will update you once I'm at work.

Leith: And remember, this is different!

Tilda sent a thumbs-up and then slipped her phone back into her bag and picked up a copy of Selma's book—they were piled high on the coffee table in place of magazines. She relaxed back into the orange sofa and opened to a random page toward the front.

> Our brain is a supercomputer. Long gone are the days when we believed that the brain we're born with is the brain we're stuck with. Our brain is not set in stone—or neurons. Our brain is a marvelous plastic organ that can rewire itself. You can learn new things and overcome old patterns, habits, and issues at any age. You have around 100 billion neurons each with thousands of ever-changing synapses. The possibilities for you are endless. You can rewire your brain, forge stronger connections between some neurons and prune back others, and, in doing so, bring about new thoughts, emotions, and experiences.
> A new you.
> A new life.
> A new reality.

Huh? Tilda reread the page, but her brain was still unable to process the words. She clearly needed a new brain to understand Selma's book.

Suddenly the door opened, and Tilda was jolted back to reality as the most vibrant-looking woman she'd ever seen stepped into the room. She was shorter than she'd looked in the clips online, with bright red hair and intense dark eyes. She wore a lime-green shirt and camel-colored bell-bottom pants, and sparkling jewels adorned her ears and her fingers. She was making way for a woman beside her whose left arm and leg were both invisible.

"Remember, Sun Jung, she's not even half the woman you are."

"And I was always the better half. See you next week." Sun Jung beamed as she headed for the exit.

The force of nature turned her attention to Tilda. "I'd apologize for keeping you waiting, but you're probably used to it."

Tilda nodded. She was right.

"I'm Selma. Come in."

Tilda followed Selma into the office and took a seat while the older woman continued chatting. "When Leith called and told me what was happening to you, I'll admit I was curious. It's fascinating. Your business inspires my clients. We give out your merchandise at our retreats. How could one of the women responsible for This Is A Sign be diagnosed with invisibility?"

"You tell me," Tilda said jokingly.

Tilda noted that, just like the waiting room, Selma's office was a stylish explosion of eclectic furniture, bold colors, and celebrity photos. On one wall hung three framed quotes from Tilda's business.

Rule your mind or it will rule you.

Whatever you think, you are right.

What consumes your mind controls your life.

Selma watched as Tilda read the quotes. "My dear girl, one should always practice what they preach." She seated herself in a red chair, giving Tilda the once-over. "When were you diagnosed?"

Tilda fiddled with the cuff on her shirt. Where to begin? "This has all been rather sudden."

"Bad news always is."

"True."

"You've lost your nose."

"Yes," Tilda said. "Plus my hand, my ear, and, as of this morning, my left foot."

Selma's eyes shot down to Tilda's feet. "No wonder, in those shoes."

Tilda opened her mouth to say something but stopped. Instead, she glanced at her shoes. They had seen better days, certainly, but they were comfy.

Intense eyes locked on Tilda. "So, what's going on?"

Tilda had a feeling Selma was not interested in the long version of events. "I was diagnosed two weeks ago. I'm trying to be proactive."

Selma screwed her face up. "Awful word, that, dreadfully overused. Instead of describing yourself as proactive or reactive, ask yourself if you're in a state of flow or a state of resistance."

Tilda had no idea what that meant, so she forged on. "Leith made this appointment for me—"

"What have you done for yourself?"

Tilda thought for a moment. "I went to a meeting run by the ISG."

Selma gave a snort. "The one run by Brenda Harvey?"

"Yes."

"Sweet Jesus. Did you feel like throwing yourself under a bus afterward?"

Tilda liked Selma already. "It crossed my mind."

"Did the meeting make you feel better or worse?"

Tilda considered this. "Worse."

Selma leaned forward slightly in her chair. "You get what you focus on, Tilda. Those women focus on the invisibility. It's no wonder we can't see them." Selma took a notepad and pen off the table beside her. "I've been in your shoes, Tilda. Well, not literally. I would never be caught in those, even in my darkest days."

Tilda glanced again at her shoes. Selma had a point. Unless you were milking cows, there was no excuse for such footwear.

Selma forged on. "I've been where you are: frightened, overwhelmed. And I found a way to change that and become a new version of myself. A visible version. And in finding that formula, I've been able to train fifty other therapists across three continents, to share it with tens of thousands of women who have beaten this condition. And that is a fact."

Tilda had to ask. "Why hadn't I heard of you before?"

"Have you heard of the leading researchers and experts in the fields of melanoma, or diabetes, or myasthenia gravis?"

"I've never even heard of myasthenia gravis."

"Because you've never needed to. The same goes for invisibility. Up to this point, it didn't exist in your world. But just because you don't know about something, doesn't mean it doesn't exist at all. My life's work has been about making this disorder more well-known. More visible. Delivering proof that it's a treatable condition. The published research is there. The data backs me up. Anyone who says otherwise is either a liar or ignorant. And there's no excuse for either in this age of information."

"My doctor says there's very little research into invisibility, and no treatment."

"She's right. There's no pill you can take to alleviate symptoms. Nothing she can prescribe. But there is a treatment, and I should know, because I developed it."

Tilda watched Selma carefully. Tilda had no reason not to believe her claims. And part of her did. Another voice, the one that always rang out when Leith talked about her visits to her psychic, was screaming with cynicism and doubt.

Selma continued, "Now, I know there's a voice in your head telling you to run for the door right now because I'm a charlatan."

Tilda squirmed in her seat. Speaking of psychics. . . .

"And it's that voice that we're starting with today. It's that voice we're here to address." One eyebrow went up slightly. "Have you read my book?"

Apart from the page of hieroglyphics in the waiting room? "No."

"Do you have any idea what I do? How I help?"

"Therapy?" Tilda sounded unsure because she was. She was suddenly embarrassed that she was so unprepared.

Selma sighed, clearly annoyed. "My training is in traditional psychoanalysis and psychodynamic therapies, but now my sole focus is on the invisibility program I've created. Using neuroplasticity, I'm going to change your brain . . . or, rather, you will change your brain, but I'll show you how."

Tilda didn't have time to respond.

"How do you see the world, Tilda?"

That was a big question—surely therapy should start with some basics, like allergies and prescribed medications. "I . . . ah . . . er . . ."

"How do you see yourself?"

Tilda scanned the room, as if the answer to that would be spray-painted on one of the walls. "I . . . well . . ."

"Can you answer these questions?"

I'd try if you'd just shut up, thought Tilda. "The world . . . life . . . is complicated."

"And you?" Selma watched her carefully.

Tilda was stumped. "Not so complicated."

Selma scribbled on her notepad and then said, "Describe yourself to me."

"Nice . . . enough."

Did Selma roll her eyes?

"I love my kids," Tilda offered.

"That's something you feel, not who you are."

This was more difficult than she could've imagined. "I'm a mother. A good friend."

"Two roles you play."

Tilda paused. She searched for suitable words to describe herself but came up completely blank. Her brain had gone on strike.

"It's a much more difficult question than you'd realize. How about this: When you're driving, or in the shower, or going about your day, what thoughts fill your mind?"

"What do you mean? Like when I leave the house and wonder if I turned the iron off?"

"You iron?" Selma glanced at Tilda's crumpled pants. "I'm more interested in your internal dialogue. How you speak to yourself. When you're cooking, driving, as you're trying to go to sleep at night, what are you thinking?"

Tilda shrugged. "I get anxious sometimes."

Selma nodded as if she was getting closer. "That's what you feel. Tell me about the thoughts you have that lead to that. How you talk to yourself."

Tilda wanted to throttle Leith for getting her into this. "I don't think I talk to myself."

"My dear, everyone who has invisibility also has an internal dialogue. One hundred percent of cases. No exceptions."

"What's this got to do with becoming invisible?"

"Everything." Selma sighed. "You're in bad shape. You need to meet PEARL."

Tilda glanced at the door. Yes, perhaps someone else *would* suit her better. "Is she another therapist?"

"No, she's the nastiest person you'll ever meet."

Oh boy, Tilda thought, *this just keeps getting better and better.*

"And she lives inside your skull."

Tilda was really lost now.

Selma turned her notepad to a fresh page and scrawled:

PEARL—acronym for Program Everything and Always Repeat Loop

Then, using her pen to point at the words, she explained, "Ninety-five percent of what you think every single day is from a record of your past. Everything you've ever experienced, ever thought, and ever felt is stored here, in what I call PEARL. She is the subconscious, a massive data bank of information. She's extremely literal. She doesn't analyze the information she stores. That's not her purpose. She's just a program of your past, tagging information and feeding it back to you on a constant loop, whether that information is actually helpful or not, or true or false."

Tilda stared at the word *PEARL* on the notepad and tried to wrap her head around everything Selma was saying. "Why do you call her nasty? If PEARL records everything, then doesn't she record the good as well as the bad?"

Selma's eyes lit up, as if Tilda were a child catching on to an important lesson. "Yes, but like the supercomputer she is, PEARL recognizes patterns of information, so despite memorizing everything, she will prioritize information she deems a match to previous data. So if you've experienced trauma as a child, and continued having negative experiences in your life, the program that PEARL feeds back is influenced by that. Does this all make sense?"

Unfortunately, it did. "This PEARL has been recording information since I was a child?"

"Yes. In fact, since before you were born. By the time you were seven, most of her major programs were installed."

Tilda felt ill. "If you'd met my parents, you'd know that's very bad news for me."

"You're not alone there, dear." Selma gave her a wry smile. "PEARL knows 'you' and feeds you a loop of thoughts and internal conversations that feel familiar, no matter how awful they are. PEARL reminds you of who you are, and anything outside those known programs will create discomfort." She tapped the notepad to make her point. "How you see yourself. How you see the world. All the conversations you have with yourself are programmed in PEARL."

Tilda's brain hurt. Or maybe that was PEARL. It was a lot to take in.

Selma sensed that. "Homework. Over the next week, start writing down the repetitive thoughts you have in a notebook. Listen to your internal dialogue, how you speak to yourself, the imagined conversations you have, and make a note of them. I give examples of these in chapters three through five in my book. Read them. You have sixty to seventy thousand thoughts a day, and over 90 percent of those are the same thoughts as the previous day. Observe some of those repetitive thoughts and write them down. Don't be too attached to them . . . just observe what's there. Get to know PEARL."

"You think my thoughts are the reason I'm disappearing?"

"What I think is unimportant. It's what you think." Selma nodded, as if this was information Tilda would be pleased to hear.

"But I'm responsible?"

"The great thing about being responsible for creating a mess is that you are also responsible for cleaning it up. And isn't that so much better than being at the mercy of someone or something else?"

"Now you sound like Leith." Tilda didn't mean that as a compliment.

"Good. She's a very smart woman."

Much to Tilda's surprise, Selma stood, indicating that the session was over. "That's enough for today. Be sure to make an appointment for next week."

"Is that it?" Tilda glanced at the clock. It had been barely thirty minutes, and the session cost a mint.

"What more did you expect?" Selma asked.

"I thought you'd ask me about myself, get to know me."

"I can't do that until you know yourself," Selma said. "I'd suggest you also buy my book on the way out and start reading. The endnotes contain links to the data from my studies and papers I've written."

Tilda was surprised that Selma didn't seem more interested in her. "This isn't quite what I expected."

"'Expectation is the root of all heartache.'"

"Shakespeare," Tilda snapped.

"What did you *expect*? An immediate cure?"

"I *expected* more questions, about my past."

"You get what you focus on, dear. Focus on the past and you'll get more of the same."

The woman spoke in riddles.

"Surely you need to ask more questions, so you can come to a professional conclusion about me. What do you think about me?"

Selma gave Tilda a friendly pat on the back as she guided her out the door. "You're about to learn that what I think is of very little consequence. It's what you think that's important."

16

If you're waiting for a sign, this is it.

—ANONYMOUS, on the wall at This Is A Sign

This Is A Sign was located in a converted warehouse: spacious, light-filled offices with internal glass walls and big windows with ocean views. The interior was an homage to many of the company's more successful posters, as well as some that Ziggy and Leith had made up just for their employees.

Busy bees don't make honey, happy bees do.

If you're waiting for a sign, this is it.

Be the reason someone smiles today.

The team of eight loved their jobs and worked well together. Hours were flexible, employees were valued, and there was genuine respect for one another. Tilda knew much of this was thanks to Leith and Ziggy. They were as passionate about the business now as they had been when that first pack of cards had sold out. Tilda was involved in all major decisions, but her enthusiasm for work had waned over the past couple of years. She figured the three of them balanced one another out, a theory she preferred to espouse rather than dig deeper into herself to find out what was missing creatively.

"Morning!" She gave the team a collective wave and headed for her office, only to have everyone stop what they were doing and greet her with overly cheery enthusiasm.

Eve at reception called out, "Hi, Tilda. Good to *see* you."

Min, who ran their social media, called out, "Looking good, Tilda."

And then Sam from sales did the same.

Tilda changed course and headed for Leith's office. "You told everyone?"

"*Everyone* is an exaggeration," Leith said. "They needed to know why you haven't been at work."

"I didn't want anyone knowing yet," Tilda said.

"Not sure when this is going to sink in, but the missing nose is a dead giveaway," Leith said. "It's better that everyone *nose* about it."

Tilda glared at Leith. "I started the nose jokes."

Leith looked at Tilda, deadpan. "And there are so many of them. I just don't know which one to *pick*."

Tilda spotted Ziggy making a beeline across the office. Ziggy's real name was An, but only his Vietnamese mother called him that. His Australian father had nicknamed him Ziggy and it stuck. He was tall and lanky, with a passion for his family, meditating, and branding, in that order. He'd been big on hashtags and inspiring memes before they were even a thing. He'd encouraged Leith and Tilda from day one, with their quirky little pack of cards. Unlike Tom, who'd thought it was beneath him. In fact, he often told Tilda that Ziggy didn't stimulate him intellectually, and he would do what he could to get out of couples' nights.

"Come here, Tilly." Ziggy marched into Leith's office and folded Tilda into a tight embrace.

Ziggy was a hugger.

He held her for a long time, and then, pulling back slightly, he put his hands on her shoulders and looked her square in the eye. "I see you."

Awkward. "Thanks, Ziggy."

He meant well.

"I need to work." Tilda gestured toward her office, and he stepped aside.

"Here if you need me, Tilly," he called after her.

Tilda escaped to the quiet of her own office, trying to ignore all the concerned looks. Accepting support was hard. Having people care and tell her they were there for her had always been difficult. She'd been raised as the only child of warring parents, a war that stopped only when her father died. Then, much to Tilda's surprise, her mother grieved the man she'd fought for so long. She was deeply unhappy. Now, decades later, Frances had emerged on the other side, much more interested in her family, and certainly her granddaughters. But for Tilda, it was too late; she had already been marked. She didn't really know how to be cared for, evident in her choice of a husband. Even in her friendships she was uncomfortable receiving support, preferring to work out her problems alone. Or at least, she tried to. She was extremely fortunate that her friends understood her and wouldn't leave her alone for long.

There was a knock on the door, and Yumiko stuck her head in. "I've sent you the list of quotes for the next quarter, with a couple that are hard to source. Are you okay to look that over today?"

"I'm not dying, so yes," Tilda snapped, and then felt bad. "Sorry. I'm a bit thrown that you all know."

"Don't be. Leith just wants you to be supported. And we all care." Yumiko entered, her eyes widening slightly as she took in Tilda's nose.

"Yes, my nose is missing," Tilda sighed.

Yumiko handed Tilda a T-shirt. "I had this made up for you."

Tilda flattened it out on her desk—a red cape flying across the front, with the words "Invisibility is a superpower" underneath.

Tilda laughed, the tension evaporating. "I love it."

In the early days of the business, the internet had yet to be swamped with memes—in fact, a meme still maintained the meaning evolutionist Richard Dawkins had given it—so Leith and Tilda had spent many a night over a bottle of wine, choosing quotes from books like *The Oxford Dictionary of Quotations*. While the early Affirmation Cards pack sold like hotcakes, and This Is A Sign was profitable right from the early days, the invention of the inspirational meme had proven to be very lucrative. And made expanding their product line easy. The company hit its first pothole when Leith and Ziggy signed off on a range of Greek philosophers' quotes that couldn't actually be attributed to Socrates, Plato, or Epicurus. It was Tom who'd first pulled them up on it over Friday night drinks.

"Every single quote needs to be sourced. Now more than ever," Tom said. "You'll end up in trouble. And if you're going to quote a translation, for Christ's sake make sure it matches the original."

"I don't think Socrates is going to sue us," Leith said. She was always the first person to challenge Tom, aware that if Tilda did it, she'd pay for it later.

"No, but you'll lose all credibility." Tom's second novel hadn't sold at all, so he wasn't offered another book deal. He was now a senior crime reporter at the *Daily Herald*. While not completely unsupportive of Tilda's business, as he certainly liked the income it was starting to generate, he expressed disdain that the public had embraced something as inane as Tilda's business but not the brilliance of his book.

"You also need to check that anything you quote is in the public domain," Tom continued. "And that it's not being misquoted, like 'To thine own self be true.' Shakespeare must be turning in his grave that a line from Polonius is now being used by self-help junkies."

"What do you suggest?" Leith asked.

"You need to hire someone to make sure that every single quote is legitimate and legally available for use. And investigate the broader context of each quote. I know you think the bloody universe is looking after you, but you're a business and need a lawyer as well."

A month later, Yumiko had started working for them. Yumiko had a law degree and a passion for literature and language. She also believed she talked to Nature Spirits. That one thing aside, she was brilliant at her job and was now a part of the This Is A Sign family. More than that, she was a part of Tilda's family. They often grabbed dinner or hung out together.

Unlike Ali and Leith, who were both happily married, Yumiko was divorced. She understood single life after forty. She knew it was both liberating and exhausting. Doing everything alone was empowering, but sometimes it would be nice to have someone else pay a bill or mow the lawn. Or to have someone to show up with at couples' events, where single women weren't really welcome. So Yumiko was the friend Tilda turned to most often after Tom left.

Now Tilda gave Yumiko a hug. "Best T-shirt ever, thank you."

"Is it you, though? I *can't see* you wearing it."

Tilda flicked Yumiko with the shirt. "Don't you start. Leith's jokes are bad enough."

Yumiko's long dark hair was pulled tight into a topknot and jiggled as she laughed. She was forty-two, looked thirty-two, and still dressed from head to toe in surf brands that she got free from her ex-husband's surf shop.

Yumiko turned her attention back to work. "There's a quote attributed to Einstein, but I can't find a source. Also, you need to look over the contract for Golden Gyms."

"I'll take a look at them before the meeting," Tilda told her.

Yumiko stared at Tilda . . . or at the wall behind her. It was difficult to tell.

"Anything else?" Tilda asked.

"I'm just checking your aura. It's good. Very strong. You've got this."

She was surrounded by nutbags, but Tilda managed an invisible thumbs-up at this supposed good news. She might not be able to see her nose, but at least her aura was visible.

Yumiko disappeared, and Leith marched in.

"I want to hear all about Selma. How was it?" She made herself comfortable in one of the armchairs in front of Tilda's desk.

"It was an outrageously expensive thirty minutes."

"Isn't she a powerhouse?"

"She's definitely unique."

"What's the plan?"

Tilda shrugged. "I have to write down my thoughts for the next week and then return for another ridiculously expensive session, with those thoughts in hand."

Leith's eyes narrowed slightly. "Don't do it if you're going to mock it."

Tilda caved. "I'm trying not to."

"You know, Selma only works with a few select clients now. She's trained other people to do the day-to-day sessions. Her focus is on the retreats and events. She speaks to thousands of women each year—women who would kill to get one bloody session with her. Show some gratitude."

Tilda perched herself on the edge of the desk. "Okay, I'm sorry. I didn't realize she was such a big deal. It's not what I expected, that's all."

"Just go with it."

"Go with the flow," Tilda said, with arm movements.

"That's not as crazy as it sounds. Our thoughts shape our view of the world, and yet we wake up each day and just let that old program of thoughts roll out and color our experiences."

"Yes, I've heard all about PEARL."

"I love Selma's acronym. Very clever."

Tilda stared at Leith. "I am going to do as Selma asks. The twins are freaking out over this. I promised I'd try everything I can to . . . fix it."

"But you don't think that's possible."

"I don't know. You seem to think it is. Yumiko, Ziggy, Selma . . . A lot of smart people seem to think it's possible. I don't know what I think."

"Well, start working that out. Observe your thoughts and write them down."

"What if doing that makes me miserable?"

"You're already suffering, Tilly. Buddhists say that the root of all suffering is in our attachment, including to our emotions and thoughts. What Selma is asking you to do is let go and just observe what comes up. Don't be attached to it."

"I need a notebook first," Tilda said, realizing that was a silly request. They had a warehouse full of them downstairs. Motivational notebooks were big business.

"I'll get one." Leith disappeared out the door.

Tilda sat for a moment, wondering what fresh hell she was in for. Then she quickly collected her bag and her jacket and bolted for the exit. She fully intended to write down her thoughts, but she didn't want anyone, even Leith, bearing witness to what went on inside her head.

17

It is only with the heart that one can see rightly;
what is essential is invisible to the eye.
—ANTOINE DE SAINT-EXUPÉRY, *The Little Prince*

It was a twenty-minute walk from home to the office. Weather permitting, Tilda would commute to work on foot, because she enjoyed the energy of her buzzing little suburb. Today, Middle Bay had a more subdued feel to it and she wondered if it was weighed down by winter . . . Or was it her mood that was impacting how she viewed everything? She felt lost. She knew that Leith would be annoyed that she'd left the office before writing in a notebook, but the thought of doing so made her feel vulnerable.

Tilda spotted Paige's Pages, the local bookshop, up ahead and decided to stop in and see if they stocked any books on invisibility. It was a regular haunt of hers, and she often attended the author signings and talks. Tom hated the place because they never carried his books. Tilda liked it even more now.

The bell on the door jangled as she entered and scanned the store, its wood floors and oak shelves crammed with books. In one corner there was an eclectic collection of sofas and seats, and a scattering of coffee tables. It was quiet, with one woman perusing the fiction section, and a staff member tidying the children's books. With her cherry-red ponytail and rosy cheeks, she looked barely older than a child herself.

Tilda made her way through to the health and wellness area and found the shelf that housed books about various medical conditions. She was surprised to see half a dozen titles on invisibility, including *The Truth About Invisibility*, the book Gurinder had given her, which was also the one she'd been reading when she met Patrick. She certainly wanted something more hopeful than that. Tilda picked up another title and read the first few pages. It was rather dry and academic—not quite what she was after. She slid it back onto the shelf and opened a book called *The History of Women and Invisibility*. She read about various references to invisibility in myths and literature and noted the beautiful illustrations. As she put the book back in its place on the shelf, she noticed a small book beside it titled *She Remains to Be Seen*. She removed it from the shelf and opened to a random page and read.

Naturally, one question you'll be asking is why you didn't know more about this condition. There are multiple reasons. Patients in the early stages of invisibility become masters of masking the condition. Then, in the later stages, they often change their daily routines so they aren't subjected to unwanted attention in public. But mostly, importantly, you only ever see what you're looking for in life. As I battled my invisibility through stages 2 and 3, friends and family continued to see me and bear witness to the progress of my condition, but to strangers, it was as if I was already at stage 4. People simply didn't see me. Occasionally someone would notice my condition and stare, but generally I was exactly as the condition implies: invisible.

Interestingly, though, I started noticing more homeless people in my neighborhood. I realized there was a woman in my apartment block who lived with a physical disability. We're now friends, and I often marvel that I lived one floor above this incredible woman for over two years before I even saw her. As people lost sight of me, I started to see others more clearly. What I discovered is, we only see what we want to see, what we're ready to see, and what is already a part of our world.

Tilda flicked to the back of the book to read more about the author and noted that she was a psychologist and university lecturer. Then Tilda noticed the book's dedication.

To Selma, who helped me see.

Tilda chuckled. That made sense. She closed the book, noticing a woman close to her own age inching up beside her, somewhat tentatively. Tilda made room for her and saw the woman reach for *The Truth About Invisibility*. Tilda saw that she was wearing a glove.

"My doctor gave me that book, and it was depressing," Tilda said.

"Oh." The woman stalled. "I'm not sure where to start."

"Can I suggest this one instead?" Tilda handed her *She Remains to Be Seen*.

"Aren't you buying it?"

"I have a similar one that I'm still reading."

"Thank you."

The woman smiled and took the book to the counter, while Tilda left the shop and continued toward home. She reflected on what she'd just read. She paused at a crossing, waiting for the light to change, and spotted a woman wearing large ornate earrings. When the breeze blew her hair back, Tilda saw that her ears were invisible. The woman noticed that Tilda was staring, and quickly smoothed her hair down as she turned and walked the opposite way, not waiting to cross the road anymore.

The light signaled to walk, and Tilda made a beeline for the park, the route she often took on the way home. She wandered under the row of jacaranda trees, smiling at a woman with a dog who walked by. There was an off-leash area for dogs nearby, and she occasionally brought Buddy there.

"Tilda!"

Tilda turned at the sound of her name, realizing Gurinder was seated on a park bench she'd just passed.

"Hello, Gurinder. I didn't see you there."

Gurinder had a newspaper folded on her lap. Her dog, a Shih Tzu, sat calmly at her feet. It reminded Tilda of a joke Tabitha had once told her: What's a Shih Tzu? A zoo without animals. Tilda knelt and gave the dog a pat.

"What a cutie. How old?"

"Fourteen. Still likes his daily park jaunt, though." Gurinder moved her sunglasses off to the top of her head. "How are you going?"

Tilda gave the dog one last rub under the chin and then sat on the bench next to Gurinder. "Not too bad. I'm adjusting."

"Did you check out that support group?"

"I'm attending my second meeting this afternoon." Tilda didn't mention that she was attending reluctantly, not sure if it was the right place for her.

Gurinder clearly approved. "Have you told the girls?"

"Yes. And they responded as expected. Holly lost it, Tabitha was stoic."

Gurinder smiled. "People are born the way they are and don't change."

"I wonder if that's true."

Gurinder angled her body toward Tilda. In this moment, she was a fellow school mum rather than Tilda's doctor. "How about your mother? I remember meeting her at a few events. It must be difficult for her."

Tilda squirmed, in uncomfortable territory. "I haven't told her yet."

Gurinder's expression shifted, not in judgment, just curiosity.

"She's away at the moment, and I feel like these things are best shared face-to-face. My mother is . . ." Tilda searched for the right description. "Let's just say Holly is a lot like her grandmother. I'll tell her when we're together so I can support her through her . . . reaction."

"You'll be supporting her, rather than the other way around."

"We have a complicated relationship."

"Oh, I understand. My mother drives me crazy."

Tilda laughed. She'd met Gurinder's mother several times. "Your mother is an excellent cook, though. I remember her dishes at the year 12 fundraiser."

"Yes, she despairs that I can't cook well. Practicing medicine isn't enough. I should also be the perfect wife and mother."

"I've seen you with your family, and I suspect you balance it all better than most."

Gurinder didn't respond.

Tilda glanced down at Gurinder's newspaper and realized it was the Indian daily. Although it was folded, she saw a headline about the Indian high commissioner stepping down and another announcing the death of a Bollywood actor. Both important enough stories to make the front page of India's news, and yet local stories would be very different.

"Was he really famous?" Tilda asked, nodding at the photo of the actor.

Gurinder flattened out the newspaper, running a finger over the actor's face. "Oh yes. When I was fifteen, I thought I would marry him. Along with millions of other girls."

The two women laughed.

A woman about their age jogged by, headphones on, sporting a baseball cap and sunglasses. Tilda noticed that she was wearing only one glove. Gurinder clearly noticed it as well.

"How did I miss this before?" Tilda asked.

"It just wasn't a part of your life," Gurinder said. "We look at the world around us and assign value to everything. We notice the things that are familiar or important, and often miss the things that aren't. You didn't know much about invisibility before your diagnosis because it's never been of value to know anything about it."

Tilda thought about when Holly had been struggling at school and her teacher suggested that she might have ADHD. Tilda and Tom had been thrown into a completely new world of psychometric testing and neurodiversity. Tilda had never heard the term 2e before it was applied to Holly, but suddenly it became a major part of their lives. Same with Jack's autism. Tilda had known nothing about ASD until Jack's diagnosis. And now she was more attuned to whether someone was on the spectrum or had symptoms of ADHD.

"My god, Gurinder, what else aren't we seeing? What else do we miss that's right in front of our eyes?"

18

We rise by lifting others.

—ROBERT INGERSOLL, *nineteenth-century lawyer and writer*

The Invisibility Support Group members were all taking their seats as Tilda arrived. She received a weary greeting from the troops, and immediately regretted coming, but allowed Brenda to herd her into one of three empty chairs. She noticed a hip flask floating a few inches above the seat on her right.

"Carol? I can see your hip flask."

"And yet not my hip. Life is cruel," came the reply.

Perhaps Carol was right, and life was cruel. Would Tilda eventually see it as so? She hoped not. Someone slipped into the empty seat on her left.

"Sorry, sorry . . ." The woman plunked her bag down near her feet, spilling some of its contents. "Shit . . . sorry," she said. "Carry on," she announced loudly to Brenda. "I'm all ears." Then leaning toward Tilda, she whispered loudly, "Not really . . . my ears are gone."

Tilda took in the walking cyclone. She was a wild mess of brunette waves and freckles, wearing a long, boho-style skirt and a bunch of jangling bracelets. She thrust one of those jangling hands out.

"I'm Erica."

Tilda immediately liked her. She looked like someone who would shake things up a bit. "I'm Tilda. And this is Carol."

Erica got extra brownie points for not looking too shocked by Carol's state of complete disappearance. "Carol, you're nothing but a hip flask. I admire your commitment to booze."

Suddenly Tilda liked Erica even more.

"I was a teetotaler my whole life," Carol said, "and look what good it did me."

Brenda cleared her throat. "Ladies, I'm speaking."

"So are we," Carol snipped.

Brenda looked surprised, clearly unused to Carol, or anyone, challenging her.

A sweet smile replaced her shock. "Perhaps you'd like to start today, Carol."

"I'm looking forward to summer."

Tilda was surprised by Carol's positivity.

"Good for you, Carol," Brenda said.

"Because I've decided that this summer, I'll be naked. No point wearing clothes. Everywhere I go, I'll be naked, and no one will know, unless I trip over a tit."

Erica reached across Tilda and held her palm up. "High five, Carol."

After the sound of a slap of hands, Erica spoke.

"My turn."

Brenda tried to interrupt but only got as far as "I'll say who's next" before Erica said, "I'm Erica. Woke up without ears and after some invasive tests on parts of my body that are more rears than ears, my doctor gave me the details of this group and a prescription for antidepressants."

"You'll need that prescription after this meeting," Carol said.

Erica grinned in the direction of the voice. "I like you, Carol."

Tilda decided she liked both women. It was an enjoyable tennis match of banter on either side of her. Hurricane Erica was a breath of fresh air, while Carol was turning out to be the most colorful person in the room despite being completely imperceptible.

Brenda coughed again, and everyone turned to her. "It starts with us, ladies. We must advocate for the correct terminology. We are not disappearing—"

"Speak for yourself," Carol muttered.

"We suffer from invisibility. There is a difference."

Tilda noticed Erica scrolling on her phone reading something, before putting her hand up.

Brenda seemed to approve of Erica's newfound manners. "Yes, your turn to speak."

"The dictionary states that to disappear means 'cease to be visible.' While the meaning of invisible is 'unable to be seen.' Same thing."

Brenda's tone was measured. "But when discussing this condition, one is correct and one isn't."

"Who says?"

"The Invisibility Advocacy Organization."

"Isn't that the organization that runs this support group?" asked Erica.

"Yes." Brenda's lips were so pursed they'd now disappeared.

Erica politely continued. "And you're the president of that organization?"

Brenda nodded. "Annually voted in, that's right."

"She counted my hand as up in that vote, but it wasn't," Carol whispered.

Erica looked as if butter wouldn't melt in her mouth. "To clarify, you're the one who has declared the difference between the two terms, and which one is appropriate?"

Brenda visibly bristled. "Are you trying to cause trouble?"

"Not at all. If I'm identifying myself a certain way, I just want to know the source of the definition and why that label is important." Erica's tone was respectful, which seemed to appease Brenda.

"Until recently, Australian doctors used both terms. In the US and UK, the term 'invisibility' was adopted some time ago, so I advocated for that. I feel that as sufferers we've lost control of enough things in our lives. At least we can control what our disease is called."

Erica nodded. "And bravo to you for leading. Thank you, Brenda." Erica started clapping, which led to others giving a smattering of applause. But Erica wasn't finished. "You believe this condition occurs because of a loss of control?"

"I never said that," Brenda snapped. "But this diagnosis means we experience a lack of control over our own bodies."

"Could that be what triggers the condition in the first place?"

Tilda watched Erica in admiration. She was driving at something, but it was difficult to know what yet.

Brenda, clearly irked, took a calming breath. "No one knows what causes invisibility, and here, in this group, we don't discuss unknowns."

Erica tucked a lock of hair behind one of her invisible ears. "If they don't know what causes it, everything is an unknown."

"We focus on what we know. How our week has been. Practical advice. How to deal with depression and anxiety."

"What about positive things, or funny experiences?"

"Erica, I understand this is all new to you, but in my experience as a long-term sufferer, there's nothing funny about this."

"Fair enough," Erica said.

"Any other questions?" Brenda asked the group.

Erica's arm shot up. She sounded like a wind chime with the clanging sound her bracelets made.

Brenda ignored her for a moment, searching the room for other options.

"My hand is up," Erica called out.

"Someone else's might be too," Brenda said.

Carol's voice piped up. "Waris, is your invisible arm up?"

Waris chuckled. "We should all be up in arms, dear."

Brenda was annoyed. "What's your question, Erica?"

"Can men have invisibility?"

Brenda clearly approved of this question. "It's not unheard-of, but it's not common. Generally, male sufferers are older. We had a male member of this group about twelve months ago. In fact, Harry, are you still here?"

Crickets.

Brenda continued. "Like most men with invisibility, Harry was diagnosed in his seventies, but the overwhelming percentage of sufferers are women over fifty."

Erica's tone shifted. "Brenda, a friend of mine who also has invisibility suggested that it might help protect women. Her husband has a temper."

Brenda studied Erica for a moment. "That must be awful for your friend. Tell her that statistics have shown no differences in cases of intimate partner violence."

Erica's shoulders slumped. "Oh, okay."

Brenda softened. "There's no research to suggest that women bring this upon themselves as a protection mode, Erica. Come and talk to me in private and we'll discuss how best to support her."

"Sure, I'd appreciate that."

"Who's next?" Brenda asked.

An older woman with invisible arms stood. Tilda hadn't heard her speak before.

"My ex has finally made an offer, but with solicitors' fees and everything, it's less than even I expected."

"We knew he wasn't going to fight fair, Sharon," Brenda said.

"I've got no savings and won't be able to afford to buy. And with the rental crisis . . ." Sharon's voice wavered. "The stress is making me ill."

Brenda put her hand up. "Stay after the meeting. We'll talk then. You'll be okay, I promise." Then she turned her attention back to the others. "Anyone else want to share today?"

Gianna jumped to her feet—her shoes were the only visible part of her. "You all know I love being a bus driver, but my boss is suggesting I take a desk job. People are refusing to get on my bus. Everyone thinks it's haunted," she said.

"They can't force you out of your role, Gianna. I'll give you a number to call for free legal advice." Brenda gave the group a sweeping stare and then abruptly ended the meeting. "Anyway, ladies, we're finished for today. Same time next week."

"Is that it?" Erica said to Tilda and Carol. "I expected more . . . support."

"Support groups are like bras—some aren't that supportive," Carol said. "I know a pub nearby. Shall we go for a drink?"

"Does the Pope wear a dress?" Erica said.

"I need a double after that." Tilda watched as Erica collected her bags and jacket.

Piled high like a packhorse, Erica gave a cheery, "Let's go, girls."

Tilda, Erica, and Carol's hip flask made for the door. Tilda briefly turned and saw Brenda putting the cookies away, the weight of the world clearly heavy on her. Or was it the weight of how she viewed it?

19

Friendship is born at that moment when one person says to another,

"What! You too? I thought I was the only one."

—C. S. LEWIS

Fifteen minutes later, Erica, Carol, and Tilda were perched on stools around a table at the Nag's Head Tavern. With its wood-paneled walls, wood floors, and cozy booths, it harked back to an era before pubs were all owned by hipsters or gamblers. The fireplace was a welcome respite from the chilly town hall they'd just come from. Erica was trying to get the barman's attention while they all chatted. "I think we should just form our own support group," she said.

"I'm in," Carol said.

"Me too." Tilda had decided that the other meeting had done more harm than good. She'd tried it twice and felt despondent both times.

"Why do you think those women keep attending the meetings?" Erica asked.

"Because, in a strange way, they feel seen while they're there," Carol said.

"And less alone," Tilda added. "At least, that's why I came back. It's important to have support, but maybe we can do that with wine and laughs."

Erica agreed. "Let's have our own meetings here. Unless they don't serve our types." She turned her attention to Carol. "So, what's your story?"

"I don't have a story."

"Everyone has a story."

"Mine's more of a haiku: short and leaves me confused." Carol sighed. "I started disappearing on my fiftieth birthday. It all happened very quickly after that."

"That's it, that's your story?" Erica asked. "Did anything out of the ordinary happen on your fiftieth?"

"You mean apart from losing my legs?"

"Yes."

"If you're looking for a correlation, research shows there's none," Tilda said.

Erica rolled her eyes. "Research funded by pharmaceutical companies that want to pump us full of pills."

Tilda hoped she hadn't misjudged Erica. She liked her, but she didn't want to be lectured on conspiracies.

Erica waved at the barman again. "What's it take to get a drink around here?"

Tilda held her phone up and clicked a few photos of the barman over Carol's invisible shoulder.

"I'd pose, but there's no point," Carol said.

Tilda laughed and clicked a few more photos, this time in Carol's direction. "I'm a photographer. I just figure if he doesn't serve us soon, I'll email a photo to management with a complaint," Tilda explained.

Erica whistled at him this time but still got no response. "What am I, invisible?"

A beat passed, and then the three women cracked up.

"Brenda was wrong—*this is funny!*" Erica said.

Carol's hip flask floated through the air and landed on the table. "Take three glasses from the bar. He won't see you."

More raucous laughter followed as Tilda walked over to where the free water sat on the bar and took three clean glasses. Erica then filled each with a shot of whisky.

"Why do you think your flask is visible but your clothes aren't?" Erica asked Carol.

"I was wondering the same thing," Tilda admitted.

"My doctor thinks it's because I've only just taken up drinking. She said that the flask might also disappear once it becomes a quote, unquote 'more integrated part' of who I am." Carol chuckled. "She knows bugger all about this, like most people."

The women toasted, "To being seen." Tilda tried to lock eyes with Carol but didn't know where to look and hoped they wouldn't be jinxed with seven years of bad sex. She had enough issues.

"My husband left me on my fiftieth birthday," Carol blurted out.

"I knew it," Erica said. "There's always something."

"I don't know if it correlates," Carol said. "It was completely unexpected. I thought we were . . ."

"Happy?" Tilda asked.

"In it for the long haul," Carol said. "What's happy? I don't know, but I never thought he'd leave. I was all dressed up, waiting to go to my birthday dinner, when he came home with 'that look' on his face. He couldn't even wait—he had to tell me immediately. Twenty years of marriage, and he couldn't even fake one more night to celebrate my birthday. Anyway, he left, I called friends and canceled, then I cried for eight hours, fell asleep, and woke up with no legs."

"To be fair, I was legless on my fiftieth too," Tilda said, making Carol laugh.

"He eventually apologized. He'd been unhappy for a long time. Said he never wanted to hurt me, but that I sucked the fun out of everything."

"Wow, that's harsh," Tilda said.

"No, he had a point." Carol sighed, as if resigned to this past of hers. "It's taken me a long time to admit that, but I was glass-half-empty for years. In fact, the glass was often completely empty. I can be negative. I was hard on him, but harder on myself."

"In what way?"

"It's embarrassing to admit this now, given my condition, but I was obsessed with my weight. It controlled our lives. Let's say he wanted to go out for dinner . . . I'd say no because I was always on a diet. Or he'd want to go out for lunch on the weekend, but I'd choose to go for a run instead."

"You don't look fat." Erica had zero filter, but Carol cackled.

"I've always been a size eight, but god forbid I gained a kilo. I was so hard on myself. I realize that now. With every gram I gained, every wrinkle I got, he still told me I was beautiful. He tried. He really did. And I treated him with disdain. I now know it's because I couldn't understand how he could see me as beautiful. He genuinely loved me, but I took him for granted," Carol admitted. "He organized a dinner for my fiftieth, and all I did was complain. For weeks. I didn't want a late night. I didn't want to eat or to drink too much. I didn't want cake. He snapped. It's taken me three years to work out my role in our divorce. Ironically, this disease has also taken the focus off my appearance. It doesn't matter if I put on weight or have wrinkles now."

Tilda thought about her own relationship with the mirror and how it had changed dramatically since her diagnosis. Instead of criticizing her wrinkles, she'd been memorizing them, fearful that she'd wake up one morning unable to see herself at all.

Erica was nodding as if Carol's story confirmed something for her. "What about you, Tilda?"

"Nothing like that," Tilda said. "I was sitting at my computer and noticed my little finger was missing."

"Nothing happened leading up to that?" Erica asked.

"I actually thought I was having a good week," Tilda said.

Erica pulled her mass of hair back, tying it up with a band from around her wrist. "You're a photographer?"

"Yes, but I have a business, so in recent years my focus has been on running that rather than taking photos."

Erica continued digging. "Do you feel creatively fulfilled?"

What a question! Tilda stalled, then said with a nervous laugh, "Gosh, I need another drink to answer that."

Carol's hip flask filled her glass.

"You don't feel creatively fulfilled?"

Erica should have been a reporter.

Tilda tossed back the whisky. "Honestly, I hadn't thought about it in those terms until this very moment."

And it was a moment. Tilda absorbed what should've been obvious to her—that for some time now there had been growing discontent in her life. Or perhaps it had always been there, but the luxury of financial stability had allowed it to intensify. Tilda was staring at a painting of three geese flying over a field. It reminded her of the print of the duck at the doctor's office, and she wondered what it said about her life that so many important moments took place in the company of awful bird art.

Erica and Carol waited for her to speak.

"I have a business I'm proud of, working with people I love. It has been a difficult, joyous, interesting journey. It's ensured my financial security, and as a single mum that has been an incredible relief. I wouldn't change that. Admitting I'm unfulfilled diminishes something truly special . . ."

"But?" Erica urged her on.

"But my dream when I was young was to be a portrait photographer. I imagined my work hanging in the State Portrait Gallery. Instead, it's on coffee mugs." Tilda's body absorbed this. "Bugger," she whispered.

Erica continued to push, although more gently now. "What happened?"

"Life happened . . ."

"But it's not how you envisioned it?"

"Life never is. Not everyone gets to live their creative dreams." Tilda refrained from mentioning Holly, who did just that. Instead, she looked at Erica. "Not everyone is good enough. Or lucky enough."

"Who told you that?"

Tilda felt ill. She didn't like where this conversation was headed. "I don't believe any of this contributed to my diagnosis."

Carol knew when a shift in gears was needed. "What about you, Erica?"

Erica fell silent for a moment. "Abusive husband. Mike is . . . crazy jealous. We're separated."

As shocking as it was, it wasn't quite what Tilda had been expecting. "I don't understand how that correlates with your invisibility."

"You wouldn't unless you've lived with someone who's pathologically jealous. The constant accusations wear you down. You change the way you dress. The way you behave. I never wanted to do anything to set him off. I tried to be invisible for years. Turns out I was very good at it." Erica poured herself another shot of whisky.

"What did he make of your invisibility?"

"Didn't notice. He never really saw me anyway. By the end, even when we had sex, it was with the lights out. He was used to me covering up. Mostly so he didn't accuse me of being provocative, but also to cover . . ." Erica's voice tapered off.

"Bruises?" Carol asked.

Erica nodded. "It's why I left. Although those bruises healed more quickly than the emotional ones."

The conversation had moved into uncomfortable territory for Tilda.

"I've been reading a book that explains how our thoughts and emotions can contribute to this." Erica shuffled through her bag and drew out Selma Nester's book. "This is hands down the best book on the subject, and Selma Nester states that not only have we created this, but we can uncreate it. I'm on a waiting list to see one of her therapists, but that could take months."

Tilda had no idea why she didn't share then and there that she'd had a session with Selma. She knew she should, but she felt guilty. Here was someone who desperately wanted one, and yet all Tilda had needed was one call from Leith to be bumped to the top of the queue. Because of the very business she'd just complained about. Tilda tossed back her whisky and then noticed the flask midair, filling her glass again.

"You look like you need another shot," Carol said to her.

Erica pushed the book across the table. "Take it. I have another copy."

"Carol can have that one," Tilda said.

"Perfect. We can discuss." Erica passed the book to Carol.

"I'll give anything a go at this stage." The book made its way into Carol's bag, visible on the floor, while the remainder of the whisky filled their glasses.

"Anyway, it took every ounce of courage to leave my marriage. He still calls, promising he's changed. But I've been strong. That man took enough of my life without taking this as well." Erica waved both hands down her body with the confidence of a woman who knew she was attractive. "Now that he's gone, I fully intend to fight this invisibility thing."

Suddenly, the barman appeared. Young, bearded, with a man bun and a smile that suggested he thought he was charming.

"Sorry, I didn't see you." He glanced at the whisky glasses, clearly confused. "Can I get you two ladies anything else?"

"You can get us another barman," Carol snapped, causing the young guy to jump back and look around the room for where the voice had come from.

Erica pretended to look worried. "Holy shit, is this pub haunted?"

Blood drained from the barman's face. "I'll just get the manager."

The ghostly voice spoke to the frightened barman again. "No need for the manager. Just grab us some fresh glasses of whisky . . . and perhaps some for yourself."

20

The most regretful people on earth are those who felt the
call to creative work, who felt their own creative power restive
and uprising, and gave to it neither power nor time.
—**MARY OLIVER,** Pulitzer Prize–winning poet

Tilda knew Mary Oliver's words by heart because she'd taken a photo of an artist at work and added Oliver's quote to it. Solid sales followed; Tilda saw the poster everywhere, including at her hairdresser's salon, where she stared at it with a quiet unease whenever she had a cut and color.

Now, as she walked home, she thought about that poster, and the quote, and her own creative regrets that she'd just unleashed from their cage. She'd never admitted her dreams of hanging her work in the State Portrait Gallery to anyone but Tom. His response had been to tell her she was funny. That riled Tilda.

"I'm not being funny. I'm serious."

Tom looked at her as one would a child—if destroying a child's dreams was your intention—and told her she needed to be realistic. "Tilda, you're not Man Ray or Cartier-Bresson."

"No, I'm Tilda Finch."

"You know what I mean. You're a decent photographer, but those men were visionaries. The career you want is unrealistic and doesn't pay the bills."

"You didn't think This Is A Sign would pay the bills, and it's starting to."

"If you average out all the hours you've put into that business, it's still in the red."

Always negative.

Tom never loved me.

Tom left and never looked back.

I wasn't enough for him.

I'm not enough.

Tilda stopped in her tracks. So this was PEARL!

Oh. My. God.

It was the first time she'd clearly observed the way she spoke to herself. And it was shocking.

Shut up!

Good comeback, loser.

Whoa!

It had been a boozy yet interesting afternoon. Surely she didn't always talk to herself like this! Didn't the Irish say that what whisky couldn't cure, there was no cure for? She'd had three whiskys and was still having these thoughts. That was a problem. What had Selma said? Observe the thoughts, start watching them, but don't be too attached to them and certainly don't believe them.

You'll believe anything.

That wasn't true. She didn't believe that she'd created this condition in herself, did she? Selma did. Leith did. Erica did. But she didn't? Listening to Carol talk about herself had certainly made her uncomfortable. She could relate to a lot of what she was saying. Not entirely. Tilda had never had a gym membership and couldn't imagine ever giving up carbs, and yet she did regularly beat herself up about putting on weight. She'd gone up one size in her jeans but refused to throw out the smaller size because that's where she felt she belonged. And last summer, shopping for a new swimsuit had been an exercise in self-loathing. There were also the times she stared in the mirror, pulling the skin on the sides of her face up. There wasn't enough collagen in the world to turn the tide on that, but she'd heard thread lifts were an excellent alternative for those who didn't want injectables. Not that she'd have one, but by god she'd thought about it, and had even googled it.

Did Tilda hate what she saw in the mirror? Honestly? No. And certainly not lately. Yet she didn't love it. Sometimes she barely liked it. She was just starting to understand how hard she was on herself. How had she never realized this before?

She tilted her face upward and took a deep breath. She turned her thoughts elsewhere. There were so many positive things to focus on. She was healthy, apart from the disappearing thing. Her girls were happy. She had deep friendships. She was proud of the business, loved the team she worked with, and had financial security. She had a good life. Contentment. But it was time to admit that something was missing. If only she could put an invisible finger on what that was.

Tilda stopped and savored the sun. It was a sensational winter's day, cold but not windy, so it felt warmer than it should have at this time of year. Her mood shifted.

"Anything is possible," she whispered.

And that's when she spotted Patrick—wearing blue jeans and a faded denim jacket over a grey hoodie—leaving the café where she'd first met him. He reached up and adjusted his aviators, and Tilda's heart skipped a beat. It took a moment for her to even see his cane.

Without thinking, she called out his name. He turned toward her voice and smiled, waiting for her to catch up to him.

"Hi, Patrick, it's—"

"Tilda! Third time lucky."

The last time a male had been so happy to see her was when she'd rescued Buddy from the pound.

"Yes, very random," she said.

"Nothing is random."

Whisky or not, Tilda was now feeling a little embarrassed and not sure what to say.

He must think I'm an idiot.

Ah, yet another charming thought to jot down in the notebook.

"You know what I think?" he said.

That I'm an idiot?

Tilda shook her head, which confirmed her previous thought because Patrick obviously couldn't note visual cues, then said, "Er . . . no."

"We're meant to know each other. Let's have dinner."

Tilda was completely thrown by his suggestion and his enthusiasm. Fortunately, there was just enough alcohol left in her bloodstream to prevent her from overthinking things. "I'd love that. When?"

"What are you doing tonight?"

In the space of a second, a struggle took place in her head. If she said, "Nothing," did that make her look like a lonely sad sack who had no life? If she responded, "I'm busy," would that ruin the moment?

"I know it's last minute and you're probably busy," he said. "It's just that I'm going overseas tomorrow for three months."

She went for it. "Tonight is good."

He was clearly thrilled. "There's a little place called Mongoose just up the road."

"I know it."

"Shall we say seven?"

"Perfect. I'll be there," she said before she had time to screw up what was the best offer she'd had in years.

"Excellent." Patrick grinned. "I'll finally get that whisky I ordered."

Tilda genuinely hoped he was referring to his running joke and not the fact that she smelled like a distillery.

21

Dating means two things; disillusionment or a racing heart.

—MAE WEST, actress and singer

It took approximately five minutes for the excitement to pass and for Tilda to regret agreeing to dinner—there's nothing like a great opportunity to start a war inside your head. She headed straight for Ali's bakery for some moral support. Jack was serving a customer so ignored her, focused on the task at hand. She could see Geoff in the kitchen pulling a tray of loaves out of an oven. He spotted her and gave a wave.

"Hi, Geoff. Ali around?"

"She's taking the day off." He placed the tray on the stainless-steel counter. "Anything I can help with?"

Tilda was disappointed she wouldn't get to offload to her friend, so she turned her attention to the tray instead. "Just some bread. Smells delicious."

"I'll bag one up for you."

While Geoff grabbed a loaf in his mitted hand, Jack turned to Tilda as the other customer left the store. "Holly tells me that you're disappearing. That's no good. She's beside herself."

"Jesus, Jack. Way to go, mate." Geoff gave Tilda an apologetic look as he walked to the counter and handed her a bagged-up loaf. "Careful. That's hot."

Tilda gave Geoff a wink and then tapped her phone on the machine Jack was holding out. While Ali and Geoff never charged her, she had a deal with Jack that she'd always pay him. "Holly's lucky to have you, Jack."

Tilda made her way back to the street, now with the added worry that Holly wasn't coping with her illness too well. How could she go on a date when her daughter was *beside herself*? By the time Tilda arrived home, she was looking for a way out.

The timing is wrong.

You're not good with relationships.

"It's not a relationship," she said out loud. "It's one bloody date."

But PEARL had a point. Tilda needed to focus on her health, not put herself in the totally vulnerable position of meeting a hot man for dinner.

You know you get anxious.

Wow, PEARL was bringing out the big guns. It was true. Leith told her it was perimenopause, but Tilda had been feeling anxious a lot lately. She'd been filled with confidence once, a long time ago. Lifetimes.

● ● ●

"Have a drink with me," Tom said.

Tilda's whole body lit up. She wanted this man. They left the writers' festival and went to a nearby bar, where even Tom's bravado wavered. The sexual tension between them was unnerving. He began to tell her about himself, but Tilda put a finger to his lips.

"I'm dating a lot . . . which means I listen to a lot of stories. And that takes up a lot of my precious time." She watched his pupils dilate as she whispered, "How about you kiss me first and we see if there's chemistry. If not, we go our separate ways without wasting time. But if there's a spark, I'd be happy to hear your story."

And so Tom kissed her.

Tilda should've listened to his story first.

● ● ●

She marveled at that version of her. Bold, completely confident in her appeal. It was so different now. Dating in her fifties really was the depths of hell on hell's hottest day.

She'd done it only once since the divorce. At Yumiko's urging, she'd joined a dating app.

Yumiko helped Tilda put together a profile that made her look fabulous, or perhaps pretentious, while pretending not to care one iota what people thought of her. Then she started searching for potential suitors.

"What career field?" Yumiko asked. "Do you want someone in banking, retail, education? How about a hot tradie?"

"I don't know. Anything, as long as he's employed."

"Try setting the bar a little higher," Yumiko said. "Hair color?"

"A man interested in me will probably be grey."

"Star sign?" Yumiko continued.

"Really? I don't care."

"You need a water or fire sign." Now Yumiko was an astrologer. "How about age?" Yumiko turned her attention away from Tilda's phone and back to Tilda. In her low-rise cargo pants and tight Rip Curl tank top, she looked more like one of the twins' friends than like one of Tilda's. "A younger guy might be just what you need."

"I need that like a hole in the head," Tilda said. She felt insecure enough. "No one younger or prettier than me, thanks." Finally, one thing she was sure of.

Yumiko shrugged and did as she was told. "Next, political persuasion. Liberal, conservative, swing voter?"

"I don't want a swing voter. It suggests commitment issues!"

Tilda had to admit, searching for love this way was more time-effective than going to the pub. She was able to cut to the chase, quickly and efficiently. Yumiko posted the profile and within minutes Tilda was inundated with thumbs-ups, the app's way for members to let someone know they looked all right. She then did what any sane woman who'd been out of the dating scene for decades would have done. She freaked out.

"I can't do this, Yumiko! This is so far outside my comfort zone it's in Kabul."

"You think it's easy for me?"

"You're ten years younger than I am."

"And Japanese. Some men think they're getting a compliant little man pleaser. They don't want me—they want an Asian fantasy," Yumiko said. "Nothing like adding some racial exoticizing to the Tinder experience."

Tilda took a moment to consider this. Yumiko was cool and whip-smart, yet even she had her issues with dating.

"We all just want someone to see us for who we are," Yumiko said.

"I'd be happy to have a man who was kind to me," Tilda said.

"Maybe you'll find that man on here." Yumiko waved at the app on the phone.

Tilda beat herself up over her cowardice. She was single. She used to be more fearless. Quite frankly, she wouldn't mind some sex. Tilda nodded at the phone. "Okay, swipe right or whatever."

Tom was lucky. Tilda had bought his share of the house, and he'd walked out the door and straight into a new home and life where there were no ghosts to haunt him. But for a long time, Tom was still embedded in the walls, whether she liked it or not. He'd been in every room, sat on every piece of furniture. God knows he'd made the final decisions when they were decorating, so even though she'd wanted a beige couch, they ended up with a deep red one. Then he'd left and Leith had smoked him out in a saging ceremony. But it wasn't until Tilda renovated and bought new furniture that Tom's presence was cleared. The house was hers alone now. And she loved it. But she had yet to christen it with another lover.

"This guy looks good." Yumiko tapped the phone screen.

"'I enjoy rock climbing and hiking on weekends,'" Tilda read, pausing right there. "I'd never see him on weekends!"

"You like walking."

"To the beach and back with Buddy. Or to your place for a drink. No-where that requires a compass."

Yumiko scrolled through more profiles. Most of them indicated that there were a lot of fiction writers on the site. Boats were clearly fash-ionable. Also, a lot of men didn't know the difference between *you're* and *your*.

"Even I won't settle for that, and English isn't my first language." Yumiko paused at one profile. "How about this one?"

EasyGoingGuy.

He was pleasant-looking, and his profile was delightfully free of bullshit.

Yumiko sent him a thumbs-up and stood to leave.

Tilda grabbed her arm. "Where are you going?"

"I have a date, and if you follow through here, you will too."

Yumiko gave Tilda a hug and headed for the door. Tilda was alone and online just as EasyGoingGuy replied. They began messaging each other. Cautious details. Playful banter. Careful disclosures about their lives. His name was Rob. He liked to surf. His favorite season was autumn. He played chess.

They agreed to meet the following weekend. Tilda tucked the can of spray paint (which apparently works like mace) Ali had given her into her handbag and made her way to a restaurant for her first date in eighteen years. She paused near the entrance and waited for Rob. When he arrived, he didn't look dangerous. He looked nervous too. There was no lightning bolt, but it was easy. They talked over a couple of drinks and he ended the night by telling her just how fabulous she was. It was music to Tilda's ears. The following few days were filled with the constant pinging of texts and an enjoyable second date. On date three, she threw caution to the wind and went back to his place for average sex, and then an awkward conversation.

"I'm not ready for a relationship," he admitted.

Tilda got up and collected her clothes. "You could've mentioned that before . . ."

Rob smiled, one of those smiles that may have worked on women once, but at his age looked empty. "I'm just being honest."

Tilda stared at him, amazed that he viewed this as honesty.

"I'll be in touch," he said.

He never was.

If anything, Tilda was relieved. She'd known from their first date that it wasn't a good match but had allowed herself to be swept up in the fantasy anyway. She retreated to lick her wounds. She deleted the app and decided that being single was much easier. And yet here she was getting ready for another date. No doubt there would be all sorts of weird complications that she really didn't have the desire to navigate. And none of those complications had to do with Patrick's vision.

Patrick is gorgeous. He wouldn't ask me out if he could see me.

I'll say something stupid.

Or boring. I'm not interesting. I never do anything interesting.

I'm fat.

He said he was going away for three months—maybe I should delay until he returns and I'll have time to lose five kilos and do something interesting and address this anxiety I feel about dating.

Thanks, PEARL!

Plus, Tilda really couldn't go out with Patrick now that she'd glimpsed the mess inside her head. Unfortunately, she couldn't cancel—she didn't have his number or even a last name to look him up. Instead, she did a quick assessment of how she would hide her condition from him. He couldn't see her missing bits. Or maybe he could. He might still have some sight. Either way, she didn't want anyone else noticing. That would add to her anxiety, and she wanted tonight to be as easy as possible.

You have nothing to wear.

She'd really stirred up the hornet's nest going to see Selma. Now that Tilda had some awareness of her, PEARL never shut up. She imagined PEARL to be a tiny woman with a large capacity for complaining—plus a blue rinse, funky glasses, a fondness for tea, and a judgmental attitude toward anyone who drank anything but tea, especially if that choice was alcohol. Maeve would hate her.

"You can back off, PEARL. Tea won't get me through this date."

Tilda tore through her wardrobe. She couldn't do anything about her nose, but she could style her hair over her ear, and wear gloves. She chose a deep green blouse, black jeans, and stiletto boots. She left her hair hanging loose, something she rarely did anymore. She gave herself a spritz of perfume and then checked herself out in the mirror.

To her absolute mortification, her neck was fading away.

Tilda grabbed a scarf and wrapped it around her neck, but it didn't go with her blouse.

"Christ almighty."

The doorbell rang—the groceries!

Tilda ripped off her blouse and slipped on a black turtleneck. Not as sexy, but then neither was a floating head. She raced downstairs and carried her groceries inside, shoving them into the pantry and fridge, and rebagging Maeve's. She grabbed her keys and ran out the door and down the road carrying Maeve's groceries and the cat kibble she'd bought days earlier. She wasn't even out of her neighborhood before her feet hurt. She needed to cancel. She couldn't just not show up. That was bad manners in any situation, but surely it was worse when you were a no-show for a date with a blind guy?

Through the squeaky gate, she rapped on the door, which Maeve opened in record time.

"Don't you look nice," Maeve said. "Who's the lucky guy?"

"How do you know it's a guy?"

"You're wearing heels."

So much for her bad eyesight.

Tilda carried everything into the kitchen.

"You want a whisky, love?"

"I'd better not, Maeve. I'm still sobering up from a few this afternoon."

Maeve waved at Tilda's stilettos. "And you don't want to trip down a gutter in those."

"Er . . . no." *But thanks for the image I'll now have in my head all night.*

"Remember, safe sex. You don't want any more kids at your age."

Tilda had no idea how old Maeve thought she was but felt flattered that anyone would think she was still fertile.

Maeve waved Tilda off at the door. "I look forward to hearing all about it."

Tilda raced back to her house, being extra careful not to trip, and reapplied her lipstick. She couldn't bear to look at herself in the mirror. She was about to fall into a sobbing heap when she remembered: Patrick wouldn't know. He wouldn't notice her nose, or her ear. He wouldn't notice the greys that were sprouting up through her faded blond locks. And even if he did, if he could see them, did it matter?

Yes! Cancel. You can't go out looking like that.

"Shut up, PEARL! This is me. If he doesn't like it, he can bugger right off."

PEARL was silent, and Tilda stared at her reflection and in that moment admitted that she looked nice. A glimmer of something surfaced.

Defiance.

"I will not cancel."

She watched herself, as if waiting for a response.

Defiance.

She grabbed her bag and her gloves and walked out the door.

"I look nice." She did, and for once she believed it. "I look lovely."

She repeated this mantra to herself until she entered the bar and saw Patrick waiting for her.

22

Spend time with people who help you see the world differently.

—ALI, referring to Jack

Patrick looked like he'd stepped off the cover of *GQ*—handsome in blue jeans, a black shirt, and an expensive wool jacket, wearing slightly tinted glasses instead of the other, darker ones she'd seen him in. Tilda's stomach did a flip. The guy was totally out of her league but seemed completely unaware of that. She'd milk it while she could, but eventually someone was bound to let him know. Maybe even their waiter.

They were seated at a table in the back corner, not far from the roaring fireplace. The ambient lighting helped ease her earlier concerns as well. They both had a whisky in front of them and Tilda felt warm and relaxed. Patrick seemed to be a regular at Mongoose. Staff and a few customers called out to him, and he greeted them all by name when he heard each voice.

"Do you frequent the same places because of your disability?" she asked.

Patrick faced her in mock horror. "Do I have a disability?"

Tilda was just about to apologize when he laughed.

"I come here regularly for the same reason sighted people do," he said. "Excellent food."

Tilda was grateful he couldn't see her face burning. "Patrick, I hope I don't ruin the evening by saying the wrong thing all the time."

"Me too. Don't ruin it." He laughed again. "Tilda, I have no problem with you being curious about how I get around. People usually avoid the topic." He leaned forward slightly and spoke as though he was sharing a secret. "With some people, I can almost hear them thinking, 'Don't mention the blindness,' as though they'd be the ones breaking this news to me."

Tilda laughed.

"Shall we get the conversation about my sight out of the way?" he asked.

"I'd appreciate that." Tilda was surprised by her own eagerness to confront this and move on. "Are you completely blind?"

"I'm legally blind, if that's what you're asking."

"Does that mean you can't see anything?"

"That's not the best question to ask. Why don't you ask what I *can* see?"

Tilda wished the floor would swallow her up. "I'm sorry, I'm not sure how to approach this."

Patrick smiled. "Head-on, Tilda. I understand you're curious. To answer your question, I can see more during the day. Not so much at night. I can still see light, some shadows and outlines too—but nothing defined. I know what's around me, without the details."

Nothing defined, no details. No wonder he saw me, Tilda thought.

"The lighting isn't great here, so I don't see much." He gestured at the space around them. "But generally, I see enough to have an awareness of my surroundings."

Tilda relaxed more, silently thanking the dim lighting. "Is that why you can surf and then walk back up the beach without a cane?"

"Yes, but also because it's familiar territory. I've been surfing these beaches since I was a kid."

"Were you born blind?" Another question she wouldn't ordinarily ask.

"No. I was diagnosed with retinitis pigmentosa—RP—when I was fourteen years old. My sight was fine until my early thirties, when it deteriorated. I had some tunnel vision and night blindness. It has stabilized again over the past few years, so fingers crossed I'm okay for a while."

"I see." Tilda could have kicked herself for her choice of words, but Patrick seemed to sense that.

"Tilda, I don't get offended every time you use that phrase." He grinned and sipped his whisky.

"I feel like I make a fool of myself every time I speak to you." She decided to get it all out there. "Like when we met in the café, and I said you needed a Yoda stick!"

"And then I picked up my white cane?"

Mortified silence. But only for a moment because Patrick began to laugh. Really laugh. So much so that Tilda joined in.

"How could you have known? I felt for you. The benefit of being blind was that I couldn't see the look on your face when I left the café."

"I'm sure it was idiotic," Tilda said. "That's why you paid for my coffee."

"Is that what you think?"

"I wasn't sure what to think."

"I paid for your coffee in an awkward attempt to flirt with you," Patrick said. "And because I was kicking myself for not asking you out then."

It was so different from her interpretation at the time. "I misread that."

"Clearly. I get the impression that you're completely surprised that I did."

"I am, but pleasantly so," Tilda admitted. "Thanks for answering my questions."

"Any others before we move on?"

"Yes. How do you manage to look so good?" she blurted out.

Patrick was clearly delighted by this. "You think I'm good-looking?"

Now she was embarrassed. "I mean your clothes. You're stylish."

He reached across the table and took her hand in his. It was both electrifying and calming at once.

"I'm stylish? Not good-looking?" he asked, teasing.

Her cheeks burned. "Well, both."

"That's good to know. I haven't seen myself clearly for years, so things might've changed."

The warmth from his hand was making her feel flushed, and she prayed she wasn't about to start sweating. "What I'm trying to say, rather inarticulately, is how do you know what to wear?"

Patrick cocked his head to one side, amused. "You want to know how I can leave the house in something reasonably coordinated?"

"I find that difficult to do, and I can see."

"I stick to certain styles. I have Braille labels attached to my shirts, so I know what color they are. I only wear these glasses"—he tapped the side of them—"at night, because I don't need as much protection from light then. And I'm told they look trendy."

Tilda laughed. "They're very cool."

"I'm flattered." He gave her one of his sexy grins. "I think you're gorgeous."

"Oh, that's . . . well . . ." Tilda wiped some imaginary crumbs off the table with her free hand.

"You don't believe me when I compliment you because I'm blind?"

"Patrick, it's clear that my foot-in-mouth tendency is more of a problem than your lack of sight, but still, you don't know what I look like."

Patrick squeezed her hand. "I can see that you're probably five-four without the boots you're wearing. I can hear a heel. I think you're wearing jeans tonight. You have a slim build and small hands. I noticed that when we met and shook hands. You have shoulder-length hair."

He was very astute. Although he hadn't picked up on her invisible neck or nose.

"Strawberry blond," he added.

Her stomach dropped. Could he see more than she realized?

"But I only know that because I asked the waitress at the café when I paid for your coffee," he admitted.

Tilda laughed. He was incredibly easy to talk to. She was surprised by how relaxed she felt. They chatted about the café where they'd met, the various beaches he had surfed, and then her children. He didn't ask what her girls did, but instead what they were like, which Tilda found refreshing. All of her concerns about what to wear and how she wasn't ready for a date now seemed distant and ridiculous. He felt familiar, and yet she barely knew him.

"What do you do, Patrick, for work?"

"I'm a pilot." Patrick waited a beat and then let out a loud laugh. "I'm joking, Tilda. I wish I could see your face."

"I believed you. I was just working out how you'd do that. I imagine you could do anything you put your mind to."

"We all can. That's what the mind is for," Patrick said. "In fact, I do fly. Stephen and I hang glide, but I go tandem."

Tilda gave a clap. "I knew it. You *are* a pilot."

"For fun, but to answer your question, I'm a musician. Sound producer and composer," he said.

Tilda wasn't surprised. He had an air of creativity around him. "What do you play?"

"Several instruments, but mainly piano and guitar."

Her eyes took him in, every line, every stray lock, the grey hair at his temples, the curve of his chin. It was an unusual experience to be able to do that on a first date. "How do you read music?"

"I studied for years before my eyesight started to deteriorate. Stephen and I grew up playing music together. Once I was diagnosed, my mother made sure I learned the Braille system for notes. I don't use it often, but I can. Music is something you feel and hear, not something you see. It's an invisible art form."

Tilda was impressed. "You're lucky. I wish I'd learned to play an instrument."

"It's never too late."

Tilda shook her head. "At my age—"

"What's age got to do with it? My grandmother just started and she's ninety. She'd always wanted to learn piano and figured she'd better get to it before she got too old."

Tilda glanced down at her missing hand. Hardly a good time for piano lessons, so she changed the subject. "Are you going on tour? Is that why you're going away for three months?"

"Sort of. It's a little complicated . . ."

Oh, here we go. He's married or something.

"Stephen and I have a business with his wife, Moe—Toolbox. We spend three months a year in Los Angeles, working and writing music."

"Lucky you." She was about to ask for more details but was interrupted by the waiter with their food. Tilda watched Patrick dig into his barramundi. There was nothing to indicate that he couldn't see it. She thought about what Selma had asked her in their first session, about how she viewed the world.

"How do you see the world, Patrick?"

"Great question." He paused for a long moment, thoughtful. "We knew I'd eventually lose my sight, so my mother took me traveling. I was fifteen, and on a trip to London we went to Highgate Cemetery. There was one headstone that said 'The Celebrated Blind Traveller.'"

Patrick could weave a tale. Tilda was enthralled. "Who was he?"

"James Holman. He traveled the world solo in the early 1800s. It was a rare achievement for anyone in that era, but even more extraordinary because Holman was completely blind. He said, 'I see things better with my feet.'"

"Incredible."

"He inspired me. I started thinking about how I saw the world even before I lost my sight. How do I perceive the world? Everything is a matter of perception."

Tilda was fascinated but didn't quite follow that. She knew that Gustave Flaubert had said there is no truth, only perception. It was on a range of merch that sold its socks off during the pandemic. "What do you mean by that?"

"Every single one of us sees a different world. You and I might experience the same event, but our reactions to that event will be different. How we perceive things shapes our experience of the world," Patrick said.

Tilda tried to wrap her mind around this. It wasn't new information. Leith spoke like this. Even Yumiko did. And they flogged it at work. Tilda had once stared at a new poster for an hour, contemplating its meaning. It read: "We don't see things as *they* are, we see them as *we* are." A quote often attributed to Anaïs Nin, who had in fact taken the words from a Talmudic text.

At the time, Tilda had read and reread that quote, emerging somewhat satisfied that she understood it. Somewhat. Her perception of it at least.

"I wonder if Holman really perceived the world through his feet," Tilda said.

Patrick nodded. "We'll never know how others comprehend the world. I do know that while Holman may have been blind, he saw the world more clearly than most. His ability to connect with the world around him made him a hero in my family. As soon as I graduated high school I traveled for a few years, with him as my inspiration."

"Where did you go?"

"Where didn't I go? I hit all the usual places, but it was the unusual ones that really shaped me. I cycled across Iran. I walked the Kumano Kodo in Japan. I traveled overland all the way from Singapore to Vienna."

She could listen to him talk all night.

"Do you still travel? Apart from to LA?"

"I do. I have just enough sight that it's really not a problem, but even if that sight went, I'd still give it a shot," Patrick said. "I was in Indonesia recently. I practice Merpati Putih, a Javanese martial art. It helps a lot with my mobility. I went over to learn more about it."

Martial arts, hang gliding, surfing. "Is there anything you don't do?"

"Sure, lots, but I don't focus on those things."

"I feel incredibly dull by comparison."

"I doubt that," he said. "Do you travel?"

"I used to, a lot. I did the required London stint in my twenties, like a good Aussie. I traveled around Europe. I've taken my daughters backpacking around Southeast Asia a couple of times. I spent a month in Mexico before lockdown." She'd forgotten how much she loved traveling. It had been a few years.

"You'd be fun to travel with," Patrick said.

There was a moment, almost awkward, where the suggestion of future adventures settled between them: walking the Camino de Santiago, drinking vodka on the Trans-Siberian Railway, waking up next to each other in Paris and Prague, listening to jazz in New Orleans. In the space of a second, all these adventures took place in Tilda's mind. But she pushed them away to focus on the moment. She'd learned the hard way to never make plans with men.

Patrick was relaxed, as if settling in to know more about her. "Talk to me about your photography."

Tilda was surprised by his enthusiasm. When was the last time a man had been interested in her? Asked questions? Wanted to get to know her?

She thought for a moment, and then spoke. "When I'm really focused on a subject, looking through that lens, I forget everything else. In that moment . . . it's the union between me and the present."

"How old were you when you started?"

Another question!

"Early teens. My father gave me a camera and really encouraged me, so I threw myself into it. Initially I found it was a way to connect with him, but eventually it became a way to connect with myself."

"I'd love to see your work, but hearing you talk about it gives me a clear sense of your talent."

Tilda found Patrick so attractive. He was well-educated, well-spoken, well-traveled, and . . . well, sexy. Conversation flowed easily, and in the blink of an eye they were the last patrons in the restaurant as it closed. Afterward, they stood on the footpath outside the bar, both clearly reluctant for the night to be over.

"I had a great time, Tilda."

A flood of electricity ran down Tilda's body. That switch had not been flipped in a very long time. "So did I, Patrick."

"As much as I enjoy randomly running in to you, how about we swap numbers?"

They exchanged numbers and then Patrick reached for her hand and drew her in. Not too far. Not for a kiss, but close. It was intimate and yet comfortable. "I'd love to see you when I'm back."

"I'd like that," she said, but she wouldn't get her hopes up. Three months was a long time.

"The next few months will be busy for me. Long days, and the time difference, but I'll definitely call."

Tilda loved that he'd clarified that.

Patrick ordered his Uber home. "Can I drop you on the way?"

"I'll walk. I'm not far from here." Tilda preferred this—she didn't want to be in a situation where she felt obliged to invite him in. She'd had a confusing week, and her growing attraction to Patrick only added to that.

When his ride pulled up beside them, Tilda wasn't sure whether to shake his hand or give him a hug. Instead, he reached out and touched her face. It was such a tender gesture that Tilda almost teared up.

"I'm so excited about meeting you, Tilda."

Tilda made her way home feeling like there was potential all around her.

23

Perhaps the biggest tragedy of our lives is that freedom is possible

yet we can pass our years trapped in the same old patterns.

—TARA BRACH, psychologist and author

Tilda woke to sun streaming through her window and dreamy contentment. She loved her bed. The clean sheets she'd put on the day before. The comfortable mattress she'd bought after the divorce, because she no longer had to cater to Tom's bad back.

Curled up under her quilt, she floated for a moment in the state between asleep and wakefulness, as her brain waves moved from theta to alpha and into low beta. She'd never noticed that transition before. Thoughts of Patrick drifted in and she recalled every detail of last night. She couldn't fault the evening. Even her foot-in-mouth moments were minimized to only a toe or two. It had been one perfect moment after another, strung together like fairy lights, gorgeous and magical. From the moment she spotted him and her stomach did *that* flip—the type of flip it hadn't done for a very long time—to the moment they said goodbye.

I'm so excited about meeting you, Tilda.

He won't call.

Aaaand PEARL was awake. It was the first time Tilda had truly observed how her brain woke up. She attempted to return to the happy reruns in her mind, but PEARL had other ideas.

That good-looking comment made you look like a fool.

And you realize you arrived with half a tank of whisky and then had two more. You drink too much.

For once PEARL had a point. Tilda got up and made her way into her en suite, where she always left her phone charging at night. There was a text from Patrick. A surge of happiness shot through her. It was completely unexpected. He'd been clear that he was away for work and would call when he could. There was comfort in his clarity. But there he was . . .

> Morning, Tilda. I enjoyed last night immensely. Hope you have a beautiful day. Patrick x

Tilda read the text three times. It was perfect. Not too much, or too little, or too confusing. Just right.

She began to type.

> Hey, Patrick

Delete the word hey.

> Hi, Patrick

Sounds weird. Delete.

> Well hellooo

God no. Delete.

> Me too. A lovely evening. I hope the trip goes well . . . Tilda x

Finally! She pressed Send and then regretted the ellipsis.

This was tough, and it had only been one dinner. But the timing of his going away worked for her. It took the pressure off. She had enough things to fill her mind, including the nagging old fishwife PEARL whom she'd only just discovered but now was aware of constantly.

She slipped out of her pajamas and checked herself out in the mirror. Every part of her body got a look, on full rotation. Nothing else had disappeared, but nor had any of the missing bits reappeared.

It was relief and disappointment in equal measure.

Tilda dressed and walked downstairs and then, after making a coffee, grabbed her notebook to write down some key conversations she was having with PEARL. Tilda noticed that some of her internal dialogue was conversational: with people from the past or present or simply with herself. Other times, it wasn't a two-way conversation at all. PEARL just talked *at* her, like one of those oblivious old negative Nellies who rarely drew breath.

She sat in the sun on her small terrace out back, pen poised.

It's too hard. What's the point? A few nice dates and then it's difficult. Complicated.

He'll want someone younger eventually.

I'm too old to date. Men my age all want much younger women. I'm left with the octogenarians.

I'll be alone forever.

I've put on weight. I need to fast today and try to drop three kilos.

I'm tired. Exhausted. Worn out. Alone. No one helps me.

No point doing these stupid exercises. It won't work. Nothing works. And soon I'll be completely invisible.

She slapped the notebook closed and grabbed Buddy's leash. He heard the jangle of it and raced to the door.

"Who's a patient boy?" His tail thumped on the wood floor. She clipped on his leash, grabbed her camera, and headed onto the street. It was a glorious day. Crisp air, blue skies. She could smell the salt in the air and hear the waves a block away.

They made their way down to the beach, with Buddy yanking at the leash when he spotted some dogs that he regularly played with. Tilda unclipped him and he took off. Pure joy, pure power. He bolted toward the pack, greeted with leaps and chasing and bum sniffs.

If only meeting men were that easy.

Tilda lifted the camera and focused, taking a series of shots just as a large mastiff mounted Buddy from behind.

Wonder what the inspirational quote for that photo will be? she thought. Perhaps she could pitch it as a Wednesday mug. *Happy hump day!*

She watched as the mastiff's attention turned elsewhere and Buddy took off, running in circles. She had to envy the joy he found in that. She'd been running in circles for years and didn't see the appeal.

She saw a group of surfers up the north end of the beach and thought of Patrick. How was it that at her age, just when she thought she'd healed the hurt and grown up, one date with an attractive man was enough to rewind the clock thirty-five years?

She'd been with one person for so long, going into that relationship young and gorgeous and filled with certainty that she was loved, and she'd come out the other end older, bruised, and unsure of everything, especially her own worth.

Life with Tom had almost destroyed her. There had been loud warning bells right from their first proper date, three days after meeting at the writers' festival. During dinner he received a series of phone calls from an ex, which didn't sound amicable. Tilda was so attracted to him that she didn't question it, or the fact that he'd continued to take them throughout their dinner. Just as the check arrived, he left the restaurant to argue with the woman on the phone. Tilda paid. She ignored the clanging bells. Within hours, and in the years that followed, the warnings had been drowned out by the sex. Wild, clawing, constant sex. Everywhere, anywhere, all the time. It was the one thing they got right. They both admitted that it often felt like the glue that held them together. Not their girls. Not the years that passed. Not their history. Not love. It was his scent that would catch Tilda as he passed her on a hot day. Or the way he'd grab her wrist as she walked by. This intense physical connection completely blurred the emotional destruction that was taking place. The stonewalling. The gaslighting. Leith had been telling her for years that Tom was emotionally abusive, but Tilda didn't see that then, and she was only realizing it now. Years after he'd walked away.

The thing was, Tom had never hurt her physically. He'd never even yelled at her. But he was never wrong. And he could be cruel. The first time she'd experienced his coldness was during an argument that started when she'd asked for some of his time. He was always busy. Work. Himself. The girls. And he was a caring father, so it had taken Tilda a very long time to realize that care rarely extended to her. He was the type of dad who enjoyed being with his children. He read to them most nights. He marveled at their milestones and achievements, and included Tilda in this. When this happened, Tilda always felt like they could move mountains together, but their time was spent with the children. He never prioritized alone time with her, and that's all she really wanted—time. So after weeks of his not having time, she finally confronted him.

● ● ●

"Tom, I'd like to have dinner with you tonight. Just the two of us. I could book that Italian place you like."

Tom exhaled, seemingly annoyed. "Tilda, I'm really swamped with this edit."

"You still need to eat," she snapped.

He ignored her. Didn't respond, didn't even glance her way. Weeks of her bottled-up emotions exploded into tears.

"Why won't you spend time with me?"

If there was one thing she'd learned over the years, it was that her tears repulsed him. Angered him. He was not the type of man to wipe them away.

He barely looked up from the computer. "Because I'm busy. Fuck, you push things."

"Don't you want to spend time with me?"

His jaw was clenched.

"I feel like you don't love me."

"I don't love you." Now he looked up, his gaze ice cold.

She felt as if the rug had been pulled out from under her.

"What do you mean you don't?"

"I don't love you."

"Have you ever?"

"I don't know."

Like a pathetic, needy girl, she clutched at him. "I love you."

He pushed her away, an impenetrable wall around him. "You always know the worst time to pull this shit."

"What shit?" Tilda didn't understand him at all.

He stood, the force of his sudden movement knocking his desk chair over. "I'm so stressed and you always make it about you."

Later that night, after sobbing herself empty on the couch, she tiptoed back to bed. He was sound asleep, softly snoring. She slid under the covers. It was a king-size mattress, but the distance between them felt insurmountable. She lay as still as possible, trying not to move too much, or make any sound that would wake him. She could feel his rage toward her even as he slept. At some point she slipped into a dreamless sleep, only to wake later as she had countless times before, with him clambering out of bed for an early-morning surf. She lay there feeling broken. The open, gaping wounds of the night before had made her body ache.

An hour later, she was still hiding under the covers, imagining all sorts of anguish to come, when she heard him return from the beach. As always, he went into the kitchen, and before long, she could hear the coffee machine. To her surprise, he brought her a coffee in bed and sat beside her. He didn't seem to notice her heartbreak that still clung to the walls.

He spoke first. "I didn't mean what I said."

"You said you didn't love me."

"I didn't say that."

"That's exactly what you said."

"I meant in that moment. You always choose the worst time to have an argu-ment with me."

"I didn't want an argument. I just wanted to have dinner with you."

"I'm snowed under with work and stressed about money."

"We both are, Tom," Tilda said. "But spending time together and being united is the key to coping."

He pursed his lips, defensive. "You ask the wrong way."

Tilda rolled her eyes. "I've tried telepathy, but you didn't pick up on it."

Tom took a deep breath as though dealing with a child. "I accept that I was mean."

Mean didn't cover it. He'd taken a sledgehammer to her heart. "You said you don't love me."

"I know this is hard for you to understand," he said, "but I don't all the time."

Another sledgehammer. "Ever?"

"I have . . . moments," he admitted.

And again. He was a regular demolition man. Tilda's voice was barely a whisper now. "Moments?"

"Yes, like when you're not expecting anything from me, and not hounding me."

It was as if they were speaking different languages. "You mean expressing a need?"

"It's impossible to love someone all the time." Tom looked exhausted. Probably from wielding that sledgehammer.

Tilda was deeply wounded. "I love you all the time."

He looked incredulous. "Even when we argue?"

"I might not like what you're doing or saying. I might not like you much in that moment. But love never leaves the room."

"That's you. I'm not like that." As was always the case, Tom spoke in riddles. "All I know is that with you, there is no breeze."

"Breeze?"

"Ease," Tom said in a tone suggesting anything but.

"Breeze? You're a destructive cyclone. How can there be any breeze when you're so difficult?" Tilda stared at him. His face was stone. Carved marble. It was a certain look he'd get when he was immovable.

●   ●   ●

That was all in the past now, but she never wanted to repeat the same mistakes. It was easy to be swept up in Patrick and their date. People's true colors didn't come out until much later, and by then it was too late. By then, your heart was in their hands, to do with whatever they wanted.

Buddy made his way back to her and she slung her camera over her shoulder and clipped his leash on again. He fell into step beside her, glancing up regularly as they made their way back up the beach path and onto the quiet road that led back to their street. Handsome, loyal, always thrilled to see her.

"I think I should just stick to you, eh, boy?"

Love hurts.

PEARL had the last say, again.

24

Over the next few days, Tilda carried her notebook everywhere and regularly jotted her thoughts down. As each day passed, she became more aware of the voice inside her head. Of PEARL. She became an active observer of her own internal dialogue.

The results were horrifying.

Tilda discovered that she had nasty self-talk going on all the time. *All the time!* She was outright mean to herself. She'd never have herself as a friend if she had the choice—PEARL was a grade A bitch.

How had she missed this before? How had she not known?

When Tilda was making dinner, the voice said: *I shouldn't eat. I'm really fat. I've piled on the weight. I've been saying I'll go keto for ages, but I never do because I'm a total carb hound. And completely unmotivated. I'm weak.*

Then, in the shower: *I'm a blimp. I could float above the city and advertise sporting events.*

All day long. An internal dialogue. Or conversations with people that never took place. Or conclusions about things that had yet to even play out. And all the feelings and stress associated with it all.

I'm useless, can't take a decent photo.

I need to do it myself or it doesn't get done.

I haven't heard from the twins. What if something's happened?

I should remind them not to go into car parks alone at night.

I've got no willpower. I've eaten the full bag of chips.

I'm in my fifties now.

Time is running out.

What's the point? Love hurts. I can't trust. I look old. I deserve to be invisible. Why me? Blah blah blah blah blah blah blah blah.

Bad things happen to good people.

Page after page of scrawled vitriol and confusion and pain.

The more she wrote, the more she thought about the quote from Buddha that Yumiko said could be attributed to him, unlike most Buddha quotes on the internet: "May all beings have happy minds."

Her mind was not a happy mind. It was a war zone. And then Tilda thought about the poster she'd seen in the café: *Your reality is a reflection of your thoughts.* And she finally got it.

Selma had asked her how she viewed the world, but she hadn't understood the question, let alone its significance. Intellectually she understood the concept and had even discussed perception with Patrick at dinner. But a week of observing her own thoughts had really driven the concept home and she now understood how *her* interpretation of the world was shaped by this running dialogue in her mind. Thanks to PEARL, Tilda's world was a place where struggle was a given. Disappointment was expected. Joy was short-lived, therefore something to be wary of. There was a sense of ever-present doom, so embracing joy felt like testing fate.

That wasn't to detract from the great beauty Tilda saw around her. Or the contentment she felt during visits from her daughters, and nights with her girlfriends. Tilda appreciated her life, and she was grateful for many things. That's why Selma's question had confused her—in a life where she had so much to be thankful for, in a world where there was so much beauty, why had she never been truly happy? Why did she feel that if she ever dared grasp at happiness, it would be snatched away?

She'd never been one to reflect too deeply on her childhood. It was uncomfortable when she did. She had always been aware of that, if not of PEARL's programs around it. But now, pen poised, she considered how her early years were connected to this constant sense of impending doom that permeated her life. Peace between her parents was always on a knife-edge. She'd be happy when things were good, desperately wanting their truce to continue, but always knowing it could end at any moment. And there were all the events she looked forward to, only to have an argument arise before they left home, ruining whatever the occasion was. There were the countless promises made in moments of peace, about time they'd spend together as a family, always broken the same day when yet another argument broke out. And then there was the day her father promised to take her out to shoot photos.

Tilda's love of photography had been nurtured by her father. It was the one activity where they really connected, and where Tilda felt seen by him. When they were taking photos, her father appeared relaxed, and she adored him. On this particular day, they planned to take the camera to the beach, but first—and there was always something else that came first—he had to get rid of "that bloody tree" because he was sick to death of sweeping up the leaves. Despite a complete lack of gardening skills beyond the rake, Lloyd Finch was adamant that he knew how to cut it down. But the spotted gum had been around longer than the madman with the axe, and as the tree tumbled, it took her father with it. An hour later, Tilda went outside, only to discover his crushed torso. It had been so incomprehensible that she'd continued to casually walk toward him, calling out to ask how much longer he would take to be ready.

When she spotted the blood on the grass, she was snapped back to reality and began to scream for her daddy.

Since then, despite his lack of presence in her life while he was alive, her father's absence had been palpable.

Tilda put her pen and notebook down. She realized that she'd kept happiness at arm's length, certain it would be snatched away if she dared to let it any closer. And it might be. There were no guarantees. But instead of giving herself permission to aim for happiness, she'd remained in the familiar state of fear of loss. It wasn't living. It was surviving. And it had to change.

She lifted her pen once again, as PEARL spoke. More a whisper this time.

You've done well.

25

The problem is you're afraid to acknowledge your own beauty.

You're too busy holding onto your unworthiness.

—RAM DASS, psychologist and spiritual teacher

"I'm deleting my Tinder account." Yumiko was regaling the others with yet another dating debacle. A guy who'd told her about his recent trip to Thailand and admitted he'd only contacted her because he wanted to see what it was like to date an Asian woman. "I've decided it's not a dating app. It's a smash-my-self-esteem app."

"I'll miss your Tinder stories," Ali said. "They remind me to work on my marriage."

"Geoff's a diamond," Leith said. "You two won't ever divorce."

"Well, if I ever considered it, Yumiko would change my mind," Ali said. "I mean seriously, she's gorgeous and still gets treated like that. With my thighs, no one would even swipe left."

"Right," Yumiko said.

"No need to agree with me."

"It's swipe right, not left."

"I thought you were agreeing about my thighs."

"Lots of men like thick thighs." Yumiko dipped a cracker in some hummus. "I wish mine had more shape."

"Geoff says it gives him something to grab hold of," Ali said.

Yumiko sometimes joined Ali and Leith for drinks at Tilda's, and tonight the four women were seated around Tilda's firepit. It was a gorgeous night, a blanket of stars above them.

The fire wasn't the only thing keeping Tilda cozy. Patrick had texted that morning, out of the blue.

Knock, knock.

It had taken Tilda a moment to realize that it was Patrick, and that his message required a response.

Who's there?

Yoda.

Yoda who?

Yoda best!

Tilda laughed out loud. That's so cheesy it's funny, she'd replied.

Was thinking about you—hope you have a good day. x

You too, Patrick. A nice evening. x

And that was that. Short, sweet, and surprisingly easy.

"What are you grinning about?" Leith asked her.

"I'm not grinning."

"You look like an ad for compact sex toys. Like you've got a special se-cret." Leith was a shark. She knew something was going on.

Tilda knew it was best to out herself. "I met this guy—"

All three friends froze mid sip of wine.

"At the café," Tilda continued. "He started talking to me, and he made me forget all about all of this invisibility stuff."

"Because he saw you," Ali said.

"That's the thing. He initiated our conversation, which was friendly—sparky, even—but . . ." Tilda hesitated.

The three women leaned further forward, waiting for all the details.

"He's blind."

Leith slapped her leg. "Excellent. I like him already. Drinking at the café."

It was like talking to a toddler. "Not drunk blind. Physically blind."

"You mean like Stevie Wonder?"

"Yes."

"Then how did he see you to start a conversation?" Ali asked.

"I don't know," Tilda said. "I didn't even realize he was blind until he walked out."

"Did he run into something?" Leith asked.

Tilda rolled her eyes. "No, he had a cane."

Leith gave her a cheeky wink. "All the better to spank you with."

"Oh my god, seriously?"

"Listen, I once dated a guy with one leg, and he hated how people tip-toed around his disability, especially when he couldn't tiptoe." Leith cracked up.

"I shouldn't've said anything," Tilda snapped.

"Clearly you're attracted to the guy, or you wouldn't have mentioned him to us," Leith pointed out.

"Plus you've got your own disability now, so you get to make disabled jokes," Yumiko said, as if it were fact.

"That's not how it works," Tilda said.

Leith stared at the wall, trying to come up with something. "Invisible jokes? Yumiko, help me out."

Yumiko jumped right in. "Maybe something along the lines of, 'I went to see my doctor about my invisibility, and she told me she couldn't see me right now.'"

"That's not funny." But Ali snort-laughed anyway.

So did Leith. "We can have a field day at work. This Is A Sign can do a whole invisibility range."

Tilda had been waiting for that. "Give me time to tell my mother before we release the mugs."

Leith's eyes widened in disbelief. "You haven't told Frances yet?"

"I need to work out how to broach it," Tilda said.

"I'd say the missing nose might be the conversation starter," Leith said.

Ali placed another log in the firepit. "Why haven't you told your mum?"

Leith waited, an eyebrow raised. "Yes, why, Tilda?"

Tilda poked the flames with a stick. "You tell me, Leith. You obviously have an opinion on the matter."

"Because a teensy little part of you thinks I might be right, and that your past has created your current state of invisibility. You're worried that telling your mum about this might open the door to confronting your childhood."

Leith could read her like a book. Tilda steered the conversation away from her mother. "I'm not finished with my story about the guy."

"You're not? There's more?"

"A few days later, I bumped into him at the beach."

"Is that because he didn't see you?" Yumiko giggled.

Tilda rolled her eyes.

"I'm following," Ali offered.

"We chatted, and that was that. But then I ran into him again two days ago."

Leith clapped her hands together, clearly loving the story. "Holy hell, the synchronicity. The universe really wants you two to go out."

"That's what he said. So we did."

All three friends stared at her, mouths agape, like a row of carnival clowns.

Leith looked seriously surprised. "And you've only just mentioned it now?"

"I was processing everything. It was too early to talk about it," Tilda said.

"I've been worried about your mental health as you absorb this invisibility thing, and you're telling me you've been dating?"

"One date, yes."

"And how was it?" Ali asked.

"Wonderful. He's smart, funny. He's a musician and—"

Leith held her hand up. "Stop. Wait. Blind, local, musician . . . You went out with Patrick Carpenter?"

"You know him?"

"He didn't mention that he's one of the Carpenter brothers?"

Tilda wasn't sure where this was going. "I also met Stephen on the beach."

Leith was so excited she stood. "You met them both? You went out with Patrick? Oh my god, Tilda, do you really not know who they are? Didn't you google him?"

Tilda shook her head. "I only looked for him on Facebook, and there were, like, over a hundred different Patrick Carpenters."

"They were probably fan sites," Leith said.

Yumiko dipped another cracker in the hummus. "I can't believe you didn't google him."

Tilda threw her hands up, exasperated. "I didn't know his surname until a few nights ago, and I've been busy since then. I'm sure, given some wine and some time alone, I would have." She turned to Leith. "Who is he?"

Leith spoke slowly, for her friends who clearly didn't understand. "Stephen and Patrick Carpenter."

"I've never heard of them," Tilda said.

"Me neither," Yumiko admitted.

Ali shook her head. "Add me to that list."

Leith sat again. "Okay, maybe you've heard of Toolbox?"

Ali and Yumiko nodded simultaneously.

"Oh right, them. I have the app," Ali said. "Jack uses it when he's stressed."

"I've got Toolbox." Yumiko waved her phone at Tilda. "I love it."

"He mentioned something about a toolbox, I think. What is it?"

Leith visibly centered herself before launching in. "Patrick and Stephen launched a health and wellness start-up called Toolbox over a decade ago. It's grown into a website, an app, and an online community worth about a billion dollars."

Tilda spat her wine everywhere.

Ali grabbed her glass of soda water and tossed it over the wine, washing it across the stone pavers as Leith continued.

"They're the granddaddy of meditation apps like Calm and Headspace," Leith explained.

Tilda's gut filled with lead. "You mean he's one of you?"

Leith looked at her in disbelief. "You really do forget the demographic that pays your mortgage."

"Maybe that's why he asked me out. Stephen was talking about This Is A Sign. Maybe Patrick thinks I'm woo-woo too," Tilda said.

Leith rolled her eyes. "I wish you wouldn't use that term. It's really condescending."

Tilda looked chastened. "Gotcha."

"Maybe he just liked you," Yumiko suggested.

"You manifested him for a reason," Leith said.

"Actually, I randomly met him."

"Nothing is random." Leith was on her phone, bringing up Toolbox on Instagram. She thrust her phone at Tilda, whose heart sank as she scrolled through the glossy account with a million followers. Photos of Patrick and Stephen surfing, hanging out in the studio, one with a small child, another with Patrick meditating.

She pushed the phone back at Leith as if it were scalding hot. "That's enough. He meditates."

"What's wrong with that?"

"I thought he was a musician."

Leith laughed. "He is. They write all the music for their programs and meditations."

"He seemed so *normal.*" Tilda was serious. She was gutted.

"Oh my god, you're judgmental."

"I'm not at all. I put up with you. And Ziggy. I just . . ."

"What?"

"His expectations of me will be so high. Like yours are. But I can handle yours. I can't handle his."

"Listen to yourself. He'll think this and expect that. Bloody hell, Tilda, one date, which you enjoyed, but then you learn this and it's over. You have him pegged." Leith exhaled dramatically.

Tilda hated it when Leith was right. "My glass is empty," she mumbled, holding it out.

"Your life motto," Leith mumbled back.

Yumiko grabbed the bottle and poured. "You've had the weirdest couple of weeks, Tilda."

"You're not wrong," Tilda agreed.

"And that photo of him drying off after the surf . . . wow." Yumiko, right again.

"A billionaire? I'm not comfortable with that," Tilda finally admitted.

"Maybe not a billionaire. Not Afterpay or Canva, but serious money." Leith shrugged.

"Honey, you might not be *that* wealthy, but you pull your own weight," said Ali, the voice of reason.

"That sort of money . . . it changes everything. I'm not comfortable with it. He'd have so many women after him." Tilda's thoughts were quickly causing her to back away.

"Maybe that's why he likes you," Yumiko said. "He senses that you're genuine. Plus you have your own money."

"He's actually gone overseas for work, which turns out to be a blessing."

"Don't sabotage this because you don't think you're worthy of it," Leith said. "Just go with it. What have you got to lose?"

"Everything," Tilda said.

Leith grabbed her friend by the shoulders. "Darling Tilly, you're already losing everything. You're losing yourself. Just let go. Step into the unknown. That way, all that you've lost will be replaced by something even better."

26

After her friends left, Tilda trawled through both the Toolbox website and app. Users could study different meditation styles, and access tools to help reduce stress, combat sleep issues, and navigate difficult times. And there were prompts to address trauma and lack of self-worth. For the skeptics, there was a whole area breaking down data and scientific research into easy-to-read articles, with links back to reputable studies.

There were also a bunch of links to programs the company funded, including one that provided practical, financial, and emotional support for those who were losing their sight, and, to Tilda's delight, one at Jericho Creek Animal Shelter: "Because our four-legged friends are the greatest mindfulness teachers we'll meet."

What had gone from one enjoyable date had turned into a swarm of wasps in her skull. Tilda closed her laptop and walked into the kitchen. PEARL was screaming at her to back away from the freezer, but she ignored the voice and pulled out a tub of cookie-dough ice cream. It was after midnight. She was quite drunk. And now in a total spin over Patrick.

This is why you shouldn't date.

Right, because everyone I've dated is rich, successful, and hot.

Why is everything so bloody difficult?!

Back on the couch, she dug into the ice cream and battled her brain. She knew the wine wasn't helping. Nor would the ice cream. But she was now aware of something deeper and way more destructive. She was aware of her programs. And by observing them, she was also able to ask herself what was really going on, deep down. She'd met a perfectly lovely man, who had been clear and kind in his interest, and yet here she was imploding because, surely, he must be deranged to think she was a suitable match for the likes of him.

It's because he can't see you.

Tilda shook that thought from her head. That completely diminished his intuition and intelligence and the way he perceived the world around him. It was pure ignorance to question his ability to know what he wanted just because he couldn't see.

Tilda scraped the bottom of the ice-cream tub and put it on the coffee table.

You have no willpower.

I know, PEARL.

And you're fat.

Not fat . . .

And a man like Patrick is so far out of your league, he's on Mars.

Tilda was sick and tired of this constant self-deprecating dialogue that took place in her head. "Why is he out of my league? I'm financially stable. I started a company from scratch too. He's interesting, and if you'd bugger off, PEARL, I'd be pretty interesting as well. And yes, he's hot . . . but I'm not exactly an ogre." Tilda rolled her eyes. "He probably talks to himself also." She licked the spoon and placed it in the empty tub. "It's got to be deeper than that."

Give him time; he won't choose you either.

There it was. PEARL had brought out the trump card.

Tilda realized that was a primary program that had repeated on a loop for years. As an only child, caught in a war zone, she always felt alone and unseen. Her parents were too needy and damaged to ever put her first. To choose her. Tom had substantiated that belief in countless ways throughout their marriage, and certainly when he told her he was leaving.

"*You don't know her. It just happened, Tilda.*"

"Don't kid yourself, Tom. These things don't just happen. She wasn't just walking down the street and suddenly tripped over and, surprise, fell onto your penis. It doesn't just happen. It's a choice. You chose this. You chose her."

Tom watched her with . . . was that pity?

"I didn't choose her," he said. *"I just don't choose you."*

The echo of that conversation could still be heard in her mind. Tilda wondered if it would ever die out. It had reverberated through her soul for five years now. That he'd left wasn't the problem. How he'd left was. He was Paris, firing an arrow into her most vulnerable spot. The man who should've loved and protected her had instead reconfirmed everything she already thought of herself.

I'm not lovable.

I'm not worthy.

No one ever puts me first.

She noticed Pirate sitting at the door, watching her. "Stop judging me, Pirate."

You're judging yourself.

Tilda wasn't sure if that was PEARL or Pirate sending mind-signals, but it hit hard. It was true.

She constantly judged herself.

She picked up Selma's book. She was halfway through now and things were starting to make more sense. And, paradoxically, less sense. She'd thought she knew herself, but now she could see she wasn't even close. Tilda started reading, to see if Selma had some answers for her tonight.

> One of my clients is the CEO of a major corporation. Meg is intelligent, successful, with a doting husband and nice kids. She appeared to have it all until she began to disappear. Like many women, she'd been so busy going through the motions of her life and carefully projecting one version of herself to the world that she was completely unaware of her unremitting internal dialogue.

Self-worth is entirely based on how you see yourself. Nothing else matters. How others see you is not your concern. Honest observation of self will be entirely superficial until you start observing PEARL. By observing PEARL, you'll soon recognize what you truly think of yourself, and from there you can bridge that essential gap between self-worth and self-love.

Tilda put the book down and thought about how she presented to the world. She was calm, and she appeared confident and successful. And yet behind closed doors she'd accepted a relationship that she'd known for years was destructive and that bit by bit had eroded her self-esteem. Now she understood: the reason she had allowed this man to play such a pivotal role in her life was that she didn't think she was worthy of more. She didn't think she was worthy of having a man choose her, show up and truly love her. She realized with horror that she'd spent years worrying about how Tom saw her, rather than how she saw herself. She'd ignored her own needs. She never took time for herself. She'd ignored her creative yearnings. She'd ignored the war inside her head. She'd hollowed out her soul for Tom and still wasn't enough for him. He had shown his disinterest in a million different ways, and still his opinion of her had been so important that she'd lost sight of her own. She'd lost sight of herself.

Tilda stumbled into the bathroom to look at herself head-on in the mirror. That was a big realization. Wasn't it those types of epiphanies that were the source of miraculous healings? A quick scan showed that not only were her missing body parts still AWOL, but her left arm had joined them. She could have a field day with this and joke that she'd joined the arm-y. Tilda just wished she found it funny. It should be funny. Looking at herself now, it was a ridiculous sight.

A wave of exhaustion washed over her.

She regretted looking in the mirror. She regretted going out with Patrick. And she certainly regretted meeting with Selma and letting PEARL out of her cage. Even in her wine-and-sugar-soaked state, she thought about a quote from Tolstoy's *Anna Karenina*: "Rummaging in our souls, we often dig up something that ought to have lain there unnoticed."

She walked into her bedroom, stripped, and clambered into bed. She couldn't even be bothered turning any lights off or brushing her teeth. As she drifted off to sleep, she wondered what she'd dug up from her soul— and what on earth she'd do with it now.

27

A woman is like a tea bag—you can't tell how
strong she is until you put her in hot water.

—ELEANOR ROOSEVELT

The following week, Tilda marched into Selma's office, notebook in hand. "I was going to cancel, Selma, but I felt I should at least explain why I don't think this treatment is working for me." Tilda waved her notebook around. "You asked me to write down my thoughts, which I've been doing. However, I think it's best I stop now."

Selma gave her a kind smile, as if she understood. "Take a seat, Tilda."

Tilda did as she was told and suddenly burst into tears. "Shit. What's wrong with me?"

"Nothing is *wrong* with you."

"I'm so bloody negative. I'm awful to myself. Cruel. I'm more horrible to me than Tom ever was."

Selma agreed. "It comes as a shock, doesn't it, when you first take note?"

"It's not normal."

Selma handed Tilda a tissue. "Unfortunately, it is."

Tilda wiped her eyes. "Other people are like this too?"

"Most people have no idea. They are afraid of their thoughts, their feelings, their pain. They keep busy so that their minds are never quiet enough to observe PEARL." Selma took the notebook from Tilda and opened it to the first page. "May I?"

Tilda nodded. "Go ahead, read it. If you can find a way to fix this, you're a genius."

"You've already taken the first step by observing your internal dialogue." Selma started reading. "Hmm . . . oh yes, 'I'm fat, I'm an idiot, old, not attractive.' Yes, very black-and-white thinking, Tilda. And you're psychic too: 'He won't call, won't like me' . . . ha! You also read his mind . . . 'I'm sure he thinks I'm dull.'"

Tilda blew her nose. "I need another tissue."

Selma handed Tilda the box from her desk.

"I'm drowning in negative thoughts."

"You'll learn to swim. Don't fight it. 'The only way to make sense of change is to plunge into it, move with it and join the dance.'"

Tilda dropped a wad of tissues into her bag and took some fresh ones from the box. "Seriously? You're quoting Alan Watts to me? You know he died an alcoholic?"

"Of course. I was at his memorial back in '73. Drank like a fish but was exceptionally wise." Selma looked down at Tilda's scribbled notes again. "You're committed to negative self-talk. PEARL works overtime for you."

"I despise her." Tilda sniffed.

"She's only doing her job, dear." Selma chuckled into the notebook as if she was reading something funny. "You predict all sorts of calamities. Your daughters . . . poor fragile things can't look after themselves. And do you really think they'll be attacked in a car park?"

"It's crossed my mind."

"By a clown?"

Tilda's silence confirmed the truth in what she had written.

Selma went on. "Shopping at Westfield must be stressful."

"It could happen," Tilda mumbled.

"Certainly, but it probably won't. Anything is possible, but you need to start being realistic about what's probable." She tapped at something Tilda had written. "You *choose* to tell yourself that you're fat and lazy, rather than remind yourself that you're an attractive woman who has worked hard for her success and deserves to sleep in sometimes and not feel guilty because you didn't walk the dog."

Tilda blew her nose. "I don't choose to be mean."

"You do. It's a choice. You can also choose to be kinder to yourself."

"You make it all sound so easy."

"It's a matter of training yourself. It becomes easier once you're aware of it."

"Anything else?" Tilda felt quite defensive now.

"You're polarized. No middle ground. For example, Tom *never* loved me. Even I know that's not true, Tilda, and I've never met him. Don't get me wrong, he sounds like he has the emotional maturity of a turnip, but then you're somewhere in the same veggie patch, dear." She tapped at the final item on the list. "And you make everything personal before you have any evidence that it's in any way related to you. You just assume you know what's going on in someone's mind."

"I don't think I do."

"You literally think you do. For example, who is this man whose mind you can read? In your notes you say he won't call."

"Patrick. We went out to dinner recently, but it won't go further."

"Whyever not?" Selma flashed her a smile. "Is he nice?"

"Very."

"Excellent. Any reason to think he won't call?"

"Apart from his being a male?"

"Are you concerned your invisibility will put him off?" Selma asked.

"No," Tilda said. "He's blind."

"In what way?"

Tilda was a bit thrown by Selma's question. "He's visually impaired. He can't see."

"Oh, is that all? I thought you meant really blind."

"He is *really* blind. He can't see."

Selma appeared frustrated by Tilda's response. "What does it mean to see? To truly see? Look at this world we live in. Everyone is blind. Dear girl, you're as blind as a bat or you wouldn't be here. You've lost sight. Of yourself. And if you can't see yourself, how will anyone else?"

Tilda froze, a wave of something rising from the tips of her toes, up her legs, her torso, her arms, her face. A sense of knowing.

Finally, she spoke. "I have lost sight of myself."

"When I asked you in our first session how you see yourself, you said you didn't know. It's in here." Selma handed the notebook back to Tilda. "Every one of these thoughts has an associated emotion: anxiety, anger, resentment. You always feel *something*."

"I'd never connected the dots, but it should be obvious. If I'm miserable, it's attached to my thoughts, and vice versa."

Selma's tone softened. "Exactly, but here's the kicker: every single one of those feelings also releases a flood of chemicals, which can be wonderful if you're feeling good. Bring on the dopamine, serotonin, and oxytocin. But when you're in a negative loop, you're releasing stress hormones into your nervous, endocrine, immune, and digestive systems. Your entire body lives in fight-or-flight mode. And you know what happens when you live like that?"

Tilda stopped annotating her homework notes and looked at Selma, aware that she wasn't going to like the answer.

"You can get sick."

Tilda let that sink in. "What do I do?"

"Over the next week, get to know PEARL more. Befriend her."

"I don't need a friend like PEARL."

"Of course you do. PEARL can be a source of great support. You just need to change the program she's running so you'll receive more helpful feedback."

"So that's the key . . . changing the program?"

"Yes."

Tilda tapped the side of her head. "It's all in here?"

"Yes."

Tilda pulled a face. "But it's exhausting dealing with my own thoughts."

Selma said, "There are other things you can do to help. They're all in my book. Affirmations, visualizations, creating mind movies."

Tilda let out a laugh. "Seriously? Aren't those things self-help fluff?"

Selma raised an eyebrow. "I'm peer-reviewed, Tilda. I don't prescribe fluff. These activities help you override the negative beliefs and create positive changes, first in your mind and then in your life. Even something as simple as decluttering can support change. Is your house in disarray?"

Tilda immediately became defensive—a habit of hers that was only now becoming clear to her. "I'm not a hoarder, if that's what you're asking."

"Did you hear me ask that?" Selma snapped.

Suitably chastened. "No."

"Then stop making things up."

"Is my house cluttered?" Tilda asked the original question and thought about it for a moment. "No, but there are things tucked away that I've been meaning to address for a while."

"Your external space is often a reflection of your internal world."

Tilda glanced around Selma's office, as if mentally tallying how many times she'd need to visit it. "And how long will it take to fix me?"

"How long's a piece of string?" Selma said.

"Needs to be long to tie this mess together."

Selma slapped her pen down. "Tilda, you're not broken. You're human. You can change if you commit to this, but it will take a while. There's no quick fix. You're changing neural pathways that will lead to a new set of programs being installed. To do that, you need to really face this current version of PEARL. Listen to the internal dialogue without being attached to it. Just observe it. Is it true? Is it correct? Is there any evidence to back a thought up? It's okay to feel overwhelmed. You need to walk through the flames now to find out why you speak to yourself this way." Selma was quite worked up, which made Tilda feel like she was on the precipice of something big and exciting. "Why are you so hard on yourself? Why don't you think you deserve a good relationship, or happiness? Why don't you see yourself as the worthy, wonderful woman you are? Why?"

Tilda transcribed what Selma was saying in a large scrawl as a reminder for later and then closed her notebook. "Thanks, Selma."

"So, are you going to continue with our sessions?"

"It's too late to stuff the genie back in the bottle." Tilda paused for a moment, following Selma's advice and observing how she felt. "I feel better now—I know I'm up for this challenge."

Selma stood. The session was over.

Tilda went to leave, but Selma stopped her at the door.

"One more thing, dear." Selma's grey eyes bored into Tilda's. "Nothing about this journey is linear. It's a spiral toward deeper truths."

28

There is one friend in the life of each of us who seems not a
separate person, however dear and beloved, but an expansion,
an interpretation, of one's self, the very meaning of one's soul.

—EDITH WHARTON, author

"They forgot my spring rolls." Leith rifled through the bag of Thai
takeaway, removing each container and placing it on the boardroom desk.
"False alarm—here they are."

"Emergency over," Tilda said, then grabbed one, dipped it in chili sauce,
and took a bite. "Ow, hot, hot."

"You do that every week," Leith chided.

Tilda shrugged. "Who am I to break tradition?"

Tilda, Leith, and Ziggy had dinner together every Monday after work,
usually in the office. Conversation was a mix of work and personal. It was
a way for them to connect at the start of each busy week once the office
was quiet and most lights dimmed. In summer they'd watch the sun set
over the ocean from the window of the meeting room, but at this time of
year it was already dark.

Tilda relaxed back in her chair. "Where's Ziggy?"

"He's spending some time with Lulu." Leith grabbed a paper napkin
and wiped her mouth. "She's dropped out of uni."

Tilda stopped mid-bite. "Is she okay?"

"Downward swing."

Lulu had been to hell and back with anorexia in her early teens. Years of therapy and then six months in a clinic had helped her recover by the time the kids all did their final exams. Fortunately, Lulu had been well enough again to graduate with her gang: Tabitha, Holly, and Jack. Tilda knew that recovery was an ongoing process, but Lulu appeared healthy and happy with life now, especially since going to university.

"I'm sorry, Leith. I've been so caught up in my own problems recently that I had no idea you were dealing with this again."

"It's all happened quickly this time," Leith said, pushing her stir-fry around her plate.

Tilda noticed that Leith wasn't eating much.

"She's smart, Leith. And she's worked hard to be healthy."

"You know, all the spiritual work, all the personal development, all the stupid bloody kale smoothies can't stop a freight train like this still hurtling into your life. I don't know if Ziggy and I failed Lulu, or if she came to this earth to test everything we believe."

"Probably both."

Leith looked crestfallen. "You think we screwed her up?"

"We all screw our kids up. It's inevitable. It's just to what degree. You and Ziggy are the best parents. I'm sure the damage is minimal."

"We chose the road less traveled and now we don't know where we are," Leith said dramatically.

Tilda laughed. "You'll find your way. Well, Ziggy will. You're useless at reading maps."

They shared a look, and both cracked up.

"You're incredible, Leith. She'll be fine. Drop the guilt and pass me the pad thai." Tilda started heaping the noodles on her plate. "Besides, you've talked me into some of this self-development shit. You don't get to renege on it."

Leith stared at her, the kind of long, hard stare that only a best friend can get away with. It left Tilda feeling uncomfortable, as if Leith could see into her soul. "I'm glad you're seeing Selma." Leith's voice wavered. She broke eye contact and busied herself with the green curry and rice on her plate.

They'd known each other since they were eighteen. They had raised their daughters together. They had experienced the wild and wacky journey of This Is A Sign together. Tilda couldn't imagine what she'd do if anything ever happened to Leith.

If she disappeared.

Tilda hadn't considered the impact of her disease on Leith until this moment. Leith had been driving her to be better, to explore, to do the work. Tilda had framed it as Leith pushing her alternative beliefs on her, but the reality was way more complex. They were each other's north and south in the world, and if one of them disappeared, the compass would be off. Not once had Tilda considered Leith's fears around her disappearing.

"How are you coping with my diagnosis?" Tilda asked.

Leith froze. "What do you mean?"

Tilda shrugged. "I was thinking, if you were disappearing, I'd be devastated. I haven't thought to ask how this is affecting you."

Leith was surprised. "Yeah, right . . . yes, well . . . definitely . . . it's been . . ." Leith's chin wobbled. She placed her hand on her chest, visibly trying to calm herself, but to no avail. Instead, she burst into howling tears. "Oh god, I'm sorry, yes, it's horrible. I can barely sleep. It's total shit!"

Tilda rolled her chair over to her friend and gave her a hug. "Let it out," she said.

"You're going to beat this, Tilly; I can't live without you."

"I'm not dying!"

That started Leith crying again. "One of us will die first."

Tilda handed Leith some napkins. "You've got a lot going on with Lulu and you're upset about me. Let's not add death on top of that."

"Okay." Leith pulled herself together and blew her nose. "That feels better. I needed a howl."

They took a moment to just sit together. The room calmed.

Tilda broke the silence. "All good?"

"Much better."

"Can I ask you something?"

Leith nodded.

"How do you see the world?"

Leith raised an eyebrow. "Interesting question."

Tilda sighed, the frustration of the past few weeks surfacing. "Selma asked me this in our first session."

Leith leaned back in her chair, her head on the headrest, and looked up, as if reading from the ceiling. "'I think the most important question facing humanity is, "Is the universe a friendly place?" This is the first and most basic question all people must answer for themselves.'"

"Einstein. Although there's some conjecture over that one."

"Yes, but it's worth considering anyway. Selma has asked the same question: Is the universe friendly? Is life just tough, or can we find happiness? I think we all come to a conclusion about that, whether we realize it or not. And that influences everything."

Tilda already knew the answer, but she asked anyway. "You see the universe as friendly, don't you?"

"I do," Leith said. "I see life as a glorious, grand adventure. Even when my best friend is disappearing, and my daughter is struggling. Both those things are very painful, but I still see the universe as loving and playful."

"What do you mean by playful?"

"When you lean into the experience of life, synchronicities occur. Nothing is a coincidence. It gives life a magical quality," Leith said. "How do you see the universe?"

"I see it as a place where there is great beauty, but I believe that any time I experience happiness, it can be snatched away from me. I live in a constant state of . . . impending doom."

"Living on a knife-edge as a child can color your world in that way."

Tilda absorbed this. While Leith had delivered her message in a matter-of-fact tone, there was much to consider.

"What else did Selma ask you?" Leith asked.

"She asked how I see myself, and I can't answer that."

"The sessions are going well, then?" Leith chuckled.

"How do you see me?"

"Gosh, Tilly . . . You're funny, whip-smart, got a sassy attitude I love. You're a sucker for a sob story, especially one with four legs."

Tilda nodded, but Leith continued.

"Loyal, nurturing, independent, creative, quite intuitive, although I suspect not fully embracing that yet." She thought for a second, and then added, "You're also extremely wise when advising other people, yet you don't really use that wisdom on yourself. Shall I continue?"

"How can I be in my fifties and not know who I am?"

"You don't recognize these things in yourself?"

Tilda thought about that for a moment. "I guess, but I'm insecure, obsessive, incredibly hard on myself. And ignorant. I thought I was content until I met PEARL. Now I know I have zero self-worth."

Leith smiled at her friend. "Not true. You're just shining a light on those aspects of yourself. You are what you focus on, and right now you're focused on the negative because you're exploring it. But it's not the whole you. Our internal dialogue is more complex than that. PEARL could also at times be your cheerleader, your counsel, your greatest fan. But right now, you're observing the negative chatter."

"I'm a mess."

"Everyone is, Tilly. Look at me tonight."

"You're not hard on yourself."

Leith shook her head in disbelief. "Of course I am, but I've been doing this work for years now." Leith used her chopsticks to fish a piece of tofu from one of the curries. "Also, unlike you, I've spent over two decades with a man who wakes each day and chooses to hold me up, not tear me down. Ziggy is my cheerleader. He sees the best in me even when I can't see it in myself. It makes a difference."

"You think Tom did this to me?"

Leith took Tilda's hand across the table. "No, darling, you did this to yourself. He certainly played the role you cast him in, but the story is yours." Leith's phone buzzed and she grabbed it and read. "It's Ziggy. I need to go. Lulu has driven off in a rage."

"I'll come with you."

"No, you should stay out of it so she has somewhere to go to if she needs to get away from us."

Tilda nodded. Her goddaughter had arrived on her doorstep several times over the years. "You go. I'll clean up."

Leith gave Tilda a hug and then grabbed her bag and disappeared out the door.

Tilda had another mouthful of noodles and then cleared the remains of dinner and took them to the kitchen. There was so much to unpack. Why, despite having had the most balanced upbringing of any of the kids, was Lulu the one who struggled so deeply? And why was life so glorious one minute, but add one struggling kid to the mix and the sun simply didn't shine as brightly? Was the universe still friendly then? Leith thought so.

Tilda turned the lights off as she moved through the building. She stopped by her office to grab her bag and noticed a pile of new photographs that Ziggy had placed on her desk. The graphics team had worked their magic on them, each quote perfectly placed and set in a fabulous font. She would sign off on these tomorrow. Tonight, her mind was busy with Lulu and Leith. She tossed the photos back on her desk and then froze, examining the photo on the top of the pile. A photo she'd taken ages ago of two surfers walking side by side along a beach.

One of them was Patrick.

And on the photo was more of the Einstein quote that Leith had just recited.

"God does not play dice with the universe."

29

Someone I loved once gave me a box full of darkness.
It took me years to understand that this too, was a gift.

—MARY OLIVER

Maintaining brain health as you age is essential, and there are many ways to do that. Hobbies such as learning a new language or musical instrument are shown to be beneficial. However, combating invisibility requires more specific brain exercises, and the most effective are those where you're visualizing a future in which you're healthy and happy.

Visualization is a tool that is commonly used by elite athletes. The brain doesn't know the difference between a real event and an imagined one, so by imagining repetitive actions, such as getting that basketball through the hoop, an athlete can create new circuitry in the brain and yield a better outcome on the day of the game.

The same techniques can be applied to your life. By using visual exercises, you can become very clear on what you want and create the neural circuitry to achieve it.

Tilda closed Selma's book and turned her attention back to her computer and the collage of photos on her vision board.

There was a woman jumping for joy, a very visible woman with her arms up in the air; a woman seated at a table with friends, laughing; a man holding a woman in a loving way; a woman at an art gallery; a vibrant older woman. Looking at the collage made Tilda smile. Despite her initial skepticism, this had been a very beneficial exercise. It really clarified how she wanted her life to look and made her feel good about the likelihood of achieving it.

With the vision board done, she looked at the next exercise on her list: decluttering.

This was going to require some assistance, so she poured herself a whisky first and then went to the garage.

When Tom left, Tilda had packed much of their life together into boxes and stored them in the garage. Holly and Tabitha had still been in school, and between parenting them and running her business, Tilda simply didn't have time to deal with the things Tom had left behind.

Literal and metaphorical.

Then, after the twins left home, she couldn't be bothered. But since her last session with Selma, Tilda couldn't stop thinking about the boxes, and how they needed to go.

She lugged them inside and put them in a corner of the living room. She couldn't even remember most of the contents. She did know there was a hot-pink vibrator in one box, an engagement gift from girlfriends. She could also vaguely remember a set of Humpty Dumpty salt and pepper shakers Tom had got her. The rest was a mystery. She eyed these boxes full of items she'd once thought so precious and now felt no attachment. Zero. Just trepidation.

She wanted them gone. They were a glaring reminder of hopes and dreams that had died with her marriage. She was tempted to toss the lot, but they called to her like a siren's song.

She grabbed the notebook to write down thoughts, as Selma had asked her to.

I don't have time to deal with these boxes.

Tom never made time for me.

I feel anxious.

I need to get rid of these boxes. Like Tom got rid of me.

He didn't get rid of me. He just didn't choose me.

Tilda paused, her pen hovering over the page.

He didn't choose her.

He never had.

Worse, though—by staying, nor had she.

It was time.

She tore off the packing tape and ripped open the boxes. And, like Pandora, she had no control over what would unfold next. A life and love she didn't even recognize spilled onto the floor. She tossed aside ceramics and art and carvings. Wedding presents for a marriage as dead as Elvis. (Although Yumiko had once sworn she'd spotted him on a beach near Byron Bay.)

There were books that would go to charity, and a kimono from a trip to Japan. The vibrator was there, smaller than she remembered, but the salt and pepper shakers weren't.

One box spewed photos of Tom and cards he'd written all over the floor, the floor he'd left her sobbing on when he walked out. He hadn't predicted that outcome when he wrote them. Had he? Many of the cards read like he was sending birthday wishes to a colleague, not a wife. Skimming through them was like ripping her chest open again. It was now five years since her marriage had ended, and yet Tilda was hit with a tsunami of grief. She felt weighed down by the passing of time. She'd been so young, so in love, so sure the marriage would last. Funny how during the most transient time of her life, she was naive in the belief in things lasting: love, her youth, time to achieve what she wanted to in life. Reading Tom's birthday and anniversary cards was like trying to decipher the Voynich manuscript. She grabbed a giant bag and threw most of them out, keeping a select few for the girls.

More and more things went into the garbage bag. Things that she'd previously thought were precious now held no importance. A past life spread around her house. The meaningless contents of these boxes and the absolute dread she'd had for years about facing any of the things that symbolized the failure of her marriage. And something shifted. The story she told herself about the boxes changed. The story she told herself about Tom changed.

Tom hadn't left her for a younger model, as she'd told herself in her story. He'd had a series of unsuccessful relationships with other women over the years, but none of them were the reason Tom and Tilda weren't together. Tom had left because they weren't happy. Because they couldn't connect. Maybe because he didn't love her, but that didn't make her un-lovable. He was just one person on a planet of eight billion. Tom wasn't the enemy. In many ways he was a good man, just damaged. While he had no doubt been cruel at times, Tilda's cruelty to herself was worse. She'd stayed, tiptoeing around his needs and his rejection of her. It was a life built on eggshells. Impacting her in ways she never imagined.

Tilda's mind replayed something that she'd read in Selma's book.

> You will turn the people in your life into whatever you need them to be so your internal narrative is right. If you expect to be rejected, you will draw into your life people who will reject you. But once you begin to understand PEARL, you can you understand the roles you've given to those around you.

Tilda clearly saw the role she'd cast Tom in. Over the past few years, her version of him had taken on a life of its own. But it wasn't entirely true. Tom wasn't the cause of her low self-worth; he was the result of it. She'd drawn in someone who regularly confirmed what she felt and thought about herself. God forbid she was wrong about herself.

Tom could be a downright bastard, but he was also funny and loved his girls. He'd never complained when Tilda or Tabitha brought home an-other stray. He encouraged the twins to embrace their individual gifts, and on the nights when he was relaxed and at ease, he'd sit with Tilda and talk for hours. Those nights had been like red diamonds. Rare, and so valuable. It was one of the great mysteries of their marriage, that two people who could share nights like that were so completely incapable of maintaining it.

With the boxes done, she turned her attention to the rest of the house. She intended to wade through everything in her life until she found herself again. Or maybe for the first time ever. Tom was only one aspect of a greater whole that needed addressing. She needed to go deeper. Every drawer, every box, every cluttered corner was a chance to uncover herself.

The night turned into days as she looked at things on shelves, in cupboards, under beds. How the hell had she ended up with so much baggage when she never went anywhere interesting? She tore the house apart, and with it her own emotional state. Would a good declutter fix things? She was on a mission to find out. This felt different from the renovations she'd done on the place to exorcise Tom. This was more personal—the little things that had accumulated over her entire life.

In one suitcase she found an old photo of herself, head thrown back, laughing, stunning with youth and potential. Her first serious boyfriend, Grant, also a photographer, had taken it. On the back he'd written, "You are a light in the world. Don't ever change."

Don't ever change? Tilda had changed so drastically that she barely recognized herself.

The life she'd planned had disappeared. Now Tilda had actually started disappearing.

She was getting more than she bargained for by opening these boxes.

She was now crying on the floor, surrounded by a mound of stuff, clutching Grant's photo of her as though it was the last bar of chocolate on Earth.

She remembered how she used to laugh more. How spirited she was. Rebellious. Creative. Freethinking.

Life had sidetracked her.

The more she released externally, the more her internal world followed. It wasn't a breakdown but a breakthrough, and it had been a long time coming.

By the next day, Tilda had thrown away all souvenirs of her marriage apart from some carefully chosen cards, gifts, and memorabilia she'd placed in two shoeboxes—one for each of her daughters.

It was their history now.

30

In all chaos there is a cosmos, in all disorder a secret order.

—**CARL JUNG**, psychiatrist and psychoanalyst

Selma seemed impressed at their next session.

"It's no longer a pity party. It's something else I feel," Tilda told her. "The minute I started decluttering . . . I had to move. I couldn't sit still."

"A common reaction. These emotions sit in our body, and we'll do anything to not feel them, so we keep moving."

"That's how it felt. I needed to move, and suddenly I was tearing the house apart."

"I'm no Marie Kondo, but a declutter is an excellent way to clear things internally as well. You're making real progress."

"My life is in complete chaos."

Selma smiled at her. "Jung said that chaos and coherence cohabit."

"And this"—Tilda searched for the right word to describe how she was feeling—"energy?"

"Sit back and close your eyes for a moment, Tilda."

"Now?"

"No, next week," Selma snapped.

Tilda did as she was told.

"Take a deep breath and just sit with yourself. Ignore your thoughts, especially the ones that are telling you this won't work."

Tilda's next thought was how perceptive Selma could be.

"Let your mind drift down to your left leg. Scan it. See how it feels. Any sensations there? Then turn your attention to your right leg and do the same. What do you feel? Don't overthink this. Just observe. No attachment."

Tilda had done enough yoga with Leith over the years that she was familiar with yoga nidra, and this was similar. She took her time, scanning her legs, and then her arms, noticing tension, stress, and . . .

"When you're ready, open your eyes and tell me what you felt."

Tilda opened her eyes and looked straight into Selma's gaze. "Rage. I feel rage in all my limbs."

"No wonder you can't stop moving."

"I want to move."

"I can imagine. And where does this rage come from?"

Tilda looked down at her disappearing hands. Where to start?

•   •   •

Tilda watched the fly crawl across the dashboard of her father's Holden Commodore. For hours it had been dive-bombing her, and now it was within swatting reach. But if she moved, the heat would once again bear down, making it difficult to breathe. Sweat ran in rivers down her legs and arms. How much longer would her father be?

There was a rap on the driver's side window, and she turned to see him open the door. Finally!

"Whatcha doing with all the windows up?"

Windows up, doors locked, because she feared the shady-looking characters who were coming and going from the pub. Those were probably the people her father was here to do business with, so she remained silent.

"Here's a lemonade. It'll cool you down." His smile suggested he thought he'd be up for parent of the year for bringing her a drink. She'd been sitting in the hot car outside the Railway Hotel for nearly three hours now. She knew that from the Seiko watch her parents had bought her recently for her tenth birthday.

"Can we go?" Tilda asked.

"Soon. I'm handling business."

Tilda took a long drink through the straw and watched out the closed window as her father walked back into the pub.

• • •

Selma watched and listened as Tilda relayed this story. Then waited.

"It's just one example, a common one. The rational adult in me gets it. I've made my own questionable life choices. He was doing his best, right?" Tilda paused before admitting, "But it also makes me so angry. The disinterest and neglect. I was a kid."

"No wonder you chose Tom. Disinterest and neglect are familiar to you. But why did you stay?"

"With Tom? The usual reasons. The kids. Money. Because I loved him. Because I didn't know better."

Selma watched her, and then said, "Over the next week, you're going to start observing this rage and whatever else you feel by sitting in meditation for at least fifteen minutes a day."

Tilda blinked a couple of times, aware that her rage had just transferred onto Selma. "Is there an option B? Perhaps mixed martial arts?"

Selma's silence was her answer.

"I'm too busy to meditate."

"There's a Zen saying that you should meditate for twenty minutes a day unless you're extremely busy, in which case you should meditate for an hour."

"Buddha clearly didn't have my inbox to deal with," Tilda snapped.

Selma put down her notepad. "I'm not asking for blood. Research shows that the average person spends around forty-seven percent of their day on autopilot. The same habits, routines, and thoughts. If you want to change your life, you must change PEARL, and meditation is the best way to do that. You'll find links on my website to music and meditation apps I recommend."

Oh, the irony. "I think I know one," Tilda mumbled.

"It's time you observe this rage, before it devours you."

31

It's time for women to stop being politely angry.

—LEYMAH GBOWEE, activist

"Rage," Tilda said. "Apparently, I need to address it."

Tilda, Erica, and Carol were deep in conversation at their weekly Nag's Head Tavern get-together. They'd never seen their original barman there again, and instead the women were now served by CJ, who went by the pronouns they and them and always attended to Tilda and Erica. Not Carol, but two out of three wasn't bad.

"I don't know what to think," Tilda said. "Am I filled with rage?"

"No one's filled with one thing; we're a rich tapestry of all things," Erica said.

Erica could work for This Is A Sign, Tilda thought.

"All women carry rage," Carol piped up. "Rage at the inequalities and the injustices. Rage about every time we've had our boundaries disregarded, only to be accused of being unreasonable or a ball-breaker or crazy for pointing them out. Rage at every unwanted touch and the constant feeling that we're unsafe in the world. Rage, rage, rage, for the girls everywhere who are only now learning that they do not count in a man's world, and all the older women who are invisible and have been discarded. Rage."

Tilda stared in Carol's direction, speechless.

"Crikey," said Erica.

Carol lifted her glass to her invisible lips. "Imagine how angry I'd be if I didn't drink."

The three women laughed.

"Holy shit, Carol. I didn't know you had that in you," Erica said.

"To be honest, nor did I, but hanging out with you two for the past month has got me thinking about things differently. Plus, I've been reading Selma's book."

Tilda had come clean with Carol and Erica about seeing Selma. Now Erica grilled her each week, saying she felt like she was seeing Selma "by association." Tilda still felt guilty. She knew Leith had pulled strings, providing her with an opportunity that Erica would kill for. Erica was extremely motivated about reversing her invisibility. She was trying everything from crystal healing to past-life therapy. She was also taking a few psychology courses through the Open Universities. She was smart and strong, and it baffled Tilda why this vibrant woman was disappearing. But she was, more so each week.

"I love that chapter where Selma says that rage often emerges in your forties," Erica said.

"Same," Carol said.

Tilda tapped the cover of Selma's book. "Apparently, women sacrifice a lot of themselves in their forties."

"Self-sacrifice is the greatest form of self-sabotage," Erica said.

Tilda chuckled. "I'm just learning that now."

"And in return for the sacrifice, you thought you'd be seen and loved."

"Crazy."

"You weren't crazy for wanting love," Erica said. "That's an essential human need."

"Tom treated me like I was crazy. Then I'd get angry. And he hated that. He often told me that he didn't love me because I yelled."

"Would he yell back?"

"Never," Tilda said. "He'd stonewall me."

"Stonewalling is classified as psychological and emotional abuse." Erica's latest subjects at Open Universities were getting a workout.

"I understand why. It's soul-destroying."

"I bet you don't yell now," Erica said.

It took a moment before it dawned on Tilda. "I haven't yelled in years."

"What changed?" asked Carol.

"My marital status." Tilda grinned.

"What do you think was the most difficult thing to get over?" Erica asked.

"Interesting question." Tilda thought for a bit. "His entitlement. He held me accountable for every perceived failure, but acted how he wanted because he felt he had the right to do so."

Erica nodded while Carol made a sound that indicated she was listening.

"I wouldn't even be going over all of this now if it wasn't for this bloody invisibility," Tilda said. "I don't need to rehash this history. I just need to heal those wounds."

Both Carol and Erica lifted their glasses.

"To healing wounds," Erica said.

"Time wounds all heels," Carol added. "What's your plan?"

"Selma suggested meditation."

"I meditate every morning," Erica said.

"Me too," Carol added. "Well, for the past month, since reading Selma's book."

This surprised Tilda. "And how's that going for you both?"

"Early days," Carol said. "But I feel the benefits. My head is clearer. Obviously, you still can't see my head, but I can feel a difference. I'm not as reactive. It's as though I have just a little more space to reflect on how I'll respond."

"Perhaps that's the space where we rewire PEARL," Tilda said.

"I attended a crash course in Vipassana meditation," Erica said.

"Is that the silent retreat?" Carol asked.

"Yes, ten days, and not easy, but I highly recommend it to anyone who seriously wants to learn how to meditate," Erica said.

Tilda was curious. "You just meditate for ten days? Sounds relaxing."

Erica gave a snort laugh. "Yes, if you call digging into perdition relaxing."

"Would it help me face this rage?" Tilda asked.

"Honey, a ten-day silent meditation doesn't just help you face your rage. It helps you blaze right through it."

32

The quieter you become, the more you are able to hear.

—RUMI

Many studies have been conducted into meditation. It is now widely recognized to not only alleviate stress but also have cognitive, psychological, and neurobiological benefits. Any online search will lead to academic research on the benefits of meditation for a range of conditions, including depression and anxiety, cancer, high blood pressure, irritable bowel syndrome, ADHD, Covid-19, and more. The health benefits of a regular meditation practice are considerable. However, my interest is the brain, and how meditation fast-tracks changes to the circuitry there. There are structural differences in the brains of experienced meditators in regions important for learning and memory, changes in areas of the brain associated with compassion and self-awareness, and in the region responsible for stress responses—fight or flight. Importantly, meditation helps to quiet the brain's chatter and stop the mind from wandering.

Meditation teacher and spiritual leader Chögyam Trungpa said in his book *The Myth of Freedom and the Way of Meditation* that meditation is "the creation of a space in which we are able to expose and undo our neurotic games, our self-deceptions, our hidden fears and hopes."

The primary focus of my research has been in addressing these neurotic games, self-deceptions, fears, and hopes. The way to do that is to first meet and then observe PEARL. In my work, when a client becomes an objective observer of PEARL, they can then actively reprogram it. The most effective way to do this is to meditate. Meditation helps you observe, examine, deconstruct, and even replace thoughts, changing the program. This leads to a happier, healthier mind, resulting in a happier, healthier life.

Tilda closed Selma's book and stared across the garden—although "garden" might be an exaggeration. It was large enough for a tree at the rear and a few potted plants—a frangipani, a bottlebrush with bees already buzzing around its red blooms, some herbs and spinach—in addition to a firepit, a daybed and some lounge chairs. Pirate had a favored spot on the back fence. Buddy had a dog bed he slept on during the day.

Tilda's terrace and small yard caught the afternoon sun all year round, but in winter, Tilda would light the firepit. Today, she was curled up in front of it on her daybed, thinking about her conversation with Erica and Carol, yet another set of smart people who espoused the benefits of meditation. She needed to stop overthinking this. She decided to get her daily twenty minutes of meditation out of the way, and headed back into the house before she could talk herself out of it.

She changed into comfortable clothing, ensuring that she was neither too hot nor too cold. She'd eaten but wasn't full. She'd peed. She switched her phone onto silent and set the timer for twenty minutes. That should go quickly enough.

She cleared a space in the living room. She was sorting through a few final boxes and had found some childhood toys she wanted to show the girls when they came for dinner tonight. She moved the toys aside and sat cross-legged on the floor, on a large cushion.

Closing her eyes, she took a few deep breaths.

She remembered that her gas bill was due but pushed that thought aside.

And she had that pumpkin that needed to be used. Perhaps she'd make soup.

Stop.

She pushed that thought aside.

She'd forgotten to ask Maeve about booking her annual flu shot.

Stop.

She pushed this thought aside too.

She focused on the breath around her nostrils as she exhaled and then wondered what Melody Lee from high school was up to these days. Tilda hadn't thought about Melody for years—perhaps since high school. She returned her focus to her breath but realized her underwear had crept up her bum, so she yanked it out before checking her phone.

One minute and twenty-two seconds had passed.

"Faaaaark!"

This was going to be harder than she'd thought.

She tried again.

She closed her eyes and focused on her breath.

And off went her brain, like a Melbourne Cup favorite out of the gate, which just made Tilda think about how cruel horse racing was, which reminded her that she needed to pick up cat food.

Then she remembered the time she'd slipped arse over tit going into the supermarket. That had been so embarrassing that she'd wished she were invisible.

Invisible. What did that even mean? Would she still exist if she couldn't be seen?

A fart couldn't be seen, but it definitely existed.

Tilda opened her eyes again.

Two minutes twelve seconds.

"Get it together."

And again . . .

Chatterchatterchatterchatter, upward swing, downward dog, Eiffel Tower, spaghetti sauce, the smell of rain, need to sweep the yard, when was my last dental check, Hindenburg disaster, who the hell would go up in a blimp anyway, Patrick . . . Patrick . . .

Patrick.

Tilda conceded defeat. She was a failure at meditation. And, ironically, now needed to clear her head. She grabbed her phone, deleted the timer, and returned to the garden, throwing another log in her firepit. Meditation was stressful. Lying on her daybed in the afternoon sun was the solution. Her phone vibrated, and one glance told her that an incoming cloud was about to intrude on her moment in the sun. Her mother was FaceTiming.

"Hi, Mum." Tilda noticed that her mother's ear was pressed to the camera. It often happened, and Tilda would remind her that they were on camera and then they'd go through the dance of her mother working out what FaceTime was. But today, Tilda spoke to her mother's ear, noting with some irony that it was visible.

"Tilda. I've only got a moment, but I haven't heard from you for a while."

"Well, I know you're on the road, Mum."

"Joyce and I've been having a marvelous time. We visited a lovely little town last week with a fabulous museum dedicated to glassblowing. Can't remember the name . . ." Frances yelled through the phone. "Joyce? Joyce, what was the name of that glassblowing town?" Silence for a moment, and then Frances returned to Tilda. "She can't hear me. She's changing a tire."

Tilda's mother was the least likely candidate in the country to embrace the grey nomad life, but she had. While she had a townhouse about twenty minutes from Tilda's place, she'd also invested in a campervan with her neighbor, Joyce, and the two of them regularly hit the road. Travel had never seen a more mismatched pair. Joyce was a wisecracking eighty-year-old who'd once owned an inner-city pub. She was the perfect foil for Frances, who had an air of fragility about her and was more buttoned-up than an Edwardian boot.

"Where are you now?" Tilda asked.

"Ballarat. I'm not a fan."

Frances said exactly that about most places she visited but continued to travel. Tilda suspected that Joyce's company was the appeal, more than the lifestyle. Joyce was gutsy, and while Frances triggered a protective instinct in most people, Joyce was different—she pushed Frances out of her comfort zone.

"We're on our way back home for a few weeks, so I'll see you soon."

Tilda was tempted to tell her mother that she might not *see* her, but that conversation could wait until her mother was home. "Great. Keep me updated." They disconnected.

Tilda sat for a moment. Even the sun on her face couldn't chase away the anxiety that now clutched at her. Her mother's latest trip had given Tilda time and space to absorb the diagnosis in her own way. It wasn't that she didn't want to tell her mother; she did, and she would. But that conversation would also be laden with feelings of guilt—that she was hurting her mother, or worse, disappointing her. She'd always felt responsible for her mother's welfare. At least since her father died and her mother spent months in bed grieving him, emerging only to embark on a string of relationships. Some men tried to save Frances; some men tried to control her; one lovely man named Morty tried to love her and included Tilda in that quest. Tilda liked Morty a lot and felt safe when he was around. But for some reason, her mother didn't know how to function without the drama, so Morty was sent packing. After each participant in this destructive parade, Tilda would look after her mother.

"Don't you ever leave me, Tilly," Frances would say.

"I won't," Tilda would assure her, staring at the door.

Now more than ever, Tilda needed to face her invisibility, so she'd be prepared to handle Frances's reaction to her disease. She didn't need crippling guilt to be added to the fear and confusion she was already experiencing.

Tilda marched into the house, sat back down on the large cushion on the floor, placed the headphones over her ears, and pressed Play. The meditation she'd chosen was fifteen minutes long. What could go wrong?

Fifteen minutes later, after following the instructions to a tee, Tilda was curled up on the floor in the fetal position, sobbing.

33

In the process of letting go you will lose many things
from the past, but you will find yourself.
—DEEPAK CHOPRA

"You're throwing out an awful lot, Mum."

"You'd better believe it."

Tilda spotted the look Holly and Tabitha shared when they saw what she was doing to the house. Grave concern, while they maintained a cheery facade. It would be exactly the look they gave her before locking her in a nursing home.

"You should've seen this place a week ago," Tilda said.

Another glance.

"I'm not losing my mind, if that's what you're worried about," she snapped, stepping over a pile of old weights she'd listed on Marketplace. As much as she dreamed of having toned arms, those barbells were never going to be used. "Or maybe I *am* losing my mind," she continued. "I've discovered that my mind isn't fun. It's mean. And tiring. And might have something to do with this invisibility. So I'm rewiring it. It's called neuroplasticity."

The twins shared yet another worried look, but Tilda ignored them and ushered them into the living room, where she'd piled some boxes that she wanted them to go through.

"These are my childhood things. Toys, schoolbooks, love letters from teenage boyfriends . . . they're all going." Tilda tossed a poster of Boy George and some plastic cockatoo earrings in a bag.

"What's this?" Tabitha said.

Tilda glanced over her shoulder to see that Tabitha was holding up a bag of grey powder that Tilda had put on the coffee table. "My cat's ashes. He died when I was seventeen. I forgot I had them."

Tabitha dropped the bag back on the table, and Tilda noticed Pirate slink from the room.

Tilda ripped open a new box and scattered the contents. A couple of dolls, some stuffed animals, two clowns, and a koala that might've been taxidermy. "I had kept these for my kids, but then I had you two and life was so busy they just sat in storage. These were my toys when I was a little girl."

"Didn't your parents like you?" said Holly.

Tilda refused to bite. "I'd like you to both choose something, for any future grandchildren I might have."

"I'm not having kids," said Tab. "I'm going to be the cool aunt."

"Same," said Holly.

"Being an aunt will be difficult if neither of you has kids. Now choose something."

They both stalled.

"I know it's a tough decision," she said, feeling sentimental.

"It's not that," Holly said. "They're creepy."

"They're vintage," Tilda explained.

"They look like they'll come to life and stab us in our sleep." Holly had been blessed with Tilda's imagination.

"Rubbish. They've been in this house for years."

Holly wasn't sold. "Sealed in a box in the garage. But they're out now."

"Choose a bloody toy," Tilda snapped. "It's meaningful!"

Tabitha picked up a rabbit, and Holly grudgingly took a bear—the two smallest toys in the lineup. Tilda grabbed the remaining toys and tossed them back into the box. The girls were right. They were creepy, especially the clowns. The next day they were going to charity and could come to life at night in new homes.

"Mum, can we talk to you about our twenty-first?" Tabitha said.

Tilda noticed another shared "nursing home" glance but ignored it while she carried the boxes out of the room and dumped them in the hall. "Good idea. The date is creeping up on us." *Like those clowns tonight,* she thought.

"We've decided to have a costume party," Holly called through the wall to her.

Tilda dropped the final box and paused for a moment. Holly and Tabitha both hated costume parties. She gathered herself and returned to the living room, where the girls were still standing, clutching their heirloom toys.

"You can sit. I'm not going to bite, or melt."

"No, just disappear," Holly mumbled, but she sat down beside Tabitha on the sofa.

Tilda settled in an armchair and waited for the girls to speak—or lie to her, as she was expecting.

Tabitha started. Bad move. She was a dreadful liar. "Holly and I were talking about it and thought the cocktail party idea was lame and wanted something a bit more fun."

"But Holly, you've wanted a cocktail party since you were ten." And Tabitha had gone along with that.

"Exactly," Holly said, as if that was the point. "I was ten. I've changed since then. Tab has changed. We've all . . . um . . . changed."

Holly carried that off well, but she was an actress.

"A costume party?" Tilda said. "Any particular theme?"

"We figured Party Like a Pagan would be fun . . ." Tilda could see that Tabitha was really struggling.

"Jack said he'd bake some ghoulish desserts. The whole thing will be frightfully fun," Holly added, her conviction almost Emmy worthy.

Tilda nodded and pretended to think. "What will I go as? That's a tough one. I really should make an effort, right, seeing as the whole theme is because of me?"

Both girls did their best to look confused, making "Huh, what are you talking about?" noises, until Tilda's stare broke them both down.

"Okay, we don't want you to be embarrassed," Holly admitted.

This was like a punch to Tilda's gut. "I won't be embarrassed. I'll be proud. It's your twenty-first." As soon as she said it, she knew it was a lie. She *would* be embarrassed.

"You haven't even told Frances about your diagnosis yet," Tabitha said. (She and Holly both called Frances by her first name behind her back, and Grandma to her face.)

"She's away, and I've been busy."

"Doing what?"

"Dealing with it. Coping and doing this"—she motioned around the living room—"is my way of trying to find a way to bloody well beat it."

Holly's chin wobbled. "We know, Mum, and we're really proud of you."

"Oh, shit, come here." Tilda scooped Holly into her arms. "Let's just stick to your original party idea, okay?"

"Dad will be there . . ." Tabitha was clearly gauging how her mother would react to this.

Faux smile. "Obviously he'll be there." And then, "He doesn't know about me, does he?"

"Of course not," Tabitha said.

Another concerned glance between the twins.

"You really need to stop doing that. It's not like *you're* invisible or I don't have eyes!"

"Mum, he's bringing his new girlfriend," Holly said.

"Oh." Tilda's smile faded. "He's seeing someone?"

Silence filled the room while the weight of that sank in.

Finally, aware that the girls expected something, she said, "It must be serious if he's bringing her to your twenty-first." Tom's girlfriends were usually more invisible than she was.

"Seems to be," Holly said.

"And you like her?" Tilda asked.

"We've met her a few times. She's nice."

"Good . . . good . . . I'm good with that." Tilda shrugged. She wasn't good with that, and everyone in the room knew it. "It's not about him," she admitted. "It's about me, looking like this. He'll rock up happy with some embryo, and I've got no nose. Or neck."

Holly and Tabitha nodded. They understood. It's why they'd chosen the one type of party that they despised, so she could hide from their father.

"A costume party? I guess I could go as a skeleton, because I have no body." She guffawed loudly, before caving. She really had no choice. "It's not the party you wanted. Or planned."

"Same could be said for you, Mum," Tabitha said. "You didn't plan this, but you're doing such an amazing job fighting it that we want to support you."

"We need to do this," Holly said. "You're so determined to do everything alone, but please let us help."

Tilda suddenly realized that her decluttering efforts weren't just external but internal as well. She was facing her past. All these items she'd locked away, along with her childhood toys, were now free to leave her life. Including the belief that she had to do everything alone. The belief that no one was ever there to support her. Her friends were, and her gorgeous girls were. And a costume was the perfect solution to her predicament.

"Come here." She drew both her girls into a tight hug. "I love you two. Thank you. A costume party is a great way to support me. Let's make it the best costume party ever."

Tilda held back her tears of gratitude for her thoughtful girls. "I might go as a ghost, under a bedsheet. I'll get sheet-faced and party my arse off. Literally."

34

This Is A Sign had once produced a tea towel that said, "You can't accept new things while your hands are holding on to the past." Tilda felt like her hands, and certainly her house, had now been cleared of so much history. The final boxes of clutter were sitting in the hall, ready to drop off at the charity bins. The whole house felt different. And so did Tilda.

Now it was time to meditate. She was determined to meditate daily, despite the grief and anguish that had surfaced yesterday. It had caught her by surprise, as had the intensity of it. But she'd remembered what Selma had said about this not being a linear journey but rather a spiral of deeper truths. She felt like she'd faced and released a lot yesterday, and afterward she'd slept soundly.

Tilda opened her laptop and searched through the recommended section of Selma's website. She noticed that the Toolbox meditation app was listed there, but meditating to Patrick's app wouldn't be relaxing. It would be weird. Instead, she downloaded another app called Easy Peacey, which hopefully would live up to its name. Then she remembered the retreat Erica had told her about. Vip-passion-something.

A quick search and she easily found Vipassana. It wasn't as obscure as she thought it would be. There were centers all over the world that over a million people had attended. The meditation style was apparently the style practiced by Gautama Buddha over two millennia earlier. It was a process of sharpening one's awareness of the changing nature of mind and body, leading to a deeper understanding of one's own suffering and ego, and ultimately anicca, or impermanence. The founder was a Burmese-Indian businessman, S. N. Goenka; his life had been profoundly changed by the teachings, and so he wanted to offer people everywhere, regardless of faith or financial circumstances, the opportunity to learn how to meditate. There was much to admire about the organization. There was no charge for the retreat; it was funded by donations, and participants gave what they could afford at the end.

Tilda checked the schedule for the center closest to her and saw that there was a retreat coming up. Without overthinking it, she filled in the application, answering a lot of questions about the state of her mental health, and pressed Apply. She didn't have to go through with it if she got a place. She would still have time to consider it. But she was curious.

Then, feeling like she'd just done something incredibly positive, and *different,* she sat on the floor to meditate. She put on her headphones, pressed Play, and began.

She shuffled on the cushion.

Music.

A voice, female . . . not too jarring, but also not too airy-fairy. The woman sounded practical and calm, telling her to take a deep breath. And then another . . . and another . . .

Tilda followed the instructions. Simple, clear.

Her mind still wandered, but the instructions and music helped draw her attention back to the task. Thoughts came up, but she dismissed them. PEARL yelled at her, but Tilda ignored her. PEARL's voice fell silent. Tilda drifted, her thoughts appearing and then passing . . .

Twenty minutes later, Tilda opened her eyes and marveled at how relaxed she felt. Had it been a mystical experience? No. Had she achieved total peace? Not at all. Had her mind returned to daily concerns and worries? Yes. But by following the instructions on the app, Tilda had been able to maintain a state of calm that she'd previously thought impossible. And it was lovely.

Her phone rang beside her, and a shiver of delight ran through her as she answered. Timing!

"Patrick, hi."

"I'm sick of texting and wanted to hear your voice, Tilda."

His voice was deep, with a touch of gravel. She'd hated her name growing up, but when Patrick said it, it became a name deserving of songs.

"How have you been?" he asked.

"Fabulous. How about you?"

"I've been thinking about you a lot."

Was that a hot flash? Tilda stood, putting Patrick on speaker as she walked into the kitchen to make some iced tea.

"I've been thinking about you too, Patrick." Tilda decided to fess up. "I mentioned you to my friends recently, and my friend Leith told me about Toolbox and how well-known you are."

Patrick was clearly pleased. "You mentioned me to your friends?"

There was that heat again. "Briefly. In passing."

"But you mentioned me."

She could hear him smiling. "Yes, Patrick. I did." She liked that he was teasing her.

"What did your friends say?"

"Leith pieced everything together and then told me you're a bit of a big deal."

"Only in my mind, Tilda," he said with a laugh. "And perhaps my mum's."

Tilda put some ice cubes in her glass. "Your Instagram account would suggest otherwise."

"Oh, that's for Toolbox, not for me. People are interested in the company. It's not like I have my own groupies or anything. Well, there's one, but she smells like frankincense."

"I'm sure she's a VIP customer of mine."

Patrick laughed. "We could probably match up our email databases."

Tilda tossed the tea bag into the sink and headed back into the living room. "When you told me you were a musician, I pictured an early-nineties cover band."

"I wish! That's how we started out," Patrick said. "Stephen and I were planning to be the biggest thing since Oasis when I was diagnosed."

"So how did you go from rock star to meditation king?"

"You want the long or short version?"

Tilda settled into the sofa. She could listen to him speak all night. "Long version, Patrick."

He chuckled. "When I was two, my father took off, leaving my mother a brief apology note but no forwarding address. Child support was paid monthly, but that's the only contact we had for years. Turns out, he'd been diagnosed with retinitis pigmentosa, same as me. He couldn't deal with it and bailed. Didn't tell Mum why. Just left."

"Have you had any contact with him since?"

"Yes. Mum tracked him down to ask about his family history when I was diagnosed. He has since stepped up and is very regretful. I get it. He didn't have the tools to cope with the diagnosis and had a few extremely dark years. Anyway, he'd been on a journey of personal development and ended up at an ashram, where he learned how to meditate. In the long run, his absence was to my benefit."

"Your father taught you to meditate?" Tilda asked.

"He did. Instead of teaching me to ride a bike and hit a ball. He taught Stephen too. Steve wasn't coping with my diagnosis. He felt guilty, like I'd taken a bullet for him."

"It's like survivor's guilt," Tilda said. "Does he still struggle with it?"

"I think the guilt is still there, but it's also our normal now," Patrick said. "But he pushes me to be better, go further, take risks."

"How does meditation help you?"

"It helps me see clearly."

"What do you mean by that?"

"There are many ways to see, Tilda."

Tilda was silent for a moment.

And then he said, "Have I put you off?"

Tilda considered this. In the past these subjects hadn't been of interest to her, but lately, with what she'd learned and discovered, she was eager to discuss them. "No, you speak the same language as my best friend. I'm interested, but a few steps behind."

"I'll just wait while you catch up."

"That could take a while. Two left feet."

"And the one that's always in your mouth."

"And that one." Tilda laughed. "Did you find it difficult to meditate at first?"

"Of course. I still do. But the benefits outweigh the struggle. When I began meditating, I was suffering from Charles Bonnet syndrome, which can accompany vision loss. It's a condition where you hallucinate. I'd sometimes see images when I closed my eyes, but mostly for me it was shapes and flashes of light. When I meditated, and experienced the void, I also experienced complete darkness. It was incredibly . . . comforting. A relief. And really motivated me to continue meditating. Over the next year, the hallucinations just . . . stopped. It gave me hope that I have some control over the progression of this," Patrick said. "Have you ever tried meditation?"

Tilda burst out laughing. "Coincidentally, I'd just finished meditating when you called."

"Nothing is a coincidence."

"I'm a total newbie. I'm not in your league."

"There is no league," Patrick said.

Tilda fessed up. "I just applied for a Vipassana course."

"That's the Premier League."

"Have you done it?"

"Uh, yeah . . ." He sounded like he was skirting something. "If you intend to do Vipassana, it's best we discuss it after you finish. I don't want to color your experience."

Now she had to do the course. Damn it.

"Tell me more about yourself," Patrick said. "I want to know everything."

Tilda felt herself melting into a puddle. When had a man ever said that to her? Ever been so present and curious?

"I'm fifty-two, and I look it," she blurted. Totally out of left field.

"I'm forty-eight, and I have no idea how I look."

"I'm too old to have more kids."

"One of the reasons my marriage ended is that I don't want kids. I would never risk passing on this condition. So I'm glad you already have kids. That expectation isn't there."

Wow. He was really putting it out there.

"I've just . . ."

She wanted to tell him about her invisibility. She *needed* to tell him. He had been so open and honest with her.

"You've just . . . ?" He waited.

She couldn't. Not yet. Maybe never.

"I've just realized that I built a business with a friend on the back of countless quotes I actually don't understand."

That wasn't quite admitting her invisibility, but it was big for her.

"When Leith and I started this business, I never really thought it would end up being my career. I went along with it without questioning whether it all resonated with me."

Patrick made a sound, as if he really understood that. "Someone once told me that the aim is to make decisions in our youth that our older selves won't understand."

"I like that," Tilda said. "Apart from the bit where you insinuate that I'm older."

"It's my turn to have my foot in my mouth."

"Now we're matching," Tilda said.

"I like matching with you, Tilda."

Swoon. Seriously. Tilda was swept up in the romance of it all, savoring every second, and yet, with Patrick, she trusted she was going to land somewhere safe.

After a marriage built on eggshells, this was a wondrous place to be.

35

Same journey, different maps.
—TABITHA FINCH, on being a twin

Gurinder Majumdar's practice had a personal feel, rare now even in small towns. Tilda always felt comforted in the waiting room, knowing she was in good hands. There was only one other patient waiting, a man with a toddler strapped into his stroller. The father looked exhausted and didn't glance her way, but the little boy did. He stopped trying to break free from the stroller harness and just stared at Tilda. She waved, and he smiled back. She played peekaboo behind her hands, which sent him into a fit of giggles. His father absentmindedly ruffled his hair and mumbled, "What are you laughing at?"

Tilda realized that the father hadn't noticed she was there. While that was disconcerting, she took the opportunity to stick her tongue out at the toddler, who thought it was hilarious.

"Tilda?" Gurinder's voice interrupted their play.

Tilda gave the toddler a wave and made her way into Gurinder's office and took a seat. Gurinder closed her office door and then turned to Tilda, taking in her appearance. "I see your condition has progressed a little more quickly than we'd hoped it would." She brought up Tilda's file on her computer. "But your latest bloodwork all looks good. No underlying issues that we're dealing with here."

"That's a relief," Tilda said. "I'd hate to have a vitamin B deficiency on top of completely disappearing."

"I'm pleased to see your razor-sharp wit hasn't disappeared," Gurinder said, but it didn't sound like she meant it. In fact, given their encounter in the park a few weeks earlier, Tilda was surprised by how brusque Gurinder was. She'd always been professional first, but today was next-level.

"Get undressed and let's take a look."

Tilda drew the curtains and did as she was told. A few minutes later, Gurinder was speaking into a handheld recorder, taking notes.

"Patient's last visit a month ago. Clothes continue to mask the disorder, however now completely invisible: right ear, nose, neck, left breast, right hand, left foot. Currently disappearing: both arms, left leg . . ."

Tilda noted her own thoughts—something she was doing more and more of.

Of course my condition is progressing rapidly. I'll be like Carol and completely disappear soon.

Is Gurinder judging me? I think she is. She's always judged me because I'd take wine to the school fete. She never really liked me.

Typical me. All the decent parts of my body are disappearing, but my fat gut is still as clear as day.

I am so negative.

Take control of this.

How do I feel? Anxious and a bit embarrassed lying here naked.

Replace with a positive thought.

I think my vagina is nice.

Whaaaat?

Ten points for not farting.

Okay, my positive thoughts need work.

Tilda checked out and stared at the woman feeding the duck. That print was becoming something of a lifesaver. Despite her harsh judgment when she'd first seen it, she was now incredibly fond of how very ordinary it was. She wished she was ordinary, with a normal life, one in which nothing much happened, and she didn't feel special, or different. Instead, she was extraordinary, a statistical anomaly. She'd ended up as *that* woman—the one who didn't just feel invisible but also became invisible.

"That appears to be it. You can get dressed, Tilda."

Tilda looked down at her underwear and noticed that the elastic was loose on one leg. When she was younger, she'd always worn good underwear. You never really knew when you'd suddenly find yourself stripping down—whether you got lucky and found yourself with a guy, or unlucky and found yourself in an ambulance. Either way, it was always best to be prepared.

She hadn't been prepared for anything but a night of Netflix for ages. She made a note to buy some decent underwear.

She quickly redressed and took her seat again, turning her attention to Gurinder. Her doctor looked tired. Frazzled.

"How are you coping, Tilda?" Gurinder wasn't looking Tilda in the eye like she usually did. Today, she seemed preoccupied.

"I'm actually feeling good," Tilda admitted.

"You're still attending the support group meetings?"

"Now and then. I've made a couple of friends through it. Not sure how helpful the group is, though."

"Why do you say that?"

"It's an extremely negative environment," Tilda said.

"You can understand that," Gurinder said. "They're all suffering."

"That's the problem," Tilda said. "I've been seeing someone who has helped enormously. The sessions with her have . . . shaken things up."

Gurinder nodded her approval. "What's your therapist's name?" She had her pen poised.

"Selma Nester."

Gurinder dropped the pen and stared at Tilda in dismay. "I don't want you to get your hopes up."

Something inside Tilda snapped. "She doesn't give me hope. She gives me faith. Faith that I can beat this."

"Tilda, you'll be disappointed."

"I'm already disappointed. And frightened. And sick to my stomach at the very sight of myself. But Selma helps me." Tilda was worked up now. "I feel better about myself. I feel happier, and I'm not sure if I've ever, in my entire life, felt happy."

"She's a snake oil seller," Gurinder hissed.

How could Gurinder say that? The evidence was there to support Selma's work. Why were so many medical professionals adamantly against Selma when the data and research backed up her claims?

And then Tilda noticed Gurinder's finger.

Or, rather, the lack of it.

Gurinder had been trying to cover it up, writing notes on a pad rather than using the keyboard and computer. But now she knew that Tilda had seen it. She didn't say a word; she just slid her hand away, down beside her leg.

"Gurinder?" Tilda's voice was barely above a whisper.

Nothing.

"Selma has helped me," Tilda said. "Remember when you diagnosed me? You were the first one to tell me it's about how I see things."

"I can't discuss this, Tilda."

"Why not?"

"Because it's never just the finger."

The two women locked eyes for one very long moment. A wordless conversation conveying heartbreak and sisterhood and Gurinder's absolute refusal to speak of her finger.

"I'll see you in a month." Gurinder stood and opened the door for Tilda.

"What if I can't see *you*?"

36

A vibrant orange dress, gold bejeweled slippers, and her red hair knotted back—over-the-top, but a look Selma carried off with unapologetic flair. Normally the very sight of Selma in such an ensemble would have lifted Tilda's spirits, but today, her thoughts were with Gurinder.

"She wouldn't discuss it with me."

"You were there as her patient, Tilda."

Tilda felt ill. "Please tell me this bloody thing isn't contagious. That I didn't give it to her."

"It's not contagious."

"She thought I was insane, seeing you."

"Thoughts can change, you know that. But don't *tell* her how this helps, *show* her."

"How?" Tilda held her invisible arms out. "I'm still disappearing, despite all this work on myself."

Selma chuckled. "Tilda, it took you over fifty years to get to this point. Healing might take more than a few weeks."

Tilda knew Selma was right. "I wish there was something I could do for her. I don't know what to make of it."

"Why do you need to make anything of it? She obviously has invisibility."

Tilda shook her head, talking to herself as much as to Selma. "But she's so together and smart and gorgeous."

"So are you."

Tilda gave Selma a look as if she really didn't believe that. "I don't compare to Gurinder. She's a brilliant GP. I'm just . . ."

"Just what?"

Tilda shrugged. This was making her uncomfortable. In lieu of answering, she turned and stared out the office window. The blue sky went on forever. She spotted a plane in the distance. How she wished she were on it.

Selma wasn't going to let this go. "Many women would wonder why you have invisibility. You have a successful business."

Tilda turned her attention back to Selma. "I've been broke, so I'll never take the security my business provides me for granted. It's just . . ." She stalled.

"Go on."

"Something is missing."

"What's missing? What would make your life more complete?"

"My daughter Holly says she refuses to have a plan B, because when you have one, that's what you get. And she's right. I was so busy building plan B that I feel like I never tried my plan A."

There. She'd said it.

Selma watched her for a long moment. "You've never told me what your daughters do."

"Tabitha is studying to be a vet. She's a passionate advocate for animal rights."

Selma made a note of that and then asked, "And Holly?"

This was always awkward, not because Tilda wasn't immensely proud of Holly but because talking about her always led to the same reaction from whomever she was speaking to. "Holly is an actress."

Selma continued making notes. "My goddaughter is an actress. Did a commercial for some breakfast cereal recently. Difficult path to take, the arts. I guess you're supporting her?"

"No, Holly works."

"Good on her. Anything I might have seen?"

"She's in *Warlord*."

Selma's eyes widened slightly at this. *Warlord* was one of the hottest TV shows in years. It was a phenomenon. "Your daughter is Holly Finch Hyland?"

"Yes."

"Even I know that show," Selma said. "I watch it with one of my lovers."

It was the first piece of personal information Selma had revealed, and what a surprising snippet.

"Well, that explains a lot." Selma didn't explain what *that explained* but instead said, "What's it like to have a daughter who got her plan A?"

Interesting question. People usually asked about the fame, or side-stepped it, trying to act cool, which of course just made them look even more starstruck. Holly had always wanted to be an actress, and when she started going for auditions it happened quickly. She was still at school when she was cast in a daytime soap. After two years of her juggling that show and her final years of school, Hollywood called. Right after graduation, she'd headed to the US, where she was cast in a thriller called X about a killer virus spreading around the world. What might have been a fizzer of a film under normal circumstances had luck on its side, as it was released the same month that Covid-19 really hit and the world went into lockdown. People everywhere felt the filmmakers were psychic. Or had inside information. The three lead actors were propelled into a sort of celebrity status. By then, Holly had another indie film under her belt. She had returned to Australia and was living with Tilda during the first lockdown when that film was released on a streaming service to a positive reception. Holly was then offered the lead in a new series filming in Australia. Season one had been a mammoth success, and they were now filming season two.

Holly was doing what she loved, and that brought Tilda great happiness. And it was a thrill watching Holly on the show. But she'd be lying if she didn't admit it was also bittersweet. Holly believed in herself in a way Tilda couldn't even comprehend until recently. She wondered, if her own childhood had been different, would believing she deserved happiness have been easier?

"Plan A?" Tilda repeated. "She never let anything else get in the way or struggled for her art."

Selma let out a laugh. "Fascinating how many creative people still use those types of phrases—'struggle for your art,' 'don't sell out,' 'creativity requires suffering.' But then they're all up in arms that people don't respect the artist, or pay the artist, or that governments don't fund the artist. All artists should be compensated the way Holly has been, but the mentality of lacking starts within the artists themselves."

"I never considered that." Tilda thought about all the times she'd worked for exposure rather than money, because that's what artists did. Holly never had. At just seventeen, she had negotiated a higher-paying contract with the TV show, because that's what she believed she deserved. "Holly has always believed in her own worth and now wakes up each day and does what she loves."

"And you don't?"

"I enjoy what I do, but I've still never gone for my dream."

"And why do you think that is?"

"You tell me."

"These memories that keep coming up about your childhood . . . anything there?"

"Everything is there." Tilda paused, that rage rising again. "What I experienced as a child left me feeling unworthy. Happiness eludes me. And yet I know my parents loved me and tried their best. The shitty stuff isn't the whole story. I also experienced love and laughter and good times. I now understand that we get what we focus on, so I'll no longer focus on the pain, or the heartbreak, or the belief that I'm not deserving of happiness."

Selma broke into a very slow clap. "Tilda, you've found the answer."

Tilda laughed a little, relief and emotion washing over her.

"Are you worth plan A, Tilda?"

"That's the big question, isn't it?" Tilda opened her bag and took out the photo Grant had taken of her and handed it to Selma.

Selma read the words on the back out loud. "'You are a light in the world. Don't ever change.'"

"How do I become her again?" Tilda asked.

"Why would you want to? She's young and beautiful, yes, but without your wisdom." Selma waved the photo around. "You don't want to be this child again. You want to be the best version of you now. Empowered, passionate, and confident in her self-worth. You want *her* to march into your head and tell PEARL to sit down and shut up because she's in charge now."

A shiver of excitement ran through Tilda. "Damn right I do."

"Your next challenge is to celebrate yourself."

Tilda was up for anything now. "Okay, where do I start?"

"A new outfit, a great haircut, a fabulous pair of heels."

Whoa, that was an unexpected shift of gears. Tilda bristled. "Are you suggesting appearance matters?"

"It's not about appearance. It's unhealthy to focus solely on appearance. But, my dear girl, it's extremely healthy to do what it takes to feel good about yourself."

"Everything you just suggested is about how I look," Tilda pointed out. "Maybe I need a facelift."

"There's a difference between being in denial about your age and embracing it. Some women can carry off a facelift, but it's not for you." Selma sighed. "The symbolic annihilation of women by the media is so complete that the media's not even the enemy anymore. We are our own worst enemies. The most rebellious thing we can do now is to not care about what others think of us. Our own opinion of ourselves must be the one we value. To know who we are and express it—emotionally, intellectually, spiritually, *and* physically, if we so choose. And that doesn't have to be through clothes or makeup. One of my clients took up flamenco dancing, and the way she carried herself and viewed her body changed. Another client has tattoos. It's your body, your appearance."

"I do like wearing dresses in summer," Tilda admitted. "And I always feel good after a cut and color."

"So do I, dear." Selma patted her hair.

Tilda wondered how old Selma was. She was sensational, not just for her age but for any age. She had wrinkles, and creases, and lines. She was beautiful. Her eyes sparkled, and her face had life and laughter written all over it. Her zest for living was clearly apparent.

She was ageless.

"How else do you celebrate yourself?" Selma asked. "Think about it as if it's your birthday every day."

That didn't help. If it weren't for her very pushy girlfriends, Tilda probably wouldn't even acknowledge her birthday at all. Tom certainly never had, so she often felt it was easier to ignore it. "Honestly, Selma, my birthday is just another day."

"No day should ever be just another day," Selma said. "Let's start small. You're struggling with the word *celebrate*. How about *treat*? How do you treat yourself?"

Tilda thought for a moment. She loved traveling, but it had been ages since she'd done that. "I like a couple of cookies while I watch TV."

Selma looked at Tilda as if she were speaking Martian. "Anything else? A bunch of flowers? A massage? A movie?"

"Not really . . ."

"Weekends away? A bubble bath?"

Tilda had a light-bulb moment. "I renovated my house a few years ago. After Tom and I broke up."

"That's a wonderful celebration of self. Have you done anything else more recently?"

Tilda was really digging to come up with something. "I bought a new camera lens a month ago."

"It's time you treated yourself. Don't you agree?"

"Does this help fight invisibility?"

"If you don't see yourself, who else will?" Selma said. "It's an act of love to acknowledge yourself. You can't expect others to do that for you if you don't do it for yourself—don't you agree? If you don't think you're worth the time to have a massage or take that dance class, then you certainly don't think you're worthy of bigger things."

Tilda nodded. "I'd never thought about it before."

"Exactly. It's clear you've built a good life, Tilda, but where is the sparkle?"

Tilda was determined. Excited, even. "I think I'll go shopping. And to the gallery. And maybe I'll buy some Dom Pérignon . . . and bathe in it," she said with a laugh.

"You do that. Celebrate yourself. For everything you've achieved. For who you are," Selma urged. "You celebrate your friends, your daughters, your pets. Time to celebrate you!"

Tilda's eyes glistened. Selma was right.

"Say it," Selma pushed. "'I promise to celebrate myself.'"

"I do, I do . . . I promise to celebrate myself. I'm bloody well worth it." Tilda roared with laughter, just like in the photo she was holding, but better.

37

I am convinced that any photographic attempt to show the complete man is nonsense. We can only show, as best we can, what the outer man reveals. The inner man is seldom revealed to anyone, sometimes not even the man himself.

—ARNOLD NEWMAN, photographer

Tilda stood in front of one of Arnold Newman's self-portraits at the State Portrait Gallery and thought about how right he was. Only recently had she been revealed to herself.

She moved around the room from photograph to photograph, stopping, admiring, absorbing. Some were portraits of famous people, others not, but all the ones she loved captured the life and pain and joy and humanity in the subject. She knew that was a lot to ask of a single photograph, and yet that's what she loved about portrait photography. The possibility. It wasn't the camera's job to render all that, but hers. The photographer's.

It had been a long time since she'd been to the gallery. Not because she was too busy or because she didn't want to go, but because it anguished her. Reflected in these faces was her own failure. Her failure to follow through on a dream. Plan A. To be an artist. To have *her* work hanging here.

During her mad declutter, Tilda had pulled out her father's art binder. It had been tucked away for years, along with her dreams. Her father had given it to her about twelve months before he died.

"I once fancied myself a bit of an artist," he'd said at the time. "I used to store my sketches in here."

Tilda remembered this, as if it were yesterday. Her father's pride as he opened the binder and showed her some of his sketches. The smell of the leather. The mixed emotions she felt as he shared this with her, but mostly her desperation for the conversation to continue. It was so rare that he ever spent time with her, and certainly not precious moments like this.

"I've never seen you draw," Tilda said.

He stared off into space. "Yeah, well, drawing doesn't put food on the table."

And then a shadow crossed his face, and the moment was over.

They didn't discuss it again. The divide between the man who'd once held artistic aspirations and the father who was always angry and withdrawn was too much for Tilda to traverse at such a young age. But he did encourage her to take photos. She'd show him her latest and he'd give a nod and tell her, "Not bad. Keep at it, Tilly."

And then he'd died. Suddenly, and traumatically.

After his death, the binder became one of Tilda's most treasured belongings. It was the vessel to hold her favorite photos well into her twenties. She ran her hands across the familiar texture and held it up to her face, the scent of worn leather bringing back a wash of memories of her father and the years after he died. With care, she untied the strap. Inside were photos she'd taken in high school and university, right up to when she'd met Tom. Grief came over her and settled in her chest.

She'd been so talented. She was comfortable admitting that now. Photograph after exquisite photograph, portraits of people captured moments of intense emotion on their faces. Close-ups showed lines around eyes that spoke of both laughter and pain. There were photos of her mother; one documented that familiar look of fragility she wore so well. But the second one—of her mother watching Holly in a school play—caught Tilda unaware. Frances gazed at her granddaughter with fierce pride, as if willing her to succeed. Other photos included those of some old friends Tilda had lost touch with, her flatmate from university, Leith, a woman she'd met while traveling in China, a doctor she saw when she fell off a bike in Wales. A self-portrait just before she met Tom. Gorgeous, of course, although she'd hated it at the time.

Tucked away in the back sleeve were some of her father's sketches. One of her mother wrapped in a bedsheet, suggesting they'd once loved one another deeply. That image alone meant so much to Tilda. An indication that she had indeed been born from love. Another sketch was of a bird in the very tree that killed her father. He'd been so talented, but he was programmed to believe he couldn't make a living from his art, so he didn't try.

What was her excuse?

Often, it was the very same justification he'd given her. It didn't put food on the table. Although ironically, for her it had. But mostly, she just didn't feel she was good enough.

Tilda asked herself what she was worth as an artist, as she now stood in front of a large portrait of a young woman. The piece was called *Maiden* and had been taken by the subject's boyfriend, a photographer with considerable talent. The woman was laughing and beautiful, her face flawless in its youth. The photographer had captured his subject in the late-afternoon light, a glow of gold behind her. It was a stunning piece, and yet one more celebration of youth. Where was the crone? Where was that photo?

Tilda's phone buzzed in her pocket; she took it out to turn it onto silent, and saw that the text was from Patrick.

> Hi, Tilda. Was thinking about you. How's your day?

The ease of the man!

> I'm at the State Portrait Gallery standing in front of a sensational photo that I'm not sure if I love or hate.

> Can you talk?

Tilda looked around—she was the only person in that area of the gallery.

Yes.

His response was immediate—the phone rang.

"Describe it to me and let's work out how you feel," Patrick instructed before she could even greet him.

So she did. And while they quietly chatted, someone opened a glass door at the side of the gallery and a light wind whipped through, bringing with it some leaves and the promise of spring brushing around Tilda's legs. Tilda didn't recognize the winds of change. She was too busy talking to Patrick.

38

Constant use had not worn ragged the fabric of their friendship.

—DOROTHY PARKER, writer

A couple of hours later Tilda entered El Torero, a small Mexican restaurant not far from the office. Leith and Ali were seated in a corner booth and both visibly did a double take when they saw her. After the session with Selma, and the gallery visit, Tilda had stopped for some retail therapy. She was now wearing black jeans with new boots and a new burnt orange top. Selma was right. It felt good to treat herself.

"Do you have bad news?" Leith asked as Tilda took her seat.

"Why would you think that?"

"You call and say you want to meet us here for dinner, then you walk in looking . . . fabulous. I don't think you're dying, but something's off. I mean, apart from your not having a nose. Or neck." Leith stared at her, as if trying to put her finger on something.

Tilda ignored her and scanned the restaurant. She liked the rustic, vibrant feel—colorful murals on the walls, distressed wood tables, and a tiled bar along one side.

"So, is there a reason for this dinner?" Ali asked. "Apart from to admire that new top on you."

"Selma says I need to celebrate myself more. Add sparkle to my life. You two are my sparkle."

"Aw, you're my sparkle too," Ali said. "Both of you."

"Also, something happened that reminded me that life is so bloody short, so we need to drink margaritas more often," Tilda said. "I went to see Gurinder, and her finger was missing."

"Jesus." Leith pulled back. "It's not contagious, is it?"

"No. I've already asked that."

"How awful," Leith said.

"Poor Gurinder. At least she has you," Ali said.

"She won't discuss it with me." Tilda shrugged. "Selma says I need to show her that this treatment works, not tell her."

"Good point. Be a beacon to others." Leith's eyes narrowed. "You certainly seem different."

"I'm wearing a new top and boots." Tilda waved at the waiter for a margarita.

"No . . ." Leith was homing in. "It's something else."

"Okay. Don't get too excited, but I've been meditating."

Leith laughed so hard people turned to look at them. "And?"

"And . . ." Tilda took the leap. "And you might be right. I feel a lot better."

Leith pointed at the ceiling. "Was that a flying pig?"

"Definitely a flying pig," Ali said, chuckling.

Tilda rolled her eyes. "Settle down."

Leith wrapped her arms around Tilda. "I'm proud of you."

"There's more." Tilda braced herself. "I've been offered a place in a Vipassana course."

"Who are you, and what have you done with my best friend?" Leith kidded.

"But I can't really disappear for ten days." Tilda realized what she'd said, and all three of them cracked up.

"I'll fire you if you don't," Leith said.

"And you know Jack loves pet-sitting," Ali added.

Tilda grabbed her phone and forwarded Ali an email. "See if he's okay with such short notice. I haven't accepted it yet, but if I do, he can stay at mine." She slipped her phone back in her bag. "Tell him I've just decluttered my house."

Ali shrugged. "I never thought it was cluttered."

"Turns out I was good at storing shit," Tilda said with a laugh.

Their margaritas arrived and they toasted to *decluttering*. Then, over a feast of fajitas, enchiladas, and their favorite fish tacos, the three women dug into the recent weeks of their lives.

Ali told the others that Jack had been on a date. "He took her some of his salted caramel fudge," she said. "Holly assured him that was how to win someone over."

Tilda agreed. "His fudge *is* amazing."

"What's happening with Lulu?" Ali asked Leith.

"She's taking some time off from uni to work out what she wants to do. She's been able to stop herself spiraling this time, so all good for now."

Tilda took Leith's hand and gave it a squeeze. No words were needed, their relief obvious.

"Have you heard from Patrick?" Leith asked.

"Regularly," Tilda said. "There's never any pressure, or expectation. It's easy . . ."

"But?"

"No but."

"Your face says there's a *but*."

Ali nodded. "Definitely a but."

"That's just my face. I have a but-face." Tilda shrugged. "Okay, there's a but . . . The timing is all wrong."

"No such thing as bad timing," Leith said. "Everything happens when it's meant to."

"I'm disappearing."

"He's the perfect boyfriend if you do," Ali said wryly.

"I took your advice about trying something different. And while I feel different, nothing has changed physically."

Ali nodded toward a table of four men near the door. "All four of those blokes turned and watched you as you walked in. I think they saw your visible bits."

Tilda had noticed that. How many moons had it been since that had happened?

"Just keep doing what you're doing," Leith encouraged. "It often takes some time for change to catch up with the desire for it."

Tilda held up her margarita. "Cheers to that."

Leith clinked her own glass with Tilda's. "So, I did some digging on Patrick."

"Leith!" Tilda was mortified. And admittedly curious. Both emotions showed on her face.

Leith took a tortilla chip from the basket and crunched on it. "Not in a stalker way. We have mutual friends, so I asked around. Salt of the earth, apparently."

So far, Tilda had found that to be true.

"He's exactly what Selma is talking about. Sparkle. Celebrate yourself by giving someone great a chance. Allow someone into your life who will celebrate you! Seriously, Tilly, you deserve a good man."

"Who says he's interested?"

Ali shook her head in disbelief. "He's overseas and he's in touch. He's interested."

"When Patrick gets home, have some fun with him." Leith lowered her voice. "It's time you exorcised you-know-who from your vagina. Voldecock."

Two margaritas was clearly Leith's limit.

"You need to break that drought," she hissed across the table.

It *had* been a while. Tilda just hadn't met anyone since her divorce. Until she'd met Patrick and a light came back on. She didn't yet know what Patrick was to her, but she knew that his texts made her day. She knew that her mind often wandered to thoughts of the stubble on his chin, his long fingers, the curve of his wetsuit over his chest. That thought alone was enough to flood her with a heat she hadn't experienced for a very long time.

Apart from Tilda's brief liaison from the dating app, she had been with only one other man since her divorce. The night of her divorce, and two months after the disastrous fling with Rob, Tilda had an even worse experience.

She shagged Tom.

The very man she'd divorced just hours earlier.

39

Tilda stared at Tom's house. She'd never been there before, but she figured it was divorce day, so why not jump in an Uber and check out what he'd done with the settlement she'd paid him? She was drunk and everything looked a little hazy, but the inner west terrace was a surprise. It looked so . . . homey.

A porch light was on. A tree at the front had recently been clipped back, the cut branches placed in a neat pile next to it. Suddenly, the front door opened. Tilda jumped back behind a large grevillea, peeking through a branch to see Tom leaving the house with a tall blond woman—early thirties, attractive, with legs that went on forever. She was carrying an overnight bag. Tom was wearing linen pants and no shirt, like the middle-aged wanker he was.

Shit. Now Tilda was stalking her ex-husband on the day of their divorce. Just when she thought she'd hit rock bottom, she had discovered a new low.

Tom and Long Legs chatted for a moment, and whatever he said made the woman laugh. Strange, because Tilda hadn't found him funny in years. Long Legs touched something on Tom's bare arm and Tilda noticed a bandage across his shoulder. Had he hurt himself having wild sex with her? Then she kissed him on the cheek and with a wave, hair swinging around her shoulders, she opened the gate and walked toward Tilda. Tilda edged further into the bush, relieved when the woman crossed the road to a small car, got in, and, a long minute later, drove off.

Tom watched until the car turned the corner. He opened the letterbox and took out an envelope. Tilda waited for him to go back inside, but he noticed an attractive woman walking a dog.

"Hi, Natalya."

Of course he knew her.

"G'day, Riesling," Tom added.

Tilda had to hold back from saying "For fuck's sake" out loud. The dog looked more like a Guinness.

"Hey, Tom. Nice evening."

"Great evening," he said.

Tilda felt hot lava rising. His marriage was officially over today, but fortunately he was surrounded by beautiful young women, so yes, lovely evening.

And then, to Tilda's utter horror, Natalya's labradoodlepoodlepanda or whatever it was lunged toward the grevillea and began to bark. Tilda pushed herself further into the branches, trying to find a secret door that would allow her to disappear. Where were the Saucepan Man and the crew when you needed them? But it clearly wasn't that type of tree, because there was nowhere else to go as Tom, being the hero he was, told Natalya to step back and moved toward the tree. Interesting—he'd never been that much of a hero when he and Tilda were married, but three hours being divorced obviously suited him, and he came in guns blazing.

"Tilda?"

Tilda stumbled out of the bush, ripping her shirt as she did.

"Tom! Hello . . . hi, good to see you. I was just . . ."

"You're bleeding."

Tilda looked down and noticed the tear in her sleeve, and blood seeping through.

"I know," she said cheerily. "And I was in the neighborhood—"

"In my tree," Tom said with a grin. He wasn't angry. He was amused.

"Yes. And thought I'd stop by for a bandage."

Tom and Tilda stared at each other.

"See you later, Tom." Natalya pulled Riesling along the footpath. Away from the weird old people.

Tom's eyes didn't leave Tilda. "Come inside, and I'll get you a Band-Aid."

Tilda did as she was told—a habit that she'd got into with him the day they'd met.

Ten minutes later, Tilda was having frenzied sex with Tom while the ink on their divorce papers dried. Afterward, she regretted everything. They barely knew what to say to each other. She looked around at the place he now called home and took it all in: the open-plan space, sleek appliances in the kitchen, dark leather sofa, glass coffee table. None of it appealed to her at all. Had he always wanted a home like this? Her gaze rested on him, and she noticed the patch on his arm was hanging loose.

"You got a tattoo?"

He shifted uncomfortably but didn't respond.

"Marking the day?"

"I used a mobile tattoo service. She came by tonight."

Long Legs.

Tilda noted that the tattoo was a phoenix. "Rising from the ashes."

Tom pressed the dressing back over his arm. Tilda suddenly understood why she was there—that, stupidly, she still wanted him to say he'd made a mistake. That he did indeed choose her. Not because she wanted him back, but because it would vindicate her, prove that she hadn't wasted decades.

Silence.

"I should go," Tilda said.

Tom clearly had no desire to stop her. "I'll see you out."

Tilda dressed, and a few minutes later they gave each other an awkward hug.

They hadn't spoken since.

40

In each significant relationship, we just want to be seen.
—QUEENIE ASHCROFT

Tilda walked home from dinner feeling on top of the world. Her thoughts drifted to Patrick—he'd be home in less than two weeks. This both excited and terrified her. She'd had time to not only adjust to her invisibility but also address some deep-seated issues. But now she realized she was only beginning to scratch the surface. Would she be able to balance her own healing journey with a relationship? She knew that was a leap—there'd been no relationship talk. But she was also old enough to know that there was a connection between them that they were bound to explore.

She listened now as PEARL rattled off a list of reasons why a relationship with Patrick wouldn't work, but even PEARL was silenced as Tilda approached her house and noticed someone standing at her front door.

Damn it.

"Mum, what a surprise." Tilda paused at the front fence, secure under the cover of darkness.

Frances Finch waved her phone at Tilda. "I was just about to call you, wondering where you were."

"Out for dinner. Mexican."

"On a weeknight. Lovely. A date?"

"With Leith and Ali."

Frances's smile faded. She'd never warmed to Tilda's friends. "Lovely."

Frances said "lovely" a lot and rarely meant it. Tilda watched her mother, aware that this calm moment was about to end at any second. Holly probably got her melodramatic streak from her grandmother. In fact, they were very close. Holly saw Frances as passionate and quirky. Tilda found her mother manipulative, using guilt and faking fragility to get her way. It was always about Frances. Now she stood on Tilda's doorstep, slender in a navy skirt and a silver turtleneck under a red wool coat, her long grey hair messily pulled up on top of her head and wrapped with a red scarf. A slash of lipstick in the same color completed the look. She was gorgeous, with an etherealness that she used to her advantage.

All through her childhood and beyond, Tilda had taken care of her mother, making sure she didn't upset her. It's why she was in turmoil right now, about to turn her mother's world upside down.

"We should go inside," Frances said. "It's not safe, two women alone on the street at night."

Tilda sometimes thought her mother needed a porch and a mint julep.

"We've got more of a chance of winning Lotto than of being attacked here, Mum."

"Well, I'm growing icicles," Frances sniffed.

It was crunch time. Tilda could no longer put this off. She took a deep breath and stepped into the light.

"Now, I know you're going to be upset . . . ," she began.

"Why? Is your house a mess?" Frances leaned forward and kissed Tilda's cheek.

Tilda waited for her mother's reaction, but there was none.

"I'm freezing here, Tilda. And I've seen your home in disarray before."

Tilda fumbled for her keys, aware that her mother was watching her. But there was still no response. Zero. Had the girls already told Frances and prepared her?

Tilda's invisible hand turned the lock. Buddy was waiting by the door, and she grabbed him by the collar to keep him from jumping up on her mother.

"Good boy. On your bed."

Buddy bolted back down the hall, and Tilda hung her coat on the hook by the door.

"You look very nice," Frances said. "Burnt orange is your color. And I like your hair that length."

Tilda stood in front of her mother, waiting for her to mention Tilda's missing parts. Her mother gazed at her, and then said, "I haven't seen you look this good in years. Are you sure you weren't on a date?"

Tilda was rattled. "Put the kettle on, Mum, while I go to the loo." Tilda bolted for the stairs and the mirror in her en suite, where she expected to see that she was visible again. She wasn't. Nothing had changed.

She furiously messaged the girls. Have either of you told Frances about my invisibility?????

Tabitha answered first. God no. Not me.

Tilda wasn't surprised. Tab had kept her grandmother at arm's length ever since Frances had suggested that the "lesbian thing" would pass when Tabitha met a nice boy. "Because a penis fixes everything," Tab had snarled.

Then Holly saw the message. No, why?

Are you sure you didn't mention something, Holly?

I promise. Not a word. What's going on? Does Frances know?

Tilda started to type a message but then decided not to tell them about Frances's lack of reaction to her invisibility. She needed to wrap her head around it herself first. Besides, she might go downstairs to find Frances hyperventilating in horror.

All good. Will chat later.

Tilda stared at her reflection. The mirror never lies. Or does it?

PEARL was screaming at her, clearly triggered by her mother's visit, but at least Tilda was aware of the program now, observing its operation, not at the mercy of it.

In fact, all the criticisms running through her head right now were in her mother's voice.

I wish you weren't alone. I had no choice. Your father died. You had a choice with Tom.

Oh dear, those jeans look a little snug.

Why do you do this to me?

Look at what you've done to me!

Don't mind me, Tilda. You go and do what you need to do. I'll manage alone.

"I have a right to my own life, my own experiences," Tilda hissed at the looking glass. "Enough. And I am enough."

She removed her glove and scarf and pulled her hair back into an elastic so her mother could have full view of her invisible hand, neck, and ear. Then she returned downstairs to the kitchen.

"I've made you a cuppa," Frances said, handing Tilda a mug that said *Thanks for all the orgasms* on it. A funny present for Tom, who'd loved it so much that he left it behind when he moved out. Also, an indication that perhaps her mother wasn't very observant today. Tilda took the mug.

"Careful, it's hot." Frances nodded at the cup and then turned and walked into the living room.

God help me, Tilda thought. How long was it going to take Frances to address the elephant in the room? And Tilda's invisible trunk? She glanced at the time; it was already nine thirty.

Tilda followed her mother into the living room and then busied herself lighting the fireplace. "Is something wrong, Mum? It's awfully late to just drop by."

Frances sat in an armchair. "Joyce and I got back yesterday, and then I met a date tonight not far from here, so thought I'd kill two birds with one stone."

Tilda was so flattered to be one of those birds.

"Your place looks lovely," Frances said, looking around.

Tilda almost fell off the sofa.

Her mother was not one for compliments. Criticism was more her style, though she always *meant* well. At least that's what Frances would say if Tilda ever brought up how critical she was: "I mean well, Tilda. I just want the best for you."

But tonight, there was something else going on. "Tell me about your date, Mum."

Frances's face lit up. "Yes, well that's another reason I dropped by. I've met someone . . . special."

Frances's bedroom had had a revolving door for years, but more recently being on the road with Joyce had been her priority over searching for that elusive "one." And it was "one" she desired, despite a history with many.

"I've known him for some time, but lately it's become more serious. I don't want you to be upset by this . . ."

Frances was seventy-eight years old but looked two decades younger, particularly in that moment, and it dawned on Tilda how deeply her mother must feel for this man.

"Why would I be upset?"

"Well, I know how you felt about your father. You were so close to him."

Tilda was floored. "Was I? Or was that something we told ourselves afterward, to soften the trauma of it all?"

Frances looked mortified. "I don't know. Maybe."

"I'm a grown woman. Dad died nearly forty years ago. You've had multiple relationships since."

"I didn't love any of those men."

Tilda didn't want to derail this moment. "Then this is excellent news. Tell me about your friend. What's his name?"

There was that light in Frances's face again. "Neville. He's a retired accountant. Sixty-seven, so a few years younger than me."

Sixty-seven? The same age as some of the men who'd contacted Tilda during her short stint on the dating app. She was now fishing from the same dating pool as her mother.

"Most men who ask me out need walkers," Frances said.

Definitely the same dating pool, but her mother was out there more than she was.

"Joyce and I were parked at a lovely spot in Mudgee, and Nev was in the camper next to us. Very well fitted out. He did it himself. He's good with his hands. Turns out we live quite close to each other, so we got to talking . . . and one thing led to another. I came back home in his van this trip."

This was all news to Tilda. "How did Joyce feel about that?"

"She's happy for me. She says that shop has shut for her, but if it's love, I should grab the opportunity. At my age, I don't have time to muck around." Frances reached into her bag and pulled out a book. "Joyce introduced me to this. She's different from anyone I've ever known before. We have long talks while we drive. She gets me thinking."

Tilda took the book: *Time to Get Real and Heal.* Her mother was into self-development now?

"Then, when I met Nev, he spoke the same language. And it's not gobbledygook, I can assure you."

"No, I believe you." Tilda handed the book back to her mother. "Mum, I'm really happy for you." She meant it. Sure, she was surprised; she'd never seen this side of her mother, but it was rather sweet.

Frances fell silent, her gaze resting on the fireplace. Something was coming, Tilda could sense it. This was where she was going to bring up Tilda's disease.

Tilda braced herself.

"Your father was . . . difficult. He liked a drink and could be moody."

That was not where Tilda had expected this conversation to go.

"You might not remember this, Tilda, but he sometimes got a bit . . . fisty."

Did Frances think Tilda had forgotten those nights? They were seared into her memory. It was deep, lifelong trauma that she was only now dealing with.

Frances turned to her. "I think I pretended to mourn him—always choosing inappropriate men and then saying that they couldn't live up to him. That was easier than being open to love and risking the same thing happening to me again."

"I've always suspected that was the case, Mum."

A flicker of relief crossed Frances's face. "He loved you, though. And I know you missed him."

"I did, but things are never that black and white. I also wished him dead on more than one occasion, so when he died my grief was mixed with a lot of guilt." Tilda held her mug up. "We should have put a shot of something stronger in these."

Frances chuckled, and then her eyes widened. "Oh goodness, I've just realized what that mug says."

Nothing wrong with her eyes.

Frances collected both mugs and stood. "I'm very glad we've had this chat. And I look forward to introducing Neville to you."

Tilda was disappointed. They were just digging into things that needed to be said. She followed Frances into the kitchen, wanting to know more. To ask more questions. She watched as her mother put her mug in the sink and then tossed Tilda's mug into the recycling bin.

"You don't need that mug putting a damper on a morning coffee with a new man," she explained.

Tilda didn't argue. She'd been meaning to toss it anyway.

Frances picked her glasses off the counter. "And I hope that happens for you soon. You deserve it, Tilly. We can't let the past define our future."

"I agree, Mum. Although I'd like to discuss the past with you. I feel like we've touched on it tonight, but there's so much more to say."

Frances held her hand up to stop her daughter. "Tilda, we've lived in the past for far too long. I don't want us to waste another precious minute there."

Mother and daughter stood facing each other for a moment, and that one look said everything that needed to be said. About all those years of trauma. Frances's guilt about what Tilda had experienced. Tilda's deep wounds from childhood.

Tilda knew her mother was right. She had work to do alone, as did Frances. There was no need to dig up the past together. At least not now. As Thoreau said, "Never look back unless you are planning to go that way."

Frances's gaze drifted to Tilda's ears. A moment passed, and then she touched the earring on Tilda's visible ear.

"Did you lose an earring? Aren't these the ones the girls got you for your fiftieth?"

Tilda nodded. She could barely breathe. She'd put only one earring on, figuring there was no point adorning an ear she couldn't see. "The other one is upstairs."

There was no denying it now. Her mother wasn't good at hiding things. She had no idea about Tilda's illness.

"They're lovely. They really suit you. But it's a bit weird to be wearing just one." She headed for the door. "I'll bring Nev to the twins' twenty-first shindig."

The shock was reverberating through Tilda's body, and her voice now sounded forced. "I look forward to meeting him, Mum."

A kiss on the cheek, and her mother was out the door, headed to her car.

Tilda watched her and waited until she was safely inside, ignition on, then she closed the front door and slumped against it.

There was no doubt . . . her mother could see her.

41

Tilda sat in front of the fire for a long time, watching the flames die down to glowing embers. It had been a big week.

There is a Taoist story that tells of an incident witnessed by Confucius. Confucius saw an old man jump into a raging river and be swept over a waterfall. He was sure the old man would have drowned so went in search of his body. Miraculously, he found the old man alive and unharmed. When Confucius asked how he'd survived, the old man said, "I adapted myself to the water; I didn't fight it. Plunging into the swirl, I moved with the swirl and came out with the swirl. This is how I survived the river."

At one of their first sessions, Selma asked Tilda if she was in a state of flow or a state of resistance. It had taken Tilda all this time to understand what Selma meant, but now she understood how tightly she held on to things. To her thoughts. To her feelings. To her *self.* She understood now how letting go of these things could move her forward in life.

For years Tilda had fought the river. In recent months, she'd felt like she was adapting to it. At least trying to. Now she wanted to plunge into the swirl. The more she meditated, the more this seemed possible.

The more everything seemed possible.

Including the absolutely mind-boggling fact that her mother could see her. Tilda had always felt that her mother had never seen her, especially in the years following her father's death, so it was puzzling—even miraculous—that she could see her now. While Tilda didn't understand how this could be, she knew that it was. The limits to what she imagined to be true had shifted.

Her phone buzzed and she opened a text from Patrick, her heart expanding as she did.

> How's the meditation practice? Found enlightenment yet?
> If so, can you let me know where to look?

Tilda sent a laughing emoji and then added:

> Your guess is as good as mine. However, I was on a waiting list for a Vipassana course starting tomorrow . . . and have just been offered a last-minute place.

> Wow . . . will you take it?

> Yes.

Decision made.

> Good on you! I'll be home by the time you're done, so I'll look forward to hearing about it. Over dinner?

> I'd love to.

Tilda headed into her home office and texted the twins, and then Leith and Ali. She messaged Maeve and let her know that Ali would check in on her. Then she switched on her computer and searched for the email she'd received from the meditation retreat. Ignoring all of PEARL's objections, Tilda filled in the form, pressed Send, and plunged into the river.

42

The only conversion involved in Vipassana is from misery to happiness, from bondage to liberation.
—**S. N. GOENKA**, meditation teacher

"You'll get your phone back in ten days."

Tilda waited in line as the woman in front of her handed over her phone. She'd read the phone-free policy, but the reality seemed rather harsh. She scanned the room; it was more an office than a hotel reception area. A woman signed people in at a welcome table and then took each phone, put it in a ziplock bag with the attendee's name on it, and placed it in a plastic tub filled with dozens of others. Tilda was next in line to forgo her connection to the world. She needed to regroup. She turned on her heel and made for the exit, mumbling something about having left her phone in her car. As the screen door swung shut behind her, she sprinted down a path and took refuge behind a large tree. She could still see the office but was out of earshot. She dug her phone out of her bag and dialed Selma. It was an emergency-only number, but Selma had assured her that she didn't mind her using it. The phone rang and rang, but then, just as Tilda was about to hang up, Selma answered, sounding out of breath.

"Sorry to bother you, Selma. It's Tilda—"

More panting. "Yes, dear. Everything all right?"

"I'm not sure if this counts as an emergency . . ." Tilda could hear a muffled voice in the background and what sounded like a slap. "Is this a bad time to call?" she asked.

"Not at all. I just finished with my personal trainer. Zumba! Nearly killed me."

"Oh . . . I can call back."

"No!" Selma snapped. "I'm about to have a massage. Now's good."

Tilda would have to be quick. She was in a spin. "I signed on for a Vipassana retreat."

"Good on you," Selma said encouragingly. "When is it?"

"I'm here now." Tilda took in the bushland surrounding her and the low-set buildings scattered around the property. "But I think the timing is wrong."

"No such thing," Selma said. "Everything happens when it happens."

"I feel I'd benefit more from it at a later date."

"Tilda, remember how we've discussed your perfectionism?"

They had never discussed Tilda's perfectionism, but Selma forged on before Tilda could interject.

"Your journey doesn't have to be perfect. The timing doesn't have to be perfect. The point is to learn and enjoy and have fun along the way."

A woman in a Peruvian poncho went in the main door, and Tilda suddenly felt like she'd already failed the dress code, in her yoga sweats and oversize coat. "I understand all that, Selma, but I feel I should head home and sort this other thing out. You see—"

"Head inward, and sort it there. I'll see you in ten days."

"But something big happened," Tilda said. "My mother came by last night."

They had discussed her struggle to tell her mother that she was disappearing.

"She was bound to find out, Tilda. She must've been very shocked."

"No, she wasn't. She could see me, Selma."

A pause. "What do you mean?"

"I wasn't invisible to her."

Selma was silent as Tilda continued.

"I kept waiting for her to react, but she just looked right at me and told me I looked better than I had in ages."

Tilda waited. Another long pause confirmed that this was indeed big news.

"Are you certain no one told her?"

"No. Besides, she's transparent. Not literally, like me, but her emotions are written all over her face."

"Utterly fascinating."

"Have you heard of this before?" Tilda asked.

"There are hundreds of examples of women becoming visible again, but they're visible to everyone. This is quite different," Selma said. "There was one case in Scotland in the seventies where a woman had severe invisibility. Her husband and children couldn't see her. She also had a lover, though, and she was completely visible to him."

"Did she run off with the lover?"

"No. She stayed with the husband and disappeared altogether."

"Oh my god." Tilda wondered what choice she would've made, but then realized she'd already made a similar one, just without the lover.

"The other case I read about was even more peculiar. About ten years ago, a woman in Wisconsin was diagnosed with invisibility. She'd also been suffering from dissociative identity disorder for several years and had three primary personalities. Anyway, as her invisibility progressed, two of these personalities were affected, but the third wasn't. Whenever that personality came through, the woman was visible to everyone."

"How is that even possible?" Tilda asked.

"No one knows," Selma said. "We can only speculate. There are so many questions we still have to answer. It's why this field is so exciting. It's in those unknowns that possibility exists."

Tilda watched as a lizard the size of her foot scurried out of the scrub and up the path. Her attention turned to the view beyond the office. She was here. It might be exactly what she was looking for.

"I'll see you in ten days, Selma."

Selma sounded delighted. "And who knows what else."

43

Meditate. Do not delay, lest you later regret it.
—GAUTAMA BUDDHA, the Sallekha Sutta

Tilda thought she'd signed up for a peaceful retreat in the mountains. While she hadn't expected yoga or a spa package, she certainly thought they'd be easing into their meditations with some short sessions. Instead, right from the start, she found herself on a cushion for hours on end. The first few days had been laboriously long. And difficult.

Under any other circumstance, such as a girls' weekend with wine, the location would have been sensational. The retreat was set on forty acres of native bushland, with spectacular views across the valley. At the center of the property was a large meditation hall, where participants spent hours at a time, women on one side, men on the other. Scattered around the site were several smaller meditation pagodas, the dining room, and the living quarters for the meditators, ranging from single rooms to dormitories. Tilda was in a bare room with two metal single beds, sharing the space with a rather stern-looking roommate, who had placed a finger to her lips and lowered her eyes when Tilda first arrived and introduced herself. Tilda had been told: zip it! This was a silent retreat. No speaking. No eye contact. Follow the rules.

There were a lot of rules. Tilda had been sent a list of them via email, and had to sign a declaration stating that she'd abide by them. For the next ten days she would abstain from killing any being, stealing, all sexual activity, telling lies, and all intoxicants. After just a few hours here, she'd felt like breaking all the rules.

She had already broken one. She'd lied to the woman at check-in, telling her that she didn't have a mobile phone with her when in fact she'd finished the conversation with Selma and then hidden her phone in her bag, switched off to save the battery. Rules be damned. She was a mother and needed the phone in case of an emergency. Or to call Leith for help when she inevitably lost her mind in this place. It was, mentally, heavy going.

While Tilda quickly got the hang of the routine, she resisted every minute of it. A woman walked around the sleeping quarters at four a.m., clanging a bell for the first meditation. Tilda lay in bed, visualizing what she'd like to do with that woman and her bell, until her roommate had dressed and left.

While the worst of winter had passed on the coast, it was still bitterly cold in the mountains. No heater in sight. Tilda dragged herself from her sleeping bag and dressed and went to the communal shower area to wash her face and brush her teeth. Then, reluctantly, she headed toward the meditation hall, following a line of women reminiscent of something from *The Handmaid's Tale*. Inside, she found a cushion to sit on and remained there for hours, with PEARL.

Breakfast followed at six thirty, with the next meditation from eight until lunch at eleven. These were the only proper meals of the day. During the midday break, anyone struggling with the process could visit one of two teachers on-site to discuss. Otherwise, it was more meditating until five p.m., when first-time participants received just a piece of fruit for dinner, followed by more meditating until a video was shown on a large screen at seven o'clock.

The video was old footage of the founder, Goenka, who talked a lot about not being attached to things. During the discourse, Tilda scanned the room, taking in all the other participants, who were glued to the screen, nodding at his wisdom, chuckling at his jokes. She felt like she'd landed in a documentary showing people in the Soviet Union in the 1950s watching a propaganda film. That bit of evening entertainment was topped off with more meditating and then bed.

Rinse and repeat.

Tilda's mind felt like a swing in a children's playground when you've wound and wound the chains up and then let go. Each day, she did what she could to cope. She paced the bush tracks around the retreat until her feet hurt. With nothing else to do, she used much of her free time to pack and repack her bag, as if organizing that would help to organize her thoughts. She was at war with her mind. No distractions. No one to talk to. Nothing to read. All the women—about fifty of them, of varying ages—kept to themselves. She couldn't even make eye contact with her roommate for moral support.

The never-ending silence weighed heavily on Tilda, which surprised her. She enjoyed her solitude at home. But now she realized how she filled her time each day reading, listening to music or podcasts, taking photos, watching TV. She was always busy, which lowered the volume on the internal chatter. Here, with all those distractions removed, PEARL had a captive audience and a megaphone in hand.

So PEARL roared. Fear consumed Tilda. She worried about Holly and Tabitha, imagining all sorts of calamities. She worried about Buddy and Pirate, despite knowing they'd been left in Jack's capable hands. She worried about her mother's new relationship. She worried about work, the future, the past, a freckle on her arm being melanoma, and aliens invading Earth.

Tilda's mind was screaming at her.

Not only her mind, but also her body. Sitting cross-legged on the floor for a zillion hours a day was the definition of agony. The aim was to sit without moving for an hour by day six. Tilda couldn't sit still for five minutes, let alone sixty.

Unlike @Emmalee.

@Emmalee sat on the meditation cushion in front of Tilda. Obviously @Emmalee wasn't this woman's real name, or Instagram handle, but Tilda felt it suited her, and making up stories about @Emmalee kept her entertained. She made up stories about several of the participants, but particularly @Emmalee. Tilda spent hours a day staring at @Emmalee's ramrod-straight back. @Emmalee was about thirty, gorgeous, with an air of vegan influencer about her. She had one long, blond plait straight down her back, with never a hair out of place. She was clearly a contortionist to be able to weave a plait like that.

Even though most people wriggled and squirmed through the meditations, @Emmalee sat stock-still, a beatific aura around her as if enlightenment had come easily to her. She was the first person in the hall every day, and the last to leave. If trophies were going to be awarded at the end of this ordeal, they were already engraving @Emmalee's name.

Tilda wanted to pull her immaculate plait.

@Emmalee's perfection magnified every single one of Tilda's failures, including her stomach, which hadn't stopped rumbling. The food was excellent—a delicious smorgasbord of vegetarian dishes and salads prepared and served by experienced meditators who wanted to give back to the center. The one problem with the food was that there were certain dishes that . . . well . . . gave you flatulence. Not ideal in a silent meditation hall—although quite funny. More than once, Tilda had sat on her pillow, shoulders heaving with silent laughter as someone else's fart echoed off the walls. She knew it was immature, but she wasn't feeling like herself. In fact, she had no idea who she was. Just this seriously unhinged woman on a cushion trying not to fart, promising herself that in future she'd steer clear of the cabbage salad.

Perhaps spiritual development wasn't meant to be fun. But that didn't ring true with what she'd experienced recently with Selma. Tilda was really interested in the science of neuroplasticity. She enjoyed learning about her thoughts and emotions and how they impacted her body. Her journey with PEARL had been as exciting as it was tough. This retreat was just drudgery. And there were so many damn rules.

She also missed the meditation app she'd recently started using. Yes, the retreat was a deep dive comparatively, but Vipassana participants agreed to give up other forms of meditation if they continued with the practice. Meaning Tilda wouldn't be able to use the app once she was home if she continued with this style. It was something she needed to consider.

Every day, she gave herself countless reasons why she should leave. But she couldn't and wouldn't give up. She needed to finish. She needed to get to the end of the ten days. That was the destination. Otherwise, she'd feel like a failure.

Selma had called her a perfectionist. She had told Tilda to celebrate herself. Surely this retreat was doing just that? But in the echo chamber of her mind, with nothing else to occupy her, she found herself dwelling on a quote by Alan Watts: "The existence, the physical universe, is basically playful."

Tilda wondered: Was she missing the point? Watts suggested that, rather than being a journey with a destination to arrive at, life was a dance, and the point wasn't reaching one "particular spot in the room because that's where you will arrive. The whole point of the dancing is the dance."

Tilda sat with this. She tried to just . . . dance. And day by day, her brain felt sharper, clearer. There was no doubt that she was benefiting from this experience. But she still wasn't sure it was right for her. This was many things, but it wasn't dancing. Or at least not *her* dance.

If there was an upside to the retreat, it was that no one was looking at her. It was the first time since her diagnosis that she'd felt invisible for reasons other than the obvious. And it *was* still obvious. She checked the bathroom mirror each day, looking for what her mother had seen. She checked herself at different angles, at different times, trying to catch a glimpse of something different. How could she be visible to her mother? How was Frances so visible, dating at her age, while Tilda was vanishing into thin air? She checked the mirror more than once a day. Four or five or eight times, but nothing changed. Although, to be fair, nothing else seemed to be disappearing. Apart from her mind.

Could your mind disappear? What if her mind disappeared? What was a mind? Where was hers? Tilda couldn't get those thoughts out of her head.

What if I completely disappear?

Have I ever been visible?

What does it mean to see?

Why could my mother see me? And if she can, why can't I?

It nearly drove her out of her mind. Wherever that was.

44

You are the sky. Everything else—it's just the weather.

—PEMA CHÖDRÖN, Buddhist teacher, author, nun

Tilda was a bad person. Day seven of the retreat was proof of it. First, when the bell had clanged that morning, she'd rolled over and ignored it.

Fuck the bell.

And fuck four a.m.

She'd been having an erotic dream and wanted to decipher it. She'd been there, and Patrick . . . and . . . She'd tried to place the third person and then realized it was her roommate. It was extremely disconcerting.

It had been a bad start to the day, and she'd needed more sleep.

Afterward, when she did emerge, sleepy-eyed, she couldn't help beating herself up. She had failed to get up at four a.m., and therefore she had failed the entire retreat. She was a failure. She knew it was ludicrous to feel that way because she'd missed one meditation. She wasn't going to be shot on the beach today because she hadn't shown up. But she couldn't let it go—she'd really let herself down. And that's when the rage began. Red-hot lava bubbling inside her. She was furious with herself.

Until the lunch break, when she stood behind @Emmalee in the dining hall and transferred all her seething rage to her. She couldn't bear the woman. Her yoga gear was immaculate—pristine and uncreased—and

Tilda had no idea how anyone could plait their hair so perfectly. Tilda's own hair hadn't even been brushed today and was pulled back in a ratty elastic. She wore tracksuit pants, and her zip-up hoodie that had a yogurt stain on it from breakfast two days ago.

Each person in line moved along the food-laden table and scooped what they wanted onto their plate. Tilda spotted the cabbage salad, a no-go zone for her. And then, to her absolute delight—she may've even snickered—she watched as @Emmalee scooped not one but two large spoonfuls of the salad onto her own plate.

Later that afternoon, the fun and games began. A rumble rang out across the hall. Tilda had been deep in meditation at the time. She was finding that easier now. But the rumble was followed by a shuffling noise, and Tilda opened her eyes to see @Emmalee wriggling on the cushion in front of her.

Miss Perfect was trying not to let loose.

Tilda knew it. She'd been there. Countless participants had. The cushions should have come with a warning because of all the gas they'd absorbed over the years. Not to mention the warning that should have accompanied the buffet. Why on earth the chefs would add that salad to the menu was beyond her. Perhaps it was for a laugh.

More rumbles.

More wriggles and shuffles.

And something else.

Over the next hour, Tilda watched, fascinated, as Miss Perfect's formerly serene facade started to crumble, until eventually @Emmalee stood and bolted from the room.

Tilda closed her eyes and drifted into a pleasant meditation.

She felt vindicated. But like everything else she'd been feeling, that too passed, and was replaced by shame for finding even momentary pleasure in someone else's suffering.

Later, during one of the breaks, Tilda noticed @Emmalee seated outside in the sun, ferociously filing her nails, her plait unraveled.

@Emmalee didn't return to the meditation hall that day.

By nightfall, Tilda was battling with herself, wondering if she should break silence and ask @Emmalee if she was okay.

She didn't. There were rules. Plus, @Emmalee had triggered Tilda's own perfectionism. Tilda had spent her entire adult life holding tight to everyone and everything, fearing it would all be taken from her. Hoping that if she maintained control, she'd keep the chaos at bay.

45

Turn your wounds into wisdom.

—OPRAH WINFREY

Screaming . . . yelling . . . muffled cries . . . *She hid under the covers, trying to block out the sound.*

Tilda opened her eyes. The dream had been vivid, and her body shook with fear, as if she'd actually been back in her childhood bedroom. As though she'd never really left. Violence never leaves. It's always lurking in the shadows, whispering to you, influencing the choices you make, about men, about love, about your own worth, about everything.

She reached over to the stool beside her bed and checked her small travel alarm: one thirty a.m. There was no going back to sleep. She dressed in the dark, then slipped from the room and up the path up to the meditation hall. It was deathly quiet, a blanket of stars lighting the sky, a waxing moon making a flashlight unnecessary.

The hall was dim. One other lone figure, a woman, sat at the front. Tilda wondered what nightmares had kept her awake.

Tilda pulled up her cushion, wrapped a throw around herself, and sat down. She wanted to run. Or cry. Or scream . . . but instead, it was time to sit with it. Black, all-encompassing despair. For the child inside her, who had suffered great trauma. Her brain was in turmoil, her body a raging river of chemicals as it reacted to these memories.

"Memories are unreliable," Selma had said. "What you remember is subjective and certainly can't harm you now. What continues to harm you is your attachment to past experiences—replaying your memories, and reliving them, in thoughts, emotions, chemistry, biology."

Tilda knew that her father had suffered unspeakable violence as a child. She knew he couldn't escape this loop of trauma she was now stuck in herself. She knew he'd loved her, and no doubt never wanted to hurt her, even though he had. He didn't know any better. But *she* knew better. She'd been given the information and tools to beak this generational cycle. Now.

She sat and faced the memories. For the child in her who deserved better. For the teenage Tilda, who'd been so filled with self-loathing that she'd slept with half the water polo team in high school. For the young woman she'd been, who'd lost years to partying, obliterating herself, trying to *feel* something. For the woman who'd loved Tom but not herself. For every version of her at every age who hadn't been kind or loving to herself because she simply didn't know how. For allowing countless men to wound her so profoundly. She sat. She committed hour after hour to that cushion. To the technique. To herself. If she was going to repair her shattered self-worth, then this was the greatest act of love she'd ever display. She sank down a spiral of desolation, to deeper and deeper truths. Hiding her father's empty booze bottles before her mother arrived home. Encouraging him to sober up, get dressed. Desperately wanting his attention, so becoming a co-conspirator in countless cover-ups. Then she felt useful. Then she felt loved. And then he died, and she was left feeling lost. She had no idea who she was or what her role was in life. She rescued her mother. She rescued animals. And boyfriends. And then Tom.

But all of that was in the past. The only place it existed now was in her mind. And it was eviction time. She would not live another day feeling unworthy of love and all things beautiful. She sat, her body hurting from her cross-legged position on the cushion, but the pain inside her trumped that. Tears streamed down her cheeks. At times, sobs wracked her body. But she sat. She sat and raged and cried and felt waves of despair engulf her. Grief for the father who'd failed her and the father who hadn't. The father she loved and the father who'd left her too soon, before he ever had a chance to change and be what she needed him to be. She grieved her dad and faced the trauma of his death. She faced it all.

And by the time the sun appeared over the valley, the despair had passed.

46

Before enlightenment, chop wood, carry water.

After enlightenment, chop wood, carry water.

—ZEN PROVERB

A short time later, Tilda ate breakfast, observing how something in the air was different. She was different. PEARL was quiet. Afterward, Tilda sat on the grass in the garden and stared at the world around her.

Or, rather, she sat in the world.

It was a much warmer morning. Colors were brighter, sounds were clearer. She could see spiderwebs strung between blades of grass in the distance. The glistening of morning dew. She watched birds and bees zip between early-blooming flowers and trees. She had no thoughts of the future, and none of the past. She had no need to go anywhere or do anything. She was in the moment. She was present. She had no desire for anything. She just was.

And it was miraculous.

She returned to the hall, her mind calm. Another meditation flew by; thoughts that would normally spiral were now like wisps on the wind. At one point her body dissolved, and she became a mass of vibrating particles.

At lunch she realized she hadn't seen @Emmalee.

That afternoon, she found it hard to meditate again, but not as hard as it had been before. She'd glimpsed something wondrous that morning.

During the late-afternoon break, Tilda returned to her spot in the garden. She was still calm, but niggling thoughts had returned. She couldn't see the cobwebs on grass blades in the distance now. She ignored a nearby bird. She did, however, notice four women hurrying toward the office: it was the teacher, two retreat volunteers, and huddled between them was @Emmalee, a blanket wrapped around her, her knotted hair free of the plait. Completely unraveled.

Tilda was awash with feelings and confusion. She knew she couldn't run to @Emmalee to ask if she was okay. She didn't know her, only an invented version of her. But also, there were rules. She had to abide by the rules.

That thought passed, and another one took its place.

Rules are made to be broken.

Tilda jumped up and followed the women into the office. Everyone looked stunned to see her, apart from @Emmalee, who was now in a chair crying, clearly naked underneath the blanket. The volunteers sat calmly on either side of her, while the teacher was on the phone.

"Sorry to interrupt." After days without uttering a word, Tilda's voice sounded shockingly loud. Now she felt foolish—but being kind was never foolish. "Is there anything I can help with?"

@Emmalee didn't even look up at her, but the other three women looked as though Tilda had just offered to sacrifice someone to the gods.

Finally, Tilda blurted, "It was the cabbage salad. You should take it off the menu." She nodded as if she'd just solved a major mystery for them.

One woman scurried over to her and led her back out the door. "Thank you for your concern. She is being well taken care of."

"And the cabbage salad?"

"We'll look into it," the woman whispered.

And that was that. The woman went back inside and closed the office door behind her.

Tilda felt reprimanded. She was disgusted at herself for acquiescing so quickly, but what else could she do? She didn't know @Emmalee.

Tilda returned to her room and lay down on her bed. She'd judged @Emmalee for trying so hard, but she could see now that it hadn't really been about @Emmalee at all. Tilda had simply recognized herself in the younger woman. Tilda had wanted to do well, win at this retreat, win at meditation, be good at healing and get to her destination. That destination was to be visible again. But seeing herself wasn't a destination—just a shift in perception. Like the cobwebs in the grass. One minute she could see them, the next she could not. Given the right state of mind, she'd be able to see the cobwebs again. Perhaps she'd be able to see herself again, just like her mother could.

Holding so tightly to everything was not the way.

Focusing on the result was not the way.

She'd done it her whole life, holding on tight, trying to stop men from abandoning her, trying to protect those she loved, trying to keep her family together. If she could just control everything, maintain order, then everyone would be happy.

Only that never happened.

What if she gave herself a break? What if she let go?

Tilda sat up and reached for her bag under the bed. She unzipped it and pulled out the contraband chocolate that she'd hidden in there, just in case. Now was a "just in case" moment. Bugger the rules. She unwrapped the chocolate and took a bite, moaning. Never had chocolate tasted so decadent.

What was she doing? Why did she beat herself up for missing a meditation? Or for sneaking a chocolate? Or for not wanting to be here at this retreat? She didn't need to be here.

You've only got two days to go, you quitter. PEARL had not been placated by the chocolate.

Tilda considered this. Two days. She'd already unpicked countless knots in her mind and understood how to meditate much better. She didn't want to continue with this style of meditation. She knew that. She wanted to experiment with different styles. She wanted to have fun and feel free. She wanted to work out how her mother could see her. She yearned to be at home, searching for that shift in perception by walking on the beach and meditating to music.

Mostly, she needed to learn how to simply walk away from something that wasn't for her. Not everything had to be, just because she'd once committed to it.

She reached back into the bag and pulled out her phone, switching it on for the first time in over a week. It began to ping with a series of messages, which she ignored. Instead, she opened her camera and snapped a photo of herself shoveling the other half of the chocolate into her mouth. Leith would appreciate that. She scrolled back to a selfie she'd taken just before entering the retreat and flicked between the two shots to see the difference. Her eyes were brighter. A softening of edges.

More than anything, Tilda wanted to be at home taking photos. That wasn't PEARL trying to trip her up. It was a deep sense of knowing. She didn't need to be perfect at this or at anything. She wasn't @Emmalee. Or perhaps she was and needed to stop being her.

You're not a quitter.

No, I'm not, but maybe I need to learn to quit when my needs aren't being met.

What Tilda really needed was a sign—the irony. She aimlessly scrolled through some photos as she mentally argued with PEARL about leaving the retreat early. There weren't many photos of her, but each one documented another stage of this awful condition. Another limb lost. The inevitable progression away from all hope that a miracle would occur for her. She watched as each image flicked across the screen: some beach photos, Buddy and Pirate, Ziggy wearing a new T-shirt at work, a couple of photos of the Nag's Head pub with the barman in the background. One of . . .

Amid a rush of adrenaline, she swiped back through a couple of photos, returning to a photo taken the first afternoon she'd gone to the Nag's Head. Her hand shaking, she enlarged it.

There, seated at the table, was a petite blond woman she'd never seen before, wearing pajamas and holding a hip flask.

Carol.

Completely visible.

47

Don't spend time beating on a wall
hoping to transform it into a door.
—COCO CHANEL

While everyone watched the evening video, Tilda stripped her bed, tossed her belongings into her bags, and sneaked out the side door. She couldn't see a thing as she bolted through the bush. It was ridiculous. She felt like searchlights and dogs would be on her at any moment. She flicked her phone flashlight on and kept running up the path. She wondered if there were any werewolves out tonight, which confirmed that her imagination was alive and well, despite the hammering her mind had taken at this place.

The gravel car park was eerily silent, lit only by one streetlamp in the distance. She found her car, threw her bags in the back seat, and then, quicker than the Anglin brothers from Alcatraz, she made her escape. Her hands gripped the steering wheel, her entire body tightly wound as she drove along the mountain road back to civilization. She spotted a couple of wallabies startled by her headlights. Otherwise, the night was still. Or perhaps that was her mind. Either way, she didn't have a single regret about her decision to leave. She needed to return to the world and work out how that photo of Carol was possible.

Just before she reached the freeway, she pulled over, made a sizable donation to the Vipassana organization, and sent off a polite email apologizing for any inconvenience but saying that she'd decided to leave. No excuses. No explanations. She then checked her messages to make sure there weren't any from the girls and noticed a text from Patrick.

> You won't get this for a few more days, but I'm home now and felt compelled to reach out. I admire you enormously. Anyone who takes on the Vipassana retreat has my respect. You'll read this upon completion, so I need to fess up . . . when I attended the retreat, I only made it to day six. It wasn't for me, although incredibly beneficial and an excellent path for many wonderful people. I'll tell you the story one day soon. Face-to-face. And you can tell me yours. x

Tilda began to chuckle. It was her first laugh in over a week, and the sound of it spurred her on. She threw her head back in delight. It was hilarious. Patrick hadn't finished the retreat either. The man who'd made a mint from meditation, whose life was devoted to helping others meditate, had only made it to day six.

And here she was thinking she was a failure.

She noticed that he was online and messaged back.

> Are you around?

Within seconds, her phone rang.

"Are you breaking silence for me?" He sounded delighted.

"I can't believe you only made it to day six." She had her voice back. Tilda clicked her seat belt in and headed back onto the main road. "At least I made it to day eight. I'm on my way home."

"Come to my place and tell me all about it."

"What's your address?"

"Let's talk while you drive, and I'll give you directions."

It was wild, rebellious. Her body vibrated with ontological shock—although shock didn't really cover the multitude of positive emotions she was feeling.

Her mother being able to see her had raised more questions than answers. But being able to see Carol had transformed Tilda's small sliver of hope that she could heal her invisibility into full-blown faith.

Tomorrow, she would work out what she was going to do next, but tonight she was free. Tilda felt like life was full of possibilities. Not limits. And certainly not ones she placed on herself.

48

Barn's burnt down—now I can see the moon.
—MIZUTA MASAHIDE, poet and samurai

"You're the best GPS ever," Tilda joked, noting how quickly the two-hour drive had passed while she was chatting to Patrick. She parked and switched the ignition off.

Patrick's home was one beach north from Tilda's beach, on a large plot backing onto bushland. She'd often wondered who lived in this mammoth beach house. Turned out it was a dual residence that Patrick, Stephen, and Stephen's wife, Moe, had built together. Looking at the home now, Tilda realized four families could easily live there and not see each other for days on end.

"Some people think it's because I can't live alone, but I do live alone," Patrick explained. "We just enjoy living next to each other. We're a close family, plus I'm really involved in my nephew's life."

"It's a modern hippie commune," she said. "You're a hippie."

"I'm hanging up now," he teased.

"Okay, I'm coming in."

Tilda sat for a moment to calm her nerves, then made her way to the side gate, which lead to the private entrance to Patrick's home. She buzzed and the gate clicked, and she walked up a path through a garden, to a door ahead. It opened, and Patrick appeared in jeans, a grey sweater, tinted glasses, and a drop-dead smile. His face lit up. Like, seriously lit up. She couldn't ever remember a man being so pleased to see her.

"Welcome to my home."

She moved into his arms as if it was the most natural thing in the world. A long, warm embrace with one delicious kiss. For a few seconds, she forgot about any disappearing body parts and thought she might disappear into him instead. His lips were soft, but his hold on her was firm and made her very aware of his hands. She could smell the faint traces of mint on him . . . and something else on his breath. Something familiar. Something she wanted to deeply inhale.

He must've read her mind, because he did inhale. "I love the shampoo you use, Tilda. Vanilla?"

She made a noise to confirm that it was, not trusting herself to string words together just yet.

They entered Patrick's home and went into the main living area.

"Holy moly." She followed him through an open-plan kitchen and dining room and out to an alfresco area overlooking a pool, with direct beach access beyond it. The expansive terrace was completely set up for entertaining and outdoor living, with a barbecue, bar, seating, and a large wood table. It was night, but a full moon hung over the ocean, giving Tilda a sense of how it must look in daylight. Endless views.

"How do you see this view, Patrick?"

"Great question. My place is filled with light during the day, and I see that light. In fact, when the light is good, I still see some outlines of things. Plus, I hear the ocean, I smell it, I sense it. I know how good the waves are for a surf from that."

Tilda noticed a couple of smaller buildings at the edge of the property. "Are those tiny houses out past the pool?"

"One is an outdoor shower with a lock-up where we keep our boards. And the pavilion next to it is a meditation area."

It showed how much Tilda had changed recently that she didn't automatically roll her eyes.

"And Stephen and Moe live upstairs?" she asked.

"Yes. Their place is bigger than this. Four bedrooms and a roof terrace. I have two bedrooms here, but we run Toolbox from the studio that connects to my place over there." Patrick pointed at a covered walkway leading to what looked like another wing.

"Amazing." Tilda turned. The open-plan gourmet kitchen was filled with shiny appliances and led to a butler's pantry. "That's a very snazzy kitchen, Patrick."

"I like to cook. Do you?"

"It's right up there with a root canal for me."

He seemed delighted. "Stick with me, and you'll never have to cook again."

"Sign me up," she said with a laugh.

"Would you like some tea?" he asked.

"Something herbal, please."

Patrick made his way into the kitchen, busying himself while she looked around. His house was lovely. Every detail was beautiful. A feature wall had wallpaper that was hand-painted. There was a fireplace in one corner of the room, no longer needed as a mild night breeze blew through the open doors. Everything was in shades of brown, beige, and stone, with two rough-hewn wood lamps on a sideboard and a large coffee table. The overall effect was stylish and homey, without taking any focus from the star of the show: the view. In fact, one large sofa faced out toward the ocean—there was no television in sight. The wood shutters framing the view were pulled back, and on one wall there were several expensively framed finger paintings, no doubt his nephew's—a quirky addition to such a stunning room.

"To answer any questions you may have, I know my way around the house without my Yoda stick."

Tilda laughed. "Thanks for the reminder. Perhaps I should take my shoes off in case I put my foot in my mouth?"

Patrick gave her a sexy grin. "Or just take them off and relax."

A surge of heat came over her as she slipped her shoes off.

"You'll notice different textures on the floor. Some floors are wood, some stone, and my bedroom is carpeted. That gives me a sense of where I am in the house. We also built the whole complex with a glyphic language on the floors, walls, and counters. Plus, I've got smart technology, so there are sound cues around the house. Lets me know if I've locked doors or left appliances on—things like that."

Tilda heard a bark.

"Speaking of sound cues," he said with a laugh, "that's Hendrix."

Tilda cracked up. "Hendrix?"

Patrick shrugged. "What can I say? I'm a musician."

The next moment, a large AmStaff came bounding across the terrace and into the house.

"The dog has the run of both homes." Patrick gave a whistle. "Hendrix, come here!"

Hendrix bolted toward them, but unlike Buddy, who would have hurtled on until he bowled one of them over, Hendrix stopped short of them and sat.

"Well trained," Tilda noted.

"Early on in my RP journey, I considered getting a guide dog, but I love rescue mutts, so I trained with the cane. And since then, we've trained all our rescue mutts."

He loves rescue mutts.

Marry the man.

PEARL had certainly changed her tune.

"You've met Buddy," Tilda said. "I've also got a rescue cat called Pirate."

Patrick pulled a face to show she'd lost him there. "I don't do cats. Totally allergic."

You can't have everything.

Patrick handed Tilda her tea. "Let's sit out here."

Both Tilda and Hendrix followed him out to the terrace, where the dog curled up on a dog bed and Patrick and Tilda sat together on an outdoor sofa.

Patrick reached out and switched off the lamps. "Easier to stargaze," he explained.

Tilda relaxed back into the sofa and sipped her tea.

"How are you feeling since breaking silence?" he asked.

"I feel like I'm in the right place to do it."

It was strange, speaking again after eight days at the retreat, and she was still on a high after seeing the photo of Carol, but there was also something so calming about both Patrick and his home that it seemed like the perfect place to be. The night sky above was dazzling as they talked and laughed. At times Tilda was certain she could put her hand up and pluck a star from it.

"Patrick, do you miss seeing stars?"

"I do. You know, First Nations astronomers were studying the sky long before the Greeks. If you look up there, you can see an emu." Patrick's finger traced a shape between the stars. "Somewhere there."

"An emu?" Tilda squinted a bit. "Nope—I can see the Southern Cross, though."

"Its head is at the bottom left-hand corner of the Southern Cross," Patrick explained. "Then it stretches out into the galaxy."

"An emu?"

"There's a legend about a blind man, I think from the Papunya people in the Northern Territory. Anyway, this guy would send his wife out to collect food, but one day she didn't return home, so he went to find her. He discovered her body. A giant emu had killed her. So the blind man speared the emu and sent it up into the Milky Way, where it can still be seen."

"But not by the blind man," Tilda said.

Patrick roared with laughter at that one. "I don't know how he saw that emu." He shrugged. "There are countless ways to see things. What does it mean to see something, anyway?"

"I'm not sure." Tilda looked down at her disappearing arms. "I can't help but wonder if I'd be here with you if you could see."

"That's crazy talk." He shook his head. "Apart from the picture I have of you in my mind, I also liked the way you slammed that book shut the day we met. I liked the sound of your voice the first time we spoke. The slight scent of vanilla that surrounds you. Getting to know you has been marvelous. You're funny, creative, independent, smart . . . shall I carry on?"

"Please do." Tilda was grateful he couldn't see the tears in her eyes.

"I see you clearly."

Patrick pulled her into him, their faces inches away, their breath mingling, time suspended, until his mouth met hers. Moments later, he led her back into the house, down the hall, and into his bedroom. She felt like she should resist this, that it was too soon, but every cell in her body was screaming for him to touch her. They didn't even make it to the bed. Instead, he pressed her up against the wall.

"You're gorgeous," he growled, his lips just grazing her cheek.

I could get used to these compliments, she thought.

He kissed her. A deep, passionate, get-lost-in-it kiss. Christ, he could kiss. And with each kiss, he peeled off another piece of her clothing, until she was standing in nothing but her underwear.

"You taste delicious."

Her hand skimmed across his jeans, and she felt something straining to get out.

Wowza.

Okay, even PEARL approved.

"I need to know you," he whispered.

For the next two hours he explored every inch of her.

And it was so good. Every stroke, touch, kiss, as they got to know each other's bodies. She didn't think about any invisible bits. She felt seen.

49

I choose to make the rest of my life the best of my life.

—**LOUISE HAY,** motivational speaker and author

Selma stared at the photo. "The woman wearing pajamas. That's Carol?"

Tilda's nod confirmed it.

"The completely invisible woman from Brenda's support group?"

"Yes, that one."

"I'll be damned. I can understand why you saw this and left the retreat. It's big." Selma sounded amused. "So you ran out the back?"

"Upon reflection, I could've just used the front door," Tilda conceded.

"You weren't escaping from Pentridge Prison," Selma teased.

"It felt like it at the time." Tilda searched Selma's face for signs of judgment. There didn't appear to be any. "Do you think I should've stayed?"

"Surely by now you realize what I think isn't important."

"I don't think it was for me."

"Vipassana isn't for everyone."

"Have you ever done it?" Tilda asked.

"Oh yes, annually, for about twenty years." Selma was very matter-of-fact. "I love it."

This floored Tilda. "Yet you recommend other practices on your site."

"I don't consider myself a practitioner. I use many different techniques."

"But they advise you not to mix techniques."

"Who polices that?" Selma rolled her eyes. "They want you to give the

Vipassana practice a chance, but it's not a law. People take everything so seriously."

"Anyway, I love the meditation app you recommended on your website. I'll use that."

"Good for you. Any meditation practice is a good meditation practice."

Tilda noted that for a T-shirt. She looked at Selma. "In other news . . . I had sex with Patrick."

Tilda could almost see Selma's brain whirring.

"I drove straight to his place from the retreat," she explained with a cheeky grin.

"No wonder you're glowing. How do you feel?"

"Confused," Tilda admitted. "I feel I've been hasty. I need to focus on myself."

Selma sighed, exasperated. "What if he's part of that?"

"Maybe he is, but I have this history of losing myself in men. I need to beat this bloody thing before I even consider a relationship."

"It's possible to do both, but it's your call." Selma's jaw tensed. "Vipassana and Patrick: two runners in one night?"

"I waited until morning with him," Tilda mumbled.

Selma's voice softened. "At what point will you stop being so hard on yourself? Vipassana wasn't for you. So you left. The timing with Patrick might not be right; you can hit pause. These are just choices you're making."

"Why do they feel so uncomfortable?" Tilda asked.

"Because you're not used to putting your own needs first," Selma said. "Has Patrick been supportive of your healing journey?"

"I haven't told him about my . . . invisibility. It's too personal."

"You've been baring your soul to this man for three months. Two nights ago, you shared his bed. At what point will it be personal?" Selma smiled at her with great compassion. "Let him really see you, Tilda."

"You're right. And I know it, Selma . . . change is afoot."

"It is. I see you treated yourself." Selma nodded at Tilda's new sandals.

"Bought them yesterday." Tilda did a little dance with her feet, tapping her heels on Selma's rug, and both women laughed. "Tom used to tell me that people don't change."

"That's not my belief, nor my experience," Selma said.

"I've been thinking of that Joan Didion quote: 'I have already lost touch with a couple of people I used to be.' I look back at the past few months and marvel at how much I've changed. And then I ask myself: Have I changed, or has my perception of myself changed?"

"Excellent question."

"Are they two different things?"

"Another excellent question."

It made Tilda quite emotional to think how far she'd come. She took a moment to compose herself. "A shift in perception . . . Perhaps that's what happened when I took the photo of Carol. Something between me, the lens, and Carol. Maybe my camera caught something that the eye couldn't."

"That can happen," Selma said. "There are many examples of people capturing spirits and ghosts on film."

"I'm going to experiment by taking photos of myself. Maybe I can capture a glimpse of . . ." Tilda's voice wavered.

Selma reached across and patted Tilda's hand. "I understand."

"This photo of Carol has really stirred something in me," Tilda admitted.

"I can imagine. Especially coming so soon after your mother's visit," Selma pointed out.

"With each of these occurrences that I can't explain, I realize I, too, can experience something inexplicable. Miraculous. I can be fully visible again. I will be."

"It only takes one person to run the four-minute mile before others find they can do it too. The impossible becomes possible."

Tilda sat still for a moment. "Why do you think I captured that photo of Carol? Why could my mother see me? How can that be?"

Selma put her notepad aside, the session over. "I don't know yet, but one thing is certain: in order to properly see something, one must be fully present."

50

*I don't need anyone to rectify my existence. The most profound
relationship we will ever have is the one with ourselves.*
—SHIRLEY MACLAINE, actress and author

The next evening, Tilda was back on Patrick's terrace watching the
sun set.

"Do you remember the last sunset you saw?" Tilda asked.

"No. I wish I did. It should be marked in my memory, right? But things
like that have been a lesson for me—we never know if we're doing something we love for the final time, so I savor each moment and appreciate it
as if I am."

That would explain the grade A performance in bed.

"Come here," he said and slipped his arm around her. "Do you want to
go out for dinner, or should we order in?"

Tilda rested her head on his shoulder. She could smell his scent, and it
made her dizzy with desire again. It had been a long time since she'd felt
like this, if ever. She needed to be honest with him. Carol's photo was all
the proof she needed—she would beat invisibility, but to do that, she
needed to focus.

"Everything okay, Tilda?"

"There's something I haven't told you."

She could feel him tense up.

"Should I pour myself a drink for this?"

"It's just that . . ."

Patrick pulled away. He seemed annoyed. "No need to drag this out. You regret the other night."

She was a little surprised by his response. "No . . ."

"But it's too much for you to take on. I get it."

"It's not you, it's me."

He looked resigned to what was coming. "It always is. Dating a blind guy isn't for everyone. "

Now Tilda was annoyed. "You know, Patrick, if you'd just let me speak . . ."

He appeared suitably chastened and waited for her to speak again.

Tilda collected her thoughts and then continued. "I've been diagnosed with invisibility. It's a condition that—"

"I've heard of invisibility." His whole demeanor shifted to concern. "I am so sorry. I just made that all about me."

"It's okay," Tilda said with surprise. "It is about you, and me, and us. We're both feeling vulnerable and working out where we stand here. And while that's happening, I've been juggling this whole other thing—my diagnosis. As I'm sure you can imagine, it's been a stressful time for me."

"I don't have to imagine. I know what it's like when things start to disappear. And about being invisible to others." He ran his hand through her hair. "Why didn't you tell me?"

"We didn't really know each other, and then you were away. I've gone on an intense journey of self-discovery. It hasn't been easy, but I feel like I'm on an adventure now, rather than in survival mode."

She breathed in the sea breeze. Her mind was still clear from her days at Vipassana. She'd enjoyed a night of incredible sex. Her session with Selma had given her the courage to now be open and honest with Patrick. She was laying it all on the table.

"I've had this miraculous thing happen to me. Two weeks ago, my mother visited, and she could see me. I don't know how, but I was visible to her. And then a woman I met through a support group, who is completely invisible . . . I caught a glimpse of her."

Tilda watched while he absorbed this, then slowly nodded. He understood the magnitude of it. Then she finally said out loud what she'd barely admitted to herself in silence. "Patrick, I believe I can beat this thing."

Patrick's face lit up, and he pumped a fist in the air. "Yes, you can. You have faith."

His enthusiasm was contagious. Tilda sat forward and grabbed both his hands. "I want this with you, Patrick. But I'm afraid I'll lose momentum. I need to focus on myself."

"What if this is it, our time? You'd walk away from that?" he said.

She stroked his cheek. "I don't have a choice."

"Well, you do." He pulled her in for a kiss. "But I understand. I see you clearly, but you also need to see yourself."

Tilda held him for a long moment, and then stood up to leave.

Patrick stopped her. "Do what you have to do, but Tilda, I'm not going anywhere."

"I can't ask you to wait."

"You're not. This might be all we have. It's just . . ."

Tilda pressed for more. "Just what?"

Patrick gave her a cheeky smile. "Yoda one that I want."

Tilda laughed. "Yoda one that I want too."

51

The task is . . . not so much to see what no one
has yet seen, but to think what nobody has yet
thought, about that which everybody sees.
—**ERWIN SCHRÖDINGER**, physicist

Tilda stood naked in front of the mirror. For the first time in forever, she didn't criticize herself. She stared at her body—what was left of it—and deeply appreciated what she saw. The possibility of losing sight of herself had provided her with greater insight. She searched her face and memorized every line, every freckle. What if her face disappeared? What if this was the last version of her face that she'd ever see? Over the past few months, Tilda had discovered that she really wanted to see herself age. She'd always hated the signs of aging, but now she hated the thought of not seeing it happen. Each new wrinkle was a celebration. She loved her face.

She'd never lost her love of photography, but for the first time in years, as she set up her tripod and camera, she was trepidatious about taking a photo. Rather than just enjoying her craft, she was filled with purpose. It was a revelation. What was she trying to capture? What had happened in that moment with Carol that allowed her to be seen in the photo, and how could Tilda replicate it for herself?

For starters, the photo would need to be fully her, fully authentic. She'd been erasing her age in her photographs for a couple of years now. A wrinkle here, an edit there. But not anymore. She would not erase her age ever again.

"In order to properly see something, one must be fully present," Selma had said.

Tilda would be present with herself now.

"How do I see myself and the world around me?" she asked the camera. "Have I lost sight of myself? If so, how can I expect others to see me?"

When had she stopped looking at herself? Had she ever really looked at herself in any way other than to judge? Over the years she had criticized her crow's-feet, and the skin that was starting to sag in spots, and the weight that had crept up during her forties and now sat around her middle. Why?

She set the timer and stepped back, not posing, not trying to find a flattering angle. She wanted real and raw. She wanted to see herself in that light. She stood there naked—physically, emotionally, and spiritually. She took a whole series of photos, rapidly, then she paused to check them. Her right breast and part of her stomach were now hazy, along with her arms. Her left leg was already invisible, but now her right leg was also vanishing. Her limbs were literally fading away.

Despite this, she was still visible, just. She'd spent an inordinate amount of time judging her body, and yet now, when she was at risk of losing it, she suddenly felt incredibly attached to it.

She didn't want it to disappear.

What was so bad about putting on weight, or having wrinkles? To judge oneself so harshly was surely the antithesis of what aging was about: to experience freedom. Losing sight of herself was the tragedy, not the loss of elasticity in her face. She put the camera down and turned back to the mirror.

"Stay with me," she whispered to herself. "I like you more than I realized."

Tilda stepped closer to her reflection in the glass. She took in the lines around her eyes and, for the first time ever, felt nothing but love for them.

"Don't go. Don't disappear," she said, her voice growing louder and louder, until she was shouting at herself. "I love you. I love you. I really love you."

For the next ten hours, Tilda took photos of herself, downloaded them, looked through them, deleted them, and started again. She bared herself in front of the camera, shot after shot. She focused on what was visible, not invisible. Her tenacity, her spirit, her strength. In between, she danced. She sang. She had a long bath filled with oils, savoring rich chocolate and a glass of wine while she soaked. She lay on her bed wrapped in a satin robe and watched *High Society*, a film she loved but hadn't seen for years. She painted her toenails. But mostly she stared down the lens like it was the barrel of a gun, knowing that one shot, the right shot, would change her fate.

Each set of photographs was better than the last.

Raw.

Real.

Painful and beautiful.

She slept for a couple of hours and woke refreshed. She showered. The hot water ran in rivulets over her as she looked down. She turned the taps off and stepped out onto the mat, then turned to her reflection in the mirror again. She stood still for such a long time that the water on her body started to dry. The fog on the mirror lifted.

She looked beautiful. She could see that. Tilda was in awe of her own beauty. The absolute wonder of being alive, having a human experience. She'd spent so much time finding fault with what was in fact an utter miracle: herself.

She realized she was hungry, so she went downstairs to the kitchen and ordered Vietnamese food. When that arrived, she ate it, naked in the living room, watching a rom-com with a glass of wine.

More hours passed, until she was drowsy and deeply content. The food, the wine, the joy of time to herself being creative had been acutely satisfying. Sated, she slipped into bed and fell into a deep sleep.

She woke early, feeling more content than she'd felt in years. If not ever. She walked Buddy, savoring her beach and the warmer weather, and then returned home to meditate.

She sat on a cushion in her living room and closed her eyes. PEARL was still chattering away, but there was something else too, another part of her mind, somehow outside the program, or above it, looking over it, observing it. That observant part of her guided her into the darkness. And in one vivid burst she saw herself standing in her kitchen, laughing, filled with happiness and completely visible.

A future *her*, but now.

She opened her eyes, stunned. The vision she'd seen was everything she wanted in life, and it had felt so *real*.

Tilda returned to the camera. She could feel an energy flowing through her, a grace, something divine. She couldn't remember the last time she'd felt so creative, so utterly in the moment. She was totally present.

She clicked away and then checked the photos until she spotted the one she was looking for.

She zoomed in and examined it carefully. She was still invisible in parts. Mostly. But there . . . she could see her nose.

She ran into the bathroom, to the mirror, pressing her hands first against the glass and then to her face.

Her nose was there. Clear as day. Right in front of her eyes.

52

A miracle is a shift in perception from fear to love.

—MARIANNE WILLIAMSON, author

An hour later, Tilda lay on the wicker daybed in the garden. The grevillea was an explosion of red. She gazed at it, contemplating the passing of seasons.

"Everything passes," she said to herself. Even her invisible nose.

She ran her hands down her body. She'd dug a satin chemise out of her drawer. She'd bought it not long before Tom left in a last-ditch attempt to get him to see her, but he'd left before she got a chance to wear it. She'd never thought of wearing it for herself. Why? Why work so hard on her relationship with him, but not on the one with herself? Never again.

She felt at peace. She'd achieved something incredible. Selma called it the four-minute mile. It had seemed impossible; now nothing seemed impossible. The world looked completely different.

Her phone rang beside her, and she smiled. Patrick.

"I was thinking about you," he said, "and you know how thoughts become things, so my thoughts became this phone call."

Tilda chuckled. He spoke a lot like Leith, but his conversation never rubbed her the wrong way. Come to think of it, recently Leith's hadn't either.

"I figured I'd touch base, as a friend only," he teased, "and see how your day has been."

My nose reappeared. So pretty bloody spectacular.

Instead, she went with, "Remember I was telling you about the portrait gallery?"

"How you've always dreamed of showing your work there?"

"I've spent the past few days taking photos, and it might be the most important work I've ever done."

He sounded interested. "Photos of what?"

"Self-portraits for now. But I want to explore what makes a woman visible using other older women."

"Excellent. I love older women."

Tilda let out a laugh. "Right."

"Hey, I love all women," Patrick said. "But older women who know themselves and don't care what others think of them . . . There's nothing sexier."

In the past, when she'd felt the first stirrings of love, it was always met with some discomfort, even panic. What was she in for? Should she run? But now, in this moment, with this human, this man, she felt only a sense of peace.

"I'm blathering on, aren't I?" he said.

"No, it's like music to my ears."

They hung up, no promises, no pressure. She lay back down on the lounge chair. Buddy came and sat beside her, and she placed a hand on his head as they both lifted their faces to the sun.

53

"Hi, Tilda—nice to see you."

Tilda had been a patient at Gurinder's practice for a decade. Amber, the receptionist, had worked there for at least seven of those years. This was the first time she'd called Tilda by name. But then it wasn't only Tilda's nose that had reappeared. Overnight, Tilda's neck and ear had also returned. She was feeling pretty damn visible.

"Did you have an appointment today?" Amber asked, putting down her magazine. She had a big stack of them on her desk and was often reading when Tilda came in, but was always polite and efficient. Amber was probably in her early thirties and was wearing her usual navy scrubs and glasses, with her dark hair pulled back.

"I don't have an appointment, but I need to show Gurinder something, if she's around," Tilda said.

Amber looked thrown by Tilda's request. "Um . . . unfortunately, Dr. Majumdar is unavailable, but I can fit you in with Dr. Ly."

"I'll wait to see Gurinder," Tilda said.

Amber's eyes darted back and forth between Tilda and Gurinder's closed office door. "The doctor is on extended leave."

Extended leave? Gurinder hadn't mentioned anything. "When will she be back?" Tilda asked.

Amber forced a smile. "Hard to say at this stage."

Tilda scanned the reception area and noted the changes: some potted plants, and new chairs in the waiting room. The counter she now leaned on had new business cards propped up in a holder: Dr. Dunstan Ly. There was an empty holder where Gurinder's cards used to sit.

"Is Gurinder coming back?" she asked.

Amber's smile wavered. "Again, hard to say at this stage."

Tilda leaned across the desk. "Is it hard to say that she's bloody well disappeared?"

Amber looked like she was about to burst into tears.

"Sorry, sorry," Tilda said, feeling dreadful. "Obviously that's not your fault."

"I'm not meant to discuss it. Dr. Ly said I'll frighten the patients if I tell them about Gurinder." Amber pulled a tissue from a box and blew her nose. "Gurinder gave me this job when no one else would hire me. Single mum with no support . . . you know . . ."

"I do," Tilda said.

"I've always been so grateful to her. A regular paycheck, a good job." Amber picked up a *Woman's Day* and waved it around. "All the latest mags. But the best thing was working for someone who really saw me and believed in me."

Tilda marveled at this. Amber was so young, yet she already knew how it felt to be invisible. She noticed a photo of Amber with two children taped to the side of the counter, and some parenting magazines mixed in with the gossip rags. She realized that she'd never really seen Amber before—and apparently she wasn't the only one.

Amber lowered her voice. "How can a woman like Gurinder just disappear?"

Tilda was starting to understand how, but this was neither the time nor the place to share what she'd learned. "I need to go and find Gurinder right now, but how about we have coffee next week to discuss it all?" she said in a conspiratorial whisper.

Amber's smile was genuine . . . and so visible.

Fifteen minutes later, Tilda pulled up outside Gurinder's house. She'd been there once, years before, for Prisha's birthday party. She parked but didn't get out of the car. There was no point. It was obvious that the house was empty. There was a For Sale sign in the front garden, with SOLD plastered across it. All the furniture from the terrace was gone, and the curtains were shut tight. The shock of it made Tilda want to wail out loud, but she still had something important to do.

Tilda took a moment to steady herself, then turned on the ignition and drove back into town.

Gurinder had literally disappeared. Tilda was on a mission now to stop that from happening to anyone else.

54

Don't tell. Show what's possible.

—**LEITH,** over wine one night

Brenda was already mid-monologue by the time Tilda arrived at the support group meeting, and she wasn't pleased about the disruption.

"Tilda, you haven't attended a meeting in the last couple of weeks, so I thought you'd decided this group wasn't for you."

Tilda refrained from admitting that it wasn't. Instead, she adjusted the mask that was hiding the return of her nose. "I've got something I want to discuss."

"You'll have to wait your turn," Brenda said.

"It's rather important."

"More important than Susan's missing body?"

Tilda glanced over at Susan, and saw nothing but a head floating in midair.

"Take a seat, Tilda, and we'll get to you soon," Brenda said.

Tilda did as she was told, checking first that Carol wasn't already seated in the chair she chose. She gave Erica a wave, then noticed a hip flask on the empty chair beside her and waved at Carol too.

"I wish my head would disappear now," Susan said. "Surely complete invisibility would be better than just being a head."

A snort came from the empty seat Tilda had just waved at.

"Do you have something to say, Carol?" Brenda asked.

"Yes. I can't believe she's whining over having a visible head. I should be so lucky." Carol let out a short, sharp laugh of disbelief.

"I never make fun of you," Susan snapped.

"Because you can't bloody see me."

Susan glared at Carol's seemingly empty chair. "My daughter gets married in two weeks, and I'll look like this in the wedding photos."

"At least you can wear a hat," Carol said.

Brenda called for order. "Ladies, this is going nowhere. We all think the grass is greener on the other side. Susan thinks you're better off, Carol—while Carol would give anything to have a visible head."

"I could wear a hat," Carol added.

Brenda barreled on. "Every single one of us battles daily with this hopeless condition."

Tilda coughed, which annoyed Brenda.

"Tilda, you'll have your turn, but you can't expect to jump to the front of the queue when you come in late." Brenda looked around the room. "Who else would like to say something?"

No one spoke, so Brenda waited . . . a little longer . . . and then ceded the floor to Tilda.

"Your turn."

Tilda grabbed her bag and rifled through it. "What I'm going to show you might shock you," she said, pulling out a stack of prints. She strode across the room and thrust the photo of Carol at the empty chair. Carol took it from her, and Tilda watched as it floated in midair for a long moment.

Carol's voice shook. "How can this be?"

Tilda had printed out multiple copies of the same photo and now walked around the room, handing them out. Finally, she stood in front of Brenda and handed a photograph to her.

Brenda visibly paled. "Is this photoshopped?"

"I can assure you it isn't," Carol said loudly.

"When was this taken?"

"Three months ago, at the pub across the road," Tilda answered.

Gasps rippled around the room.

"Bloody hell, Carol, you're a freaking knockout," Erica said.

"I was," Carol said.

"You still are," Tilda said. "The camera caught it."

Brenda was lost for words, for once, but Tilda saw a flicker of fear cross her face. Everything she believed had just been challenged, and she didn't know how to deal with it. Tilda realized that Brenda's life had been built around hopelessness, supporting women with a disease for which there was no cure. Without that, she really would disappear.

She looked defeated.

Suddenly, Tilda wondered if she'd made a mistake, announcing this discovery in such a public way. Perhaps she should've approached Carol alone.

"I know this is shocking," Tilda said to Brenda. Then she turned to the other women. "I don't have all the answers, but I do have some ideas. And Selma Nester thinks they're worth exploring."

"That charlatan," Brenda said.

"No, Brenda," Tilda said calmly. "Selma is a leader in this field, with the research and evidence to back up her treatment. But there's still a lot we don't understand about invisibility. For this to be a proper support group, we need to acknowledge the fact that many women beat this and discuss all the treatment options. Otherwise, it's not a support group . . . it's a discouragement group."

A smattering of applause spurred her on.

"There are so many unanswered questions. This should be a place to explore those questions." Tilda noticed Susan's head nodding as she continued. "There's more. Recently, my mother dropped by, and she could see me."

Brenda didn't look well at all. "She was probably being nice and pretending . . ."

"Brenda, I haven't told my mother about my diagnosis yet, and I can assure you, she'd have mentioned my missing bits." Tilda looked around the room. "The key to this condition is perception. How we see. For some reason, my mother could see me. And while I was taking that photo of

Carol, there was a moment where the camera captured something I couldn't see. Looking at that photo, I developed a theory . . . We're all focused on what's invisible now, but what if we force ourselves to see what *is* visible? I decided to test it, and now I have something else to share." Tilda pulled off her mask to reveal her nose.

All hell broke loose.

Some women screamed. Others applauded. There were questions, and a cacophony of voices. Susan's head floated toward Tilda, stopping to give way as several other members of the group mobbed her. For a few minutes, it was bedlam.

Brenda called out from behind, her voice retreating as she headed for the door. "That's it for tonight." She appeared wounded.

"Wait!" Tilda called after her.

Brenda kept walking, but Tilda pushed past everyone and ducked in front of her. She handed Brenda a card. "My studio and contact details. I want to photograph you. I think I can help."

Disappearing, physically discombobulated women descended en masse. Tilda turned to them now, handing a card to every one of them. "I want to photograph you all. I'll be at the studio all day Saturday and Sunday. Call, or just drop by . . . I can't promise anything, but let's see what we capture together."

Mayhem ensued. Promises to be at the studio, questions about what to wear, discussions about whether it might actually be possible to turn the tide on their invisibility.

Tilda noticed Erica making her way through the crowd, heading for the exit. "Back in a tick," Tilda told the others, and followed after her.

She caught Erica as she was just about to slip out. "Hey, meet you at the Nag's Head later?"

Erica paused for a moment. "I can't today. Sorry."

Before Tilda could say anything else, she was out the door.

"Wait, Erica!"

Tilda followed her out onto the steps.

Erica turned.

"It will work for you too," Tilda said.

Erica glanced down at her hand, which was now missing. Her condition was progressing rapidly. "Maybe one day . . . I've got some other things I'm dealing with."

Tilda noticed a black pickup truck. "What's going on?"

Erica looked agitated. "I'm happy for you, Tilda, but I can't talk now. I have to go."

Tilda knew she needed to tread very carefully. "You said it was being with him that made you disappear."

She saw a glimmer of defiance in Erica's green eyes.

"Maybe it is," Erica said. "I don't know. But I do know that sometimes you need to make sacrifices to be with the man you love."

"Not yourself. You don't sacrifice yourself."

"I know I talk the talk, Tilda, but I'm not strong like you."

"I'll help you." Tilda stepped toward her friend and lowered her voice. "Mike is abusive. You're disappearing because being visible is unsafe."

"He's different this time. He's even driving me to these meetings."

"For now."

Erica sighed, as though deeply exhausted. "What can I say? I love him." She rushed down the front steps and hopped into the waiting car. She got in, head down, as the driver scolded her.

"Tilda?"

Carol's voice. Tilda turned in her direction.

"She's back with him," Tilda said. "I feel helpless. Perhaps I should—"

Carol cut her off. "You can't force help on someone. All you can do is light the way."

They watched as the pickup truck drove off, too fast for the quiet street.

Carol tugged at Tilda's sleeve. "There is one person here who wants your help."

Tilda smiled. "Come and I'll show you how, Carol."

55

Each friend represents a world in us, a world
not possible until they arrive, and it is only through
this meeting that a new world is born.
—ANAÏS NIN, author

That afternoon, Tilda and Carol were discovering a new world between them, or for them. They were lying on opposite sofas in the studio
at This Is A Sign—or at least Tilda assumed Carol was lying down. They'd
swapped whisky for wine and were halfway through a bottle. Old-school
Alanis Morissette rang out in the background. They had yet to take a
photo. They were too busy digging in deeply to the very marrow that sus-
tains women: friendship.

Like many women her age, Tilda understood the power of female
friendship. She was the type of woman who stayed in touch with others.
New friends were rare; Tilda preferred to put her energy into the ones she
had. But then she'd met Carol and they just clicked.

Right now, Carol was talking about her marriage. "We'd decided not to
have children. We told everyone that it was a decision we made together,
but it was his idea. I was happy to go along with that because I loved him,
and because I never really wanted children. Not the same way my friends
did. I was ambivalent. If he'd been excited about having them, then I
would've had kids and no doubt loved them. But when he said he really
didn't see himself as a father, secretly, I was happy—I wouldn't get fat. Can
you believe it? Anyway, I wasn't pushed into being childless, but I made

that decision with him thinking we'd always have each other. Then he left, and it turned out he just didn't want children *with me*. He has a son now."

"That must've been hard, Carol."

"It was. The night of my birthday, when he left . . . it wasn't just my husband who disappeared, but the hope that someone would be around for me. He got to change his mind about kids at fifty. I couldn't."

"Would you want to?"

"I'm at peace with being child-free, but if I'd known this was how things were going to turn out, perhaps I would've chosen a different path twenty years ago. I'd love a little more traffic in my life. People who care."

"I care," Tilda said, and she meant it. "I know that's not what you're talking about, but I'm really enjoying getting to know you, Carol."

"Same. Imagine something positive coming out of that bloody support group."

Tilda sat up and poured more wine. "How did you get so caught up with Brenda? She's a nightmare."

"She's my sister," Carol said, matter-of-factly.

The shock showed on Tilda's face, which sent Carol off into gales of laughter.

"You're joking, right?" Tilda said.

"Oh no, I'm serious."

More howls from Carol, which encouraged Tilda to laugh too.

"The look on your face!" Carol said.

Tilda laughed until her sides hurt. "Now I wish my face was invisible."

Finally, Carol explained. "Same father, different mothers. We didn't grow up in the same house, but Brenda spent a lot of time with us. She was always weird, but I do love her. She means well."

"How strange that you were both diagnosed with the same condition. There's no evidence to suggest a genetic link."

"My mother thinks Brenda just wants attention. I was diagnosed, and then about eight months later, she said she'd been diagnosed too. Only she was completely visible. Apparently, she'd lost a breast." A wineglass hovered in the air as Carol took a sip before continuing. "She started the group while she was still completely visible. It was about two years before she actually began disappearing, at least as far as I could tell."

"Do you think she brought it on herself?" Tilda asked. "That she got what she focused on?"

"I always joked that she had, but I never really believed it until I started Selma's exercises," Carol said. "And then when you showed us that photo today, I was sure of it. She should've been excited, but she appeared devastated."

"I know. I felt sorry for her!" Tilda stood and grabbed her camera, then fired off a series of shots of the couch, pointing the lens at roughly where Carol was lying.

Carol put on a husky voice. "Should I pose?"

"Do what you want. You could give me the finger and I wouldn't know."

"Good, because I am."

Tilda adjusted one of the lights and then snapped another few rounds. "Is Brenda married?"

"She was, to a very pleasant fellow named Ted. Dull as dishwater, but nice. They had three sons and a daughter, and then Ted died suddenly. She was left with four kids under eight."

"Jesus!"

"I never saw her cry. She forged on. To her credit, she is a warrior. A good mother. A primary school teacher, and eventually a school principal. She retired a couple of years ago. Now she volunteers at a women's shelter," Carol said. "Her kids are all wonderful, with good careers. I adore them. They're very attached to me. I've always played the role of the eccentric childless aunt."

Tilda sat with this, rethinking her incorrect assumptions about Brenda. "That's quite a story."

"That's the CliffsNotes version. Brenda's story is hers to tell, but there's much more to her than that uptight support group coordinator." There was pride in Carol's voice, and Tilda felt chastened.

"Four kids alone. She never met anyone else?"

"Well, she has this boarder, Deidre, who I've always wondered about, but if Brenda is gay, she certainly hasn't told anyone."

"Except maybe Deidre," Tilda joked. She checked her camera, noting that Carol wasn't visible in any photos, so hit Delete All. "Get comfortable."

"Tilda, I took my bra off an hour ago."

Tilda laughed. "Okay, Carol, we're going in deep now." She started shooting again, then asked, "How do you see yourself?"

Carol told her. "I never considered that before reading Selma's book. Until recently, I only thought of myself in terms of who I was married to or how I looked. But Selma's book has me analyzing how I see myself and the world. It's uneasy viewing."

"In what way?"

"I was abused by a family friend one night when he babysat me. I was seven. I told my mother, and she told me not to lie. So I tried to make myself invisible every time that man visited. It didn't help. The abuse continued for years."

Tilda had tears in her eyes. "I'm so sorry that happened to you."

Carol continued. "My PEARL tells me that to see me is to hurt me. That people can't be trusted. I spent years trying to maintain control of my body, to its detriment. But I'm also now recognizing another woman inside me who's yearning for connection, who's strong because she survived, and is now taking great pleasure in getting to know herself."

"That's the woman I see," Tilda said.

"Will see," Carol added.

They lost track of time. They laughed, they cried, and Tilda took hundreds of photos. Then deep into the early hours, Tilda saw what she was looking for. She walked over to where Carol was lying and sat on the corner of the sofa.

"I see you, Carol."

Carol took the camera. There was a clicking sound as she flicked through the photos of herself, and she began to cry.

The two women sat side by side as the sun rose over the ocean outside the window, heralding a new day.

56

Motherhood is the biggest gamble in the world. It is the glorious
life force. It's huge and scary—it's an act of infinite optimism.
—**GILDA RADNER,** actress and comedian

The hotel suite was abuzz. Tilda and the girls were in the penthouse of
the recently reopened Hotel A, the coolest boutique hotel in the city, with
a view of the harbor. The suite had stone floors, whitewashed walls, and
wood beams overhead. The rooms were filled with ornate touches like
patinaed bronze light fixtures and door handles and gold-framed water-
colors. The website described the hotel as "the perfect European hotel,
outside of Europe."

Tilda zipped up her costume and adjusted her hat. There had been
weeks of discussions before Tilda, Leith, and Ali settled on *Macbeth's*
three witches. It was a show of unity—Tilda had her two best friends
flanking her in their wild, sexy witches' britches.

Tilda could hear the girls laughing about something as they got dressed
in their larger room.

She had so much to be grateful for, so why did she feel like she was
about to vomit?

The truth was that she was filled with anxiety about seeing Tom and
meeting his new girlfriend, Laura.

Tom had been in a series of relationships since their divorce, but Tilda
had never met any of the women. The fact that he was bringing Laura to
the party spoke volumes. Tilda had considered inviting Patrick but quickly

decided against it. She thought it could be awkward now that she'd put the brakes on. When, and if, the time was right, there would be a more appropriate setting for him to meet her nearest and dearest.

For the past couple of years, Tilda had assumed she was over Tom, but being diagnosed with invisibility had left her with no choice but to dig into her past and her pain. She now understood that while she thought she was over him, and over her past, her body had been keeping score. But with everything she'd experienced in recent months, things had shifted, and she felt completely free of him. She was finally in a place where she could see the value in everything she'd experienced with Tom, good and bad, without any attachment to it.

Tonight, however, Tilda wished she didn't have to come face-to-face with his happiness. It didn't bother her that he'd found it, but knowing she had to meet Laura made her uncomfortable. She could picture her now: young, edgy, streamlined—a bit like Tom's new Mercedes. Tilda was more of a VW Beetle: vintage, and with curves, but having a bit of a re-naissance. She'd felt good about herself recently, so this insecurity was challenging.

She applied another coat of lipstick and admired her nose. She'd always thought it was too *long*, when in fact it was just perfect. She'd wasted so much time being critical of something that she was now grateful for.

She spun around in front of the mirror.

She had to stay positive. It was why she didn't want anyone but her inner circle knowing about her diagnosis. She didn't want the shock or the sympathy tonight, not when she was kicking invisibility's butt. The focus should be on the twins. Plus, she certainly didn't want any compari-sons to Tom's new girlfriend to get in the way of her healing.

"Other people's opinions are none of my business," she muttered.

Tilda combed her hair and then headed out to the lounge, just in time to see a vision of pure joy enter the room: Tabitha and Holly, dressed for their twenty-first birthday party. The costume party neither of them had ever wanted but chose in an act of solidarity with their mother. She could not have loved them more than she did in this moment. For once, the snapshot Tilda took was without a camera, and would be treasured for life. The sight of them! Resplendent in costumes that brought out their beauty and character. Tabitha was dressed as Fauna, a mystical forest creature, in a formfitting jumpsuit with a tail, and antlers on her head. Waris from the support group had painted her face earlier, thrilled to be booked for another job. Jess, who was already at the venue checking on the catering, was dressed as Flora, with flower vines wrapped around her limbs. Then there was Holly, the Harvest Queen, in a showstopping deep-green velvet dress and crown.

Tilda started to cry, which brought Holly to tears too.

"Come here, you two." Tabitha pulled her sister and mother into an embrace. "I love you both so much."

"I love you too," said Tilda.

"I love you more," said Holly.

Tilda picked up the two gift-wrapped boxes that were sitting on the table and passed one to each daughter. She couldn't believe her babies were twenty-one. How had that happened? She blinked.

The girls unwrapped the gifts, revealing identical Tiffany & Co. boxes. Each box contained a custom-made sterling silver heart-shaped locket with a brilliant round diamond and, inside, a small photograph of the three of them, the date, and an inscription: "Love yourself as I love you. Fiercely."

"I love it so much!" Holly howled.

Tabitha hugged Tilda and then passed the necklace to her. "Can you put it on me, please?"

Tilda clipped a locket around Tabitha's neck and then around Holly's, remembering when she'd constantly cover the back of their necks in raspberries and kisses when they were young. When was the last time she'd done that? That was something you only understood as the years progressed—that you'd had a final precious moment without even know-ing it. That final time your child held your hand as you crossed the road. The final time they crawled into bed with you. That final kiss on the neck. Now, as she clipped the necklaces on, she kissed their necks once more, not knowing when she might get the chance again.

Holly jumped up and ran over to her bag. "We got something for you."

This surprised Tilda. "But it's not my birthday."

"It's a special day for you too," Tab said.

Tilda laughed. "It is!"

"Mum, we're so proud of you," Holly said. "You've gone on a crazy journey—we know it hasn't been easy, but you've been so strong. It's really inspiring."

Tilda attempted to brush off their praise with a wave of her hand, but Holly grabbed it.

"We're serious. We're so inspired by the steps you've taken to change your life and to be visible again."

Now Tilda was crying.

"You've already got your nose, neck, and ear back," Tabitha said. "And we have no doubt the rest of you will be visible soon, so we figured while it might be our birth day, it's also your rebirth day."

Tilda was going to have to redo her makeup, damn them.

Holly handed her mother a tissue, and a shoebox-size box. Tilda blew her nose and then tore the wrapping off . . . a shoebox.

She opened the lid and there inside was another, smaller box, from Tiffany. They'd bought her the exact same necklace she'd just given them.

"We bribed Leith for the details," Tabitha explained.

Tilda opened the locket. Inside was the same photograph of the three of them, and the same inscription, with one difference.

"Love yourself as *we* love you. Fiercely."

57

Nothing is absolute. Everything changes, everything moves,
everything revolves, everything flies and goes away.
—FRIDA KAHLO

The Velvet Room was the grande dame of the city's cool clubs. Its eighties heyday had seen the likes of Prince, Grace Jones, and all the members of the Rolling Stones drop by when they were in town. Its time had passed and it had closed, only to reopen again recently, completely renovated and refurbished but retaining its oak bars, checkerboard dance floor and disco lights, vintage fittings, and velvet sofas and booths; nods to its former glory.

Tonight, a red carpet led to the club, which was now styled as the backdrop for a Samhain feast in keeping with the "Party Like a Pagan" theme. Jack-o'-lanterns adorned each table in the myriad rooms, spreading a warm glow. A six-foot-long grazing table—a stunningly designed combination of leaves and branches—covered in dips and dark breads, nuts and crackers and cheeses had been set up on each floor of the club. Cured meats and roasted vegetables gave way to Greek meze: hummus and tzatziki, olives and dolmades. There were cornucopias, too, overflowing with figs, pomegranates, strawberries, blueberries, mangos, grapes, and raspberries—an explosion of color, and a feast for the senses. Local handmade chocolates were piled high under doughnut towers.

Mulled wine, cider, and mead were free at the bar, as were champagne and beer from the brewery sponsoring the event. Holly's celebrity was being exploited. The whole event was free—all Holly and Tabitha needed to do was smile for the two photographers Holly's management team had vetted. For once, Tabitha had allowed Holly to have her way, but on one condition—the event would raise money for Four Paws, her rescue group.

Tilda spotted her daughters seated in a lounge area off to the side. Tab and Jess were draped across each other, the perfect symbiotic relationship of Flora and Fauna. Lulu was with them, dressed as a fairy. Tilda marveled at how much she looked like Leith at that age—peas in a pod. Everyone was listening to Holly as she held court, Jack by her side. He was wearing a suit, his outfit of choice for any social gathering, but Holly had managed to get him to wear a crown along with her. At the table next to them were Geoff and Ziggy, deep in conversation, both dressed as zombies.

Tilda spotted her mother, dressed as Morticia Addams, enter the club with a much younger, shorter, and frankly quite good-looking Gomez by her side. *Go, Mum!* Tilda headed across the room toward them.

"Love the costume, Mum." Tilda gave Frances a kiss and then turned to Gomez. "And you must be Neville?"

Tilda stuck her hand out to shake his, but instead he lifted it to his lips, giving it a Gomez-like kiss. Then he dropped the character and followed up with an affable grin. "I've heard so much about you, Tilda."

"All good, I hope?"

Frances laughed. "No, not all."

"Don't tell fibs, darling," Neville said. "You rave about Tilda and the girls."

Tilda was taken aback. Firstly, Neville had just called her mother *darling*. And even more disconcertingly, her mother was beaming like a teenager in love. She was . . . luminescent.

"Can I get you two ladies a drink?" Neville offered. "What would you like, darling?"

There it was again!

"Yes, please, a G&T," Frances twittered.

"I'm fine, thanks," Tilda said, despite being anything but. It was a lot to take in.

"Lovely to meet you, Tilda. I look forward to getting to know you." And off he went in search of drinks.

Tilda hugged her mother. "I like him. And I've never seen you so happy, Mum."

Frances gave her daughter a very sly grin. "Happy? My dear, I had my first orgasm with a man three months ago. I'm having the time of my life."

Way to ruin a moment.

"Nev needs me at the bar," Frances said, giving him a wave as she headed off, leaving a thankful Tilda behind. She didn't need to know any more details about her mother's sex life.

What next?

"Tilda? Is that you under that witch's hat?"

Of course this was next.

"Tom! Hi there." Tilda managed a "fancy meeting you here" face. "Look at you!" She waved at his costume. "The Pope?"

"A druid."

"Oh right, now I see it." She didn't. But she did notice how old he looked. And small. He'd once been a giant in her eyes, but tonight he looked rather average.

Tom gave her a somewhat awkward hug.

"Tilda, this is Laura."

And there was his new girlfriend, standing before Tilda, smiling at her, clearly also wanting to be seen.

Tilda's costume helped hide her surprise. Laura wasn't a pretty young hipster. She wasn't cool. She was attractive, but in a somewhat ordinary way. Mid-forties, and curvy under her druid's dress, with sharp features, short dark hair, and a lovely smile, which she aimed at Tilda now.

"Nice to finally meet you, Tilda."

"You too, Laura." Tilda held out a satin-gloved hand, but instead Laura leaned in for a friendly hug.

This wasn't what Tilda had expected. She stopped a passing waiter and grabbed three flutes of champagne, passing one each to Tom and Laura. "We should have a toast . . . to the twins."

The three of them clinked glasses, and then Laura said, "And to you both, for successfully raising two amazing people. Congratulations."

Tilda was thrown. Laura was genuinely acknowledging Tilda and Tom's bond as parents. Together. She wasn't guarding her territory; she was being respectful. Tilda wasn't sure whether it was the glass of fizz she'd already downed or the mouthful of this one, but she liked Laura.

"Where did you two meet?" Tilda was genuinely curious.

"At work," Laura said. "I really wasn't looking to meet anyone, but then this bozo asked me out for coffee." She gave Tom a light shove, and the two of them laughed.

Tilda pretended she was in on the joke with her own chuckle and took a large swig of champagne. "Are you a journalist?"

"God no. I'm an account manager."

Practical. That would appeal to Tom. I was useless with money.

Clearly two glasses of champagne weren't enough to silence PEARL.

Laura looked at Tom, and Tilda recoiled slightly at the look in Laura's eyes. Love. Pure love. Aimed at Tom. *I used to look at Tom like that.* She realized she'd forgotten the good parts, forgotten the man she'd fallen for, but she remembered him now, as she saw him through Laura's eyes. She had always complained that he didn't see her—but when had she stopped seeing him? Tom noticed her looking at him and smiled. It was the first genuinely caring smile he'd directed her way in years, and it completely floored her. She'd forgotten that smile of his too.

"I can't believe our girls are grown up," he said. "We did well, Tilda. *You* did well. I know most of the credit goes to you."

Was he joking? Or trying to impress Laura?

Tom told Laura that he was surprised the girls had chosen a costume party. "I always thought they hated them," he said.

Tilda shrugged. "People change."

Laura agreed with her, which Tilda found equal parts weird and refreshing.

It was surreal watching Tom and Laura together. Tilda couldn't deny the connection between them. But there was something else there that she just couldn't put her finger on.

Tilda spotted Leith and Ali on the dance floor. She wanted to be with her friends, not here in this awkward triangle. She turned to Laura and gave her a hug. "I'm sure I'll see you again, Laura." And then it was Tom's turn. He pulled Tilda in for a hug and held her tight, for just a moment longer than she was comfortable with.

"Perhaps I could give you a call," Tom said. "I'm finally working on that novel we'd always discussed, and I'd love to bounce some ideas off you." He said it in a conspiratorial tone, as if Tilda would get what he was talking about and be pleased.

And then Tilda saw it: the look on Laura's face. A flash of insecurity. Achingly familiar.

"I'm sure Laura could help you with that, Tom."

"Laura doesn't have a creative bone in her body."

Tilda looked at Laura, who was smiling as if Tom was right; but her smile didn't reach her eyes. Tilda wanted to warn her. *Get used to it.* She wanted to tell her to run. Tom had been Tilda's everything. Now the huge space he'd once filled, in her life, in her heart, had been emptied of him completely. In his place was . . . a breeze.

Then Katy Perry's "Roar" interrupted, energizing the room.

"I've got to dance," Tilda said.

And she made her way to the dance floor without looking back.

58

Nobody has ever measured,
not even poets, how much the heart can hold.

—ZELDA FITZGERALD, author

A few hours later, the hotel suite was stacked with grazing plates and filled with raucous conversation and laughter. The party had been a roaring success, and the core crew was now hunkered down for the night.

Lulu lay across a large cushion on the floor, her wings beside her. She was happy and laughing—and, Tilda noticed, eating crackers and cheese. Tabitha and Jess were wrapped around each other at one end of the sofa, while Holly sat in the center, her legs across Jack's lap. While not always comfortable in social situations, Jack was at ease tonight. These were the people he'd grown up with, and he was always happy to be with Holly.

Tilda joined Leith and Ali at the table. She picked some strawberries off a platter and popped one in her mouth.

"Good work, Tilly," Leith said. "That was a sensational night. And you blitzed the whole Tom thing."

"It wasn't as bad as I thought it would be," Tilda admitted. "Our daughters are twenty-one, so that was . . . unifying. But mostly, he felt like a stranger."

"Did you see him buddy up to Ziggy all night as if they were besties? So far up Ziggy's arse I thought he'd come to the party as a colonic."

Tilda and Leith cracked up.

"I liked Laura," Tilda said. "And I felt for her."

"It's her journey," Leith said.

"It's crazy how I'd built up this idea of who she was and how he'd found the happiness that eluded us with someone else." Tilda thought about this for a moment. "What a waste of time and energy. The reality is that seeing them together made me uncomfortable because it was . . . familiar."

"What do you think that means?"

Tilda matched Leith's stare. "Same script, different cast. Nothing changes until you change."

Leith chuckled. "You sound like you work for This Is A Sign."

"At the end of the day, Tom and I were unable to see each other. I wasn't the only one who was invisible." Tilda shrugged. "I didn't see him clearly either."

Leith reached across the table and took Tilda's hand. "You've traveled far, my friend."

Tilda agreed. "And I ended up here."

The three women looked across the room at their kids, all wearing pajamas now. The room was full of life. Their life together.

Tilda thought back to the first night she'd spent with Tom. It was as clear as if it had happened yesterday. The next morning, he'd made her a coffee in his kitchen. There had been a moment when she'd looked into his eyes and seen . . . something. Their future mapped out. The full spectrum of pain and suffering and love and passion she was about to experience. If she stayed.

She'd stood, said, "I'm sorry, I need to go."

The abruptness had taken him by surprise. "Now? What about your coffee?"

"Maybe some other time."

And she'd quickly collected her things and left.

An hour later, she'd received an email:

> That was sudden. Did you see my tie-dye gear behind the
> brown shoes?

Her heart leapt, and then another email arrived:

> I'm interested in why you took off so suddenly, if you can
> put your finger on it.

It had taken her over twenty years to put her finger on it. Or perhaps she'd known it that morning, and that's why she ran.

She'd returned. Of course. Again, and again, until there was little left to return to.

But would she change anything if she could?

No. Not a thing. To do so, she'd have to change this moment. And this moment—with her glorious girls and this version of herself experiencing it—was perfect.

59

If I told you the whole story it would never end . . .

What's happened to me has happened to a thousand women.

—FEDERICO GARCÍA LORCA,

Doña Rosita la Soltera: The Language of Flowers

For weeks, each night after the office closed, the photography studio at This Is A Sign became a hive of activity, with women from the support group gathering, eager to discover the key to beating invisibility. Some women wanted to be alone with Tilda during their session, while others came in pairs or threes or fours. All of them were fully committed to the process—this experiment in seeing themselves. They faced the discomfort, had the difficult conversations, and pondered some big questions for the first time ever. They revealed their traumas, their heartbreaks, their pain. They unveiled their shame, anger, resentment, and guilt. Sometimes, someone would reach their limit for the day and go home, returning days later after observing their thoughts and their feelings, ready to dig even deeper.

It wasn't all serious. The sessions were also filled with laughter and encouragement and the incredible support that women are capable of when they love and trust each other. These were brave conversations between women who were all facing unfathomable challenges daily. Their stories varied, but Tilda noticed a common thread. All the women had experienced trauma at some stage in their lives that had made them see the world differently and left them questioning their own worth. The result was a program—their individual version of PEARL—that fed them a loop of negativity, all day long.

The world wasn't safe.

They weren't loved.

Life was hard.

They were over the hill now.

Getting old.

They weren't worthy of being seen.

The women were all shocked when they began observing their personal program.

"I thought my ex-husband was cruel, but I leave him in the dust," Lydia said.

Carol threw herself into the project, sitting in on most of the sessions, and often referring the others to Selma's book. She'd committed to Selma's exercises 110 percent, determined to heal. The morning after her own miraculous photography session, she'd seen a flash of something as she walked past the bathroom mirror. It was the first time she'd seen herself in years. She was visible again, presenting as an ethereal being. What once would have been a shocking sight to the other women in the group was now inspiring, further proof that everything really was a matter of perspective.

Selma, too, was fascinated by the project, dropping by several times. Tilda was mindful of how she framed each session, aware that she wasn't a trained therapist, but Selma's observation was that these sessions were a creative process, not therapy.

"Besides," she said, "women thrive when they explore their lives with other like-minded women. You're just facilitating what all women need—great conversations in a supportive environment."

Leith popped in most days and called the studio the Crone Cave: a space imbued with womanhood, in all its wild beauty, wisdom, and rage. A sacred place in which secrets were kept.

Tilda had never felt more inspired. The very act of seeing each woman had supported her own journey back to visibility. She had begun to see herself more clearly. It was a thrill to see her arm again. She'd celebrated the return of her foot with new sandals. The reappearance of her whole leg was cause for a celebration with her friends. Day by day, every single inch of her returned, even her hands—all but her little finger. Seeing Tilda was the jump-start each woman needed to believe in a miracle. They were given more than a photo of themselves. They were given faith that the world was full of possibilities, including their own recovery.

"Who's do we have left?" Tilda was packing up for the night while Carol went through the list of women they'd photographed.

Carol was now like a ghostly apparition in a leopard-print Camilla kaftan, her blond hair falling around her shoulders. "Anarat is in tomorrow, and you still need to finish Gianna. And Chris texted this morning—said she looked in the mirror last night and actually heard her internal voice say, 'You're a warrior.'"

"Love it," Tilda said. "We all are."

Carol nodded. "Can you believe how much time we've wasted being critical of ourselves?"

"Mind-boggling," Tilda agreed.

"I look in the mirror now and I'm filled with gratitude."

"Same," Tilda admitted.

They both paused, contemplating the magnitude of what they shared, before Carol returned to the list. "The only other people left are Brenda and Erica."

Tilda's heart sank at the mention of Erica's name. She'd texted her a couple of times but received no response. Tilda knew she should check in on her, but Erica's reconciliation with Mike had stirred some deep-seated discomfort in her, so she hadn't tried very hard.

Tilda noticed Carol watching her. The two women had come to know each other better in a few short months than some friends did over a lifetime.

"I'll call her and see if she's free for lunch," Carol suggested.

There was that familiar feeling in Tilda's limbs. Ice. Tilda changed the subject. "Have you spoken to Brenda?"

"Daily," Carol said.

"Did you explain what we're doing here?"

"She's busy, apparently."

Tilda zipped up her camera bag. "Doing what?"

"She didn't say."

"I can't understand her," Tilda said. There was an edge to her voice, but it really had nothing to do with Brenda, and Carol knew it. Both women had been completely transparent with each other about their pasts. "Surely the very sight of you should be enough to have her show up. It's as if she doesn't want to be seen."

"Perhaps she likes being invisible," Carol said.

A voice interrupted them. "I don't, but it has its advantages."

Tilda jumped—she could see Brenda standing in the doorway, though only barely. Her condition had progressed in the past couple of weeks.

Carol gave her sister a warm hug.

"Would you like me to set back up, Brenda?" Tilda asked, waving an arm around the room. "I'd love to photograph you."

"Soon, but there's something I need to do first." She turned her full focus on Tilda. "I need your help with something tomorrow morning. And we can't be seen."

"What could be more important than this?" Tilda asked.

"We need to get Erica away from her husband."

60

Men are afraid that women will laugh at them.

Women are afraid that men will kill them.

—MARGARET ATWOOD

Tilda's hands were disappearing in front of her eyes. It was at once both horrifying and fascinating.

"Let's go through the plan again," Brenda was saying.

But Tilda wasn't paying attention. She was in the back seat of Brenda's Hyundai staring at her hands, watching all the hard work she'd done unravel.

"Hello, Earth to Tilda?" Carol called over her shoulder.

Tilda managed an "I'm listening."

Her eyes drifted to the window. They were parked behind a delivery truck, down the street from Erica's house. Rows of cookie-cutter homes lined the street, and Tilda silently began to sing "We Gotta Get Out of This Place" as her hands disappeared.

"It is currently oh eight hundred hours. Mike will have left for work by now," Brenda explained, not for the first time. "When he arrives at work, he calls Erica."

"Possessive bastard," Carol snarled.

"From the time of that call, we have about an hour to get her out. He often comes home to check on her."

Carol growled again, even though Brenda had told them the same thing twice on the thirty-five-minute drive to Erica's home. In fact, she spoke like an army drill sergeant.

Tilda's hands were not only disappearing now; they were also shaking. Her whole body had gone into fight-or-flight mode. Stress hormones coursed through her.

The only thing keeping her in the car was the seat belt, and the fact that she had no idea where she was.

Brenda passed both Carol and Tilda a beanie and a mask. "Wear these. Tuck your hair up into the beanies. It's so he never recognizes us if we run into him in the future."

"You're fine, Brenda," Tilda sniped. "You're almost invisible."

"A positive," Brenda said with a chuckle.

Tilda shoved the beanie on her head, tucked her ponytail up into it, and tugged the whole thing down tight. Once she added the mask and a pair of sunglasses, even her own mother wouldn't have recognized her. She began to sweat, not sure if it was from fear or wearing winter woollies on such a warm day.

Brenda was surprisingly calm. In fact, her presence steadied Tilda somewhat. Brenda had been volunteering at the women's shelter for a few years; she understood the risks and knew how to minimize them where possible. She was very comfortable being in charge of this mission. Tilda's experience of Brenda was that she liked to be in charge everywhere, and today, Tilda was grateful for it. Brenda was wearing a big jacket and had a beanie in her lap, even though you could hardly see her. She had already put black tape over her license plate. She was taking this very seriously, but then again, it was serious.

Despite his promises that he'd changed, Mike was once again hitting Erica. It was her fault, of course, according to Mike. She'd flirted with one of his friends. Supposedly. That night, he'd punched her on the side of the head, and then cried afterward, begging forgiveness. Over the past month, the abuse had escalated, and Erica was scared. In the last week, he'd choked her and broken her finger. He'd allowed her to see a doctor—female, obviously. Erica told the doctor that she'd jammed her finger in the door. The doctor wasn't fooled.

"If you need to leave, do you have a car?"

"No, he sold it."

She handed Erica a phone. "Whom can you call to get you to safety?"

Erica called Brenda. She'd once discussed her situation with Brenda, who had told Erica to keep her number handy, just in case.

This was the just in case.

Both Brenda and the doctor agreed that Erica would be at further risk if she called the police herself. If anything went wrong, and she was left to face Mike, who knew what would happen? So instead, Brenda had put an immediate plan in place—they'd report Mike to the police once Erica was away from danger. They just had to get her out first.

Brenda's phone now buzzed, and all three women jumped. The tension in the Hyundai skyrocketed as Brenda scrambled to answer it.

"We're around the corner, Erica. We'll be there in five."

Brenda pulled her beanie on and started the car, then inched out onto the empty suburban street and took a left turn, before pulling into the driveway of one of the cookie-cutter homes. She turned the ignition off, pocketed the keys, and said, "Let's get in and out in fifteen minutes."

Tilda felt like her heart was about to gallop right out of her chest. She just wanted to grab Erica, throw her in the car, and get home herself, back to Buddy, Pirate, and her everyday life. Back to safety.

She followed Brenda and Carol up to the front door, which was open. Erica was standing there in a long black dress. Her wild hair was scraped off her face with a hairband; without a scrap of makeup, or any jewelry, she looked young and vulnerable. She was also sporting a bruised cheekbone, and her right arm was invisible. She grabbed a cardigan off the console table and slipped it on, masking the arm, and then waited for Brenda's instructions.

"You said you have two suitcases?"

Erica nodded. "They're packed and under the bed in the spare room. I also have a bag in my wardrobe. That's all I could stash away without him noticing."

"Anything else you want to take?" Carol asked.

"Just my cat," Erica said. "There's a carrier in the laundry."

"Carol, you go with Erica and grab the bags," Brenda said. "I'll get the cat carrier. Tilda, you find the cat."

Erica legged it up the hall with Carol. Tilda looked around for the cat, taking in her surroundings at the same time. It was a small, prefab-type home, but it was full of thoughtful touches: a gorgeous throw across the sofa, a cluster of crystals and a Buddha statue on a sideboard, and several framed photos of Mike and Erica on the wall. It looked like a happy home, but looks can be deceiving. The ceilings were low, which Tilda found oppressive, and there was a chill in the air that the quirky lamps, boho cushions, and rugs couldn't alter. In fact, if anything, the room was exceedingly sad. Erica had clearly tried. She'd believed in this love, yet now she had to sneak out without any of the things she'd thought made this house a home.

Apart from the cat . . . if Tilda could find it.

"Kitty . . . kitty . . . puss puss." She looked under the coffee table and then crouched down and crawled on all fours to check behind the sofa. Every inch of her being was screaming at her to get out of there, but Tilda had done enough rescue work to know that animals were victims of DV as well. There was no way they could leave the poor thing behind. "Puss puss, where are you?"

A chill crept up her spine.

She sensed him before he spoke.

"Looking for this?"

Tilda stumbled to her feet and turned to face one very angry man and one very scared cat.

Tilda felt herself disassociate.

She was watching herself standing in front of Mike. It was an all-too-familiar feeling. One she'd experienced countless times as a child. Vivid images flashed before her now. Of her father's fists pounding down on her mother. Of her mother clawing back. Of herself, standing there, screaming . . . and feeling invisible. All of this now merged with the present as Tilda watched herself literally and completely incapacitated with fear.

Momentarily.

Because today was different. She wasn't twelve anymore. This was almost forty years on, and Tilda had survived all that, and more, and she was certainly going to survive this.

She slammed back into herself, composed and strong. She'd been doing the work and was ready.

"You must be Mike." She held her hands out for the cat. "And what's his name?"

"You're off your nut if you think you're taking my cat. Or anything from here."

Mike was smaller than Tilda had imagined. Rather stocky, clean-cut, with a tattoo of an owl on his forearm. He didn't look dangerous. That's not to say he wasn't, or that Tilda wasn't in danger. But Tilda saw something in him that she'd seen in her own father and only understood later. Pain. Probably generations of trauma passed down through family violence. She knew her own father had suffered terribly at the hands of his father, only to perpetuate that trauma in his marriage. Would he have changed, given the chance? As Oscar Wilde said, "Every saint has a past, and every sinner has a future."

People change. Tilda had changed. She didn't recognize herself anymore.

Was this man a monster, as the press would describe him if things went south for Tilda here? Or was he someone who, given the chance to redeem himself, could change and contribute?

Tilda knew it wasn't her job to find out. Right now, this man was a danger. He needed help, and he needed to be held accountable. There was never any excuse for weaponizing one's pain and trauma and using them against another person. She'd just realized that the past had no power over her anymore. She was not going to cower before this or any man.

"Mike, the police are on their way here," she lied. "Don't make this any worse for yourself than it already is."

She saw Brenda come in behind her, holding a cat carrier. Without saying another word, Tilda stepped up to Mike and took the cat from him.

Erica entered the room clutching a suitcase in each hand and froze. Carol was behind her, and had an overnight bag slung over her shoulder.

Tilda was firm. "Carol, take Erica to the car."

"Get back in the bedroom, Erica," Mike growled.

Tilda spoke again, calmly. "Carol, take Erica to the car."

Mike took a threatening step forward. "If you fucking leave this house with these two, we're done."

Tilda realized Mike couldn't see Brenda. Brenda had been right. There were some benefits that came with being invisible.

"Erica, go now," Tilda ordered.

Erica followed Carol out the door. Tilda was petrified but stood her ground. She saw Brenda pick up a heavy vase. All Tilda needed to do was make it to the car, and this whole awful scenario would be behind her.

She walked over to the cat carrier and put the cat safely inside.

"I'm leaving now." Tilda backed up toward the door. "The police will be here any minute to hear your side of the story."

Mike took one threatening step toward her.

Brenda stepped up beside him.

His whole body was rigid with rage. "You won't get away with this!"

There was a ghostly whisper, right up against Mike's ear.

"Ooooooh, but Mike, she already has."

And with that, Mike wet himself.

• • •

Two hours later, the four women were safely ensconced in the neat little one-bedroom flat that Brenda had arranged for Erica. It was in a suburb not far from Tilda's, and well away from the one where Mike lived. Brenda's women's shelter had provided a fridge, bed, kitchen table, and couch. Brenda had also called on assistance from some local friends, who offered up all sorts of necessities, as well as some lovely potted plants, a big jute rug, some bright wall art, and wicker baskets.

Brenda and Carol chatted in the kitchen while the kettle boiled for tea. Brenda had left the house still holding the vase, and it now sat on the kitchen counter with a bunch of lilies in it. Down the hall, Erica was setting up the cat's litter box in the laundry. The rush of adrenaline had subsided, and in its place was a sense of euphoria. Once the cat was settled,

Brenda was going to take Erica to the local police station. They had domestic violence liaison officers there who would help her apply for an apprehended domestic violence order. It was the first step of many for Erica, but at least she was moving in the right direction now.

As for Tilda, she felt invincible. She had faced more than Mike today— she'd faced her own past, her own trauma. She'd be lying if she said she wasn't rattled. She was. But she'd also felt a huge weight lift. Not all domestic violence made the front page of the newspaper. Most injuries were to the hearts of victims, shaping their lives, their loves, and their world.

Brenda came in and passed her a mug of tea. Tilda took it, and noticed her hand—all five fingers were completely visible.

61

This is a wonderful day. I've never seen this one before.

—MAYA ANGELOU

Tilda unclipped Buddy's leash and let him loose, laughing as she watched him bolt down the beach. She made her way to the water, stripped down to her swimsuit, tossed her dress and towel in a pile on the sand, and then ran into the sea. She used to swim all the time—she loved the ocean. But somewhere, sometime, she'd stopped swimming. So as summer arrived, she'd bought a new swimsuit and now embraced a daily swim.

She greeted each wave sideways, breaking through with her hip, and then, once she was waist-deep, she dived in. Utterly exhilarating. After a while, she made her way back up the beach, where she wrapped herself in her towel and sat on the sand.

She was happy. Each day was glorious.

Buddy sat beside her, and she rested a hand on him, running her fingers through his wet coat. They both savored the sun as it dried the water running from her hair down her back.

Tilda took a deep breath and closed her eyes.

Hello, PEARL.

Hello, Tilda.

A truce had been made. It wasn't observed all the time. Not every day. Sometimes Tilda was tired, or stressed, and the negative loops would become louder and louder. The difference now, though, was awareness. She still battled fears and anxieties, and even some unwarranted opinions of herself. But mostly she was greeted by kinder thoughts.

She'd once read a quote from the *New York Times* columnist Charles M. Blow that had immediately made her think of Tom: "One doesn't have to operate with great malice to do great harm. The absence of empathy and understanding are sufficient." She'd read it again not long ago, and this time she'd thought of herself—of the harm she'd done to herself in the past, and how now, with love, and understanding, and a lot of deep personal work, she was slowly undoing it.

A breeze whipped her hair over her face, but her eyes remained closed. As her mind stilled and her perception expanded, she could hear the ocean, but it grew fainter as she drifted deeper. Time passed, until eventually she opened her eyes and wiped away a lone tear that crept down her cheek. That often happened when she was present and replete with gratitude.

She looked down at her curves in the new swimsuit and felt comfortable in her own skin. More importantly, she felt comfortable in her own mind.

Looking good.

Thanks, PEARL.

62

Her own thoughts and reflections were
habitually her best companions.
—JANE AUSTEN

Tilda watched as her father swung her mother around the living room to Perry Como's rendition of "Caterina" playing loudly on the record player. Her parents moved with grace and rhythm, doing "olden-day dance steps," as Tilda called them.

Her mother threw her head back and laughed as her father twirled her once and then dipped her.

Tilda jumped up and down, clapping her hands. "My turn, Daddy, my turn."

Frances dropped onto the sofa and fanned herself with a magazine, and Tilda's father reached his hand out for his next dancing partner. Tilda knew the drill. She stepped up and onto his feet, giggling loudly as her father then danced around the room with her standing on his shoes.

• • •

Tilda finished her story and sat for a moment, while Selma watched her.

"I've been thinking about that a lot," Tilda said. "My parents often danced. Often laughed. There were good times. The bad times overshadowed those, certainly in my mind, but they're not the whole story. Not even close. I can look at it all now and see the broader scope of it, with very little attachment to it."

"You've rewritten your story."

"The key is, it's just a story. The past. It has no power over me now."

"It's amazing how once you've exorcised the house, the ghosts can't haunt you," Selma said. "Any word from your doctor?"

Tilda's mood shifted, and her distress showed. "No. I had coffee with her receptionist last week. Gurinder sold the practice."

Selma understood immediately. "Her condition progressed quickly, then."

"I keep hoping to run into her somewhere, but who knows—maybe I have and just didn't see her."

"We can't force healing on anyone else. All you can do is be a beacon of light for others."

Tilda nodded. "Leith said the same thing. You've been a beacon to me, Selma. You're an amazing example of how a woman can age with pride."

"I know," Selma said with a smile, then added, "You're incredibly inspiring yourself."

"I know," said Tilda, mimicking Selma, and they both laughed.

Selma tapped her pen on her notepad, where she'd listed all of Tilda's now visible body parts. "What's next for Tilda Finch, now that you're completely visible?"

"Oh Selma, so much. There are great things I can imagine, and even better things I can't imagine yet." Tilda wiggled her visible little finger at Selma. "I'm so different now . . . I'm expecting the unexpected."

Selma held her palm up for Tilda to high-five, which she did. "Gosh, I like this new Tilda. You're a walking advertisement for This Is A Sign."

Tilda pulled an "I know" face. "I can't tell you how smug Leith is about that."

"I bet."

"All of this has given me a fresh perspective on the business. Taking the time to pursue portrait photography has completely banished the feeling of creative dissatisfaction I was struggling with. And strangely, it's helped me view what I've built with Leith and Ziggy differently, and I'm feeling inspired by that all over again."

Selma stood and placed her notepad on the table in front of them. "You have no more need for me. It's time to sign off."

Tilda was both upset and excited by this news. She trusted Selma and enjoyed their sessions, but she knew letting go was a part of the process.

"I will see you again, won't I?" she asked.

"Of course. Women like us are so visible—we can't help but see each other."

"I was wondering . . . I know you have a waiting list, but Carol would really benefit from seeing you. She's even talking about taking your course. I spoke to Pam and told her I'd cover Carol's costs if she took my weekly session."

"I think we can work something out. I met Carol at the studio, and it's clear she's very committed to this work." Selma started walking Tilda to the door. "Good luck, Tilda. I look forward to hearing what adventures unfold for you."

The two women embraced.

"And remember," Selma said, "it will be something very different. That's the whole point of being a new version of yourself. New things are bound to enter your life."

63

Life is either a daring adventure or nothing at all.

—HELEN KELLER

Tilda pressed the buzzer and waited for Patrick to answer.

He might not be at home, PEARL said.

True.

You should've called first, PEARL said.

True again.

He might be having wild sex with his new girlfriend or simply not want to see you.

Ah, PEARL, still some work to do.

Patrick's voice came through the intercom. "Hello?"

"Patrick, it's Tilda. Sorry, I should've called, but—" She was cut off by the clicking of the lock on the gate as he buzzed her through.

Tilda inhaled courage, checked the tuck of her shirt in her jeans, and went in. Patrick was waiting for her at the door, beaming.

"About time you came back."

It was that simple. He drew her into his arms and held her tight. "I missed you," he said.

"I missed you too," she whispered.

He stepped back, his hands still firmly on her arms. "So, how are you?"

"Visible." That one word filled her with joy, pride, and gratitude.

"Bloody brilliant! Now get your visible arse inside."

Tilda laughed. "Yes, sir."

She went inside, and breathed in deeply as she took in the endless ocean view. A view that would not, and should not, ever be taken for granted. She noticed some food out on the counter—too much for Patrick alone.

"Either you're really hungry or I'm interrupting something," she said.

"Not interrupting. I'm just throwing lunch on the barbecue for Moe and Stephen. Join us."

Easy, welcoming. Tilda laughed. "I'd love to."

"Uncle Trick!" A child's voice rang out from the side of the house. A boy of about five with a mop of dark curls rounded the corner. He paused when he saw Tilda, but she raised her hand and gave him a wave, a cue for him to come on in.

"Kai, this is Tilda," Patrick said.

Kai grinned. "Hi, Tilda."

"Nice to meet you, Kai."

"Are you Uncle Trick's girlfriend?"

"She won't be if you don't shut up and stop embarrassing her," a voice called from the garden.

Tilda watched as a beautiful dark-haired woman in her early forties appeared in the room. She was dressed in loose white yoga pants and a T-shirt that said "Bee Yourself," with a bee flying across it. Tilda recognized it as being from This Is A Sign.

"Moe, this is Tilda," Patrick said.

Moe's face lit up. "Lovely to meet you. How's that for synchronicity? I'm wearing one of your shirts."

Kai piped up. "You always wear that shirt."

"Tattletale," Moe said. "But it's true, Tilda—I love your merch."

Tilda laughed. "Next time I'll bring you some." She grabbed a gift bag she'd brought with her. "I did grab one thing for Patrick, though."

"Because I'm special," Patrick teased.

Tilda passed Patrick a mug.

"I wonder what it is," Patrick joked as he ran his hands over it. "What does it say?"

"'Drink coffee like Yoda must,'" Moe read for him.

"Love it! My new favorite mug." Patrick laughed. "Now let's get this party started."

Moe began setting the table. Tilda was given the task of preparing a salad, which allowed her the space to watch Patrick in his element but still feel like she was contributing. He set up the barbecue and threw some salmon on the hot plate. His lack of sight certainly didn't get in the way of his functioning around the house. As he added some crumbed egg-plant to the barbecue, Kai appeared beside him, and Patrick crouched down to listen to something he was saying.

"Some women might think it's a lot to take on . . . a blind guy."

Tilda realized Moe was talking to her.

"I'm sure there are challenges that go with it. I'm not naive. But I've yet to really discover one," Tilda admitted. "At this stage, I just have a lot of questions about Patrick's experience of the world."

"Careful, Tilda, this is where Moe grills you."

Tilda saw that Stephen had entered the room behind her.

"I'm not grilling . . ."

"It's fine," Tilda said. She liked Moe's protectiveness—and Stephen's. He was clearly surprised she was there. But he didn't make her uncomfortable.

"Sorry to show up uninvited to lunch," she said to him.

Stephen smiled. "I reckon you don't need an invite." He gave her a warm hug. "Nice to see you again." He gestured at her. "Literally."

This stunned Tilda.

"Patrick told me." He gave Tilda an appraising stare. "You've achieved something quite phenomenal, and it will inspire others."

"I've already found that to be true," Tilda admitted. "It's really just about seeing things differently."

"Sight is an interesting concept," Stephen agreed. "Years ago I asked myself: If Patrick lost his sight, how would he see things—and then how would *I* see things? My relationship with him is such a driver in my life. Would I see things differently, for him?"

"And have you?"

"I see things very differently now because of him."

"Not as differently as I do," Patrick chuckled, walking into the kitchen. "Can you two not scare Tilda off? I like her."

A flood of warmth washed through Tilda from head to toe.

"I've been thinking a lot about sight since meeting Patrick," she said. "I'd never considered how language is full of sight analogies. 'Wait and see.' See?"

"'Look here.' 'Nice to see you.' 'Focus on this.' See what I mean?" Moe added.

"Exactly," Tilda said. "I've really had to consider how I see the world, and how I see myself. Getting to know Patrick has opened up a new way of thinking for me, about what it means to see."

Stephen looked delighted.

"Can we all eat?" Patrick said, handing Moe some crumbed fish for Kai. She added it to a wrap with some salad, and Kai took off to his jungle gym in the yard, Hendrix close behind.

"He'll feed that to the dog." Moe sighed.

As they took their places at the table outside, Stephen turned to Tilda. "I like that you're considering what it means to see. There's a whole field of research into that. I'm sure Patrick has told you that we practice Merpati Putih?"

"The martial art? He has mentioned it," Tilda said.

"My mother's family are Javanese," Moe said. "Mum remembered seeing blind people being trained in Merpati Putih. They were able to move around by sensing energy. So we went to Java and studied."

As you do, thought Tilda. How could her ordinary little life compare to these people's lives? She had nothing to offer.

Not true. You've just cured a supposedly incurable condition.

Well, well, well, PEARL.

"What does that mean for you, Patrick?" Tilda asked.

"On a practical level, it means I can detect things around me, which gives me independence." Patrick looked relaxed. "I know how my RP could progress, but I haven't ruled out other possibilities. What's probable and what's possible are often completely different. You're proof of that, Tilda."

"To quote Shakespeare," Moe said, "'There are more things in heaven and earth, Horatio, than are dreamt of in your philosophy.'"

Tilda nodded. "We have that on a range of items at work."

"I know. I have the mug," Moe admitted.

Tilda laughed. "You must be one of our best customers, Moe."

"She collects the inspiring quotes for herself, and buys me and Patrick the unspirational gear," Stephen said.

"We're about to release a new line of that. My favorite is a T-shirt that reads, 'If at first you don't succeed, skydiving probably isn't for you.'"

Everyone laughed.

"I love it," Stephen said. "We need one for hang gliding."

"I've always thought it would be amazing to try," Tilda said. "Never have, of course."

There was a moment of silence, and then Patrick said, "Team?"

"Oh yes," Stephen said.

"What's going on?" Tilda asked.

"Be careful what you wish for," Moe said.

"More like ask and you shall receive," Patrick said.

"Am I missing something?" And then, "You're suggesting we go hang gliding?"

Stephen pushed back his chair and stood. "If you insist."

Tilda's stomach dropped a thousand feet. "Now?"

"No time like the present," Stephen said.

This family really needed to work with This Is A Sign.

"We fly off the point up there." Moe pointed along the coast.

Today's not a good day.

Say your goodbyes and leave.

These people are insane.

Do you want to bloody die?

PEARL was on a roll.

But then the new Tilda stepped in, shoving PEARL out of the way.

Grab hold, Tilda.

So she did.

64

If you don't risk anything, you risk even more.

—ERICA JONG, author

It didn't take long for PEARL to get her voice back and start screaming at Tilda. She reeled off a dozen reasons why this was a bad idea. Tilda did her very best to ignore the screeching in her head, but she sent the twins a text telling them she loved them, just in case.

Tilda knew from all the work she'd been doing on herself that fear was just an emotion. The voice in her head was just a program, designed to keep her in familiar territory, but everything about today was edging her closer and closer to a precipice. Hang gliding was only one part of that. A much bigger leap was coming with Patrick. She could feel that too. Everyone here could. It was inevitable. They were crazy about each other. But that didn't mean it didn't scare her. It would take way more courage than leaping off this cliff.

Though she was crapping herself over that too.

She watched now as Patrick, harnessed under Stephen, flew along the coast in the distance. Normally Moe would also fly, but Kai was with them today, so she remained on the ground and instead explained how it all worked to Tilda.

"See how the glider is fully controllable?"

Tilda couldn't see that but nodded anyway. To her, it looked flimsy and risky. Tilda liked to fly on things that had been through rigorous safety tests. Like A380s. This thing had taken only about ten minutes to set up. "Like a tent," Patrick had said. Tilda didn't mention that she hated camping.

"It uses the wind and thermals to stay aloft," Moe said.

This concerned Tilda, as it didn't seem particularly windy. "You talk like a pilot."

"We are pilots. You don't go up there without proper training."

This placated Tilda somewhat. "They're a long way off."

"Those things can fly forever," Moe said. "The world record is over seven hundred kilometers."

Tilda fanned herself. The heat was stifling, but she wasn't sure if the warmth was from the sun or her anxiety. She watched as the hang glider rounded over the ocean and headed back toward them.

"You feel like a bird out there." Moe sighed.

"I'm probably a chicken."

"I used to be scared of everything." Moe giggled. "Even crossing the road."

They both laughed. Tilda really liked Moe.

"I suffered debilitating anxiety until my mid-thirties," Moe said.

Tilda forgot about her own anxiety and turned to her. "I can't imagine you scared of anything."

"I took anxiety meds for years."

"What changed?"

"I met Stephen and Patrick." Moe waved a hand at the hang gliding brothers. "I changed. Here." She tapped the side of her head. "The boys introduced me to meditation. A total game changer for me. It's completely rewired my old programming around fear. Not all of it. And not every day. But mostly. Plus, when I fell in love with Stephen, I was swept into this incredible adventure with these two."

Tilda realized that "these two" were now hovering nearby, preparing to land.

"I could either run a mile, which I considered," Moe said, "or I could go for it. I've discovered that going for it, taking that risk, brings the most incredible results."

Tilda was silent, knowing she was about to face a similar choice.

"See how Stephen is pushing the bar away to slow down? He'll stall it to land. There. Patrick has removed his feet from the harness."

Tilda watched as the hang glider was brought effortlessly back to a standstill on terra firma. Kai was obviously used to this, because he patiently waited until they'd both unclipped and then ran over to his father and uncle.

A few moments later, the two women joined them.

"How was that?" Moe asked.

"Bloody brilliant," Patrick said. He reached his arm out, and Tilda took his hand, as if that was the most natural thing in the world.

"A little bit of turbulence at the northern headland, so we won't fly that far," Stephen said.

Tilda wanted to say she was happy to wait until another day, but then Patrick pulled her in and gave her a kiss.

"You ready for this?" he said quietly.

"For hang gliding?"

"For everything?" he said.

"Yes, I'm ready."

Patrick looked elated. "Stephen, strap her in!"

Ten minutes later, Tilda was flying. She'd closed her eyes in terror as they took off and the ground rushed away from her. It was more frightening than any roller-coaster ride she'd ever been on. Well, the one roller coaster she'd been on, because they scared her.

"All good, Tilda?" Stephen called from above her. His voice was reassuringly calm.

She opened her eyes.

She was soaring.

The world looked completely different from here. A thrill ran through her, and then a sense of calm. At one point, as they flew over Patrick and Moe, far below them on the ground, Tilda could see Patrick, head tilted up to the sky, as if he were watching her.

65

Change Your Mind, Change Your Life.

—DR. JOE DISPENZA, author, researcher, lecturer

Tilda opened the front door and smiled. Today, it was a bush bouquet of native beauties on her doorstep—a rustic explosion of bottlebrush, banksia, kangaroo paw, and flannelflower. She bent down and picked it up.

I'm unbelievably proud of what you've achieved. Bask in the glory of this moment. Love, P x

How she had changed over the past twelve months—and how love had changed. No pressure. Ease. Support and kindness. Lovely long dinners. Swimming. And great sex. Lots of that. She felt so much love now, from her friends and family, from Patrick, but most importantly from herself. Her own self-care for the past year had been the latchkey that threw the door wide open to the full force of love in the world. She thought she'd known love before, but she'd never known this. Patrick was a wondrous part of it all, but he was a result of her happiness, not the source of it.

PEARL had not been completely silenced—that was not the way the mind worked—but Tilda had made peace with her. PEARL was often a cacophony of positive conversations, cheering Tilda on with kind words and care. Other times, she was still a bully, but Tilda had more patience with her. She also didn't accept everything PEARL said as truth, and often disagreed with her criticisms, drowning out many of the negative loops.

There were still tough days, of course, particularly when she was tired, but mostly, Tilda was deeply content. Everything felt better. She'd found a way to be present for all the magic and mystery life offered her. Including full visibility.

Tilda's healing had been the metaphorical four-minute mile for other women from the support group. Several of the women she'd photographed had seen small to major improvements in their own visibility, including Brenda, who was now visible and incorporated positive thinking into the weekly meetings. All but two subjects had regained at least some visibility. The result was eighteen profound, painful, outstanding images, which had been shown at a well-known local gallery. The exhibition was called *I Am Visible*—Tilda's jubilant return to portrait photography. Each subject provided both a written and audio description of how invisibility had impacted her life, which was there to read or listen to beside each portrait. It was powerful storytelling. Word got out about the exhibition, and women flocked from all over the city to see it. It was well reviewed, with one critic calling it "compelling, raw, personal . . . the most important exhibition of the year." Then Tilda had received a call from the director of the gallery she was visiting today.

Tilda placed Patrick's bouquet on the console in the front hall, grabbed her keys, and headed for Maeve's. It was a gorgeous summer's day, her favorite time of year. She unlatched the gate and rapped on the door and waited. What was taking Maeve so long? She'd often thought about how being the only person to regularly visit Maeve meant she'd no doubt be the person to find her dead.

After that, her imagination always went straight to the cats.

Fortunately, she heard footsteps down the hall, so that particular imaginary drama wasn't going to ruin a sensational day.

Maeve answered the door holding some flowers.

Tilda stepped aside as a couple of the cats raced out. "I can't stay," she said. "I'm just checking to see if you've changed your mind and want to come with me today."

Maeve was always reluctant to leave the house. "I won't, dear. I'm best pottering around here. Just not good out there anymore."

Tilda presumed that "out there" meant in the world.

Maeve handed Tilda the flowers. "I got you these, though." They were wilting peonies from her garden, wrapped in a Dick Smith catalog.

"Thanks, Maeve, that's very thoughtful."

Maeve looked at Tilda. "You've really fallen for that chap, haven't you?"

Talk about a change of gears. Still, the very mention of "that chap" made Tilda smile, because she had indeed fallen for him.

"I can tell by the flush of your cheeks," Maeve continued.

"You know, Maeve, there really is nothing wrong with your eyes."

"I know that. Why do you keep bringing up my eyes?"

"I thought you needed new glasses after you had your driver's license revoked a couple of years ago."

"That wasn't because I failed the eyesight test. It was for DUI!"

That information was entirely new to Tilda, and it showed.

"Don't judge me. I can see from the look on your face that you're judging me."

"I'm horrified that you'd drink and drive. You could have called me if you needed something."

Maeve shrugged. "I'm enough of a burden on you."

"You have never been a burden."

"That's very sweet, dear, but let's be honest, I'm a bit of a charity case."

"I'll declare you on my next tax return," Tilda teased. "Okay, so if your eyesight is so good, why didn't you notice that parts of me started disappearing a while back?"

"What are you talking about?"

"You didn't see that my nose was missing? Or my hand?"

It was clear that Maeve had never noticed these things.

Maeve said, "I think we can agree that we've both got perfect eyesight."

"Not sure my optometrist would agree with you there," Tilda said.

Maeve reached her hand out and took Tilda's. "Then you tell your optometrist how you're the first person to see me in years."

66

I've discovered that I'm a force of feminine resilience,
the creator of my own story, and a woman whose
worth doesn't diminish with age.

—TILDA FINCH

"Shut up, everyone. You're making me cry."

Tabitha, Holly, Leith, Ali, Yumiko, and Carol were all gathered around Tilda, chattering excitedly, while Patrick stood at her side, his long fingers linked through hers. So much love surrounded them.

Patrick handed her a clean handkerchief.

He'd brought her a hanky.

"Now describe the photo to me," he teased.

"Well," Tilda said. "I've never seen myself so . . . large. Beside it, on a white plaque in black lettering, it says, '*Tilda Is Visible*. Self-portrait by Tilda Finch. Purchased by the State Portrait Gallery. Inkjet print on paper.'" Tilda gazed at her photo for a moment, absorbing every wrinkle, every crease, every mark on the unretouched image. It showcased her strength, her tenacity, her spirit. "I look beautiful."

You are *beautiful*, PEARL whispered.

Tilda looked around her: the gallery was busy. A group of tourists were following a guide from room to room. Nearby was a painting that had recently been up for the Archibald. In the distance, a Max Dupain piece. Tilda was in good company, both on and off the wall.

Ali snapped some photos on her phone. "Not quite up to your standards," she said, "but let's capture the moment."

They all leaned in for the shot, beaming, and then Tilda took a deep breath.

Leith gave her a nod. "Ready?"

Tilda stepped forward and pressed the button, and a recording of her voice rang out through the gallery.

> "What does it mean to be visible? Everything. It's what we all yearn for, in every relationship, no matter how brief. To be seen means we matter. But visibility must always begin with self. We must first see ourselves. And to do that, we must sit with ourselves and listen. Who are we really? What stories are we telling? And why?"

Tilda's voice quavered with emotion as the recording continued.

> "This photograph is the culmination of a journey I took to see myself clearly. It is the result of rivers of tears and howling at the moon and the unwavering resolve not to disappear. I discovered that I'm a force of feminine resilience, the creator of my own story, and a woman whose worth doesn't diminish with age. I see me clearly now. I am Tilda . . . and I am visible."

The recording ended.

Silence.

Tilda looked at Patrick and then thrust the handkerchief into his hand. "Now you need this."

"So proud . . ." was all he managed as he drew her in for a kiss—it never grew old.

"You did it, Tilly." Leith was openly crying. "Pass me the bloody hanky, Patrick."

"I brought one just for you." Patrick pulled a second handkerchief from his pocket and held it out to her.

Tilda laughed. She loved that Patrick and Leith got on so well. That they all did.

Tilda turned back to her photograph. She'd always dreamed of this moment, and here it was, even better than she'd imagined. But this wasn't the end of a journey, or a happily ever after. This was a moment in time that was the sum total of the changes and choices she'd made. One glorious moment, strung together with so many others, in this new life of hers. A life that kept getting better.

"Let's go, my beautiful people," she said. "The champagne is waiting."

Patrick was taking them all to lunch to celebrate. As they made their way out of the gallery, Tilda hung back. Tabitha and Holly were chatting with Patrick, her girlfriends following behind. She was supported, and loved, and blessed.

She paused briefly to take one more look at her work, and the awe-inspiring beauty of her fifty-two-year-old face, not just visible but looming large on the wall of the State Portrait Gallery. She'd done it.

She fully savored the moment—the happiness, the pride, the contentment.

And then she walked toward the exit, catching a glimpse of herself in a glass door, clear as day.

• • •

Watching her leave was a woman Tilda had once known, invisible to everyone around her. She stood in front of the photograph, and something inside her shifted. If Tilda could do it, maybe she could too.

AUTHOR'S NOTE

MEDITATION

My first attempt at meditation was as a twenty-three-year-old living in Japan. Over the next three decades, I studied several different types of meditation, including Vipassana. I highly recommend Vipassana, as both an organization and a meditation style. Tilda's early departure from the retreat was needed for her character arc. My advice is, if the practice resonates with you, attend a ten-day retreat and stick it out. It is incredibly beneficial. Many of Tilda's experiences were inspired by my time at Vipassana's New South Wales Blackheath center. However, unlike Tilda, I completed the ten-day retreat and continued to practice this form of meditation for a few years.

In 2014, I was first introduced to the work of Dr. Joe Dispenza. I've thrown myself into his teachings, and they have been instrumental in changing my life. To this day, I continue to use Dr. Joe's techniques, along with a mix of others.

For years now, I've meditated daily, and I've shared my passion for it in this book. For recommended links, and more meditation musings, please sign up for my Substack newsletter @JaneTara.

ERICA'S RESCUE

Erica's rescue is based on a real event where I helped remove a family friend and her dog from a similar situation. She then reported to the Domestic Violence Liaison Officer at her new local police station, the first step of many to ensure her safety. Her story has a happy ending, as I'm sure Erica's has.

ONE STORY, MANY VERSIONS

I've told one story about invisibility and am aware there are many versions of it in the world today. No one person can or should speak for everyone.

The same can be said for Patrick's journey with retinitis pigmentosa. I've done years of research into living with RP, initially because I was misdiagnosed with this condition ten years ago. Here, I was inspired by two people whose experiences with vision impairment helped to inform Patrick's story.